LEAVES OF RED AND GOLD

LEAVES OF RED AND GOLD

The Journey of Matthew Schipani

Scott R. Chapman

Writers Club Press
San Jose New York Lincoln Shanghai

Leaves of Red and Gold
The Journey of Matthew Schipani

Writers Club Press
an imprint of iUniverse, Inc.

For information address:
iUniverse, Inc.
5220 S. 16th St., Suite 200
Lincoln, NE 68512
www.iuniverse.com

Any resemblance to actual people and events is purely coincidental.
This is a work of fiction.

ISBN: 0-595-24131-X

Printed in the United States of America

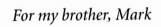

For my brother, Mark

Contents

CHAPTER 1

DEATH OF A GREAT MAN

March 1994

The loud ring of the telephone made Matthew Alexander Schipani sit right up in the bed. Ever since his father's unexpected heart attack last month, the late night ring of the phone would send a shock of terror to the core of his spine. He grabbed the phone, knocking over the lamp in the process. Matthew expressed an inquisitive and reluctant "hello" into the mouthpiece of the phone. The voice on the other end slowly started, "Matthew...this is Bradford Collins." Collins was the chief legal counsel to Lloyd Dickerson, the controversial Governor of Massachusetts. Collins continued, "Wallace Cartwright is dead...Dickerson is going on television at 7:30 to make the announcement. He wants you there." Matthew, who was now wide awake by the message he just heard, gulped and then said, "I'll be there." At that response, Bradford Collins hung up the phone. Matthew held the dead receiver in his hand for a moment. Then he put it back into the cradle. Matthew sat in the bed and stared at his bedroom wall for a few moments. The news had stunned him. He was unable to muster up enough energy to think or move.

Matthew finally pushed the sheets aside and got up out of the bed. He walked into the kitchen and looked at the clock on the wall. It was 4:30 in the morning. It was still dark outside, no sunrise yet, spring wasn't here yet. He rotely began to make coffee, filling the water and the scooping the grounds into the filter. As the coffee brewed, Matthew sat at the kitchen table silently. He began to think about how he met Attorney General Wallace Cartwright.

Cartwright had appointed Matthew to the position of Chief Legal Counsel for the state's Division of Child Protection five years ago. Matthew was only 35 at the time. At the time of his appointment, he was one of the youngest chief counsels of an executive agency. But his youth did not deter Wallace Cartwright. Wallace had faith in him. This came from Matthew's brief stint at the Attorney General's office as an assistant. Matthew made a name for himself when he won a major racketeering case against powerful politicos in the Worcester area of Massachusetts. When the time came to fill a void at the Division of Child Protection, Cartwright asked Matthew to come back to state service. Matthew returned to the agency he loved.

Wallace T. Cartwright was the Attorney General of Massachusetts for almost a quarter of a century. He had served four Governors. Wallace was a giant among lawyers. At 6 feet, 5 inches, with bright silver hair, the 69 year old Attorney General was revered by the bar. He was a legendary man in Massachusetts politics. The legend began with Wallace's service to his country at the end of World War II. Cartwright had earned a purple heart in action in the Pacific theater. From the war he entered law school at Georgetown University. He returned to Massachusetts after graduating and became one of the brightest county district attorneys the state had ever seen. He won the Attorney General's office on his first try. The past two elections Wallace ran unopposed.

Wallace inspired hope and deep loyalty among those who worked for him. He was a fair and honest boss who always made time for his staff. He lavished praised on his staff's every accomplishment. Wallace was known publicly and privately as the "Gentle Giant." This referred not only to his physical statute, but his personality as well.

While bearing this nickname, Wallace was no pushover on crime. He believed that violent crimes deserved swift and severe punishment. He would take pleasure in prosecuting the most notorious criminals in Massachusetts personally. His telegenetic appearance left the public enthralled with him. And now he was gone.

Matthew poured himself a cup of the freshly brewed coffee and lit a cigarette. Wallace was dead. So quick and without explanation. He had just had lunch with him last week and everything seemed fine. Wallace was as jovial as ever. The thought of death was beginning to envelop Matthew's mind. Just last month, he was fighting the death demon when his father, Franco almost died during heart surgery. That too was totally unexpected.

Matthew's father had been enjoying his retirement for the last ten years. Then the horrible phone call came in the middle of the night. His mother Rosa called to tell her son that his father had a severe heart attack. That phone call turned Matthew's life upset down for the next month. Thankfully, his father was beginning to enjoy what appeared to be a solid recovery.

Matthew walked back towards the bedroom and poked his head in the doorway. There was his lover, Adam Lesley, snoring away in the bed. Adam, his law school sweetheart who became the love of his life, could sleep through anything. Matthew, with a tiny smile on his lips, recalled how a few years ago Adam was taking a cat nap on a sunny warm afternoon. A burglar crawled in through the window of their home and made off with the TV and VCR while Adam snored away, unaware of the intrusion, and thankfully unhurt. Matthew mused briefly on whether he should wake Adam up and give him the news. But he decided against it. "He'll know soon enough," thought Matthew.

Matthew took a long hot shower. His mind began to drift. He thought of his days with Wallace Cartwright. "Those were good days," he thought. Matthew appreciated how Wallace had trained him and treated him so well. "Did I let him know how much he meant to me?", thought Matthew. He realized that he was poking in the shower, so he turned the water to cold to force himself to hurry. It did the trick and he finished his shower.

Matthew got out of the shower, toweled off and began to dress. He then went back into the kitchen and poured his second cup of coffee. The sun was beginning to rise. The aroma from the coffee must have reached Adam, who was now awake and stumbling into their galley kitchen. Adam grunted a brief "hi," went over to the coffee machine and poured his cup of coffee. Adam then sat down at the table and stared into space. Matthew learned over their many years together that he had to wait until Adam was ready to begin the morning conversation before he started to speak. Adam was a bear in the morning and a gentle comment could easily set off his roar. So Matthew sat and waited.

Matthew looked at Adam, marveling how beautiful his lover was, even in the wee hours of the morning. Adam was 6 feet tall with wavy black hair. He was a light skinned, biracial man who prided himself on keeping in top physical shape. He devoted himself to eating the healthiest of foods. He went to the gym at least 4 times a week. At 35 years old, Adam looked ten years younger. His skin was soft and smooth, not a wrinkle on his face. But Adam also had the one bad habit that Matthew did. He reached for the pack of Marlboro Lights and lit up. Matthew, almost instinctively grabbed another cigarette and lit up as well. Adam looked at him, grimaced and waved his hand at the smoke hanging between them to fan it away. After taking his second drag, Matthew reprimanded himself quietly and vowed he would stop smoking. It was his fifth vow this week.

Adam was finally ready to begin conversing. He said to Matthew, "what gets you up so early?" Matthew paused before responding. Then in a very soft tone said, "the Governor's office called. Wallace Cartwright is dead." Adam looked up from his stare into the coffee mug and sputtered, "...what?" Matthew looked at Adam and repeated, "Wallace is dead. Bradford Collins wants me at the State-house when Dickerson makes the announcement." Adam, now looking very confused, mumbled, "what the hell happened? I just saw him on Friday!" Matthew responded, "I don't know. Collins didn't give me an explanation. I guess I'll find out when I get there."

Matthew got up from the kitchen table and went into the study closet to find a tie. Adam followed, "let me pick one for you," he told Matthew. Adam never trusted Matthew's judgment when it came to matching ties. Adam pulled a tie from the rack, handed it to Matthew saying, "Do you think he had a heart attack or something?" Matthew reached for the tie and said impatiently, "I told you. I don't know." "Was he sick?", Adam quickly inquired.

"I don't know" responded Matthew becoming frustrated with Adam's inquisition. Adam who always believed there was a conspiracy lurking when a cogent explanation was not immediately forthcoming, replied, "maybe somebody killed the 'Gentle Giant.' You know there were a lot of people who didn't like him..." Matthew gave Adam an unapproving look. Adam continued, "I bet Dickerson is going to form a commission to investigate the death and he wants you on it!"

Matthew became angry at Adam. He said, "would you please grow up! Stop always trying to find a spy novel in everything!" Adam persisted. "No, I'm serious...maybe one of those mobsters got back at Cartwright. He really pissed them off. They may have had enough.", concluded Adam in an elevated and excited voice. Matthew's patience was gone. He walked away from Adam saying as he walked, "that's the ticket Adam! It was a conspiracy...a mob hit. And don't forget, Johnson killed Kennedy!"

Matthew sat at the kitchen table. Adam waited a few minutes and then came into the kitchen. "I'm sorry," said a contrite Adam, then adding, "I know how much he meant to you. You know how I am...I always want to find a secret or something. I love intrigue. I'm really sorry. I'm sorry." Matthew looked at Adam and then said, "yeah, I know how you are…this really sucks! It sucks! I can't believe he's dead." Adam moved over and sat on Matthew's lap. Matthew put his head on Adam's shoulder. Adam stroked his hair softly for a few minutes. They kissed and Matthew said, "I better get going." He got up and grabbed his jacket off the coat tree. "I'll watch for you on the morning news," said Adam as Matthew waved good-bye closing the outside door behind him.

The ride from his home in Cambridge down Massachusetts Avenue, or "Mass Ave," as it's known, was a quick one. The morning rush hour and congestion into Boston hadn't started yet. Matthew maneuvered his Volvo around the pot holes in the street that always plagued Massachusetts roads and cars at the end of the winter season. While maneuvering he was thinking, "Why the hell does Dickerson want me there when he makes the announcement?" This thought kept repeating itself as Matthew got closer to the parking garage near Boston Common. He could not answer his own question.

Matthew parked the car and began his walk across the Common. The bright morning sun began to warm this mild end of winter day. He noticed the sun glimmering off the famous golden dome of the Massachusetts State House as he was getting closer and closer to it. He thought, "maybe the winter is finally over." It had been a record breaking, hard and long winter in New England. The temperatures were significantly lower than normal and it seemed as if it snowed every day. The question of the day during this past winter was not whether it would snow, but how much would it snow. But luckily today it was mild, and Matthew was grateful for the break, no matter how little it might be.

Matthew ascended the stairs of the Massachusetts State House to the main entrance. Once inside he identified himself and was escorted by the state police officer to the Governor's office. He entered the outer office and was greeted by his early morning caller, Bradford Collins. "Thanks for coming Matthew," stated Collins as he shook Matthew's hand. Collins motioned to the coffee pot. Matthew politely declined. Collins curtly stated, "It's important to the Governor that you're here. I'll be back in a few minutes to get you so we can meet." He then exited through the inner door into the Governor's office. Matthew looked down at his watch, thinking, "he'd better hurry up if we are going to make 7:30." A few moments later Collins reappeared and motioned with his finger for Matthew to come through the door into the Governor's office.

Governor Lloyd Dickerson extended his hand to Matthew as he walked in the room. The Governor bellowed, "good morning Matthew. So glad you could make it. Sit…sit." Matthew sat down in the chair. The Governor continued, "we're just waiting for Eunice Harrington and then we can get started. Women…never on time for anything, not even having babies!" The Governor then turned his head away from Matthew and began to engage in muted talk with Bradford Collins.

Matthew looked off to his left, thinking about Governor Lloyd Dickerson. Here was this incredibly overweight man, known as a screamer, who would yell and scream everytime something he didn't like turned up in the press. Dickerson would inspire terror for those around him because of his frequent temper tantrums. This Governor, who by a fluke or by apathy, won the office two years ago seemed like a "one termer" to Matthew. Dickerson's television appearances were noted for his frequent fights with the press. He lacked political polish. He was constantly making incongruent policy decisions. When the press or members of his staff would point this out to him he would have a fit no matter where he was. Many of his temper tantrums were permanently recorded by the press on videotape.

Eunice Harrington walked into the Governor's office. She tried to quietly close the door behind her. The Governor looked at her and then said sarcastically, "So glad you could take the time out of your busy schedule to join us, Eunice." Harrington cowered and proceeded to the chair in the corner of the office where she sat down.

"Well, now that everyone, including Eunice is here", Dickerson said with emphasis, "I guess we can begin.", the Governor started. "Wallace Cartwright died at 1:42 a.m., this morning...," announced the Governor. Dickerson went on, "Wallace died at home. Mildred heard a thump downstairs in the house. When she got down there she found Wallace dead in the library. She called Dr. Lightner. He pronounced Wallace dead at the scene. Lightner called me and told me that his initial assessment is that Cartwright died from an overdose of pills." The Governor paused and looked around his office. He was measuring the response of the eight persons assembled before him. There was no response, Matthew stared straight ahead. The Governor moved on.

"Now I don't know how many of you are aware of this, but Wallace had lung cancer. He had been hiding it for a while now, but he was getting a lot worse. I guess he thought he couldn't hide it anymore and pretty soon everyone would know. The 'Gentle Giant' would be seen as weak. Wallace wasn't going to have any of that. So kaput! He took some pills and went to sleep!", concluded Governor Dickerson in an elated voice. With the "kaput" comment, Matthew looked at the Governor and thought, "you asshole!"

Dickerson went on in a slow and deliberate pace, as if he were telling a ghost story. "The only people that know how Wallace died are his wife, the doc and us. And that's the way it's going to stay. The people need their heroes, and damn it, in death Wallace is going to remain one!" The Governor looked around his office. Everyone, including Matthew, was nodding their heads in agreement to his last statement. "I plan to announce that Wallace died of natural causes. This will be the official cause of his death. I've talked to the Coroner's Office. They know if they want their jobs they will do as I tell them!", the Governor continued. Then with a gleeful gleam in his eye, Dickerson stated, "I will lead the state's mourning for Wallace. We'll have a day in his honor. I'll head the ceremony. It'll be great!" Matthew once again looked at the Governor with disdain and thought, "yeah, great for your ratings, you fat fuck!"

The Governor rose from his chair. They all rose in unison. Dickerson said to the group, "well, let's go to the auditorium and meet the 'talking heads.'" This was Dickerson's phrase for the press. "Even that's not original," thought Matthew. Dickerson had borrowed that phrase from President Bush. As Dickerson walked out the door, they all followed him down the hall to the press area.

They entered the press room. Matthew could feel the air in the room. It was thick with excitement. A press conference by this laissez-faire Governor at 7:30 in the morning had to mean that something important was happening. The Governor usually didn't make it to work until 11. Dickerson went to the podium. The lieutenant Governor stood to his side. Matthew and the others stood off to the left of the Governor at the rear of the staging. The Governor began with "good morning." The hot bright lights of the portable cameras flipped on and the flashbulbs began to pop. The Governor began his formal remarks.

"Ladies and gentleman of the press and my fellow citizens of this great Commonwealth. I have a short statement to make this morning and there will be no questions to follow. I have the sad duty as your Governor to inform you that at approximatoly 1:42 this morning, Attorney General Wallace Cartwright died at home. He was discovered by his loving wife of 33 years, Mildred. At this hour it appears that the Attorney General died of natural causes. He was 69 years old." Dickerson took a dramatic pause before continuing with his remarks. He put his head down briefly.

Governor Dickerson looked up and continued, "funeral arrangements will be announced later today by this office. I intend to personally head the funeral ceremonies. Effective immediately, Bradford Collins, my chief of staff will be the acting attorney general of Massachusetts." The flashbulbs continued to light up the room. Matthew looked out at the thirty or forty press members in the auditorium. They were hanging on the Governor's every word. Even Matthew's friend, Shannon Watson, who had a lesser opinion of the Governor than Matthew did, was astutely listening.

Dickerson once again took a dramatic pause. When he looked up from the podium, with tears in his eyes that only a true politician can muster up at the opportune moment, Matthew looked away. "Well, he's winning the Oscar today.", thought Matthew. The Governor continued, "Wallace Cartwright was a giant among the citizens of Massachusetts. He served this Commonwealth and his nation with dedication and honor. I am personally overcome with grief, as is my wife, Ida. We extend our personal sympathies to the lovely Mildred. We'll be visiting with her later today. I am sure that many of you here are as sad as I am at this moment. We will all miss Wallace. Thank you for coming this morning." With those comments, the Governor stepped away from the podium and walked to the exit. Matthew and the others dutifully followed. The reporters yelled questions to the Governor that would not be answered. Dickerson kept on walking.

Outside the Governor's office, Dickerson shook hands with those who had joined him at the press conference. Matthew noticed that his mood was light. He was smiling profusely as he thanked everyone for coming. Matthew shook the Governor's hand. Dickerson looked him in the eye and said, "give me a call after all this ceremony crap is over. I want to talk to you further." Matthew responded, "okay," smiled and walked away.

Matthew descended the steps of the State House and walked across the stark Boston Common back towards his car. Matthew pondered about the Governor's departing comment to him. "Why was I there today? What was the point? What does the fat fuck want to talk to me about?" Matthew looked at his watch. He realized that he still had plenty of time before he needed to get into the office. He decided to take a moment and sit on one of the benches on Boston

Common. He sat quietly. He began to reflect on his life and his journey to becoming a lawyer and to attending press conferences with the Governor of the state. Matthew reached way back in the recesses of his mind, back to the beginning of his professional career.

CHAPTER 2

BACK TO THE BERKSHIRES

October 1978

Matthew cruised down the highway in his shiny blue 1968 Ford Mustang. The radio was playing *"Ain't No Mountain High Enough"* and Matthew turned it into a duet with him and Diana Ross. Matthew looked through the windshield of his car at the beauty that surrounded him. He stared off into the hills that met the road. He took in the beauty of the vivid fall colors on the changing New England trees. Leaves of red, gold and orange surrounded him on both sides of his car. It was a picture perfect postcard day. A day that made New England famous. As he continued to drive, he reflected on how much his life had changed in the last six months. Only a few months ago, he was driving on the freeways of Los Angeles. The view there was much different. Bumper to bumper traffic, hot steamy days and smog filled views.

Matthew continued his drive. His appointment was about forty five minutes away. He turned down the radio. Diana was finished singing. He thought about his California days. The times in southern California were heady times. To have escaped that scene in one piece was truly remarkable, Matthew thought. What began as a promise to a new world after completing his degree at USC, ended in a warped sense of reality, and an intense exposure to the darker side of life.

In 1972, Matthew began at the University of Southern California. It was the "ivy league of the west". He loved his college experience. The education and college living had agreed with him. Matthew graduated four years later, number 12 among a class of 585. His degree was in sociology and political science. After his graduation, Matthew went to work in a home for disturbed adolescents in Long Beach. He didn't make much money there, but he enjoyed the job. To deal with his economic crisis he fell back on his family. Matthew took the invitation offered by his widowed uncle and moved into his uncle's home in Long Beach.

In his early 20's, strong and lean, Matthew took advantage of the sexual freedom of the '70s. For the next two years he explored the gay scene of southern California. He became sexually promiscuous. He was a regular at the Los Angeles gay clubs. The disco fever that infected the clubs provided the perfect setting for Matthew to shine. He was an accomplished disco dancer.

At 6 feet tall, with blond hair, blue eyes and a body that showed the benefits of regular exercise, Matthew was desirable to many men in the gay bars. Little did they know that his beautiful, bright blond locks came from a package. His Italian heritage had given Matthew dark brown hair. But that didn't matter. Everything was cosmetic and could be changed. Matthew took advantage of his popularity. He would frequently leave the bar with a new man on his arm at least three or four times a week. They would have sex and it would end at that. There was no romantic commitment; no relationship established, only sexual pleasure. Matthew prided himself on his sexual stamina. He would frequently tell his friends he was at his "peak". He also prided himself on the fact that many men, of different shapes and sizes, found him desirable. He would have a different type for each month. His "flavor of the month", as he called it. When he left California the flavor that month was blond, blue eyed 'surfer' guys.

The radio was playing *"Dim All The Lights"*, one of his favorite Donna Summer disco songs. Matthew turned the radio up and began to sing again. He tapped his hands on the wheel in an attempt to keep the beat of the song. As he continued toward his destination, driving through the hills of Western Massachusetts, he continued thinking about the party scene in California. But the party and sex scene quickly gave way to the overpowering bad memories of southern California. "Damn, if I could only keep remembering the fun times", exclaimed Matthew as he turned the radio off.

Matthew's uncle, Francesco with whom he moved with in Long Beach was in fact a gay man. Uncle Francesco was widowed at an early age. He had no children. In fact, he was only twenty years older than Matthew. Many in Matthew's family did not know Uncle Francesco's "secret". Before Matthew accepted the invitation to live with his uncle, he made it clear to Uncle Francesco that he was gay. Matthew was surprised when his uncle confided in him that he too was gay. Matthew had always heard that Uncle Francesco was a "ladies man", but his uncle insisted that this image was for business purposes only.

Matthew thought he could take comfort in living with his gay uncle. At least he could be open about who he really was, not like when he was living with his parents in the Berkshires. But Uncle Francesco had a hidden agenda when he confided in Matthew his little "secret". Uncle Francesco was involved in the transportation of illegal goods over the border from Mexico. He wanted his nephew to be part of the operation.

Matthew was quickly lured into assisting his uncle by promises from Uncle Francesco. These promises not only included receiving a great deal of money for a relatively safe task, such as making telephone calls and dropping off packages, but also included sexual favors. Uncle Francesco had many connections in the gay world. In fact, Uncle Francesco boasted that he knew actor Rock Hudson personally. Uncle Francesco would reward Matthew with providing young men, usually wanna-be actors, to wet Matthew's sexual appetite. But everything came with a price, and before Matthew knew it he was over his head and sinking fast.

On his final night in California, Matthew made a desperate call to his mother, Rosa, pleading to come home immediately. Earlier that evening he had been severely bruised and beaten by a friend of Uncle Francesco's, as his uncle stood by watching. Matthew had screwed up on a delivery. His uncle's friend said that Matthew was "too busy sucking cock" and had lost a lot of money. Matthew would have to be taught a lesson. Uncle Francesco stood by and watched the lesson being administered.

After his uncle and his assaulter left the home, Matthew climbed up the stairs on his hands and knees to his bedroom. He quickly packed a small suitcase. A few hours later while Uncle Francesco who had returned, was sleeping in his bedroom, Matthew snuck out of the home. He drove the car to a pay phone and made his panic call to his mother. He asked her to wire a ticket to LAX to get him home in the morning. Rosa, without question or inquiry, sent the ticket. Matthew boarded the Boeing 707 four hours later and returned to the east coast. No questions were ever asked by his mother, and Matthew had not heard from Uncle Francesco since his return to Massachusetts.

Matthew's day dreaming was interrupted by the loud blare of a horn from a passing tractor trailer in the other lane. Matthew had been so distracted that he crossed over the center line without noticing. He corrected his driving and continued down the windy stone lined road. Matthew was about five minutes outside his appointment. He was scheduled to meet with a 6 year old girl about allegations that she had been beaten by her mother.

Matthew had started working as a child protective social worker for the state a few months ago. He worked out of the Berkshire Division of Child Protection office. It was an incredibly challenging job, but Matthew was growing to like it. He felt he was doing good for society. In the few short months on the job, Matthew was exposed to the severity and sinister side of child abuse and neglect in such a magnitude that he never knew existed. The job not only required dedication and skill, it also required the ability to ferret through the most despicable form of crime against children: child abuse by a parent or parents.

Matthew enjoyed the people that he worked with in the Berkshire DCP office a great deal. The office had 26 staff ranging in age from early 20's to mid 40's. There was a mixture of old and new staff, with a variety of backgrounds and experiences. Matthew was assigned to a child protective investigation unit. The primary responsibility of this unit was to investigate reports of abused or neglected children under age 17. He shared the office with five other social workers: Sarah, Gail, Sharon, Michael, and Janice Pierce, who would end up becoming one of his closest friends.

At first Matthew was not open about his sexual orientation. He wanted to make sure that his colleagues liked him for his professional abilities before they found out he was gay. If they could see him as a skilled social worker and be accepting of his orientation, then everything would be fine. Most people in the office could do that. So Matthew became more open. But as open as he became, he never let on his sexual attraction and eventual crush on his coworker Michael Wade.

Michael was a 23 year old black, former college football player. He was the subject of many daytime fantasies for Matthew. Matthew was sure that Michael Wade possessed one of the best bodies in the entire state. He was 6 feet 2 inches tall, with a wide and muscular chest. His biceps were bigger than Matthew's thighs. Michael was strikingly handsome and had a charming personality. Those daytime fantasies got Matthew through many a stressful day. However, Michael Wade's sexual interest was purely heterosexual. Matthew would have to stand in line. Michael was the stallion of the office. The single women, and a few married ones too, were pursuing him. Matthew had decided that Michael and Janice would make a cute couple. He made a mental note to try to encourage that.

Matthew's own love life was blooming. He was deep in the throws of a new relationship. He had met Darren Warner shortly after he returned from California. They met at a gay bar in the City of Springfield, called "Fever". Darren was 22 years old, shorter than Matthew and was in the Marine reserves. Matthew was very attracted to the butch attitude of this weekend warrior. The first night they met they went home to Darren's and had hot, passionate sex. Only a month later, they had moved into together and were setting up home. Matthew knew that he was becoming obsessed with Darren. He wanted to be with him all the time. Matthew was very jealous when they would go out to the bar and other men would try to pick up Darren. He decided he would have to learn to deal with this jealousy.

Matthew turned into the trailer park in Westfield and pulled up to number 7. He stopped thinking about his personal life, past and present, and focused on the task at hand. He would conduct his investigation and then return to the office to complete backlogged paperwork.

The investigation ended as many did. The parents were upset and belligerent toward Matthew. They were furious that someone had reported them to DCP for abusing their child. The mother strongly denied that she every physically abused her daughter, Mary Kate. The father gave permission for Matthew to interview the child alone. Mary Kate insisted that the bruise on her face came from falling down while she was playing. Matthew noticed that this frail child had a look of fear in her face as she spoke to him. He believed that her parents had coached her on what to tell him. Matthew determined that even though he could not substantiate any child abuse, he was going to make sure that a social worker from his office would make a follow up visit to check in on Mary Kate. He was afraid for her and he did not want to let Mary Kate fall through the cracks.

When Matthew returned to the office he began to tackle the paperwork sitting on the corner of his desk. Not only was the actual process of completing a child abuse investigation time consuming, the documentation required was equally as burdening. Matthew would repeat this routine many times over the next year.

As the year progressed, the names and faces would change, but the investigation would be basically the same. Parents, either deliberately or through neglect were hurting their children. The only noticeable change over the year was that the number of cases was continuing to grow. What had started out as a challenging job was now becoming an impossible one. More cases, more paperwork, and not enough time to do it all.

One exciting development for Matthew as he began his next year at DCP was his relationship with Janice Pierce. Matthew and Janice had become very close in the last year. They not only worked closely together, but on a personal level they were becoming very good friends. Matthew and Janice would frequently work the "Hotline", which was the DCP after hours organization for emergency cases of child abuse. They would be on-call during the evenings and week-ends on a regular basis. By their nature, these after hours calls were true emergencies that required a quick response to assess the safety of children. They usually involved serious child abuse or child death cases. They required the highest level of social worker skill. Matthew and Janice were tested both intellectually and emotionally on almost every call.

They spent many evenings and weekends together driving all over western Massachusetts and the Berkshires responding to the emergency calls. Their work relationship became like two police officers who had been partners for years. They knew each other's unspoken cues. They knew how to safely get out of a dangerous situation. They also knew how to play "good cop/bad cop", to their advantage to insure that their investigations provided for a safe outcome for the children that they were involved with.

Janice also brought much joy into Matthew's social life. A straight woman, who enjoyed the company of gay men, Janice would frequently go out to "Fever" with Matthew. She was a hit at the gay bar. Janice was a tall, svelte woman, with soft brown skin. She had an engaging personality and contagious laugh. Janice would light up the bar when she entered it. Janice was a transplant from Brooklyn, New York, who came to western Massachusetts to obtain her Master's degree. Once she finished her degree she began working at DCP. She decided never to return to New York, it had gotten "too crazy", as Janice frequently told people. Janice Pierce made the Berkshires her home.

One evening after a long day of emergency responses, Matthew and Janice decided they deserved a drink. They were only a few miles from "Fever" so they chose to go there. The one drink turned into two, and then three, and more. Janice decided it was time to dance. She too, like Matthew, found disco music to be invigorating. With their beepers attached to their collars, so they could hear if they went off, Janice and Matthew tore up the dance floor to the disco beat. The pulsating lights reflecting off of the huge disco ball infused them with energy.

As they were dancing, Janice kept poking Matthew in the side. "Look at that cute guy over there…he's checking you out!", she told Matthew. Matthew smiled and kept dancing. Finally, Janice decided to stop and said, "let's go over there and talk to the cutie!" Matthew blushed, saying "no", but Janice pushed him along from behind. Janice walked up to this very handsome tall man, with wavy black hair and high cheek bones. She extended her hand and said, "hi! We wanted to meet you." Matthew shook his head. He was blushing. The man shook Janice's hand and then Matthew's. He introduced himself as Scott Houston. Once Matthew heard his name, he smiled a knowing smile.

Scott Houston was known among Matthew's friends as the "hunk of the bar." Matthew had never seen Scott before. Now looking at this gorgeous man for the first time, Matthew knew why Scott had this title. He remembered how his friend, Ken Rivers, was constantly talking about Scott and how much he wanted to sleep with the "hunk of the bar." As they stood there and engaged in small talk, Matthew thought, "wait till Ken finds out I met Mr. Wonderful!"

Matthew was impressed by Scott Houston. Although it was small talk, it was clear that Scott's personality matched his stunning good looks. He was a genuine, down to earth person, who was warm and engaging. He appeared very comfortable with himself. "No wonder he's the star of the bar!", Matthew told himself. After about fifteen minutes, Janice in a very obvious fashion, excused herself from the conversation. This left Matthew and Scott alone.

Three dances and two hours later as the bar was closing, Matthew and Scott ended the evening by exchanging phone numbers. Janice was elated. Over the past year she had developed a strong distaste for Darren and she had made that clear to Matthew.

Matthew went home and crawled into bed next to a sleeping Darren. The evening and the weekend, although full of work, had ended on a high note for him. He had fun with Janice and he had met Scott. Matthew hid Scott's phone number in his sneaker, as he was sure that Darren had been going through his wallet for the past couple of months trying to see if Matthew had been cheating on him. He had not, but Darren was still probing. Matthew placed his head on the soft pillow and tried to fall asleep. He was thinking about Scott Houston in a sexual fashion. Little did Matthew know that the relationship between him and Scott would transcend the sexual bounds, and on this evening he had met one of the most important men in his life. But as he lay sleeping, erotic scenes of sex and waterfalls infused his dreams.

As the new decade approached, Matthew and Darren's relationship took a decided turn downhill. The relationship which had been marked with occasional physical confrontations, was becoming increasingly physically violent. Almost everyday of the week, Matthew and Darren would engage in physical confrontations. They would be followed by apologies, mostly offered by Matthew who for the most part was not the initiator of the violence. Then they would have sex, as if that were to wipe the slate clean and erase the violence. It had become an unhealthy pattern of interacting. Matthew felt trapped in the relationship. He was still obsessed with Darren, even though he knew that it was wrong. When he would think about leaving Darren he would remember Darren's regular comment that "nobody else would want you...you're nothing great." Matthew believed that. Matthew knew about domestic violence, but in gay relationships, domestic violence was unspoken. People looked away...and Matthew felt very alone.

To cope Matthew would spend more time away from Darren. He would spend this time with Janice and Scott. They had become his refuge amidst the chaotic relationship at home. But they were not enough. He still had to go home to Darren and that was very difficult for him. Matthew also began to fear for his life at times.

During the summer of 1979, Darren purchased a .357 Smith and Wesson revolver. Matthew told him he didn't like guns and was opposed to having a gun in the house. Darren didn't care. He responded, "I need it for the reserves. We have to carry all the time. Who knows when terrorists will attack! Look at what's happening in Iran for christsakes!" So the gun remained in the house or on Darren's hip. Darren always had an explanation for everything, and although Matthew never saw him bring the revolver with him to reserves, he accepted Darren's reasoning and let the issue drop. Darren found power in the gun. He was constantly toting it around the house and showing it off at inappropriate times to friends. He would bring out the gun and strut around, feigning shooting the gun. A few times he pointed it at Matthew in front of friends, thinking it was funny.

It was around this time that Darren became increasingly controlling over Matthew's day to day activities. He would call him repeatedly at work, as if to check in on Matthew. He demanded to know where Matthew was going after work or on the weekends. He wanted to know what Matthew was doing and with who. Matthew complied with Darren's demands. Although Darren would frequently be in parts unknown to Matthew, he did not in turn demand from Darren an itinerary of where he was. He was afraid to do that.

One evening when Matthew tried to stand up to Darren and refused to tell him where he was going, Darren became furious. The argument became so explosive that Darren took a hammer, smashed the tank and sparkplugs on Matthew's Honda 650 Nighthawk, disabling it so Matthew could not leave. When Matthew told Darren later that evening that he had to get the motorcycle fixed, Darren responded, "fuck you. If you had done as you were told, none of this would have happened. You pay to have it fixed!" And Matthew did.

Matthew also changed his posture during their physical fights as time went on. He would not strike back at Darren. Rather, he would stand there like a punching bag and endure the abuse. On more than one occasion, the abuse was so severe that Matthew actually blacked out. He was becoming ashamed of who he was as a man. When questioned at work about new scratches or bruises visible on different parts of his body, Matthew would always have some explanation that left out the true source of the injuries. He began to feel as if he was a battered wife...or maybe a battered child, in an adult's body.

For New Year's Eve 1980, Darren bought Matthew a gift that he would come to cherish more than he did his actual relationship with Darren. The holiday season had been difficult for both of them. Money was tight and this only exacerbated an already violent and destructive relationship. True to the pattern, Darren tried to make up for the physical abuse. As they were getting ready to go over their friends, Ted and Pete's house for the annual New Year's Eve party, Darren left the house for a few minutes. He returned with a black Labrador and Dalmatian puppy in his hands. "Happy New Year's", he said to Matthew as he placed the puppy in Matthew's extended hands. Matthew was shocked and thrilled with his gift! The tiny puppy began to lick his face.

A few moments later there was a knock on the door. It was Matthew's mother, Rosa. She walked in with a bag of puppy food and assorted dog toys. Matthew put the puppy down and she ran around the kitchen floor. Matthew, Darren and Rosa then began debating names for the new member of the family. Jokingly, Rosa said, "why don't you call her 'Diana', after Diana Ross?" They laughed together, paused and then looked at each other. They realized that this name was perfect for Matthew's puppy. Matthew was completely enthralled with the singing star Diana Ross. He had every record she produced and had bought videotapes of her movies. The name fit this little puppy to a tee. Diana the dog came into being that New Year's eve.

The beginning of the new decade brought with it a twist in Matthew and Darren's sexual relationship. It was becoming increasingly odd to Matthew. Darren had become fixated with pornography. Most of the male pornography he bought featured young, teenage boys. Of course the movies had the disclaimer that all the actors were over 18, but it was clear that their appearances in the movies was because they looked younger than 18. All Darren could talk about was how "cute" these young boys were. Everytime Matthew and Darren went to the mall or a store, Darren would be staring at teenage boys and make sexual comments to Matthew about them. This made Matthew increasingly uncomfortable.

When they would go out to "Fever" together, Darren would frequently seek out young men who clearly were not of drinking age, but through charm and flirting had obtained entrance into the gay bar. A few times Darren would bring these young men over to Matthew. He would introduce them and flirt with them in front of Matthew. Later he would tell Matthew that, "maybe we should have a threesome…it would brighten up our sex life!" Matthew would get angry at Darren and walk away. The threesomes never happened, but Matthew wondered often if twosomes did.

Matthew realized that this obsession of Darren's was becoming out of control. One evening, Darren's actions again illustrated that. They were out to eat with Ted and Pete. They went to a local family restaurant which was famous for its sandwiches and fair prices. As they were sitting drinking their coffee after dinner, Darren remarked to Ted, "look at that one", motioning with his head toward a table in the corner. When everyone looked to see who Darren was talking about, it became apparent that he found a 12 or 13 year old to be sexually exciting. Ted and Pete said nothing, but Matthew bellowed, "that's sick!" Darren laughed saying in response, "that's good chicken. I bet it's tasty!" Ted injected changing the subject trying to calm things down at the restaurant table. Pete gave Matthew a strong disapproving look, as if Matthew could take control or had some responsibility for Darren's obsession. Little did Matthew know, that this event would be a telling sign of what the future held.

Matthew found stability at his work, which did not say much about how his life in general was going. To find stability amidst the chaotic world of child abuse was not a good sign. In his third year at the job, the role of child protective investigator was becoming increasingly difficult. The child abuse cases continued to grow in his office. More children were being removed from their parent's custody by the DCP workers. The cases were becoming increasingly difficult and complicated. The nature of the abuse to the children was becoming more heinous. He would work well beyond the 40 hours a week he was assigned. Sometimes this was out of dedication, sometimes to avoid the volatile home environment he found himself in, and sometimes for both reasons.

Matthew was also appearing in court more often then he ever had in the past. He found himself entranced by the courtroom experience. Matthew had a childhood dream of becoming a lawyer. It must have come from all those *Perry Mason* shows that he watched with his mother. So Matthew decided to apply to various law schools in Massachusetts. Darren told him that he was "being an idiot" and that he would never get accepted into law school. Darren would take advantage of this subject to further insult Matthew. He would constantly berate him, telling Matthew, "you'll never get into law school…you're not smart enough…you're wasting your time and money." But this did not deter Matthew. He hoped as he waited for the response to his applications. Matthew had even applied to Harvard Law School. "What the hell…why not!", he thought. Scott and Janice were supportive to Matthew's application for law school. They would tell him that he should pursue this dream. "You're definitely smart enough!", exclaimed Janice one evening when Matthew was talking about his goals. Scott joined in "I think you would make a great lawyer!".

Over the next summer while testifying in a care and protection proceeding, Matthew met a lawyer who would become his friend and legal mentor. The beginning of their relationship certainly would not have indicated how instrumental Attorney Phillip Styles would become in Matthew's life. Their relationship started in the context of the child abuse case that Matthew was testifying as a witness for the state. In the case pending before the court, Attorney Styles represented a child who had been severely abused by his parents. DCP was slow to act in removing the child. But finally he was removed, and the parents were challenging his continued placement outside of their home. Attorney Styles was insisting in court that DCP and Matthew, as the assigned social worker, were not doing enough to protect this child from future abuse. The cross examination of Matthew by Attorney Styles was intense and condescending. At one point the DCP lawyer objected, "your honor. Counsel for the child is continuing to badger the witness! There is no need for this!" The objection was sustained. After another half hour of pointed cross-examination, it ended. Matthew was told he could step down from the witness stand. A relieved and tired Matthew walked out of the courtroom.

Matthew stood in the hall of the courtroom looking for a friend to join him for lunch. He felt a tap on the back of his shoulder. He turned and there was Attorney Styles. Phillip Styles said to Matthew with a smile, "I think I owe you lunch." Matthew looked at him perplexed at the invitation, considering the beating he had just received on the stand. After a moment or two, Matthew responded, "okay, I guess". Phillip invited him to follow and they went across the street from the court to a bagel and deli shop.

During their lunch Phillip and Matthew talked about social work and child protection. Matthew spent most of the lunch just sitting and listening. He found Phillip Styles to be incredibly interesting. Phillip had been a former child protection worker in New York City. Some of what he described as seeing in that job made Matthew cringe. Phillip moved to Springfield in the late '60s to attend law school at Western New England Law School. He decided to go to law school because he wanted to work in the area of child protection and advance legal issues on behalf of children. Phillip said, "I know you think I was being a dick to you in the courtroom. But I was doing my job. You have to hold DCP to the line in order to get the bureaucracy to work. That's what I was doing in the courtroom. It was nothing personal. It's my job." Matthew shook his head in agreement. While intellectually he agreed that there was nothing personal about what happened, emotionally he felt it was personal. "I guess I'll have to adjust", thought Matthew as he contemplated Attorney Styles remarks.

Matthew spoke with Phillip about how he wanted to be a lawyer also and that he had applied to law school. "I think that's wonderful", responded Phillip. Matthew thanked him and Phillip went on, "No, I really do. I think you would be a good lawyer. I may have given you a hard time today, but it's clear that you are an educated and dedicated man. You did good work on that case. If you can do a good job at

DCP then you will do good in law school." Matthew responded, "I hope so. I really want to do well there." Phillip offered, "please let me know if there is anything I can do to help." Matthew responded, "thanks."

During their lunch Phillip also discussed another subject that Matthew found interesting and disturbing at the same time. "I have a daughter…she's 6 years old", Phillip Styles told Matthew. Matthew smiled at the photograph that Phillip took out of his wallet. Phillip then went on to explain that the probate court denied him custody of his daughter when he and his wife were divorced. When questioned why, Phillip responded, "the court has a problem that I am living with a man and that he and I are lovers. The court loves mothers and hates homosexuals. They think we're going to screw in front of her or something. It's really ridiculous. My law partner, Octavia and I are working on the appeal. Meanwhile, I can't see her…", he sadly concluded as his voice trailed off. Matthew looked at Phillip and saw a man in pain. "That really sucks…it's backwards thinking", Matthew stated. "I know", responded Phillip. Matthew replied, "it's kinda scary to think these judges are so narrow minded." "It's really scary!", exclaimed Phillip.

Matthew then gave Phillip a rosy picture of his relationship with Darren. They talked about the local gay bars and shared 'war stories' of weekends in Provincetown. Phillip suggested that they should get together for dinner one night with their respective partners. Matthew agreed, but thought to himself, "Darren would think it was boring. He'll never go." Matthew further thought that he wouldn't want Darren to meet Phillip for fear that he might embarrass Matthew in front of this very bright and engaging attorney. Realizing that their lunch had gone on much longer than planned, Matthew said, "I've got to get going. I have to be in West Springfield in an hour for an appointment." The lunch ended with a firm handshake between the two and Matthew's promise to call Phillip's office soon to set up dinner.

In the fall, Matthew and Gail were approached by the Berkshire DCP director, Susan Warrington, to work on a very confidential investigation that was about to begin. They met with the director and four other social workers from DCP offices in Greenfield and Springfield in her office. Director Warrington explained that they would be assigned to a highly sensitive and delicate investigation. The director began, "we have received information that two priests who have been working in various dioceses throughout western Massachusetts have sexually abused up to 100 teenage boys over the last 10 years. You are going to work as teams and interview as many of these boys as possible. This investigation must be kept under wraps. Publicity could compromise its effectiveness. Therefore, you cannot talk to any of your peers in your respective offices about the nature of the investigation. I will be coordinating the investigation with Deputy Commissioner Sands from Boston." The director went on about the logistics of the investigation including coordination with the State Police.

This new investigation was to be one of the most difficult professional experiences for Matthew. It brought him much closer to his partner for the investigation, Gail. But it was also very difficult not to share details of the investigation and receive emotional support from his dear friend Janice. But he and Gail made the pact not to disclose the information. It was only several months later when the investigation was completed that they were allowed by Susan Warrington to confirm the rumors about the nature of the investigation.

A typical day during this prolonged investigation started with Matthew and Gail meeting with the other social workers at a coffee shop in Northampton. It was midway geographically for the six social workers who were paired into three teams. They also found the ambiance of Northampton to be an enjoyable and relaxing way to start each day. The social workers would review with each other the previous day's activities and what was planned for the day ahead. Each day would consist of at least four or five interviews with possible victims and their families. The pace was intense, but the number of potential victims was so high that they needed to work at that pace before the word spread and evidence started to disappear. Many times an interview with one family would yield the name of a new possible victim that was not in the original report. As the weeks wore on, Matthew and his colleagues were becoming tired, burnt out and punchy about the investigations. But they pursued on, stress and all.

The holiday season was approaching as the investigations were beginning to come to a close. Frequently, Matthew and Gail would have discussions about how the investigations were affecting their religious beliefs. The season only magnified the depth of their discussions. Both Matthew and Gail had been raised strict Catholics. They had both attended catholic schools. Gail graduated from a catholic college. Matthew had at one time thought of becoming a missionary priest. The facts that their investigations were uncovering about these priests were irreconcilable with what both Matthew and Gail had been taught and believed about priests all these years. Yet, the discussions about religion and the priests violation of the religious teachings were compelling to Matthew. They made him think a great deal about his perceptions of the catholic church. They also made him think about how he as a gay man fit into the church. This was a church that condemned his homosexuality and yet hid the fact that many of its priests were pedophiles. "Something is wrong here", said Matthew to himself.

The two principals in the case were Father James Simpson and Father Leo Wolfe. They were both in their late 50's and had been priests for over 25 years. They had served in many different parishes throughout the Connecticut Valley. They also had been mysteriously reassigned on many occasions. Matthew and Gail learned that they mystery of their reassignments was not that deep. Anytime a parent would confront one of the priests about his or her concerns regarding their contact with the parent's son, a quick reassignment would occur. Then the abuse would start all over again, with fresh, new victims for Father Simpson and Father Wolfe.

The information that Matthew and Gail were receiving during the investigation was incredibly incriminating. The information was consistent with that the other social worker teams were receiving as well. The typical victim in these cases was a 13 to 15 year old male. The child had been encouraged by his parents to become an altar boy or to be active in the church. The priests, who maintained regular contact whether they were assigned to a parish together or not, would have many outings for the altar boys. These included overnight trips, camping trips, beach trips and sometimes nights at the rectory. It was typically at these events that Father Simpson and Father Wolfe would take advantage of these children sexually.

The abuse was classic. It would begin as an offer to massage the tired young boy after a busy day of physical activity. Over time it would escalate. In many cases there were repeated acts of oral and anal intercourse with the children. They boys were regularly told that they were "helping" Father Wolfe and Father Simpson to relieve the stress of being a priest. They were told that by engaging in sex they were helping the priests to be "better priests so they could carry out their mission." Threats also accompanied the abuse. But the threats were covert. The boys were told that they could not tell their parents about the abuse, and if they did they would be "betraying the church". So the boys remained silent, and guilt ridden. They knew that what was happening felt wrong, but telling about it seemed to be worse than the actual abuse. It wasn't until Matthew or one of his colleagues confronted the boys that the disclosures came. Then there were many crying, scared and damaged boys who needed reassurance and comfort from their families and the social workers.

Matthew could understand how difficult this abuse was for these boys. Not only did it raise questions of their sexual preference at a time of identity searching, it also challenged the core of these teenagers religious beliefs. Matthew would become very angry about this.

"How could they do this to this kids? They've taken away so much…their sexual identity and their religion." Matthew and Gail frequently talked about how Father Simpson and Father Wolfe had not only violated these boys bodies, but their trust and faith in adults and in God was also violated.

Many of the parents who were confronted with the revelations about what happened to their sons were horrified. They did not want to file criminal complaints and nor did they want DCP to pursue it further. It challenged the parents also. Not only did these revelations raise the issue of religion, they also brought up the taboo of homosexuality. It challenged parents own decision making about the access they granted the priests to their children. When Gail and Matthew would try to explain that the priests were not homosexual, but rather pedophiles, it was a rare parent that understood. Most parents wanted the priests and DCP to go away. Matthew and Gail also were on the receiving end of many parent's frustration and anger about the situation. They were accused many times of being on a 'witch hunt' and trying to persecute these priests. Matthew found this to be hard to deal with. They were doing their job and trying to protect children. But the parents just wanted to make believe it never happened.

As the investigation entered its final phase, rumors throughout the community were spreading like wildfire. Matthew and his colleagues were glad that most of the interviews were done. The final interviews usually were nonproductive as the rumor of what was going on would cause parents to either refuse to meet with DCP or children to just shut down about the abuse. Even Matthew's mother had heard the rumors and questioned him about them. "Mom…you know how rumors get started, just ignore it.", he told his mother. Matthew knew that if he divulged to his mother what was really going on he would lose his job. His mother responded that she would go and pray for the priests and pray that the rumors were not true. Matthew thought that maybe her prayers could help.

During the last week of the investigation, Gail insisted to Matthew that they were being followed as they drove to their appointments. Matthew told Gail, ",,,you're just burnt out and becoming paranoid. Nobody's following us…nobody is that interested in what were doing." However, a few days later Matthew came home to find tacked on the outside of his apartment door a piece of notepaper. On the paper, in crude writing was an itemization of where he and Gail had been for the last three days while conducting their investigations. The writing, which Matthew did not recognize, included the names and addresses of their investigations and how long they had spent at each home.

Matthew tore the paper off the outside door. He ran into the apartment and called Gail. "I told you someone was following us!", she said. Then she added, "do you think somebody wants to hurt us?" Matthew responded that he didn't know. He told Gail that he would let Susan Warrington know about the note tomorrow. As he was concluding their frightened conversation Darren walked in. Matthew said, "gotta go, Darren's home" and hung up the phone. Matthew asked Darren if he had seen anyone strange around the house lately. Darren replied he hadn't and then asked "why?" Matthew explained he found a piece of paper tacked to the door. He showed it to Darren who looked at it and then asked, "what does it mean?" Matthew indicated that it reflected the addresses and times of the investigations that he had been doing with Gail the past few days. Darren said, "that's weird" and walked away without any further interest in the subject.

The investigation concluded with Matthew and Frank Livingston, a supervisor from the Greenfield office who had been working on the investigations, being chosen to interview the two priests about the allegations. Both priests were now inpatient at a psychiatric unit of Our Lady of Hope hospital in Holyoke. The night before Matthew and Frank were to meet with the priests, Matthew received a call from Susan Warrington. Father Simpson had left the hospital and boarded a plane to San Juan, Puerto Rico earlier that evening. It was a one-way ticket. They didn't know about it in time to get him at the airport. Father Wolfe remained in the hospital.

The next day Matthew, Frank, two state police officers and an assistant district attorney went to the hospital to interview Father Wolfe. When Matthew walked into the conference room for the interview the first thing he thought was, "I hope he's not wearing his collar", referring to the traditional catholic garb. Matthew was relieved when Father Wolfe walked into the conference room, accompanied by his therapist, in regular street clothes.

The interview was much different than Matthew anticipated it would be. It seemed like a catharsis for Father Wolfe. After being advised of his Miranda rights, Father Wolfe readily waived them. He confessed to sexually abusing the teenage boys. The high drama of the interview, which it appeared that Father Wolfe was calculatingly building up to, was when Father Wolfe implicated his fellow priest, Father Simpson as also being responsible. In fact, at one point during the interview, Father Wolfe attempted to lay the responsibility for the abuse on Father Simpson. "He forced me to do it…he blackmailed me. He told me he would tell the Bishop.", Father Wolfe told his inquisitors. Matthew had the task of reciting more than 58 names of teenage boys to Father Wolfe. The purpose of this exercise was to verify whether children that DCP had interviewed were actual victims. As Matthew read the names from his list, Father Wolfe responded with dramatic pauses and gestures. He would then explain in explicit detail what sexual acts he had engaged in with the child Matthew had identified. He also indicated that some children had been sexually abused by both himself and Father Simpson.

Some of the names Father Wolfe did not recall. When pressed by Matthew, he would respond, "I probably did it with that one too." After saying this about ten or twelve times, Matthew became very angry inside. But he did well in hiding his anger. Matthew was furious that this man could not even remember the names of some of his victims. This was extremely disturbing to him. "They were only little sexual play things to him...their names didn't matter", Matthew thought as he was writing, while Father Wolfe was continuing to explain what happened with the children.

The investigation was finally over. Father Simpson never returned to the states and his location on the island of Puerto Rico was never determined. There was no criminal prosecution of Father Wolfe. The district attorney maintained that he could not get a jury to convict a catholic priest. Father Wolfe was reassigned. Matthew never found out where. He didn't want to know. He only hoped it was somewhere where there was no access to children.

About a month after the conclusion of the "priest investigations", as Matthew was now calling them, he found the impact of those investigations to be weighing heavily on his soul. He was questioning more and more his religious beliefs. As he was driving to a routine investigation he passed his old catholic church from his youth. He pulled into the parking lot, got out of the car and walked into the church. There was no one else present in the church. Matthew sat in a pew and stared at the large crucifix hanging over the altar. Alone in the church he began to yell in his mind at the crucified Jesus. "Why do you let these things happen? What did these boys do to deserve this? This shouldn't go on! You have let me down!", he told God.

Matthew sat in the church for almost an hour. He continued to stare at the crucifix and continued to be angry at God. Silently tears fell from his eyes. When he stood up to leave, he never let his stare leave the crucifix. He walked out the church door. God had not answered his questions. "Maybe there is no answer", he thought.

As Christmas was around the corner, Matthew and Darren went to the mall one evening to finish up their shopping. Matthew caught Darren staring at a young teenage boy. He yelled at Darren who promptly responded in his usual fashion, telling Matthew to "fuck off!" They continued to walk through the mall and continued to argue. The argument grew and then went to other subjects in their relationship.

The argument continued during the drive home. Matthew told Darren that he was unsupportive to him during the recent weeks when work was so stressful. Darren responded, "get a new job...I don't give a shit if your job stresses you out. It's not my problem!" Matthew persisted, "you could have been supportive to me during these heavy duty investigations. It was hard on me. It was long hours, no support. But you just bitched at me all the time." Darren responded, "too bad", as he continued to drive down the highway. Matthew went on, "how about that day when I came home and found the note tacked on the door with my itinerary for the day. That was scary...but you couldn't be bothered." Darren looked across the car seat, intensely stared into Matthew's eyes and said, "I had you followed. I wanted to know what you were doing, so I paid Doug to do it."

Matthew stared back as Darren returned his eyes to the road. "What!", he screamed. Darren started laughing and said, "I told you. I was the one who had you followed. You wouldn't tell me what was going on, so I decided to find out myself. You guys were easy targets. Not very creative...always the same route. Gail pokes when she drives too. Anybody could have picked you off if they wanted to!" Matthew shook his head in disbelief. He started to say something but Darren put his hand up to Matthew. "I would shut up if I was you", he told Matthew. Matthew shut up and the subject was never raised again. Inside he felt bretrayed again. Betrayed by Darren, betrayed by the priests, betrayed by God.

The following week began a stressful period for Matthew. His anxiety was as he knew that the acceptances to law school would be coming shortly. He was leaning on Scott and Janice, and now his new friend, Attorney Phillip Styles for support. They reassured him and helped him deal with his fear of rejection. Darren couldn't be bothered with the law school matter. He told Matthew, "If one of those schools is stupid enough to let you in and it's in Boston, count me out. I'm not moving to that fucking city!" Little did Darren know, but that comment gave Matthew strength. He now was placing more hope in getting into law school. If Darren was not going to move with him and he was accepted at one of the three schools he had applied to in Boston, Darren would stay behind and their relationship would finally be over. Boston sounded just fine to Matthew; in fact it sounded inviting.

The letters began arriving shortly before New Year's. Matthew had been accepted at Western New England School of Law in Springfield. While he was excited about this, he still was placing his hopes on getting into one of the Boston law schools. A day before New Year's 1981 Matthew received two letters. They were from Suffolk University Law School in Boston and Harvard Law School in Cambridge. Matthew brought the letters, unopened to his office and put them in his desk drawer. He was sure they were rejections. "Harvard was just a joke anyway. I could never get in there.", he said to himself.

Matthew and Darren went to Ted and Pete's annual New Year's Eve party. They both got very drunk and decided they better not drive home. They ended up sleeping over. In the morning, a clearly hung over Matthew woke to find himself in bed with a major headache. He wanted to go check the acceptance letters. He walked down the hall of Ted and Pete's second floor and took a long hot shower which finally sobered him up. Matthew drove to the office. Using his key to gain entry on this holiday, he went down to his office and opened his desk drawer. He pulled out the letters from Suffolk and Harvard. He read each letter two or three times. He had been accepted for the fall semester at both law schools. He could not believe it! He yelled, "all right!", in the empty office and began to run around the office laughing and singing, "I'm going to law school!" over and over again. Matthew paused momentarily. "Thank God nobody's here…they'd think I've lost my mind!", he said out loud.

He sat down at his desk and called his parents, Rosa and Franco. They were very excited for him and praised him upon his acceptance. He called Scott and Janice. They were thrilled. They decided to go out to dinner, the three of them. He called Darren and left a message on the answering machine that he was going out. He purposely did not leave the message that he had gotten accepted to law school.

After dinner that evening Matthew, Scott and Janice went to "Fever". They danced away in celebration of Matthew's news. Phillip Styles arrived later and upon hearing the news joined in the celebration. While dancing, Matthew realized that a major door in his life, both professionally and personally had just opened for him. He knew that he needed to walk through that open door to his new life.

CHAPTER 3

ON TO THE NEXT CHAPTER

February 1981

Matthew's acceptance to Harvard was tempered by Darren's revised decision that a move to the Boston area would be good for him as well. Matthew thought that his acceptance to law school would provide the easy way to end the relationship. Just move on to a new chapter in their lives. But Darren was intending upon making it difficult. By indicating that he too was moving to Boston, Matthew felt that his 'no pain' plan was being taken away from him. Once again the control over his day to day existence would continue to be exercised by Darren. Darren would ruin Matthew's law school career.

Matthew had talked to Gail and Janice about going to counseling to address how to end this relationship now that the easy way out was taken away from him. They had encouraged him to do so, but Matthew felt trapped. He knew that he needed help, and yet he could not move forward to seek it. So Matthew did nothing and let the world operate around him. He spent the next several weeks just going through the motions of life. He was becoming noticeably more depressed. His friends at work could measure his depression in the way he was gaining weight, always looking tired and seeming scattered brain most of the time. This was not the Matthew they had come to know over the years. Even his job was beginning to suffer. Janice had offered to help Matthew with the break up. She said, "just tell him that you will be under a lot of stress in law school. Tell him the stress of having a relationship and all the responsibility that comes with it will take away from school. It's neutral…it doesn't make him look bad." While Matthew agreed this sounded like a good plan, (in fact it almost mirrored Matthew's plan), he never took Janice's offer for assistance. The break up conversation never took place. Matthew was too fearful of Darren's response.

Matthew's friends began to distance themselves from activities that would involve Darren as well. A minor event one evening provided the last straw for Gail, who vowed that she would never attend any activity that involved Darren again. Matthew had invited friends over from work for a spaghetti dinner. Trying to be the Italian cook that his mother was, Matthew put every effort into the dinner for ten. He even bought Lambrusco wine, which he hated, because his mother had said it was a traditional wine with spaghetti. The dinner itself was a success. Matthew's friends poured on the accolades about how good the food was. Darren was abusive in his response, "it's spaghetti sauce for Christ sakes!" he replied when Matthew asked him what he thought of the dinner.

After dinner Darren poured drinks for everyone. While sitting on the couch discussing the latest news and gossip, Matthew began to crunch the remaining ice in his drink. Darren lashed out. "Would you stop that shit! It's annoying. You're 27 years old, not 7. Stop being such a baby and act your age!", he screamed at Matthew. Matthew turned red and immediately spit out the ice that was in his mouth. The room became silent for a few moments. His friends, especially Gail, stared at Matthew. Sharon changed the subject quickly to set off the awkwardness that had set in. The evening then progressed quietly without further comment from Darren. But to

Gail, this was a sure sign of Darren's control over Matthew and she did not like it. Further, she felt it was humiliating to do this in front of Matthew's friends. She knew that Darren's berating Matthew had embarrassed him. The next morning she let the other friends know her vow, but she never said anything to Matthew. She did not want to hurt his feelings further.

The gray dark days of February made Matthew more depressed. He could not hide it. Even his supervisor at work was now noticing. She took Gail aside one day and asked, "what's going on with Matthew? He seems out of it all the time." Gail just shrugged her shoulders. She would not violate Matthew's confidence in her and disclose what she perceived to be the problem. She was too loyal to her friend, even though she disapproved of his lover.

Many times during the month February, Matthew would leave work or his last appointment and just drive in his car with no particular direction or destination in sight. He would drive around trying to figure out how he got into all of this and if he could ever get out. At times he was even reconsidering law school. "I can't deal with Darren and studying at the same time.", he would think. Then he would become angry with himself and more determined to go to law school. Law school was something that he had always wanted to do. He had dreamed of it since he was a child. Darren was not going to take that away from him. Matthew became resigned to the fact that Darren would not leave his life and that he was going to Boston with Darren in town. "I'll just have to deal with it.", he decided.

However, one cold damp day in early March changed all that. It began as a typical work day for Matthew. He had an investigation that involved a 15 year old victim of sexual abuse named Craig Talbot. The investigation was as routine as most, but this teenager struck the rescue cord in Matthew. Matthew went to meet Craig at a runaway shelter in Springfield. The shelter was an old Victorian house in a neighborhood surrounded by crime and drug addicts. The shelter was a small oasis of safety, in a neighborhood that had clearly seen better days. Matthew hated going to this shelter and would always schedule his appointments there during the day. He did not want to be caught in this part of the city after sun down.

Craig Talbot was an attractive, muscular teenage boy with jet black hair. Matthew and Craig met alone in the conference room of the shelter. The conference room offered privacy and comfort which was conducive to interviews. It must have been a library at one time when the shelter functioned as a grand home in its early days. Matthew appreciated old architecture and old houses. He especially liked the walls of the conference room. They were lined with floor to ceiling bookcases. "I want a room like this someday", he thought to himself.

Matthew and Craig spent three hours speaking. Craig detailed how over the past two to three years his mother and father had sexually abused him and prostituted him to their friends. Craig was not shy with his language. He spoke explicitly. The abuse started initially with Craig joining his parents in their sexual activities. Both his mother and father would perform sex acts on Craig. The abuse escalated to his parents bringing friends, and then paying customers to their home to have sex with Craig. Some of the sexual activity had been videotaped by his parents. The abuse also included group sex. "One time…", Craig said to Matthew, "I had to give two guys head while my mother was shoving a dildo up my ass. I liked sucking the guys cocks, but your mother shoving a big black dildo up your ass…now that's disgusting!" Matthew calmly listened as he took notes while Craig continued with the details. Craig told him that he finally decided that having sex with his parents was "too weird" and he told them he wanted to stop. They didn't agree and the sex continued against his wishes.

Craig continued on with his soliloquy. He told Matthew that finally, he "couldn't take it anymore". So he ran away to his aunt's house in Springfield. However, she was not sympathetic to him. Once he was calmed down in her house she called the police who already had a runaway warrant for him. He was returned to his parent's house and his father severely beat him while he was anally penetrating him. "No one gives a shit about me – I'm just a piece of meat!" Craig exclaimed.

"Do you want to see the bruises on my ass?", Craig asked Matthew. Matthew politely said, "no…that's okay. I believe you." The night before he ran away again Craig had been involved in an orgy with seven adults. They had tied him up and "two guys tried to fuck me at the same time. It hurt so bad. When everybody left and my Mom and Dad were passed out, I took off", he told Matthew. He found out about the runaway shelter on the street from a friend he had met on his second day as a child of the streets.

Craig then began to turn the tone of the interview into a flirtatious tone. "Do you think I'm sexy?", he said to Matthew with a smirk on his face. Matthew ignored the question and moved on. But Craig again interrupted him, "Come on man, do you think I'm hot?", he asked Matthew. Matthew responded, "Craig, that isn't my job. My job is to make sure you are safe. I'm not here to talk with you or decide if you are sexually attractive. Plus, I'm an adult…you are still a child. You shouldn't try to find sexual approval from adults." Craig guffawed and said, "yeah, right…you know you want me." Matthew again ignored Craig's remarks.

Matthew ended the interview by explaining to Craig what the process would be so that he would not have to go back to his parent's house. Matthew explained that he would return tomorrow to take Craig to the juvenile court so he could be placed in the state's custody and then probably go to a foster home.

"Good", said Craig. "I want to get the hell out of this shelter. Three guys have hit on me already…they want to suck my cock. I've had enough of that shit!" Matthew could not understand this direct change in attitude by Craig. A few moments ago he was trying to flirt with Matthew. Now he was condemning the sexual acts. Matthew stood up to leave. Craig said to him in a loud and forceful voice, "I ain't no faggot, you know!". Matthew just smiled and then reached forward with his hand and shook Craig's. "I'll see you tomorrow.", he told the young boy.

When Matthew was driving back to the office he thought about Craig's comment that other boys in the shelter were coming on to him sexually. Matthew found that many victims of sexual abuse had characterized what may be an innocent situation into a sexual one. Maybe it was true that some of the boys were trying to become sexual with Craig, but Matthew thought that this most likely was Craig's perception. It struck him funny that many victims of sexual abuse think that sex is the primary factor in every human relationship, no matter how superficial, that they may establish. Then he thought that this was sad. It was distorted and could have a devastating effect on future interactions and relationships for Craig. He thought of Craig's remarks to him. This too made him sad. They were misdirected and harmful.

Matthew found Janice dutifully working at her desk upon his return. He leaned over and gave her a kiss on the cheek. "Do you want to go for a drink after work?", he asked her. Janice readily accepted the invitation, she had been going through a tough week. She had three overdue investigations and the time clock was her worst enemy. Matthew sat at his desk and began to try to get through his own pile of paperwork. "Oh shit!", he said out loud. "I'd better call Darren and see if it's okay if I go out." Janice looked at him and smirked in disapproval. Matthew picked up the phone and dialed home. The answering machine picked up. Relieved that he did not have to quarrel with Darren about where he was going and with whom, he left a curt message on the machine. "I'm going out with friends for drinks after work. I won't be long. See you later."

Matthew and Janice spent a few hours at the "townie bar" in Westfield. They were joined by Sharon and her lover Louise. Kendall showed up as they were ready to go, so they ordered another drink. It was a fun, light evening with his friends. They all knew that they had to get up for work the next day so the evening was an early one.

Matthew arrived home to an empty driveway. "Good", he thought, "...some peace and quiet for awhile." His new apartment that he and Darren had moved to last month was in a two family house, located on a quiet street in Lenox. Matthew's friends had nicknamed the place the "Hurricane House" because of its dilapidated external appearance. But the inside of the home was spacious and well kept. Matthew was glad they had moved from their tiny apartment to this home. It was also good for Diana. It gave her more room and there was a yard behind the house that she could run in. The yard was filled with beautiful trees and Matthew could hardly wait to see their burst of fall color come several months down the road.

Diana greeted Matthew with a running bark as he came through the door. He reached down and hugged her as she licked his face and waged her tail profusely. At eight months old, Diana was becoming bigger and stronger every day. Her tail was a lethal weapon. When she got excited she wagged her tail so hard that a mug or glass on the coffee table was not safe. If her tail would hit it, the glass or mug would go flying. Matthew would laugh. Darren would yell. Matthew gave Diana her "scoobies", as he called her dog biscuits. As she was eating them he looked at her, thinking as he frequently did, "...would Diana Ross be angry that I named my dog after her?" Matthew always decided that Diana Ross would not be angry with him because he loved his dog. Naming her after Miss Ross was a sign of his affection for her and a compliment, thought Matthew. It made him laugh. He grabbed a soda out of the refrigerator and went to the kitchen table to check the mail. He looked down at the table and was shocked by what he saw lying there staring him in the face.

There, with the letterhead of the Commonwealth of Massachusetts, was an investigation letter with Darren's name at the salutation. The letter stated: "Dear Darren Warner: The Massachusetts Division of Child Protection has received a report that identifies you as responsible for the sexual abuse of George Bridges. An investigator from this office will be meeting with you on March 7, 1981 at 2:00 to discuss these allegations. You may have an attorney present if you desire. If you have any questions please call me at the telephone number above." The letter was signed by Paul Stafford, an investigator from the DCP office in Springfield.

Matthew sat down in the kitchen chair. He read the letter over and over again. He did not speak. The letter, which was an exact duplicate of the letters he had issued to persons when he was conducting child abuse investigations, caused panic in him. His mind began to race. "Who was George Bridges? How old is he?", thought Matthew. "Where did this happen? What did Darren do? Does anybody at work know about this?" Matthew could not stop these questions from racing around inside his head. "Do I know this kid? What the hell did Darren do with him? Do they think I had anything to do with this? Am I going to be fired?" His head began to hurt as the questions continued to spin around.

Suddenly Darren walked in the door. He didn't even have his jacket half off when Matthew stood up and held the letter up in Darren's face. Matthew burst out, "what the fuck is this?" and threw the letter at Darren. Darren picked up the letter off the floor and began to laugh. "Poor baby", he said to Matthew in a sarcastic tone. "What's wrong? Is mister Matthew a little upset?" Matthew stood right in front of Darren's face and screamed, "tell me what the hell is going on!" Darren who was enjoying Matthew's anxiety said, "are we a little bit nervous? Oh poor baby, what's wrong? Your career flashing before your eyes?" Matthew continued in his verbal assault. "I said, tell me what the fuck is going on! This isn't funny. I want to know what's going on right now!", he yelled.

Darren turned and went to grab a drink of water. He drank the water, put the glass down and stood right in front of a fuming Matthew. Darren coldly stared at Matthew without saying a word. He raised his hand and smacked Matthew across the face. "Now sit down before I knock your ass on the floor!", he yelled at Matthew. Matthew turned and cowardly did as he was told. After a few moments of silence Matthew in a much calmer voice said to Darren, "please just tell me what this is all about." Darren responded, "shut the fuck up! I'll tell you when I'm ready."

After what seemed like an eternity, but in reality was only was a few minutes, Darren began to speak. With a devilish smirk on his face, Darren began his tale. "George is this really hot blond 14 year old. He's all smooth…no hair on his chest. He loves getting his cock sucked. He's got a great dick…it's thick and hard. He can shoot his load three or four times in an afternoon!" Matthew sat frozen in the chair as the words Darren was uttering were echoing in his ears. His mind was telling him that what he was hearing was not true, but yet he knew that it was.

Darren continued on. "I met George right before Christmas, outside the high school. Every Thursday when I get out of work early I cruise down by the school and talk to the kids. They love my Trans Am and I take them for rides in the car. We usually drive to the woods and party. Sometimes I smoke pot with them or have a few beers. These kids are really curious, you know? They get a little high or drunk and they'll let you give them a blow job. I've met about five or six kids over the last few months." Matthew put his hand up to stop Darren from talking. Darren looked at him and said, "you wanted to know. So just sit there and be quiet or I won't tell you any more!"

Darren sat down right next to Matthew and continued with his story leaning into Matthew and speaking in a purring seductive tone. "Sometimes I've brought some of the kids home here and fooled around with them. These kids are great. They can keep it up all day." Matthew could feel his heart beating faster and faster. He felt like he could not breathe. Darren went on. "George is real special to me. He's my favorite. Like I told you, he's got a great dick. He shoots a real big load. Lately he's been loving to fuck my ass. He's real good at it. In fact, I even told him I wanted him to do a threesome with you and me and he wants to." Matthew quickly interrupted, "that's disgusting!" Darren leaned into Matthew's face, saying "fuck you! So anyway, let me show you how special George really is. Once you see this you'll want to be sucking that cock too!"

Darren got up and went into the bedroom. A moment later he returned with Polaroid pictures in his hand. "Here take a look", he said to Matthew as he threw five or six pictures on the kitchen table. Matthew looked away. Darren sat back down and held the pictures up in Matthew's face. They showed a young blond boy, naked with erections. A few of the pictures showed him ejaculating. Matthew presumed this was George. "Don't you want to suck that big fat cock?", Darren asked Matthew. "You're sick!", replied a now shaking Matthew. Darren leaned back in the chair and said, "well I may be sick, but I'm getting that chicken almost every day." Matthew looked at him and tried to obtain a calm voice, but when he spoke he was very loud. "This is fucking disgusting!", Matthew bellowed, "...and it's illegal!" Darren responded, "who gives a shit! Its fucking fun and he loves getting his cock sucked!" Matthew reached across the kitchen table and grabbed the investigation letter. "What about this?", he said to Darren throwing it into his lap. Darren picked up the letter and crumpled it up in his hands. He looked at Matthew and said, "you think because George's mother turned me into your job that I'm going to stop? I'm having fun and nothing will stop me. George calls me all the time. I give great head and he loves it! If you and his mother don't like it that's too fucking bad! Get used to it!"

Matthew stood up and yelled at Darren, "you're going to go to jail and I'm going to lose my job!" Darren stood up too and yelled back. "I don't give a shit about your job! I'm not stopping it with George...and if you know that guy Paul that wants to come talk to me, you better tell him to bring the state troopers because I'm packing! DCP isn't going to tell me what to do!" Darren turned and stormed into the living room. Matthew sat back down at the kitchen table. His mind continued to race. The pressure on his head was intense. He held his head in his hands, shaking his head as if he could shake the demons away.

About a half hour passed when Darren came back into the kitchen. "What the fuck is wrong with you?", he screamed at Matthew. Matthew shook his head and said, "I can't believe your doing this to me. I'm sure everyone at work knows about this...you're ruining me and you don't care!" Darren looked at Matthew and said, "no, I don't care...and you and your job can go fuck yourselves!" With that final salvo Darren went into the bedroom and slammed the door. Matthew remained sitting at the kitchen table. His mind would not stop racing. His picked up the investigation letter and read it over and over. He picked up the photographs and flipped threw them. They disgusted him. He thought he should throw them out, but he decided that Darren would probably beat him if he did.

Matthew finally went into the living room and grabbed the quilt off the back of the couch. He would sleep there. He refused to sleep in the same bed as Darren. He called Diana up on the couch and laid there cuddling her. He tried to calm himself down, but his mind continued to race. He could not make it stop. Tears were streaming down his face. Matthew felt like he wanted to throw up. He got up two times and tried to do so, but was unable. He tried to fall asleep but he was not successful. He tossed and turned in the bed. Matthew was sure that this must be the worst moment in his life. This was even worse than what had happened in California. Finally, he drifted off to sleep, but it was not a sound sleep.

The morning sun shining through the living room blinds woke Matthew up. He took a quick shower and dressed for work. He took Diana outside for her morning walk. As she walked Matthew stared down the street and off into the clouds. Then he looked down at his watch. He was running late for work. He hurried Diana along, ran into the house and grabbed his notebook for work off the table. As he reached for the notebook, the investigation letter and pictures were staring up at him. "No, it had not been a bad dream", he sadly thought. Matthew looked around the kitchen corner at the bedroom door. It was still closed. Darren must be asleep. He certainly was not going to go in and wake him up. Matthew grabbed a can of soda out of the refrigerator, leaned down and gave Diana a kiss good-bye and headed out the door.

Matthew jumped into his Mustang and began his short morning commute. When he got closer to the office he drove slower and slower. "Who at work knows about the investigation?", he thought. "Does my boss know?…he must. Do my friends know? I hope not." Matthew pulled into the parking lot in the rear of the office. He sat in the car for a few minutes trying to calm himself. "I'll try to act as normal as possible", Matthew thought. He looked in the car's rear-view mirror. The stress of the situation was written all over his face. "I have to relax", he said out loud. Before he exited the car he decided that he should tell Janice about the situation. "Maybe she can give me some guidance about what to do.", he thought.

Matthew went into his office and right to his desk. He began to make phone calls about his investigations to different agencies and local police departments. He still had a lot of work to do. As he was on the phone Janice walked in and greeted him with a cheery "good morning!". Matthew half heartedly waved to her. When he hung up the phone Janice turned to him and said, "what's wrong with you?" He knew that it was written all over his face, but he responded, "just a little hung over from last night." Matthew was not ready to talk to Janice about what was going on. He couldn't deal with the demon that was now in his life so early in the morning. He would talk to her later.

Lunch time arrived and Matthew invited Janice to join him. They walked down the street to the local deli that many in the office frequented. The deli was overpriced for the small portions you received, but Matthew knew that Janice liked it there. Matthew would become infuriated with the attitude of superiority that the staff in the deli had. They acted as if you should be grateful that they would serve you. But Matthew decided that they could get a booth in the back. There he could talk to Janice about what was happening with some privacy.

About half way through their lunch Matthew said to Janice, "I have something to tell you and it's really bad." Janice looked up from her plate with a look of concern on her face. "Go ahead", she said to him. Matthew then began detailing for Janice the events of the night before. He went through every detail, including the photographs. Janice was dumbfounded. She just kept looking straight ahead at Matthew as he explained the events. Matthew finally finished his story and without any question to Janice, she exclaimed in a loud tone, "that bastard!" Matthew raised his finger to his mouth to shush her. "I'm sorry", she responded to his cue. Janice in a rushed tone said to Matthew, "you have to get out that apartment and quick! He's going to ruin your life. I hate that motherfucker for this!" Matthew hung his head down. For the longest time he did not say a word. The silence was deafening. He knew that Janice was right. He had to end this relationship. He had to leave Darren and he had to do it right away. But he was also incredibly scared about leaving and didn't know if he could do it. He explained his fear to Janice about leaving and said, "you know, he's got a gun." Janice replied, "I don't care! You have to get out there. I'll help you...we can call Scott to help too. He'll help out. Just get out!" He signed heavily. They finished the remainder of their lunch in complete silence.

Walking back to the office Matthew explained his embarrassment about the situation to Janice. She looked at him and said, "you have nothing to be embarrassed about. He's the child molester. You didn't do anything." Matthew responded, "I know. I'm just afraid what people will think..." Janice replied, "fuck what people will think! I mean, you don't have any doubts about whether he did this do you?"

Matthew shook his head 'no' and said, "especially not after I saw those pictures."

They stood out in the parking lot for a few moments and talked some more before they went back into the office. Janice told Matthew he needed to tell their new boss, Kevin Michaels about what was happening. Matthew agreed, but told her he thought it would be hard. His relationship with the new director of the office was good most of the time, but right now they were in a strained period. Janice insisted that he tell Kevin. "You just need to sit down and talk with him. You need to let him know that you had nothing to do with this…that you didn't know it was happening, and that your moving out." Matthew knew she was right. He told her that he would talk to Kevin tomorrow about it. "I can't do it today. I don't think I can handle any more today. Plus, I don't want to have him see me cry." His face bore the stress of the past few days. Matthew looked completely wiped out.

They also talked about who among their inner circle of work friends should know about this. They decided that Gail should be informed. She and Matthew had become good friends, especially during the 'priest investigations', when they were partners. Janice volunteered to tell Gail. Matthew decided he should tell Sharon, another close friend of theirs. He also told Janice he would ask Sharon if it was possible to stay at her home for awhile until this all blew over. Janice thought this was a good idea. "What about Scott?", Janice asked Matthew. He responded, "I'm going to be really embarrassed to tell him…but it should really come from me. I'll call him later. Maybe he can help me move my stuff out. I probably should get out of there this weekend." Janice agreed. They walked back into the office together, both trying to maintain their composure and act as normally as possible.

Matthew called Scott and invited himself over to his house for the evening. Scott could tell from Matthew's voice that something was wrong but he did not ask. Matthew said he would be over after dinner at his mother's. The remainder of the work day was uneventful; Matthew apparently pulled it off. Nobody acted as if anything was wrong. But inside he knew that everything was wrong.

That evening after having his second beer at Scott's house and engaging in small talk for about an hour, Scott sternly asked Matthew, "will you tell me what's wrong?" Matthew responded, "what do you mean?" Scott sat down next to him on the sofa and said, "I can tell something's wrong. I know you too well by now. What's going on?" Matthew slowly began to explain to Scott what had happened with Darren. He told Scott the whole thing was "crazy" and that he felt like he was losing his mind. Scott noticeably became angrier and angrier as Matthew explained the details. When Matthew took a break in the accounting of the events, Scott blurted out, "that little fucker. I want to go over there and smack his ass around!" Scott's face was beat red. Matthew became nervous by Scott's anger. He was afraid that Scott would actually go to the house and beat up Darren. Matthew did not need any more drama, so he quickly suggested they go to "Fever" for a drink. Scott agreed. "I need a drink!", he said to Matthew.

At the bar Scott and Matthew continued to replay the events of yesterday over and over again. Matthew asked Scott if he could get time off over the weekend to help him move. "No problem...let me know when.", Scott replied in his best effort to portray a happy tone. The music blared around them and they ordered more drinks. Matthew was furiously puffing away on cigarettes. "You should really give that up.", said Scott. "I know", responded Matthew. As the time went on Matthew became nervous that he would be in trouble for not being home. He hadn't even called Darren today. Scott told Matthew that he wanted him to stay at his house for the night. "I don't trust that asshole. He'll do something stupid. You're not safe there." At first Matthew declined. But Scott persisted and Matthew reluctantly agreed. He ordered another beer.

Scott told Matthew, "I'll call the asshole and tell him you're too drunk to drive." Matthew nodded his head, mumbling "okay" as Scott went into the phone booth in the bar. When Darren picked up the phone on the other end, Scott tried to sound as normal as possible. He told Darren that Matthew needed to "sleep it off" at his house. Darren replied, "fine…let the drunk queen sleep there" and abruptly hung up the phone on Scott.

They left the bar and returned to Scott's apartment. Matthew fell asleep in Scott's bed. He woke up in the middle of the night in a sweat. He had a dream about yesterday's catastrophe. Rolling over and looking at a sleeping Scott, he put his head back on the pillow. Darren was not here. He was safe, for now at least. Later in the evening he woke up to find himself and Scott cuddled into each other. There was nothing sexual about it. This gorgeous man who Matthew initially had sexual desires for, was now laying into him as a way to comfort his friend. It was a safe, intimate cuddle. Matthew fell back to sleep and slept through the remainder of the night.

The morning came with the aroma of coffee. Matthew joined Scott at the kitchen table of his small apartment. They sat and drank their coffee and ate muffins. Scott told Matthew, "I really want you to stay here again tonight. I don't think it's safe for you to be in that house with that maniac." Matthew demurred, saying that he did not want to be out of the house for too long because it would make things look suspicious. They began to get ready for work. Scott agreed that Matthew was probably right, "but you call me if he pulls any shit!" Scott walked Matthew to his car and gave him a hug as Matthew prepared to leave for work.

Just before noon, Matthew's boss Kevin Michaels appeared at the door of Matthew's office. "Can I see you in my office in about five minutes?", he inquired of Matthew. Matthew nodded affirmatively. He knew that this must be about Darren. The five minutes passed quickly, and Matthew found himself knocking on Kevin's door. "Come in", responded Kevin, "and please shut the door." Matthew did as he was requested and sat down in the chair on the side of Kevin's desk. How he hated when the boss told you to shut the office door. It was like going to the principal's office!

Kevin Michaels reached over to the right of his desk, picked up a document and handed it to Matthew. "I want you to read this to yourself.", he instructed Matthew. The document was the report of the sexual abuse of George Bridges. The document clearly identified Darren as the alleged perpetrator of the abuse of this 14 year old child. The document contained details of the allegations including that George had confided to his mother that Darren had been sexually abusing him for the past several months. The document further stated that Darren had threatened George if he told anyone about the abuse or refused to have sex with him anymore. Finally, the document indicated that the local police had been conducting surveillance of Darren and his home. This of course, meant that the police had been observing Matthew as well.

Matthew read the document very slowly; more slowly than normal. He was trying to avoid the inevitable. He knew that once he stopped reading, he would have to address the situation with his boss. Finally, Matthew put down the document in front of him and looked up at Kevin Michaels. Kevin leaned back in his chair and looked Matthew straight in the eyes. "I know that reading that was not pleasurable for you. I know how difficult this is for you. But, it basically comes down to this. You have a choice to make and you have to make it pretty damn quick." Kevin paused briefly. Matthew said nothing. Kevin Michaels continued. "You have to choose between your boyfriend and your career. The district attorney will be investigating this with Springfield DCP and the state police. I would strongly suggest that you get yourself out of that situation as soon as possible." Kevin stopped speaking. Matthew knew that he was awaiting a response from him.

Matthew's head was now pounding from the conversation. He began in a soft and deliberate tone. He explained to Kevin that he had seen the investigation letter that arrived at his home yesterday. He indicated that he had confronted Darren about it. Matthew did not discuss the response that he had received from Darren or provide any information about the nude pictures of George. Matthew then said, "after reading that report I've decided I'm going to move out of the apartment this weekend. My career is too important." He then asked his boss if he could have a few days off from work to deal with the move and this situation. Kevin agreed with his request authoritatively stating, "you need to get your head together and get away from that situation and that man." Matthew remained seated in the chair. He looked down. When he looked up after a few moments, he asked Kevin Michaels who at work knew about the investigation. Kevin responded that only he and his assistant were aware of the report. "No one else needs to know.", Kevin added. Matthew then asked how this would affect his employment at DCP. Kevin responded, "it will have no effect. No one is accusing you of doing anything wrong. The only thing the report says is that a DCP social worker lives at that address as well. You just need to get out of that situation. That's all I care about."

At this point Matthew involuntarily did what he did not want to do in front of his new boss. He began to cry. Kevin remained silent. Matthew then apologized to Kevin for crying. Kevin shook his head and said, "there is no need to apologize." Kevin allowed Matthew a few minutes to regain his composure. Then he told Matthew, "go out for a walk...get yourself together. Then begin your plans to move this weekend." Matthew thanked Kevin for his understanding, got up and left the office. He quickly went down the hall to the employee bathroom before anyone could see him. He washed off his face and then returned to his desk.

There was no one else present in the shared office. Janice was in Agawam for the rest of the day to complete an investigation. He did not know where Sharon and Michael were. Matthew took a quick walk and returned to try to finish up some paperwork. His mind was drifting and the rest of the work day was an unproductive one.

The weekend arrived before Matthew knew it. It was time to move out of the apartment. He wanted to do it quick, unnoticed and without confrontation. Sharon and her lover, Louise had been extremely welcoming when he asked to stay at their home. They had already set up the extra bedroom for him. Darren had left early that morning to go to work. Matthew began scurrying around the house making sure that he packed those things that mattered the most to him first. Before packing his clothes, he packed old letters, college notebooks, textbooks and many photo albums. Most of the furniture in the house, with the exception of the new television, belonged to Darren. The move would not be that burdensome physically. He wanted to make sure that he didn't forget any of his personal things and momentos that meant so much to him. He couldn't rely on Darren to return them once he moved out.

Scott and Janice were helpful as promised. They both arrived together right on time. They brought doughnuts and coffee. While helping to pack they both continued to remind Matthew that he was doing the right thing. They also reminded him that they would help him through this mess and that he "deserved better" than this. Diana just laid on the sofa in the living room, looking around and not knowing what to make of the chaos going on around her.

As the continued to pack, Scott who was in the bedroom packing clothes yelled out, "what the hell is this?" Matthew and Janice hurriedly went into the room. They saw Scott standing there holding an old shoe box. It was filled with photographs. They all walked out into the kitchen and sat at the table. Scott began digging into the box and they flipped through the photos together. Mixed among the pictures of Darren and Matthew and their friends were pictures that disturbed all three of them. There were at least a hundred pictures of naked boys in the box. The boys had to be between 13 and 16. Many included two or three boys in sexual poses or engaging in sexual contact. The pictures were obviously taken at the apartment as the background showed the living room, bathroom and bedroom of the apartment that Matthew and Darren rented. They looked at the photos and stared at each other in disbelief. "That sick fuck!", exclaimed Scott. Matthew shook his head saying nothing. Janice said, "these are gross!"

Scott grabbed the pictures off the table and put them back in the box. He walked over to the kitchen sink. "Give me your lighter!", he said to Matthew, who promptly reached into his pocket and handed his lighter to Scott. One by one, Scott burned the pornographic photos over the stainless steel sink. He stood there along with Matthew and Janice, and watched as the faucet water washed the ashes down the drain. "There", he said, "let the little pervert have a fit when he comes home and can't find his kiddie porn to jerk off to!" They sat down again at the kitchen table. The three of them began to discuss whether they should contact the police about their find. They went back and forth about it. They decided that even if they wanted to contact the police, they had "destroyed all the evidence" when they burned the pictures. Scott said, "it's probably better. That little fuck would blame you for taking them anyway. You couldn't defend yourself...it's better they're burned up." Matthew looked at the clock on the wall. Their time was running short. They returned to the task of packing.

As Matthew was placing things in a large carton he kept mumbling over and over, "I can't believe this is happening to me." He was shaking his head back and forth. His packing was slow. At times his eyes would fill up and he would slowly cry. When it appeared they had packed up everything, Janice said, "let's get the hell out of here!" Matthew nodded in agreement as he taped up the last box he had been working on.

They loaded everything into Matthew and Scott's cars. They walked back upstairs. Matthew was exhausted. He realized they had a few minutes, so he offered Janice and Scott a soda. While standing in the living room, Matthew asked his friends, "what do I tell my parents about this?" Neither Janice or Scott responded and the silence hung in the air. Then Janice said, "maybe you should tell them that he ripped you off for rent or something." Scott interjected, "look, they really aren't the greatest fans of Darren anyway. So tell them that you two had a fight and you decided to leave. They'll probably be happy about it." Matthew nodded his head saying, "I can't tell them the truth…it would kill them." Janice said, "you don't have to tell them the truth. They don't need to know. Just tell them what Scott said…say you had a fight and you decided to leave."

They finished their sodas and began to leave. "Look around and make sure you have everything.", Scott told Matthew. While walking through the house Matthew realized that there was one very important thing he could not take with him. His dog Diana. She remained sitting on the couch and Matthew looked over at her. Darren had constantly reminded him everytime they fought that Diana was his dog even though he bought her for Matthew. He would cynically tell Matthew, "you leave me and you leave her too."

Matthew walked over and sat on the sofa and hugged his dog. He began to cry uncontrollably. Janice and Scott walked out into the kitchen leaving Matthew alone with Diana. "I'm going to miss you the most.", Matthew said as he cried and hugged his dog with intensity. "You're the best thing that came out of this relationship.", he told Diana. He continued to hug her and cry. Janice came up behind him and grabbed him slowly around the waist. "Come on" she said, "we have to go." Matthew let go of Diana and took one last look at her. He cried silently as he waived good-bye to his dog and followed his friends out the door.

A few days passed and Matthew's mother called him at work. "Darren just called here and said you had moved all your stuff out of the apartment and he didn't know why." "Mom", Matthew responded, "we've been fighting a lot lately. I need to get out of there and get my shit together. I'm starting law school soon and I don't need any hassles from him. It will screw me up." His mother agreed with him. She did not question Matthew or probe for details about what happened. She stated with what appeared to be a sigh of relief in her voice, "I think this is best for you. Just move on to a new chapter in your life." The conversation ended with Rosa asking her son to come over for dinner on Wednesday. She was making one of his favorites, escarole soup. Matthew readily accepted the invitation.

Not five minutes after the conversation with his mother, the phone on Matthew's desk rang again. It was Darren. He blurted into the phone, "what the fuck do you think you're doing moving all the shit out of the apartment?" Matthew trying to remain calm, replied, "I can't talk to you now. Just please, leave me alone. Forget about me…forget I ever existed." But Darren persisted in the conversation. He yelled at Matthew, "look, I don't know where your staying right now, but I'll hunt your ass down. It ain't going to be that easy to get rid of me." Matthew interrupted. "I told you. I can't talk to you right now. Please don't call me. Don't bother me. Just leave me alone." Darren would not hang up. He asked Matthew, "where are my pictures?" Matthew attempting to sound ignorant of the subject, responded in a questioning tone, "what pictures?" Darren retorted, "you know what pictures I'm talking about! You better return them or I'll fuckin' kill you!", and with that he slammed down the phone in Matthew's ear. Matthew held the receiver in his hand for a few moments and then put it down.

Matthew got up to get a drink of water. Before he could get to the water fountain, the phone rang again. He picked it up, answering, "Investigations". The voice on the other end said, "I hope your precious little letter from your grandmother means something to you, because if you don't return my pictures by tomorrow, I'll burn the fucking thing!". With that Darren again slammed the phone down in Matthew's ear.

Matthew sat in his chair at his desk and realized that he did leave something behind at the apartment that had value to him. About two months before his grandmother died, she had sent him a long letter. In the letter she talked about her life, her accomplishments and her hopes for his future. She spoke in great detail about the war and the depression, and how it impacted her life. She spoke about the joy she found in her family, and in him. It was as if she knew that death was waiting for her. Matthew treasured that letter and he wanted it back. He had to figure a way to get the letting without dealing with Darren. The pictures had all been burned up in the sink. He had nothing to deal with. Matthew sat at his desk and pondered his next move.

The phone rang again. The police were at the office with Craig Talbot. He had been picked up for prostitution in an area known at "The Block" in Springfield. This area was know for prostitution and being frequented by gay men. Matthew went to the front of the office, thanked the police and brought Craig back to his office. He told him to sit down as he called a few foster parents to see if they would take Craig in for the night. Finally he found a family in Wilbraham. "See man, I'm becoming a big cocksucker", Craig remarked as Matthew hung up the phone. Matthew wanted to engage Craig in a discussion about the dangers of prostituting himself, but he was just too tired. He looked at Craig and said, "you need to have a little more respect for yourself.". Just then Janice walked into the office. She offered to take Craig to the foster home. Matthew was too worn out to deal with Craig, and thanked her as he took her up on the offer.

Just before the end of the work day Matthew's phone rang once more. It was Darren. He had not calmed down. Once again he asked about the pictures. Matthew promised that he would look for them and would get back to him as soon as possible. Darren ended the conversation with another threat. "Don't forget…I may not know where you're staying now. But I'm watching. Just remember, keep looking over your shoulder, cause you'll never know when I'll be standing right there ready to pop you one!" This time Matthew hung up the phone. He sat on his desk. His entire body was trembling in fear.

Matthew felt like everything was closing in on him again. Even the office walls seemed to be closing in on him. He quickly packed his notebook and folders and left the office. He drove towards New York state, driving without a destination in an effort to calm himself down. He turned on the radio. His favorite, Diana Ross, was singing the song "It's My Turn". Matthew intently listened to the lyrics. It was if the song was written for him. It was his turn. His turn to live. His turn to be happy.

That evening Matthew did not sleep well. He decided to go to the house first thing in the morning while Darren was at work. He would find his grandmother's letter and take it with him. Morning came and he drove by his old apartment. Darren's car was still in the driveway. "He should have been gone by now", thought Matthew. He pulled his car around the corner of the street, far enough down so not to be noticed. "I'll wait for a few minutes for him to leave.", Matthew said to himself. About five minutes later, Matthew noticed Darren walking to his car followed by what appeared to be a blond teenage boy. "Was it George?", he mumbled to himself. Once Darren's car was no longer visible, Matthew drove up to the house and parked his car. He went to the door and put his key in the lock. It worked. Darren hadn't changed the locks yet.

When he entered the apartment he expected to be greeted by Diana. But she was not there. A rush of anxiety came over him, but then he remembered that Darren's older brother would frequently pick up Diana during the week and take her to his farm. That way Diana had the enjoyment of the outdoors and could exercise. "That must be where she is.", thought Matthew, relieved.

Matthew began looking around the apartment for his grandmother's letter. By happenstance he went into Darren's closet. Finally he found the letter. Darren had shoved it in the inside pocket of his sportcoat. He probably figured Matthew would never look in his clothes for the letter. Matthew placed the letter in his pocket. As he was walking toward the bedroom doorway he heard the outside door open. "Oh God!", he thought. He walked out of the bedroom to see Darren and a teenage boy standing in the kitchen.

"What the fuck are you doing here?", Darren screamed at Matthew. Matthew cowered. Then he softly said, "I thought I left my high school ring here. I was looking for it." Darren screamed from the opposite end of the kitchen, "you're a fuckin' liar!" With that scream, Darren reached into his jacket and pulled out his Smith and Wesson .357 revolver and pointed it at Matthew. Matthew was frozen in fear. He did not utter a word and he could not move. Darren in a cynically soft tone said, "I told you to look over your shoulder. You don't listen to me. Now you'll learn not to fuck with me!" Before Matthew could say anything in response, he heard a thunderous blast go off and saw a burst of flame. Matthew fell to the floor in the doorway. Time suddenly came to a stop. There was complete silence after the blast. Matthew felt as if he was watching a movie when he looked up from the floor and saw Darren with the revolver to his side. He moved his head to see the teenage boy running out of the apartment. Then he saw Darren turn and slowly walk out the same door that the young boy had run through.

Matthew laid on the floor for a few minutes. He was sure he hadn't been shot, but his right ear seem deadened. He couldn't hear out of it. Matthew touched his ear to make sure it was still there. It was. Matthew finally got himself to his knees. After a few moments he stood up. He looked to his right. Next to the doorjamb over the kitchen sink was a large hole in the plaster wall from the bullet. It had missed him by about two inches. Matthew looked at the hole, felt his ear again, and then looked down at the crotch of his pants. He had urinated in his pants. He stood silently, unable to move and unable to cry.

CHAPTER 4

A CHILD'S HORROR

June 1981

Transitioning was never easy for Matthew. He had decided that the closing days of his career as a child protective investigator at DCP would be quiet and routine. This would make the transition smooth. But that was not to be the case. His beeper went off at 2:30 in the morning. Matthew woke right up, mumbling "shit" as he reached over and turned the beeper off. He had been out earlier in the evening with Scott and Phillip Styles at "Fever".

They had been dancing most of the night and he was tired. They talked about how Scott would be joining Matthew in Boston in the fall as his roommate. Scott felt he too could use a change of scenery. The Berkshires, and even metro Springfield were becoming old to him. Scott invited Phillip to join the next weekend to apartment hunt; an invitation Phillip gleefully accepted. They would make a weekend of it. This early morning beep was not appreciated by Matthew.

Matthew turned the light on and reached for the telephone. He dialed the 800 number for his job. A woman picked up on the other end and announced, "Child Abuse Hotline". He responded, "Hi. This is Matthew Schipani from the western region. I was beeped." The more alert voice on the other end responded, "Hi Matt. This is Brenda. I beeped you. Hold on, we're waiting for Janice Pierce to call in." Matthew grumbled "mm huh" and held the phone to his ear. A few minutes later he heard his dear friend's voice on the other end. Brenda indicated, "Matt, you're on with Janice." "Hi Matthew!", said Janice sounding much more awake than he was.

Brenda then described to Matthew and Janice the type of call they would be responding to. Matthew scribbled notes on a pad that he pulled out of the nightstand drawer while Brenda spoke. She began detailing the case for them. "The last name of the family is Harris. The mother is Kim, father is Wayne. About an hour ago Holyoke PD contacted us. They had responded to a call for help. When they arrived they found two children. Sally is three and Peter is four months old. Both children were severely abused. Holyoke PD immediately had them transported to WestMass General in Springfield. The children have been admitted. I'm not too sure of their current condition. The parents are at the hospital with them. Matthew was attempting to keep up with Brenda as she spoke. She seemed to be talking very rapidly for such an early morning hour. "Maybe it's me", thought Matthew.

Brenda went on with her narration. "The children are together in a room on the fifth floor. Pediatric Intensive Care. We've talked to the hospital and they are expecting you. Dr. Collin Stevens is the attending doctor. Any questions?" Matthew said, "none really…well, who's the on-call supervisor?" Brenda responded, "Ellen Bally." Matthew then said, "Janice, I'll call you at home in a few minutes about where to meet up." Janice responded, "okay" and the three of them ended the call. Matthew called Janice right back. Since he was living in Springfield with Sharon and Louise he was much closer than Janice. She remained living in the Berkshires. They agreed to meet at the hospital parking lot in about an hour.

Matthew realized he had some time to get ready. He jumped in the shower hoping that this, if not the fact that he had to go see two severely injured children, would wake him up. When he came out of the bathroom only dressed in a towel, he saw Louise sitting at the kitchen table. "Hotline?", she inquired. Matthew responded, "yeah, gotta go to WestMass." Louise stood up and said, "finish getting dressed. I'll put on the coffee." Matthew thanked her and returned to the bathroom. A few moments later he went back into the kitchen. A mug of steaming hot coffee was sitting on the table. Matthew sat down and reached for the sugar bowl. "I already put two in. Isn't that enough?", asked Louise. Matthew said, "not at 3:00 in the morning. I need a sugar rush!" He then poured more sugar into the mug. They sat at the table making small talk. While they were talking Matthew's mind was thinking about Sharon and Louise's relationship. They had been together for over ten years. Their relationship was one that Matthew truly envied. They were kind to each other, supportive and responsive to each other's needs. Sure they argued, but it wasn't any knock down, dragged out argument. They argued about topics, avoiding the personal insults that usually get thrown into arguments. Matthew enjoyed his brief time living with them. He knew that he would miss them when he moved to Boston. They were homebodies, so he knew their visits would be few and far between. He hoped the geography wouldn't terminate their relationship.

Louise worked at home. She was a successful professional artist. She supported their above average lifestyle. Certainly Sharon's weekly paycheck from DCP helped, but their home adorned with antiques and paintings was more a reflection of Louise than of Sharon. As Matthew stood up to leave, Louise said, "I'll have breakfast ready for you when you get back." He thanked her, leaned over and gave her a brief kiss on the forehead. He gulped down the rest of his coffee from the mug, grabbed his windbreaker and left to go to his emergency.

Matthew pulled into the parking lot. He waited a few moments and then saw Janice pull in with her brand new Toyota Celica. He got out of his car and motioned her over to park next to him. She got out of the sportscar and they said their "hellos", exchanged a brief hug and proceeded directly towards the lobby of the hospital.

Once inside the hospital they showed their work identification cards to the security guard on duty. He pointed them to the elevator. As they rode up to the fifth floor, Matthew said to Janice, "I am so tired. I hope this is quick." Janice just smiled. The elevator doors opened and they followed the signs to the pediatric intensive care unit. They walked down the bright hall with its shiny waxed floor towards the nurse's station. The fluorescent lights bouncing off the floor shine was so bright it bothered Matthew's eyes. They approached the counter at the nurse's station and identified themselves, asking for Dr. Stevens. The nurse held her finger up to indicate one minute and left the station.

Less than a minute later a very tall, tan handsome man approached them. "Hi. I'm Collin Stevens". Matthew and Janice identified themselves and shook hands with Dr. Stevens. He turned away from them and said, "follow me." They followed behind Dr. Stevens through the gray steel double doors. After passing through the doors, they took a sharp left into a small brightly lit room. As they entered the room, the horror of what was before their eyes smacked Matthew right in the face. Now he was wide awake.

In the bed on the left was a little girl with matted braids in her blond hair. She was asleep. An oxygen mask was covering her nose and mouth. Dr. Stevens approached the bed and Matthew and Janice followed closely behind. Dr. Stevens softly spoke to them. "This is Sally Harris. She's just three years old, last week. She has suffered incredible trauma to her body as is quite visible. She had four broken ribs, a blow to her sternum, a broken left arm...torn frenum, three broken teeth and severe damage to her left inner ear." Matthew had pulled his small pad out of his pocket. He was writing fast and furiously as Dr. Stevens articulated the injuries the child had suffered. Matthew looked over at Janice who was staring right at the face of the little child. Janice's eyes were starting to fill with tears. Janice uttered, "she's just a baby", and wiped her eyes with her hand.

Matthew looked away from Janice. He hated to see his dear friend upset. Matthew shifted into his 'work mode'. It was his way to separate from the emotion of the situation. It allowed him to deal with the situation at hand. He turned to Dr. Stevens and asked, "what's the prognosis?" Dr. Stevens responded, "its much better than she looks. I think we can stabilize her in a few days. She'll need an extended stay here to recover from all the injuries. But I hope she will make a full physical recovery. Emotional recovery, well that's another thing...", said the doctor, his voice trailing off.

Dr. Stevens then motioned Matthew and Janice to the other side of the room. They approached another hospital bed. "Over here we have Peter", began Dr. Stevens. "His prognosis is not as good. He has blunt trauma to his head. He's only four months old. My diagnosis is that he is on the verge of being brain dead. His heart will continue to operate for a short time after."

Matthew and Janice moved closer to the infant laying on the hospital bed. Many machines were surrounding this tiny human being. The infant's head was wrapped in a bandage above his eyes. It looked like a turban. His eyes were closed and swollen. Peter's head looked much larger that it should for the size of his little body. There was blood coming from his anus. Tubes and devices were sticking into his arms and legs. Matthew looked at all the medical machines around the bed. Only one of the machines made any sense to him. "Does that monitor the heart?", Matthew asked softly while pointing to the machine with a screen displaying a moving line and numbers. "Yes, it does", quietly replied Dr. Stevens.

Time seemed to grind to a halt. Matthew looked over at Janice. She had composed herself by now. It looked to him that she too had switched into her work personality. "It's amazing how we can become detached in order to deal with this shit", thought Matthew. Janice then spoke. "I hate to ask this, but..." Dr. Stevens interrupted, "it will probably be about three hours. We are pumping pain medication. He really can't feel very much. The brain will probably die within two hours. The heart will go quickly after that. There's no hope here." Matthew began to feel nauseous. He turned and looked behind him. He grabbed the hard wooden chair from the corner and sat down.

Janice moved next to Matthew. She stood off to his side and began rubbing his shoulders. "Where are the parents?", she inquired of Dr. Stevens. He replied, "they're down the hall in the waiting room. They wanted to leave, but I told them they had to wait until you guys got here. They got pissed that I told them they had to wait." Matthew asked, "is there a phone around here we can use?" Dr. Stevens pointed to the counter in the back of the room. "Just dial nine", he said. Dr. Stevens then turned and began to speak with the three attending nurses in the room.

Matthew stood up after a moment or two and went to the back of the room. He called Ellen Bally, the DCP supervisor on call. She must have already been up because the phone only rang once and she answered. Matthew went over the details of what they had learned. "Should we call the state police? The baby is going to die. This could be murder.", he asked Ellen. She responded, "I'll call them right now and get back to you. Have you asked the parents what happened yet?" Matthew replied that they had not. Given the nature of the injuries he had automatically assumed that they were inflicted. Ellen told him to hold off on interviewing the parents until she had gotten back to them. She would call the state police. "Maybe you can do a joint interview." Matthew said "okay" and hung up the phone.

Matthew filled Janice in about his conversation with the supervisor. They decided to leave the small room where the children were and talk to the nurse outside at the station. Maybe the parents had made a statement to someone when they came to the hospital. Matthew and Janice then spoke with a young nurse who began to cry as soon as she started talking about the two children. When Janice asked if the parents made any comments about the source of the injuries to the children, the nurse said, "the father hasn't said a word. The mother said the baby fell down the stairs and she thinks the little girl chased down after him and she fell. Mother told me that she found both children at the bottom of the stairs and called an ambulance right away." The nurse reached for a tissue and wiped her eyes. She then angrily said to Matthew and Janice, "I don't believe her. The injuries aren't consistent with a fall down the stairs. I think she's full of it about calling the ambulance right away too. The injuries indicate that more time went by from the time of injury to the time of arrival than if she contacted help right away."

Matthew thanked the nurse and he began to turn to go back to the children's room. Janice also turned, but the nurse grabbed her by the arm and said, "can you believe they asked us if they could go home and get some sleep because they were tired? Who in their right mind would leave their babies in this condition unless they did something wrong?" The nurse was crying again.

Janice extended her hand and rubbed the nurse's arm in a gesture of comfort. "Janice the comforter", thought Matthew. Matthew then asked, "could you tell them that we want to talk to them in a few minutes? Try to stall them...we're probably going to have the state police come here too. They're really good, so it won't take long for them to get here." The nurse shook her head affirmatively and Matthew and Janice returned to the children's room.

As they reentered the room Dr. Stevens and the nurses were at Sally's bed. Seeing Matthew and Janice, Dr. Stevens said, "I think she is finally comfortable. The pain medication is in her system. She should be able to rest for a bit." Dr. Stevens then walked across the room. He said, "now the little guy here", pointing to Peter, "well, he's not doing very well. It's going quicker than I thought." Matthew's beeper then went off. He excused himself and went to the back of the room to call Ellen Bally. Janice stayed by Peter's bed with Dr. Stevens.

Ellen Bally told him that the state police were on their way. "They should be there in less than a half hour. Sergeant Normans is coming. He says he knows you." Matthew responded, "yes" and then gave Ellen a status update on the condition of the children. He also shared with her the statements that the parents had made to the nursing staff when they arrived at the hospital. Matthew concluded the conversation and returned to standing next to his friend and work partner, Janice.

A thin nurse in the room who clearly had been crying approached them with a box of chocolates. "Here", she said, "its all we have. It was someone's birthday and they left them behind." Matthew took the box from her and Janice thanked the nurse. They each took a chocolate out of the box and brought it with them as they sat down on the chairs between the two hospital beds.

The half hour seemed like an eternity, but it really was only thirty minutes when Sergeant Normans of the state police walked into the room. He walked passed Dr. Stevens and the nurses flashing his badge at them. He went directly over to Matthew. He firmly shook his hand and said, "nice to see you again. Sorry it has to be under these circumstances." Matthew nodded and introduced Sergeant Normans to Janice. After the introduction, Normans said to Matthew, "bring me up to speed." They sat down and Matthew and Janice updated the police officer. Dr. Stevens came over as they were about to conclude the conversation. He interrupted, "the infant is brain dead. It probably will only be an hour before the heart stops."

Matthew and Janice looked at each other. Matthew put his head into his hands and closed his eyes. Janice looked down shaking her head back and forth. Sergeant Normans got up and went over to talk to Dr. Stevens. Matthew and Janice sat silently for a moment and then walked over to the doctor. Sergeant Normans asked if the injuries could have been accidental as the parents said. Dr. Stevens responded, "No way. They were inflicted injuries. This is classic child abuse."

Normans tapped Matthew on the shoulder. "Are the parents still in the waiting room?", he asked. Matthew responded, "as far as I know." Normans responded, "okay...O'Toole should be here any minute. Then the four of us will go talk to the motherfuckers. I'm going to have a cigarette. Matthew, you want to join me?" Matthew was having difficulty speaking so he just shook his head "yes". Janice added in a weak voice, "I need one too." Matthew looked at her. Janice probably smoke one cigarette a year, and that was usually after a long night of drinking. The three of them exited the room and went down the hall to the solarium.

They were finishing up their cigarettes when a tall brunette woman walked in. "Hi Paula", said Matthew, referring to state trooper Paula O'Toole. She was Sergeant Normans long time partner. "Hi Matthew", she replied while shaking his hand. "Sorry we always have to see each other in such shitty situations." Matthew lit another cigarette and so did Janice as she introduced herself to Paula O'Toole. The four of them stood in the solarium not saying a word to each other, just puffing away. Normans put out his cigarette about halfway through and said, "okay...let's go. It's showtime." With that statement Janice and Matthew butted out their cigarettes. O'Toole took two last quick puffs. Matthew and Janice led the police officers to the waiting room at the end of the hall. They passed the crying nurse they had spoken with earlier. She joined the entourage.

The nurse waited outside the door as the four of them entered the waiting room together. Sergeant Normans took the lead and took care of introducing everyone. Kim and Wayne Harris glanced up at them and nodded acknowledging their presence. An older woman sitting in the corner of the waiting room was knitting a pink shawl. She identified herself as Kim's mother. Kim and Wayne Harris held onto the magazines that they had been reading prior to the arrival of the group. Trooper O'Toole began the interview. She sat down and so did Janice. Matthew and Sergeant Normans remained standing. Paula O'Toole asked, "we need to talk to you about what happened earlier this evening." Both of the parents sat quietly in the room. Mr. Harris looked down at his magazine and opened it up again. He was flipping through it. Time passed by and neither parent responded to O'Toole's opening remark. Janice then said, "are you aware of the condition of your children?" The parents continued not to respond. Kim Harris looked forward with a blank stare. Wayne Harris remained flipping through the magazine. Janice once again, but in a firmer and louder tone, asked, "do you know what the condition of your children is right now?" Finally, Kim Harris looked at Janice. She responded in a monotone voice, "it was an accident…I forgot to close the cellar door."

Sergeant Normans then sat down on the couch across from the parents. Matthew remained standing in the back of the room. Normans began to ask the parents basic identifying questions, such as their address, place of employment, etc. Mrs. Harris responded to the questions in a flat voice. Mr. Harris remained reading the magazine, or just glancing at it. Sergeant Normans repeatedly looked over at Mr. Harris and then back at Matthew. It was clear to Matthew that Normans was becoming more and more agitated at Wayne Harris' disinterest in the situation. As he continued to ask questions, Sergeant Normans voice got louder and louder. Finally, when he had enough, Normans ripped the magazine out of a surprised Wayne Harris' hands. He looked directly into Mr. Harris' eyes and shouted, "listen asshole. You better pay attention because I'm about to arrest you both for murder if I don't get some answers here!" Mr. Harris slid back in his chair. He stared back into the face of the state police officer. Finally he spoke for the first time. "We told you. It was an accident. Can't we just leave?" A red face, fuming Sergeant Normans stood up and towered over the sitting Mr. Harris. "No, you can't leave!", he boomed. Normans continued, "you stay right here…don't move. The four of us need to talk. We'll be back in a few minutes." Normans motioned O'Toole, Janice and Matthew to get up and walk out the door, which they all did.

They walked back down to the solarium. They all lit up before Normans began to speak. He turned to his partner and said, "call in a couple of uniforms. I'm going to arrest them. Call the Lieutenant and get a search warrant too." O'Toole shook her head and put her cigarette out. She left the room and walked to the telephone booth opposite the entry to the solarium.

Normans turned to Matthew and Janice and said, "we'll take them to the barracks. We'll conduct the interrogation there. You guys are welcome to come watch. One of these motherfuckers is going to confess!" Matthew and Janice stood beside Normans. His face showed his infuriation. He remained beat red. After a few minutes, O'Toole returned. "All set", she said. Matthew said, "I have to call our supervisor. I'll be back in a few." Janice added, "I'll follow you. I want to check on the baby." They excused themselves and left the police officers in the solarium.

They walked down the hall and turned into the small room where the children were. They suddenly heard a constant beep. Matthew looked at the infant and then looked up at the heart monitor machine. The line on the monitor was flat. There were no numbers flashing. Four month old Peter had just died in front of their eyes. Matthew turned and walked out of the room. He walked to a corner at the beginning of the bright hall. He sat down on the shiny floor. Janice followed and sat next to him. Not a word was exchanged between them. They stared silently at the bright white wall across from them. At least ten minutes passed while they sat there. Both Matthew and Janice had tears streaming down their faces.

About an hour later they found themselves at a breakfast restaurant. They had ordered a big breakfast, but when it came it just sat on the table. Matthew and Janice sat in the booth, not speaking. They continued to drink what was their fourth cup of coffee and smoke countless number of cigarettes. Janice had filled her cigarette quota this evening for the entire decade. When they were done, Matthew threw some money on the table. They walked out of the restaurant together. They hugged in the parking lot, told each other they loved each other and went to their respective cars to drive home.

By the time Matthew got home the house was empty. Louise must have run out on an errand and Sharon was already at work. There was a note on the table from Louise. "Coffee's all set. Breakfast in the fridge, just pop it in the micro." Matthew didn't want any more coffee and certainly was not hungry. He took off his jacket and went directly into the bathroom where he threw up. He sat on the cold bathroom floor for a few minutes and then leaned over into the toilet and threw up again.

Matthew got undressed and went into the shower. He turned the water on steaming hot. He stayed in the shower for at least forty five minutes. He lathered up and washed himself over and over again. He felt incredibly dirty, yet in actuality his body was not dirty at all. It was his soul that was dirty. He had just witnessed one of the worst crimes to children. Matthew thought over and over again in his head about the events he had just witnessed. He had spent the early morning hours of this day watching a horrendous case of child abuse unfold before his eyes. He saw parents who were disinterested in the fate of their children. He watched a four month old baby die right in front of him. He was there when this little infant's heart beat its last beat. Matthew was desperately trying through the soap and water to wash away the filth of what he had just witnessed. It was not working.

The remainder of the summer and the remainder of his time as a child protective investigation was unremarkable in comparison to this investigation. What happened to little Peter would stay with Matthew for the rest of his days. He completed many more 'routine' investigations of child abuse. He was in court several times more. The criminal case against Kim and Wayne Harris would move slowly and occur long after he had left DCP.

One of his last court appearances was on behalf of Craig Talbot, the teenage boy who had been prostituted by his parents. Matthew had testified in the juvenile court about the abuse and against the parents receiving custody of Craig. However, the case was not successful. Craig would have to be returned to his parents. The judge ruled that Craig was a willing participant in much of the sexual activity. The judge further decided that Craig was of such an age that he could adequately protect himself. Craig's prostitution activities did not help the case. Even when he told Craig that he had to leave foster care and return to his parents, this paled in comparison to what he had seen in the hospital a few short weeks before. Craig was clearly angry and accused Matthew and the judge of not believing him. "You think I'm a goddamn queer!", he yelled at Matthew. Matthew's reassurances that he tried his best and that he believed Craig about the abuse fell on deaf ears. "You probably think its all pretty exciting, you pervert!", Craig screamed at him as Matthew dropped him off at his parent's house.

Matthew's office had a very nice going away party for him. He found himself being very sentimental at the party. The people he had worked so closely with had helped him to mature. The job had exposed him to a world he never knew existed. Through that exposure to the dark side Matthew had gained a more worldly perspective and became more knowledgeable. All of his friends joined the wishes of his boss, Kevin Michaels in a toast to Matthew's "success and happiness in law school and your legal career!" The summer had ended and it was time to move east to begin his legal training.

CHAPTER 5

HARVARD DAYS

May 1982

Matthew's first year at Harvard Law School came to a close with his last examination in Contracts. His first year at Harvard mirrored the experience that Scott Turow detailed in *One L*. It was overwhelming and Matthew was glad to see an end to this long year. The intensity and constant feeling of running against the clock had drained Matthew during the year. Always too much too do, and too little time.

However, on some level Matthew was enjoying this experience. Law school was intellectually challenging to Matthew. It was also challenging his entire lifestyle and his perspective of himself. His identify was truly that of a "law student". He could think of nothing else. It was his entire life. The only thing that Matthew really found a distaste for was the manner in which the professors treated the students. He was resentful of their condescending attitude. At times he felt as if he were back in junior high school.

Now he had to wait. Wait for the results of the examinations. He believed that he had done satisfactorily and would be able to return in the fall to continue his studies. He had no illusions that he would do as well as he had in undergraduate school. Matthew had the luxury of a summer ahead with no pressure. He did not have to work.

His parents continued to subsidize his share of the apartment he had with Scott. He loved his apartment on Beacon Street in Boston's Back Bay. But he knew that if he sat around the apartment all summer it would get old quick and he would feel trapped. He decided he had to find something to do during the summer or he would go crazy. Any type of job, just as long as it wasn't associated with the law, would suit Matthew fine.

Meanwhile, Scott was making a name for himself among the food service and restaurant industry. He was even thinking about becoming a partner with a man opening up a bistro in Davis Square in Somerville. Scott saw this as a way to eventually open his own restaurant, a life long dream. Matthew was very happy that his friend was doing so well, and reassured that both of their moves to Boston was the right decision those few years ago.

Matthew had made a few new and good friends at the law school. His friends Cathy Reed and Shirley Morin were fast becoming part of his inner circle. They had studied together, partied together, and worried together. But how law school had changed his old friendships. Many persons who he thought were good friends had fallen by the wayside. It was truly "out of sight, out of mind", for many friends back in western Massachusetts. Matthew found this to be sad, but realized that as people move and grow those who are left behind sometimes choose to stay behind.

But, Janice Pierce would never let Matthew grow without her! She was a constant visitor at his apartment. Her friendship with Scott had also grown over the past year. On long weekends Janice would be a frequent overnight guest. Matthew and she would explore the sights of Boston and Cambridge. She was a constant support to him during the anxiety days of his first year of law school. Their relationship continued to get closer and deeper. Janice had also moved closer to Matthew. She had been promoted and was now supervising child protective investigators at the Worcester DCP office.

During the week prior to finals Matthew took the bold initiative and went and talked to a fellow law student he found attractive. Jeffrey Caine was two years younger than Matthew. He was 5 feet 10 inches tall and a light skinned black man. They were in Constitutional Law together. Matthew had thought Jeffrey was gay and when they finally set up a luncheon date Jeffrey confirmed this. The night before Matthew's Contracts examination they ended up in bed together. Matthew was amazed at the sex they had. It had been a long time since he had sex. He wasn't sure if it was the time period, the stress of the next day's examination, or the intensity with which Jeffrey made love, but the sex was fantastic. Matthew knew he wanted more!

A knock on the apartment door made Matthew jump with joy. He knew it was Janice. She was spending Memorial Day weekend with Scott and Matthew. They were going to Provincetown together to celebrate Matthew's completing his first year at Harvard. As he opened the door, Janice came bounding in. She extended her arms and they hugged and kissed over and over like they always did. "Sit down", Matthew said excitedly to Janice. "Have I got some dirt for you!", he said as Janice took a place on the living room sofa. "Guess what happened?", Matthew asked gleefully. Janice responded, "what?" Matthew smiled and blurted out, "I slept with a black man!" Janice laughed and replied, "wasn't it wonderful!" Matthew retorted, "yes it was!" A momentary pause occurred and then Janice said, "And?…" Matthew giggled, looking at her. He knew what she wanted to know. Janice said, "well?". Matthew smiled and replied, "Honey…it was the biggest dick I've ever seen!" They laughed so loudly that they did not even hear Scott coming into the apartment. They looked up and Janice bolted off the couch once she saw Scott standing there.

Janice ran over to Scott and gave him a big hug. "What are you guys laughing about?", Scott asked. Matthew replied, "you know that law student Jeffrey Caine?". Scott could tell by the lilt in Matthew's voice. He smirked and said to Matthew, "you're such a pig!" All three of them began to laugh incessantly.

Their weekend in Provincetown came and went too fast. It was full of activity. They had wonderful warm weather. They spent the days walking the beach and Commercial Street. Janice spent lots of money on new clothes. "Time to get me a man!", she said. "Not in this town!", replied a laughing Scott. They ate well every night, indulging in lobster, mussels, scallops and much wine. They spent a lot of time "checking out the scenery", as Matthew called it. Matthew had decided that all the good looking gay men in the Northeast had come to Provincetown that weekend. At night they danced away at various gay clubs. Janice remained the popular center of attraction for the gay men in the clubs. Matthew marveled at how she could attract men. "Wish I had that ability!", he told Scott. Before they knew it the dancing and man watching was over. It was time to return to Boston.

Over the coming summer Matthew and Jeffrey became a regular item. They spent a lot of time together, alternating back and forth at each other's apartment. Matthew did not want to intrude on his best friend by having Jeffrey always at the apartment. So they spent as much time at Jeffrey's as they did at Matthew's. Jeffrey's roommate did not mind a new tenant for the summer. Matthew also wasn't sure about how Scott felt about Jeffrey. At first he thought it was jealousy that Jeffrey was taking time away from him being with Scott. But by the end of summer he wasn't sure why Scott was cool to Jeffrey. He also decided he wasn't going to fret about it. He was having fun with Jeffrey. He agreed with Scott that Jeffrey drank too much, but this relationship was certainly an improvement over the last one. "At least he's nice to me.", Matthew told Scott. Matthew also found Jeffrey to be incredibly attractive, and the sex remained fantastic!

Matthew never ended up getting a job during the summer. He was too preoccupied with Jeffrey. Jeffrey also had the luxury of parents who were subsidizing him. Matthew knew that summer was over the morning that Jeffrey picked him up to go to the bookstore to buy their books for the fall semester. "It went by too quick!", he told Jeffrey on their ride into Cambridge.

While Matthew was checking out of the bookstore he grabbed a *Newsweek*. Later that day when he was alone he curled up on the sofa and began reading the magazine. One article disturbed him. He intently read an article about "GRID", a new form of "gay cancer" that seemed to be appearing in alarming numbers among gay men in San Francisco and New York. According to the article this "cancer" was spreading rapidly and its source was unknown. Matthew decided that he needed to keep this magazine and made a mental note to himself to look for stories about this new disease. He placed the magazine in the bottom of his bedroom closet along with other papers and magazines that he had chosen to save for one reason or the other.

Matthew's second year of law school was almost like a blur to him. It went by so quickly in comparison to the first. Matthew felt much more comfortable in the classroom. It appeared that the professors were much more respectful. It was as if they had passed the hazing portion of law school and could now be treated as adults. Matthew would spent time between classes checking out cute men with his friend Cathy Reed. She was always on a man hunt. But she never seemed to find the right one. Matthew also noticed that it seemed that more and more he only looked at black men. He found them to be more attractive than white men. Matthew wondered if he had gotten bitten by the bug since his relationship with Jeffrey.

Matthew and Jeffrey's relationship progressed on a stable course. But their time together was lessening. School had once again eaten into Matthew's social life. Also, Jeffrey's drinking seemed to be increasing. It was to the point that it was starting to interfere with his studies. Frequently, Jeffrey would come to class unprepared. Around exam time he would be incredibly stressed out trying to catch up so he would be ready for the exams. Matthew and Jeffrey would argue about Jeffrey's lack of commitment to law school. Their arguments started to have a separation effect on their relationship. All they had left was the sex.

In the midst of his final exams Matthew received a call from Phillip Styles. He had decided to join a law firm in Cambridge and was moving in June. Matthew was thrilled! His friend, who had become his legal mentor was now moving from the west to the next town over. With summer coming they would be able to spend much more time together. Phillip told Matthew that once he got settled in they had to go out for dinner. Matthew readily accepted the invitation.

After his last exam, which was in his First Amendment course, Matthew decided to meet Scott and Ken out at a bar in the south end. They celebrated hard that evening and Matthew was flirting with everyone. Once Matthew had a few beers in him, he became an incredible flirt. Jeffrey did not join them as he was home intensely cramming for his last examination at the end of the week. Matthew seemed to forget that he already had a boyfriend, as he was dancing with almost every man that came up to him. During a rest from the dancing, Matthew was standing against the bar wall with Scott watching the dance floor. A tall, biracial man with wavy black hair came up to Matthew and asked him, "do you go to Harvard law?" Matthew responded that he did. This handsome man replied, "me too. My name's Adam Lesley. I just finished my first year. I thought I saw you standing in the halls between classes." Matthew smiled and replied, "that was me."

Adam asked Matthew to dance, and he accepted. As they walked to the dance floor Scott looked at Ken and exclaimed, "here we go again!" Before the night had ended Matthew and Adam had exchanged telephone numbers. As they were walking out Matthew said, "…I will…I'll call you next week!", to Adam as Scott grabbed him by the arm and led him out of the bar.

When they were walking home Scott said to Matthew, "you're such a slut! What are you going to tell Jeffrey?" Matthew laughed and shrugged his shoulders. "I probably won't call that guy anyway", Matthew said. "Bullshit!", said Ken, "you were in heat with that guy!" The three of them continued to laugh as they walked up the stairs to Scott and Matthew's brownstone apartment. Once inside Ken collapsed on the sofa and Matthew and Scott went to their respective bedrooms.

When the morning sun came Matthew rolled over to find Ken in his bed. "Oh shit", he mumbled. With that Ken woke up. "Did we?", asked Matthew, as the memories of their sexual encounter in the middle of the night came back into his memory. Ken replied, "we sure did! You weren't too bad for an old man!" Matthew sat up and mumbled, "fuck you!". Ken laughed in response. As Matthew began to put his underwear on he said to Ken, "we can't let Scott know about this. He'll have a field day with it!" Ken agreed, but their plan was interrupted by Scott opening the door to the bedroom. There sat Matthew just pulling his underpants on and Ken sitting naked on the side of the bed. Scott looked at them and began laughing. "Well, good morning lesbians!", he chimed.

The remaining summer weekends were not as eventful as this one. Matthew finally began working at a small law firm in Brookline as a law clerk. It was grunt work, but at least Matthew was learning the day to day basics of practicing law. Phillip arrived as promised and he and Matthew would regularly spend two nights a week going out to dinner. They would spent the evening in deep discussion about the law, Matthew's future and gay issues. Matthew looked forward to these conversations. He found Phillip to be very intelligent, sophisticated and concerned about the human condition. Scott was in full force working hard on the partnership at the bistro in Somerville. He was becoming quite successful.

Matthew also would occasionally go and meet Phillip at his office for lunch. He came to know and then become friendly with Phillip's law partners, Octavia Moon and Ruth Rogers. Both of these pretty women in their 40's were very welcoming to Matthew. They enjoyed a prosperous law practice and focused a large amount of their time on child welfare and gay civil rights issues. Matthew knew that Phillip had found his professional home with Octavia and Ruth. It was obvious from Phillip's mood in general that the move from the west was a positive one for him.

Matthew's relationship with Jeffrey continued to sour as the summer came to an end. Matthew would blame Jeffrey, telling him he drank too much. But Matthew also knew that this was not the only reason. He was afraid to get close to anyone after Darren. That had been a nightmare and he didn't want to repeat it again, in any shape or form. Matthew also felt that he was outgrowing Jeffrey. So to fill his time and avoid Jeffrey, Matthew would make the trek west and spend time in the Berkshires with his parents and Diana. When Darren moved to Florida shortly after their breakup, he left Diana with Matthew's parents. "At least he did one nice thing for me.", thought Matthew. He had decided against taking her to Boston with him because he felt his dog had too many disruptions. But when he left to return home for the weekends, he realized how much he missed Diana.

Janice continued to be a shooting star at DCP. She was well respected in her office. She broadened her horizons by joining many statewide child welfare organizations. Janice had also began to date a Latino man named Jose Gonzalez. Jose was an incredibly attractive man who was very good to Janice. He cherished her and treated her with the utmost respect. Matthew would constantly kid Janice about Jose. "Are you sure he doesn't want to take a trip on the wild side?", he would ask her. Janice would laugh and proclaim Jose to be "100 percent heterosexual!". Jose enjoyed Matthew's company and respected the deep relationship between Matthew and Janice. Matthew was happy. Jose was good for Janice.

Scott and Matthew only grew closer as time went on. They shared everything with each other; their goals, their fears, their hopes and their love. Scott dated on again and off again, but dating was not his major concern. He was an entrepreneur trying to build a successful business. He took the big leap and bought a small coffee shop on Tremont Street. By summer's end, although he was struggling, the business looked promising. Scott found his joy here. He continued with his partnership at the bistro and spent most of his time running back and forth between the two establishments. But it was clear that Scott was very happy.

The final year of law school was approaching and Matthew knew that he now had to think seriously about his future. He couldn't have his parents support him anymore. He would have to rejoin the work force, and he wanted to make sure that his first job out of law school would be one that gave him a lot of experience quickly. Phillip had talked to Matthew about working for the firm with Octavia and Ruth. Matthew was flattered, but he said he wanted to look at government jobs first. He knew, having been a former state employee, that a government job would get him into court quickly and teach him litigation skills.

After Thanksgiving 1983, Matthew and Jeffrey decided to call it quits. They were civilized when they ran into each other at the law school, but outside of school was quite different. They would call each other over and over again just to fight. Matthew would accuse Jeffrey of being a drunk, and Jeffrey would accuse Matthew of being a slut. It was a never ending circle that only stressed out both of them. They knew it had to end.

Matthew also would see Adam Lesley, the young man he had met on that wild summer weekend, at the law school. Matthew would say hello to him, but nothing further was exchanged between them. Then the Christmas shopping season came and changed all that. Matthew was walking in Copley Square looking for a Christmas gift for Scott when he saw Adam approaching. Adam walked up to him and said "hi", and they began to engage in brief conversation. Adam was also shopping and he asked Matthew if he could join him. Matthew invited him along.

The two of them spent the next three hours walking around the stores, making purchases and talking about law school. Matthew invited Adam to walk with him to Scott's shop for a cup of coffee. As they walked down the street through the new fallen snow, Adam looked over at Matthew and said, "would you ever consider going out on a date with me?" Matthew smiled, looking at him and said, "we're not on a date now?" Adam smiled back, saying, "no. I'm serious. Can we got out to dinner or something?" Matthew replied, "yes, that would be nice. How about tomorrow?" Adam accepted and as they walked through the coffee shop door they were discussing where to go for dinner.

They sat at the small corner table and ordered coffee. A few moments later Scott came out from the kitchen. Walking over to the table and seeing Matthew with a black man, Scott smirked as he caught Matthew's eyes. "Scott, this is my friend Adam. He goes to law school with me. I think you may have met him last summer when we were out.", said Matthew. Adam stood and shook Scott's hand. "Scott is my roommate. He owns this store.", continued Matthew. The three of them engaged in small conversation for a few minutes. Then Scott pronouncely said, "well unfortunately I have to get back to work. I'll be home around 10:30, just in case you two want to be alone." Scott smirked again as he left the table and walked back toward the kitchen.

Adam looked at Matthew and said, "he's gorgeous", speaking about Scott. Matthew laughed and said, "yeah, I know. That's what everybody says." Adam then asked, "are you two…?" Matthew interrupted, "no. He is my closest friend in the whole world, but no we've never been lovers. I know that some people find it hard to believe. You know, gay men, they can't have any relationship without fucking. But we do. It's wonderful and we love each other unconditionally. We don't need the sex." Adam smiled. Matthew noticed his smile more so than he had before. It was a beautiful, perfect smile. Brilliant white movie star teeth. Adam then said, "I think it's really wonderful

what you two have. I wish I could say I had the same type of relationship. It's real special." Matthew replied, "yes, it really is." They finished their coffee, waved bye to Scott and headed back out into the
winter cold.

While they were walking through the snowy streets of Boston,
Matthew was thinking about how much he loved this time of year.
The magic of Christmas. He liked the snow for the holiday, but as far
as he was concerned, it all could melt on December 26th. Matthew
was truly in the holiday spirit this evening. He had an enjoyable
shopping experience with his new friend, Adam. The store windows
all decorated with holiday splendor added to his Yuletide spirit. Matthew walked Adam to the 'T' stop. Adam lived in the neighboring
town of Medford, and Matthew was only a block away from home.
He didn't invite Adam back to the house, but rather when they were
exchanging phone numbers again, he reminded Adam to call him
before he left so they could meet at the restaurant. They shook hands
good-bye. Two men doing anything more on the streets of downtown Boston would be dangerous. The bright moon shined against
the ice covered trees. The glistening of the trees made the streets alive
with winter splendor. When Matthew laid his head on his pillow to
go to sleep he thought, "maybe this is the one."

Their first date went extremely well. They enjoyed dinner at one
of Boston's famous North End, italian restaurants. They talked all
through dinner, mostly about law school. However, they also talked
about their past and how they arrived at Harvard. Adam was from
Westport, Connecticut. He attended Trinity College in Hartford
before law school. His family still lived in Westport. He wanted to
become a defense attorney when he was done at Harvard. They
found they had a lot in common, except that Adam thought Matthew's proclamation that Diana Ross was the "biggest star there ever
was", was a little much. They talked about traditional dating. Matthew said that he would like to get to know someone before he ended
up in bed with him. Adam agreed that this was part of gay life that he

didn't like. He said to Matthew, "you meet somebody at the bar, go home and screw. Then the next morning you decide if you want to get together again. It's kinda backwards." Matthew agreed.

Adam walked Matthew home and they kissed in the hallway of the apartment building. Matthew let his sexual urges override his earlier thoughts. "Should we break the traditional dating rule?", he asked. Adam replied, "no, let's wait. It'll make it that much better." Matthew said, "you're right." They decided to meet again on Sunday for brunch. They would go to Scott's coffee shop. "He's trying to break into the brunch crowd.", Matthew told Adam. They said their good-byes and Matthew walked into the apartment.

Scott was sitting on the sofa. "No overnight guest tonight?", he asked Matthew. Matthew responded, "no we're going to try to date first." Scott replied, in a high tone, "I wonder how long that will last, mister mandingo fever!" Matthew laughed. Scott excused himself to go to bed. Matthew had a cigarette and soon followed. As he laid in his bed that evening, Matthew masturbated to the thought of making love to Adam.

The holiday itself passed quickly. The snow remained, much to Matthew's chagrin. He also decided that he really resented law school during the holiday season. School took up so much of his time he felt as if he could never relax and enjoy the holidays fully. "Maybe next year", he thought. Between driving back and forth between Boston and the Berkshires for holiday festivities, Matthew was exhausted.

Adam joined Matthew at Ted and Pete's for the traditional New Year's Eve celebration. Adam was a hit at the party and this made Matthew happy. To have his friends approval of his new boyfriend meant a lot. They spent the night at Ted and Pete's, but they did not have sex. Adam was the aggressor this time, telling Matthew it was "time to start the new year with a bang!", but Matthew held off. That evening they slept cuddling into each other. As Adam snored, Matthew laid in the bed with an erection trying to fall asleep. Just holding Adam excited Matthew and made him feel good.

Law school was in full swing when Matthew and Cathy Reed picked up their weekly school newspaper in the hall. What they read in the paper infuriated them. There was a student article entitled, "Faggots: Who Needs Them?". The article went into great deal about how homosexuals were supposedly corrupting the morals of society. The article quoted sources that Matthew and Cathy had never heard of and stated unequivocally that all gay men were pedophiles and trying to recruit young boys to "turn them into faggots." The article also blamed the exploding AIDS virus on the "wrath of God against homosexuals and their immoral lifestyle."

Matthew was standing in the hall of the law school turning red. He looked at Cathy and tersely said, "can you believe this shit?" Cathy replied, "some people are so ignorant. Just ignore it." But Matthew knew that he couldn't ignore it. The article attacked who he was as a person. The article quickly became the talk of the law school that week. Students on both sides of the issue joined forces and debated the issue of homosexuality. The First Amendment became an integral part of the debate as well. Only law students would debate for hours about whether the amendment protected speech such as this article, thought Matthew. To him it was just blatantly wrong.

Adam and Matthew talked a great deal about the article that week also. Adam was insistent that Matthew go with his idea of writing a response in the school paper. Even Jeffrey, who hadn't really talked to Matthew in several months, encouraged him to write an article. And so, Matthew did. He wrote a long response laced with statistics he had obtained from different state and federal agencies. Matthew was most proud of the part of his article which stated, "...while I respect the right of the author to express his views, I am concerned when those views are couched in questionable statistics and radical sources of material to lend support for the premise of his editorial." Matthew's response went on to say, "...hopefully in the 1980's we as a nation will work together towards becoming more enlightened and understanding of minority issues, including the rights of the gay

community. An editorial that seeks to inflame, rather than to promote that understanding and appreciation of the differences among
us, will not help in achieving this worthwhile goal."

Matthew sat and waited on the day of publication of the school
newspaper. He wondered if he would be ostracized, praised, or
would people be indifferent? To his delight, not only his friends
Cathy and Shirley lauded praise on him for his article, but many others did as well. He most appreciated the praise from those who were
socially and politically at the opposite ends of the spectrum. They
sought him out and made positive comments. One friend, Brian
Gibson, who was a staunch Reagan supporter gave Matthew one of
the most meaningful compliments he received. Brian said to him,
"you took the high road. You got the statistics and proved that the
original article was baseless. You didn't appeal to emotion, but
instead showed the facts. It was great!" Matthew blushed in appreciation and thanked his friend. They then quickly changed the subject
and began their regular jousting about the President's policies.

It turned out that the article experience was one of the most positive memories Matthew would have of law school. While he did not
hide the fact that he was gay, he didn't parade around the law school
flaunting his sexuality either. This experience became liberating to
him. He stood up and fought against bigotry and it made him
proud. Those people who were his friends remained his friends, even
with Matthew's position on the issue of homosexuality available in
black and white.

The setting for Matthew and Adam's first sexual encounter could
not have been less romantic. It happened during mid-semester when
they were studying for their Federal Courts and Jurisdiction class.
They were at the Matthew's apartment alone. Scott was working late.
He had rented the store next door and was in the process of expand-
ing his business. Always the perfectionist, Scott stayed late to super-
vise the construction of the new space. They had just reviewed
<u>Burford v. Sun Oil</u>, a case that further expanded the federal court

abstention doctrine. The case held that abstention by the federal court was necessary to avoid interference with important state activities. Matthew found this fascinating. Adam found it boring. While Matthew was re-explaining to Adam for the fourth time what he thought the case meant, Adam reached over and began to rub Matthew's inner thigh and crotch. Matthew instantly became erect. Matthew leaned into Adam and began kissing him. They began thrusting their bodies into each other. "Haven't we waited long enough?", asked Adam. "Yes!", panted Matthew. They began to pull off each other's clothes. Before they knew it they were naked and engaging in sex on the living room carpet. The sex did not last very long. They had waited a long time for this moment, and their excitement got the best of them. It was over before they knew it.

Studying was over for that night. The textbooks and hornbooks remained on the coffee table and living room floor. They got up, went into the bedroom and collapsed in Matthew's bed. In the middle of the night Matthew awoke to find Adam kissing his neck and chest. They had sex again. However, this time they were able to control themselves and make it last longer. When it was over, Adam fell right back to sleep. Matthew laid in the bed staring at the ceiling. Even though it wasn't the most romantic of settings, Matthew knew that this night would be forever etched in his mind.

In the morning Matthew sat at the kitchen table drinking coffee while Adam remained sleeping. About a half hour later Scott got up and joined Matthew in morning coffee. "How late did you work last night?", Matthew asked Scott. He responded, "oh, I was there until about 1:30. It's coming good. I think the space will be done in about two weeks and then I can buy the tables and booths. What about you? Did you guys study late last night?" Matthew responded, "not too late." Scott said, "well the living room is a mess." Matthew smugly apologized, "sorry. We got a little distracted..." Scott looked at him and smiled, "no?" Matthew replied, "yes!" Scott said, "Finally! Was it worth the wait?" Matthew gleefully replied, "it certainly was!

Adam is so hot. It was great...sweaty sex. Just like I like it!" Scott roared with laughter.

A few moments later Adam stumbled into the kitchen only wearing a pair of boxers. He waved to Scott and then mumbled, "hi". He sat down with them at the table. Scott waited a minute or two and then in a tone laced with sarcasm and humor asked, "so Adam...did you have a good night's sleep last night honey?" Matthew turned away so not to laugh. Adam smiled and said, "you told him, didn't you?" Matthew replied, "mmm hmm...and I told him it was wonderful!" Adam laughed and looked at Scott. He told Scott, "you know it was the best he ever had!" Scott smiled, "I bet it was", he replied. They all laughed. Scott sat there and looked at Adam admiring his well toned, muscular brown body and thinking, "yes, I bet it was!"

The rest of the week was a washout for Matthew and Adam. They ended up skipping classes and spent the week studying each other's anatomy rather than studying the law. By Sunday, Scott was calling them "rabbits" and asked them if they were ever going to come out of the bedroom. "My older sister, the tramp!", Scott said to Matthew.

Springtime arrived in New England and Matthew was in love. He was not only in love with Adam, but also with the weather, Boston, law school and just about everything else. He was head over heels in love with Adam. He was constantly talking to anyone who would listen to him about Adam. Nothing was bothering Matthew. Everything seemed to give him a natural high. He was also very excited about the upcoming graduation from law school. "Every queen loves a good ceremony!", he told Scott.

One early May day, Matthew's Conflict of Law class was canceled. He had an afternoon free and he decided to enjoy the warm spring weather. He had to wait for Adam to finish his class, so Matthew went to Harvard Square to hang out. He loved sitting on the stoops in the square and people watching. It was a square bustling with activity. There was so many people to watch. The square was filled with students, young professionals, political protesters, and culturally alternative people. He parked himself on one of the stoops and began watching the activity.

Matthew was smoking a cigarette and sipping on his bottle of coke when he heard a voice behind him say, "Mr. Schipani...is that you?" Matthew turned and saw a handsome young man staring at him. The face looked familiar, but Matthew was having difficulty placing it. He knew that the young man was from his past, but his brain was not making the connection. "Mr. Schipani?", asked the young man. "Yes...yes, I'm Matthew Schipani.", replied Matthew. "Do you remember me?", asked the young man. Matthew hated these situations. There was no way to hide it, just come out and say it. So he did. "You look familiar, but I'm sorry I can't seem to remember your name.", Matthew told the young man.

"Craig Talbot. I'm Craig Talbot. I met you about four years ago.", the young man told Matthew. It was coming back to him. Craig was a teenager that had been sexually abused and prostituted by his parents. Matthew had done the investigation. "Of course", Matthew replied. "I remember you now. How are you doing?", he inquired. Craig responded, "good...real good." A few uncomfortable moments passed before the next words were exchanged between them. Matthew asked, "so what brings you to Cambridge?" Craig replied, "I'm a freshman at MIT." Matthew raised his eyebrows and said, "wow! That's great. I can't believe your in college already." Craig then asked, "do you work down here now?" Matthew shook his head, "no, I'm finishing up at Harvard Law." Craig smiled and said, "I'm impressed!"

Craig sat down on the stoop next to Matthew. He lit a cigarette. Matthew reached into his pocket and lit one of his own. They looked alternately back and forth at the people in the square and at one another. Matthew didn't know what to say next and he felt uncomfortable about it. He certainly couldn't ask how his parents were. Searching for something to say, Matthew asked, "so how is school going?" Craig responded, "it's really tough. But I like it. There's a lot of technical stuff, but I think if I make it through this year, I'll be okay." Matthew said, "well hang in there. It's a great school." Matthew continued to smoke his cigarette and was checking his watch. "Where's Adam?", he thought. He was hoping that Adam would show up so he would be able to get out of this increasingly awkward situation. Craig then asked Matthew, "are you always studying or do you ever get time to go out to a club?" Matthew replied, "I get out occasionally. Not as much as I used to...but I get out." Craig asked, "have you ever been to 'Metropolis'?" Of course Matthew had. It was one of the most popular gay bars in Boston.

"Why?", asked Matthew in an inquisitive tone. Craig responded, "well, I've been going there a lot lately." Matthew asked, "do you like it?" Craig said, "yeah! It's really fun. There's a lot of hot guys there!" Matthew smiled. Craig then continued, "do you think you and I could go out there some night and have fun?", and then he grabbed Matthew's knee. Matthew picked up Craig's hand and sternly said, "don't do that!" He looked soberly at Craig and then told him, "Cambridge may be liberal, but it's not that liberal...at least not yet." Craig replied, "sorry".

Matthew lit his third cigarette. "Where the fuck is Adam?", he thought. "If he doesn't get here soon I'll have to think of something to get out of here." Craig interrupted Matthew's thinking with another question. "So, you didn't answer my question. Can we go out and party some night?" Matthew looked at him, smiled and then said, "that would be nice, but I'm sorry. I'm involved with someone and we don't go out that much to the bars anymore." Craig asked, "is it serious?" Matthew replied, "very serious".

As he butted out his cigarette Craig said to Matthew, "I think you're very cute." Matthew responded, "thank you. That's very flattering." Craig then went on to say, "I know you told me you're involved...but I have a hard on sitting here looking at you. How about we go over there to the park and I suck you off?" Matthew stood up. He looked down at Craig and raised his voice as he said, "I told you I'm involved!" Craig stood up next to him. "I know", he told Matthew. "But how about a quickie…wouldn't you like this nice piece of chicken sucking your big cock?"

Matthew turned to walk away. Craig grabbed him by the jacket and said, "come on. I give great head. How about it? It's cause of you I'm sucking cock all over the place! So how about I pay you back? The chicken you took away from his mommy and daddy pays you back with a great blow job!" Matthew pushed Craig's hand from his jacket and began to walk away. He had only taken a few steps when he turned and walked back to Craig. He went up to him and said, "look…you can't just proposition people off the street. You're going to get hurt. You better be careful! The next person may not be so kind." Craig stood and smirked at Matthew and then grabbed for Matthew's crotch. Matthew stepped back and with a quiet, but stern voice said, "you don't get it. I told you I'm not interested. I'm happy for you that you're doing well at MIT and that you've got your shit together, but I really have to go. Good luck to you."

Matthew turned again and began to walk away slowly. Behind him he heard Craig scream loudly, "faggot!". Then he felt the thud against the back of his head and heard the crash of glass at his feet. Craig had picked up the soda bottle Matthew left behind and threw it at him. Matthew grabbed the back of his head. It was slightly bleeding. He saw Craig standing a few feet away staring at him. Matthew began to run towards Craig. Craig took off. He was running quickly through the square. Matthew followed, running through the crowd. Craig was too fast for him. Matthew lost him near the 'T' station.

Matthew walked back towards the square. "Damn cigarettes!", he said to himself. "If I didn't smoke so much I would have caught that little shit!", he thought. As he held the back of his head he saw Adam standing in the square. "What's wrong?", said Adam as he approached Matthew. Matthew calmly explained the events that had just preceded Adam's arrival. Adam reached in his bookbag and found some Kleenex. Matthew held them to the back of his head. The bleeding was slowing down. Adam put his arm around Matthew and said, "let's go out and get something to eat. We'll just avoid 'Metropolis' for awhile because I don't want to run into that psycho. I'll give him a fucking bottle across his face!"

They decided to walk through campus and toward Porter Square. Matthew began to calm down about the events. He looked around at the campus and said to Adam, "I can't believe it almost over. It went by so quick. It seems like I just started here the other day." Adam smiled and said, "I hope my last year goes as quick as yours. I'm over this place!" They had a nice dinner at one of their favorite Mexican restaurants and then went to Adam's apartment. That evening, while lying in bed Matthew again became distracted with the events at Harvard Square. Adam said, "look. Just try to put it out of your mind. He's fucked up. You tried to help the kid. Obviously he still needs help. It's a big city, you probably won't see him again. Just stay away from 'Metropolis' and MIT!"

Adam reached over to turn out the bedroom light. The phone rang. It was Scott looking for Matthew. Adam handed him the phone. Scott told Matthew, "Phillip has been trying to get a hold of you all night. He's still at the office. He said it was important and he wanted you to call." Matthew said, "Okay. I'll call there now." He hung up the phone and dialed Phillip's office. The phone only rang once when Phillip answered. "Moon, Rogers and Styles Law Offices", Phillip announced. "Hi Phillip, it's Matthew", he said. "Hi Sweetie!", Phillip replied. Matthew asked, "what are you doing there so late?" Phillip chuckled and said, "oh the glamorous life of an attorney. I'm working on a damn brief. I called to find out what you were doing this Friday night." Matthew thought for a moment and said, "nothing, why?" "Well!", said an excited Phillip, "I have an extra ticket to the Attorney General's campaign dinner and I thought it would be good for you to go. I've had cases with Wallace Cartwright. He's a very good man. I want you to meet him." Matthew replied, "that sounds great. What time and where?" Phillip said, "meet me at the public library at six thirty. It's at the Copley Marriot. Dress is semi-casual." "Okay", said Matthew, "it's a date." and he hung up the phone.

Adam turned to him and smiled, saying, "so you're dating Phillip on the side huh?" Matthew laughed and said, "there's a campaign dinner for Wallace Cartwright on Friday. He want's me to go with him. He thinks it'll be good for me. I guess I should go. I just hope it isn't boring." Adam replied, "It probably will be, but you should go. It's getting about that time to find a job again!" "Yeah, wonderful!", sighed Matthew.

Adam got up out of the bed. "I think I'll take a bath. I want to relax…a nice hot, steamy bath." He continued in a purring tone as he walked by Matthew in his shorts, "yes, a real hot bath. You know the kind…where you get all sweaty and wet…and hard. Care to get wet?" Matthew smiled, sitting up in the bed. "Get wet?", he asked. "I already am just thinking about it!" Matthew chased Adam into the bathroom. Adam reached for the faucet and the steamy water began filling the tub. A few moments later they were laying on each other in the tub pouring water over each other's bodies and kissing.

Graduation day 1984 was everything Matthew hoped it would be. The sunny skies and warm temperature only enhanced the majesty of what would be one of the most important day's in Matthew's life. He graduated with honors from the most prestigious law school in the country. When he marched into the auditorium for the beginning of the ceremony with his fellow students, he heard the band playing *"Pomp and Circumstance"*. This song always moved Matthew. By the time he had reached his seat there were tears welling in his eyes.

The graduation party Scott threw for him at his shop out did the ceremony. Scott had decorated the entire store in graduation garb. His family and his friends, old and new were all at the party. Even

Diana made the trip. Scott had made her a little mortar board for her head, but she kept knocking it off with her paw.

Before he knew it he was deep in study for the bar examination. The time and intensity of the preparation was unbelievable to Matthew. He became incredibly stressed. But he knew that he had a highlight at the end of the tunnel which he could focus on to relieve his stress. As his graduation present, his parents had bought him two tickets to Honolulu leaving the day after the bar exam. Scott had purchased a ticket as well and would be joining Matthew and Adam in Hawaii. The thought of the trip provided comfort to Matthew, but he needed to get through the "quiz" first as his friend Shirley Morin called it. Matthew found the bar exam to be very difficult. He had no idea whether he passed or failed at the end of it. But at least it was over. He hoped he wouldn't have to do it again. He was physically and mentally drained. It actually took him two days in Honolulu before he could let of the stress and realize that the exam was over. He didn't have to study anymore.

On the second day in Hawaii, Matthew was standing waist deep in the warm pacific ocean. Adam and Scott were off to the side of him playing on a blow up raft they had bought. Matthew gazed at Diamond Head to his left and began to laugh loudly. Too loud. Adam quickly swam over to Matthew. "What's wrong?", he asked. Matthew continued to laugh and said, "nothing. Absolutely nothing is wrong! Everything is right!" Adam and Scott looked at each other. "Maybe Matthew has broken out of his funk.", thought Scott. He raised an eyebrow to Adam and then they both jumped on Matthew and dunk him under the water. When Matthew came up the three of them engaged in a splash fight, all the while laughing. They spent the rest of the afternoon frolicking in the water and on the shore of Waikiki Beach. To Matthew, life had returned to normal. He could relax.

About halfway through the trip Scott met a native Polynesian man named Wayne Movado. They quick fell in lust with each other and spent a great deal of time together. This allowed Matthew and Adam to be alone and they used their alone time to rekindled their relationship. However, one evening they all decided to go out to eat at a restaurant that Wayne had picked out. They sat in the bar of LeLani's Restaurant waiting for their table. Matthew loved the Polynesian decor of the restaurant. As they were waiting Matthew heard a familiar voice from the other side of the restaurant. "Are those my girls?", shouted the voice. Matthew turned around and there was Phillip Styles coming over to them. Matthew's mouth fell open as he got to his feet and gave Phillip a warm hug.

Phillip was in Hawaii for three weeks. When he booked his trip he had consulted with Adam. He purposefully planned to overlap a few days so that he could spend time with Matthew. Matthew was thrilled that his friend and legal mentor was in Honolulu to share some of his vacation. They spent the final days on the island as a group touring beyond Waikiki Beach. Wayne was a wonderful tour guide. Matthew particularly liked the windward side of the island. Adam was thrilled with the Poli Lookout. The height made Matthew feel as if he had vertigo. The vacation was a masterpiece. Matthew felt rested and rejuvenated.

It soon became fall in Boston. Matthew's favorite season. He loved the "sweater weather", as he called it. Cool days and crisp clear nights. The trees turning on Boston Common. This was the season for Matthew. But not this year. He was obsessing about the coming bar results. He couldn't enjoy the season. At times he would think about the results so much he would make himself physically ill. Adam was being supportive to Matthew, but he was involved with his own studies. Adam was not enjoying his final year at Harvard. Scott was busy enjoying the fruits of his labor as his business continued to take off. "He'll be a millionaire before we know it. Maybe I should have married him!", said Adam one night trying to joke with a brooding Matthew. Scott cashed out on his interest in the bistro in Somerville and treated himself to a new Saab. Matthew was happy for Scott, but on some level he felt a twinge of jealousy.

Matthew was working part time in Phillip's office. One day he took a message from the Attorney General's office for Phillip. At the end of the day, Phillip came out to Matthew's desk and said, "I got a call from Wallace Cartwright. He remembers meeting you at the campaign dinner. He wants to meet with you about a possible job that will be opening in December." Matthew was clearly surprised. "You're kidding!", he said. Phillip replied, "no, I'm serious. Here's the number. Ask for Doris, she's his administrative assistant. She'll set up the appointment for you."

Matthew's interview with Attorney General Wallace Cartwright was intimidating for him from the beginning of the interview when Cartwright entered the room. The Attorney General had a commanding presence. He reminded Matthew of Spencer Tracy in the movie, *Inherit the Wind*. Wallace Cartwright was the lawyer every law student dreamed of becoming. His presence in any room instantly redirected the focus of the crowd. Wallace Cartwright was a "presence" in every sense of the word. He was a powerful and legendary force in the Massachusetts legal community. Matthew was sure that he let his nervousness and intimidation ruin the interview. He left the interview feeling somewhat depressed. "Well, I guess I could work for Phillip if I have to.", thought Matthew.

November first. The change of the calendar frightened Matthew. The bar results would be out by the end of the month. Matthew was so anxious that he was becoming forgetful. He hadn't slept a full night in weeks. His anxiety was affecting his work as well. His sex life was poor, he had no desire for sex. Adam was becoming inpatient. Matthew would respond, "don't give me any shit. You'll be the same next year at this time." A few days later good news arrived via the telephone. It was Doris Sinkowski at the Attorney General's office. Matthew hadn't done that poorly in the interview after all. She was calling on behalf of the Attorney General. The Attorney General was offering him an assistant Attorney General's position beginning on December first. She reminded him that it was contingent of course on his passing the bar examination. "God damn exam!", he thought as he politely accepted the position.

Every day for the past two weeks he had rushed home at noon time to check the mail. No results. The wait was driving him crazy. One day he called Janice at work. He was in an absolute frenzy about the bar results. She tried to calm him down, but it wasn't working. So Janice invited him to Provincetown for the weekend. "I think you need a rest", she told Matthew. Both Scott and Adam thought it was a good idea that Matthew get away for the weekend. They planned to take advantage of Matthew's absence and spend a night on the town together. Matthew was very happy that they had become such good friends. He was glad they could spend the time alone without him and enjoy themselves.

It was their second brisk day in Provincetown when the phone rang in Matthew and Janice's room. Matthew picked it up. It was Scott. "What's the matter?", asked Matthew. Scott responded, "the mail's here." Matthew disinterestedly responded in return, "yeah, so?"" Scott said, "its here." "Oh shit!", exclaimed Matthew. "Janice!", he yelled. She came running out of the bathroom. "The bar results are out!", he shouted at her. "Oh God!", she said in return. Matthew yelled into the phone, "we're on our way. Don't open the envelope!". He slammed down the phone in Scott's ear.

They quickly packed their clothes and went to the car. "You drive", commanded Matthew to Janice. "I'm too nervous", he said as he threw the key ring at her. Matthew was trembling all over. The drive back to Boston seemed like an eternity. Matthew kept talking, in fact, he was babbling at times. "What if I failed? What will I tell people? Should I have studied more? I don't want to take that damn exam over again!", he kept repeating over and over. Janice was doing her best to try to calm him down, but it wasn't working. Matthew was smoking one cigarette after another as Janice pushed the speed limit to get home.

They parked the car in front of the apartment on Beacon Street. Matthew noticed his father's LTD parked out front. "What are they doing here?", he asked Janice as they walked up the stairs to the apartment. Then he remembered that his parents had been visiting his cousin in Nahant. They walked in the house together. His mother Rosa gave him a big hug. Adam handed the envelope to Matthew. Matthew grabbed it and went into the living room by himself. He sat down in the wing backed chair. He held onto the letter that held the answer to his future. He rubbed the envelope over and over again. Then he opened the back of the envelope. He slowly pulled out the letter and held it folded in his hands for about five minutes. He read the letter twice. Then he began to cry silently. He looked down at the letter and read it once again. The letter said, "the Board of Bar Examiners is pleased to inform you that you have successfully completed the July 1984 Massachusetts Bar Examination." He had done it! All the studying and preparation were worth it. He was a lawyer!

CHAPTER 6

GOVERNMENT LAWYER

November 1985

"Docket Number 85–154. Commonwealth vs. Atchinson", heralded the court officer. "Will the parties identify themselves to this Honorable Court?", he bellowed. "Matthew Schipani, Assistant Attorney General for the Commonwealth", Matthew stated. "Attorney Kathleen McEwan for the defendant, Susan Atchinson", she stated. "Are the parties ready to proceed?", asked Judge Deidre Sinclair. "Ready for trial", Matthew firmly responded. "Ready, your honor", replied Attorney McEwan.

Matthew was ready to begin to prosecute a high profile civil rights case. Typical of government service, he was thrown right into the middle of this controversial case, and he had only been a lawyer for a year. Susan Atchinson stood accused of civil rights violations and conspiracy to murder in an abortion rights case. The defendant, Susan Atchinson had founded the "Save the Babies" organization, a pro-life group that frequently protested abortion clinics and politicians offices.

One day this past winter, so the government's theory went, Atchinson incited her group to protest at the Women's Health Clinic, located in the affluent Boston suburb of Newton. As the protest intensified, the conflict grew between pro-life and pro-choice demonstrators. One of Atchinson's disciples, according to the government, was directed by the defendant to pull out a revolver and kill one of the pro-choice protesters. The victim was a young woman named Kari McDuffee. The shooter was a young man named Carter Kendall. When Kendall was arrested he immediately and proudly identified himself as a member of the "Save the Babies" organization, and confessed to the murder. After a few hours of heated interrogation by the police, Kendall implicated Susan Atchinson as part of the murder.

Kendall told police investigators that Atchinson had 'ordered' him to kill one of the pro-choice demonstrators. His said this command was given so that the "message would be heard loud and clear" that abortion was murder. In exchange for his testimony against Atchinson, the district attorney in conjunction with Attorney General Wallace Cartwright, had arranged for a reduced sentence of 20 years for Kendall. Carter Kendall was to be the star witness in the government's case against Susan Atchinson.

Attorney General Wallace Cartwright wanted a conviction. He wanted the headlines. The Attorney General wanted the notoriety that he had defended a woman's right to choose and upheld the Constitution. Matthew was chosen among the staff to bring Wallace Cartwright those headlines.

The judge ordered the jury to be brought in. While they were seated, Matthew looked around the courtroom. He had been in this courtroom many times over the past year. He loved this courtroom. It had been built in the 1940's. It's grandeur portrayed the majesty of the law. With deep cherry wood paneling on the walls, and a judge's bench that was high above the fray, Matthew thought, "this is what a courtroom should look like." Matthew couldn't stand the modern courtrooms with their veneer furniture and padded chairs. He wanted hard wooden chairs and benches in the courtroom. "The law is a serious matter and not just a bunch of people sitting around having a conversation. The furniture in the courtroom should reflect that seriousness.", though Matthew. Judge Sinclair's courtroom stood for justice and the power of the law through its construction. Long deceased judges, depicted in portraits mounted in gold gilded frames, presided over the courtroom that Matthew loved. "If I ever become a judge, this is where I want to sit.", thought Matthew.

The jury was seated in the jury box. They had padded seats, but Matthew forgave that. "They deserve to be comfortable", he thought. Judge Sinclair welcomed the jury and briefly explained the trial proceedings. As she was speaking Matthew thought about Deidre Sinclair. She was one of the first black women to sit on the superior court bench in the Commonwealth. Judge Sinclair was a no nonsense jurist who took control of her courtroom. Matthew respected that. In the halls outside the courtroom, Judge Sinclair was known for her toughness as well as her fairness. Matthew was happy when she was chosen to hear this trial.

Matthew turned his attention to the final words that Judge Sinclair was saying. "In conclusion, ladies and gentlemen of the jury, I want you to remember this axiom throughout the trial and during your deliberations. The Commonwealth must prove beyond a reasonable doubt, every element of the crimes the defendant is charged with. The defendant sits before you with the presumption of innocence and unless the Commonwealth meets its burden, the defendant must be found not guilty." Judge Sinclair extended her hand across the bench in Matthew's direction. It was his cue to begin the case. Matthew rose to make his opening statement. He recalled the advice he received in his trial advocacy course in law school. His professor constantly hammered home to the students that the opening statement of the case was the most important moment in every case. "It is where the case is won or lost." Matthew remembered his advice as he moved around the table toward the jury to begin his statement.

He had rehearsed his statement at home and almost committed it to memory. He believed that if a jury was to see an attorney read from a prepared text, the opening statement loses its power and thus the jury loses confidence in that attorney. Matthew wanted to hook the jury right away. He knew that he had to have their full attention, and keep it. His opening statement was purposefully short and to the point. There would be enough boring scientific and other evidence during the trial. He did not want to lose the jury on the first day. Before starting he looked into the galley of the courtroom. It was packed with spectators. Phillip Styles was among those assembled. He promised Matthew that he would be there for moral support, and he was. Matthew began. "Ladies and Gentlemen of the jury, my name is Matthew Schipani. I am an Assistant Attorney General for Massachusetts. I appear before you today to prosecute one of the most heinous crimes this Commonwealth has seen. The government will prove that this crime was committed by the defendant seated before you today, Ms. Susan Atchinson."

"Now I warn you up front", Matthew stated, "much to the contrary of what you may hear from defense counsel this case is not about abortion. This case is not about the right to an abortion or whether abortion is murder. This case is about the murder of a young woman. This case is about the conspiracy that went with that murder, and the violation of the civil rights of the victim, Kari McDuffee. I ask you to remember the victim in this case as you hear the evidence presented to you during this trial. Kari McDuffee was gunned down at age 23 this past winter. Only four months shy of her graduation ceremony at Boston College. Only four months shy of beginning her adult life. She was gunned down because she happened to be at an assembly of people who met to uphold the Constitutionally guaranteed right to abortion. She was among a crowd voicing her support when her life was snuffed out on that cold winter day. Four months shy of her adult life, a life that will never be lived."

Matthew moved in front of the witness stand toward the jury. "The evidence will show that in January of this year, Carter Kendall shot and killed young Kari McDuffee outside a women's health clinic in Newton. The evidence will show that Carter Kendall completed his murderous act at the command of his leader, the defendant Susan Atchinson!" With that statement Matthew raised his arm and forcefully extended it, pointing across the courtroom at the defendant seated at the counsel table with her attorney. Matthew took a few second dramatic pause and stared at the defendant, the classic "television attorney move" practiced at home by Matthew, seemed so powerful to him. The pointing finger – the accusing finger. Susan Atchinson looked straight ahead.

Matthew turned back to the jury. "Now a trial is about a search for truth", he continued. "In this case that is your most important role. To search for truth, so that justice may be served. But to get to the truth you will have to wade through a river of distractions, theories and rhetoric set forth by the defense to confuse you. But you must wade carefully through that river. You must sift through the rhetoric and distractions so that the truth can be found." While Matthew was making these statements he took his hand and flipped it sideways in a waving motion.

Matthew walked to the front of the jury box. He continued on with his opening statement. He purposely lowered and extended his voice. "The facts in this case are not complicated. Only the rhetoric is. The facts and the evidence you hear will prove beyond a reasonable doubt that Susan Atchinson conspired to violate the civil rights of Kari McDuffee and conspired to kill this young woman. The evidence will show that Atchinson founded her group, 'Save the Babies', six years ago as a vehicle to promote her view that abortion was murder. Now we all respect various views and opinions. We cherish them, develop them, and promote the right to express differing views. But when you choose to challenge the law, because you disagree with the law, you must stay within the bounds of the law. The defendant didn't stay within the bounds of the law. She crossed that important boundary."

Matthew turned briefly away. He looked out at the audience and Phillip. Then he turned back to the jury. "The evidence in this case will show that the defendant recruited young disciples to carry out her mission. Her mission of hate for those who would have abortions. Her mission to stop abortions at all costs. Now where did the defendant find these disciples? She recruited them through her literature and protests. What type of recruits did she find? You will learn that the defendant looked for young and impressionable adults. She recruited religious extremists. She recruited the lonely. She recruited emotionally unstable people. The defendant recruited those who had a need to belong and be led. The defendant recruited those who would promote her message at any cost, including being willing to step outside the bounds of the law to make sure her message was heard."

Matthew paused, caounting to five in his mind, for effect, and then continued in his sober and direct tone. "The government shall show that the defendant as time went on was not satisfied with the lawful means of protest. Initially the defendant stayed within the boundary. She would send her 'groupies' to protest at abortion clinics throughout the metropolitan area. She would hold candlelight vigils and sent mailings promoting her views. But as time passed the defendant became unhappy with staying within the bounds of the law. Her efforts weren't having an impact. In fact, more people were joining the opposite side of the issue. Her group was being outnumbered by those who disagreed with her. She was losing the battle and didn't know how to hold on. So the defendant began to intensify her recruiting efforts. She looked for more disciples to carry out her message. The evidence will show that the defendant became more and more frustrated as time went on. She had more disciples but the message still wasn't being heard. She had to do something, and she did. She decided to cross over! Cross over that boundary that separates lawful activity from lawlessness and chaos."

Matthew paused again before continuing his statement. He wanted his words, his opening statement, to resonate with the jury. Then he began again. "The defendant had to decide how to make an impact for her side. She decided the way to achieve her desired impact was through fear and intimidation. So the crossover began. It started with threats, late at night, over the phone to doctors and nurses who worked at the health centers. Mailings to health care professionals at their homes and offices. Mailings with veiled threats and pictures of allegedly aborted fetuses. Bomb threats over the phone to the health clinics. These were the activities that began the escalation. Now, the defendant could not do all the activity on her own. She had too much work to do. Too much disruption to cause. Too much intimidation to carry out for her message to have an impact. So the defendant used her deputies to carry out these tasks for her."

Matthew began to raise his voice. "Escalate and escalate, after she crossed the boundary. The evidence will show that in the year prior to the slaughter of Kari McDuffee, the defendant and her disciples increased the activity. They appeared at more clinics, more marches and incited more violence. Former disciples of the defendant will testify, from that witness stand and will identify to you that the defendant, Susan Atchinson was the ring leader of the increase in violence. The witnesses will tell you how the defendant would hold her so-called 'power meetings' where she would assign tasks for her charges to carry out. And as good little charges they carried them out to please their leader."

"The evidence will show that the defendant occasionally had to step back into the 'fun' and be a part of the activities with her disciples. The evidence will show that it was the defendant who led the group that threw replicas of supposed aborted fetuses at the Governor last year when he was campaigning for re-election." Taking two steps back he continued on. "But plastic dolls being thrown at the leader of Massachusetts were not enough for the defendant. Susan Atchinson only got two days of press coverage out of that stunt. So the defendant issued her edict from on high…to the disciples in her organization. She acted as if she were a leader on top of a mountain making proclamations to those below." Matthew elevated and bellowedhis voice, "The edict came down from the mountain. 'Kill a pro-choice supporter! Do it now!'" Matthew once again took a dramatic pause.

In a lower voice he continued on. "The state will have Carter Kendall here for you. Now, Mr. Kendall is not a nice guy. But he's already in jail. He confessed and is paying for his crime. Mr. Kendall will be here to explain to you how the defendant sent him on his deadly mission. The evidence will show how the defendant, a highly educated, sophisticated woman, knew how to take advantage of Mr. Kendall, a lonely societal reject. Carter Kendall was the perfect messenger for Susan Atchinson. He didn't question. He followed his leader's orders. Mr. Kendall will testify to you how he was given his orders from the defendant and how he carried out his leader's message via a forty four magnum revolver. And that, ladies and gentlemen is why the defendant sits here before you today in judgment."

"I asked you earlier not to forget Kari McDuffee, the 23 year old woman who was senselessly cut down at the beginning of her adult life. The defendant, Susan Atchinson, participated in and provided the impetus for the commission of the murder of this young girl who had not yet begun to live. The defendant set the wheels in motion. She shared the mental stated required for the murder. The defendant implanted her mental state in the trigger man's mind."

Matthew turned and moved slowly toward the middle of the courtroom. With a raised voice, Matthew went on. "In conclusion, ladies and gentlemen, that woman!….", pausing Matthew once again punched the air with his extended arm and pointed finger at Susan Atchinson. "That woman, set forth her disciple to carry forth her message. Kill a pro-choice supporter! Scare them all to death! Send the message…if you don't go away, Susan Atchinson and her disciples will make you go away…in a casket!"

Matthew moved behind his counsel table. With a calmer tone he completed his opening statement. "Weigh the evidence...skim out the rhetoric. Don't let them distract you or insult your intelligence. Put the pieces of the puzzle together, and when the puzzle is finished you will see the picture of the defendant conspiring to murder and violate the civil rights of a 23 year old, soon to be college graduate. Thank you for your attention and for your service to this court." With his statement concluded, Matthew sat down in his chair at counsel table.

Judge Sinclair gazed over the tall bench and turned toward Attorney Kathleen McEwan. "Counsel, are you prepared to make your opening statement", the judge asked. "Yes, your honor.", responded Kathleen McEwan. She rose from her hard chair and walked toward the jury in silence. At the front of the jury box, Attorney McEwan began her opening statement on behalf of the defendant.

"Ladies and Gentlemen of the jury, I am Kathleen McEwan and I represent the defendant, Susan Atchinson, a woman wrongly charged. Let me begin my brief remarks to you today by pointing out a few things. Counsel for the government wants you to put together the puzzle as he called it, and find my client guilty. But counsel for the government forgets that one big piece of the puzzle is missing. That piece is the evidence that will show that my client had anything to do with the tragic death of that young girl this past January. The evidence simply is not there. There is no connection. In fact, the evidence in this case will prove that my client had absolutely nothing to do with the murder except the misfortune of knowing the murderer, Carter Kendall."

Kathleen McEwan continued on with a soft conversation tone as she addressed the jury. "Counsel for the government tries to portray the defendant as a guru, a religious leader. Much to the contrary of counsel's assertions, Susan Atchinson did not have any messianic power over Mr. Kendall or any other member of her group. She did not command Mr. Kendall to shoot that gun. Rather, the evidence will show that my client feared Mr. Kendall and in fact, she expelled him from her group because of his violent views." Attorney McEwan rested her elbows on the railing of the jury box before continuing. "Look at the defendant who sits before you today. She is a 54 year old frail, church going woman. Now when Mr. Kendall comes here to testify, I want you to take a good look at him. Compare Mr. Kendall with my client. Compare this 22 year old, strong big black man, with my 54 year old client. Then decide for yourself. Who intimidated whom?" As Kathleen McEwan took a breath, Matthew said to himself, "not bad", and then refocused on his opposing counsel's opening statement.

"Counsel for the government", continued Attorney McEwan, "asks you to look through the rhetoric and at the facts. Well, the rhetoric has already begin with counsel's opening statement! Yes, we know that abortion is legal in this country. But the right to free speech is also legal. The right to protest and assemble is also legal. And challenges to the law have always been recognized as valid and worthwhile in this country. If they weren't, I wouldn't have the right to vote. The essence of democracy is challenging the rules that the government has set forth for society. And my client, Susan Atchinson and her group were utilizing one of this country's most cherished rules: the First Amendment. The right to express their views on this controversial issue."

Kathleen McEwan turned and walked back to her table. "Now, I am not going to go on and on and lecture you about this case as my brother did earlier. The evidence will provide all that you need to exonerate my client. We would agree however, with one premise of the government's opening statement and we ask you to follow that premise. Use your common sense when you hear the evidence. Use your common sense when you weigh and evaluate the evidence. When you look at it carefully you will see that Carter Kendall, the man who sits in prison for the next twenty years, is the responsible party for this crime. You will see that the government is trying to scapegoat my client in the interest of political advantage. Go beyond the politics and look at the evidence."

"The defendant would ask you not to fall into the trap the government is setting for you. Don't hold the defendant responsible for the radical actions of a sick young man who my client expelled from her lawful organization. When all is said and done in this courtroom, I trust that you will see that Susan Atchinson is a woman with a lawful and life promoting message. She has no hidden agenda. She wears her message on her sleeve. She values all life, born and unborn. The evidence will show that Susan Atchinson is innocent of the crimes she has been charged with. Thank you for your service in this most important case.", concluded Kathleen McEwan.

With the ending of the defense's opening statement, Judge Sinclair said, "I think this will be a good time for the morning recess." The fourteen men and women of the jury who held the fate of the defendant in their hands were escorted through a side door by the court officer. Matthew piled up his papers on the counsel table and turned to his 'second seat', Attorney Peter Casner. "Let's go get some coffee", he said to Peter.

They walked out through the swinging doors and into the galley of the courtroom. Phillip Styles came over to them. "Want to get some coffee?", he asked Matthew. "You read my mind", replied Matthew as they began to walk to the coffee shop located in the lobby of the courthouse.

"Well how about some constructive criticism", Matthew said to Phillip as he began to drink his coffee. Phillip responded, "I don't really have any. I thought you were pretty powerful. You laid out the theory and hooked the attention of the jury. I wouldn't have done it any differently." Matthew responded, "it's a tough case". Phillip nodded his head in agreement.

The rest of the first day of the trial was routine and unremarkable. The first witness to appear was the Emergency Medical Technician who responded to the murder scene. It was a short direct examination by Peter Casner. The EMT described the medical condition of the victim upon his arrival. The EMT matter of factly went into the injury resulting from the gun shot wound. Peter attempted to have the EMT show some emotion when he testified that Kari McDuffee died enroute to the hospital. It didn't work. This was a detached witness who was just recounting another night on the job. The fact that Kari McDuffee was killed over her political beliefs was of no consequence to this witness. He had answered a subpoena to tell a story in a courtroom. Cross examination by Kathleen McEwan was equally brief. No testimony came out on cross that hurt the government's case. The second witness for the state was the police detective in charge of the case. His examination would require much more attention. The first day of the trial concluded with only a few hours of direct examination of Detective Paul Carbello by Matthew.

Matthew returned home that evening exhausted. It had been a stressful day. Adam had dinner ready on the table when he arrived. It was one of Matthew's favorites, garlic chicken. Matthew ate rapidly. He hadn't eaten anything all day. Rather he smoked and drank coffee to get him through. His day was fueled by nicotine and caffeine. As the food settled Matthew enjoyed a cup of coffee. He summarized the opening day of the trial for Adam. He wanted to know each and every detail. Adam even wanted to know how people were dressed. More particularly, Adam wanted to know how Peter Casner was dressed. Matthew laughed. Adam had a crush on Peter. "I think he's so cute…that salt and pepper hair, it just drives me wild!", said Adam in a lilting tone. Matthew responded, "I'll make sure and let his wife know that she better keep her guard up!"

They watched the evening news together. Matthew looked over at Adam and smiled. The old Adam had returned. Since finding out last week he passed the bar, Adam's attitude had improved immensely. During the several months leading up to the bar results, Adam had become increasingly irritable about everything. Where Matthew dealt with stress internally, Adam acted it out. Everything bothered

Adam, right down to the brand of toothpaste they were using. Now Adam would begin the job hunt. He was a newly licensed attorney who was unsure about what he wanted to do with his future. "But he'll figure it out", thought Matthew. Then he grabbed the remote and flipped the channel to *Jeopardy!* so they could begin their daily competition.

During the afternoon of the eighth day of trial Matthew kept looking at his watch. He had to leave court right on time as he and Scott had an appointment with a Realtor. They were looking at a three family house in Cambridge near the law school. Scott and Matthew had been discussing over the past few months that since Adam and Matthew looked like a 'permanent thing', they needed to decide what to do about their living arrangements. Matthew did not want to lose Scott. He loved Scott. He loved living with him. Yet, he knew that Adam couldn't be at the apartment everyday while he lived with Scott. It was too intrusive. So they decided to buy a house together.

Matthew thought this was a wonderful idea, but he wasn't sure where he would get the downpayment. Scott had been doing so well in his business that he told Matthew that he could "cover it", and Matthew could repay him in the future. Matthew wasn't comfortable with this idea. He felt as if he was taking advantage of Scott so that he could accommodate the two most important men in his life. So Matthew turned to his parents. His father, Franco did not need much convincing. "I guess since we're paying for your sister's wedding in May, we can give you a wedding present now.", he told his son. So Mom and Dad came through for Matthew as they always did, and he was able to provide his share of the downpayment. Adam really liked the idea too, but he felt guilty about not being able to come up with any money down. His law school loans were going to kick in next month and he was still looking for work. Scott and Matthew did not let this deter their mission. They wanted Adam as a partner in the venture. In fact, Scott tried to calm Adam down about the issue by making light of it. "I'll just add it to all those blow jobs you owe me!", he told Matthew. They all laughed, but Scott flirted with the idea of having sex with Adam in his mind. "If you weren't with Matthew, I'd be all over you brown baby!", Scott thought. He found Adam very attractive, but of course he would never act on it. He knew how much Matthew and Adam were in love.

Matthew was able to leave the courthouse on time. For some reason the traffic was light and he made the appointment on time as well. He pulled up to the house in his now rusting Mustang that he refused to part with. Scott was already sitting there in his new maroon BMW. "Such a yuppie!", thought Matthew as he walked up to his best friend's new car. They greeted each other and walked up the front stairs to the door.

The Realtor came out on the front porch and invited them in. As they walked through the three apartments in the house, Matthew kept whispering to Scott, "I want this house...I want this house!". Scott, always the businessman, whispered back, "patience...patience." Matthew was impressed by the size of each apartment and the ornate original woodworking in the house. He loved the high ceilings in the rooms and had visions of tall Christmas trees decorating the living rooms during the holiday season. Matthew let Scott do the negotiations with the Realtor. Scott covered all the bases. He was able to make a fair assessment of the house's virtues and detractions. Through negotiation and his assessment with the Realtor, Scott was able to knock five thousand dollars off the selling price. "If you can guarantee me that price, we're interested", Scott commandingly told the Realtor. Matthew sat and smiled as Scott and the Realtor continued their negotiations. Patience was a good virtue, thought Matthew as he remained quiet and let his best friend continue to run the show.

Two weeks later while sitting at the counsel table in Judge Sinclair's courtroom, the court officer handed Matthew a note. Scott had called. The bank approved the mortgage. The closing was set for next Thursday! During the afternoon recess Matthew called Scott at his store. He was elated. Matthew told Scott, "We're 'homo home-owners'!" They both laughed.

That evening Adam joined Matthew and Scott at the *Ritz* in downtown Boston. They were out on the town for an expensive dinner to celebrate their new acquisition. They invited Janice but she already had plans with Jose. That relationship was becoming serious, and Adam joked as usual about how sexy Jose was. "He's a hot, hot Latin!", Adam exclaimed. Scott joined right in with the joking. He said to Matthew, "I bet she's a dominatrix…cracks the whip and all!" Adam replied, "beat me Janice, beat me harder!" Their laughter became so loud that Matthew had to "shush" them, reminding them that they were at a "classy" restaurant. The three of them laughed under their breath. "Leave it to the faggots to disrupt dinner at the *Ritz*!", said Scott.

A three day weekend was approaching and Matthew decided he would use the next few days to prepare for the last government witness. Adam was going to Westport to spend time with his family. Scott, of course, would be working. Matthew knew he needed the time alone to work hard on his final witness. It was his most important witness in this trial. The star witness for the government. Carter Kendall.

It was another normal trial day in the Atchinson case, with one exception. Their was an additional lawyer sitting at defense counsel table. Attorney Steven O'Connor had been brought in as a specialist for this case. Matthew and Steven O'Connor knew each other briefly in law school. They were a year apart and were in a couple of classes together. Steven O'Connor was a single woman's worst nightmare in a bar. He was a predator. He was suave, well dressed and extremely attractive. Attorney O'Connor was a prosecutor's worst nightmare in the courtroom. He took his predatory skills from the bar room and brought them with him into the courtroom. Kathleen McEwan had retained Attorney O'Connor for one role in this case. His sole purpose was the cross examination of the state's star witness, Carter

Kendall. While Judge Sinclair was attending to some administrative matters, Matthew walked over and greeted Steven O'Connor. They laughed about law school war stories. Their small talk was interrupted by the court officer announcing the arrival of the judge. "Court, all rise.", he bellowed. Matthew returned to his table. The jury was brought into the courtroom.

Judge Sinclair said to the court officer, "please bring in the next witness." Carter Kendall entered the courtroom from a side door. All six foot, four inches and two hundred seventy five pounds of him entered the courtroom. As he walked through the door all that could be seen was small slivers of daylight on each side of his head. He filled the doorway. "He looks good", thought Matthew as Kendall walked to the witness stand dressed in the suit that the state had paid for and Matthew had picked out. Matthew wanted to make sure that Kendall was dressed appropriately for the court, and more importantly for the jury. Matthew gazed over at the jury as Kendall took the witness stand. Their eyes were fixed on this witness.

"Please identify yourself to the court and spell your last name", intoned the overpaid, underworked court clerk, Clara Baker. "My name is Carter Kendall. K-E-N-D-A-L-L.", said the witness. Judge Sinclair extended her hand across the bench toward Matthew. "Mr. Schipani, you may begin your examination", she told Matthew. "Thank you, your honor.", said Matthew as he rose from his chair.

Matthew stood between the counsel table and the witness stand. "Mr. Kendall, could you please tell us when you first met the defendant, Susan Atchinson?", Matthew asked as he began his inquiry of this most important witness. Kendall's testimony during direct examination was marked by his matter of fact delivery. He described in detail, without emotion, how he had met Susan Atchinson. He told the court that they had met in 1983 when he had seen her at a rally against the state funding of abortion. "I thought she was a good speaker", he said. Kendall then explained how he approached Atchinson after the rally and asked how he could help her group. "She told me to come to her office. I think it was on Tremont street then…", Kendall said. "She gave me her card. I was there the next morning."

Matthew had Kendall trace through his involvement with "Save the Babies" and the defendant. Kendall explained how he became more and more involved with the group as time went on. He testified he was at the headquarters of the organization "almost every day". Kendall also testified that he was a member of the "Power Meetings" that Susan Atchinson would hold. "What happened at those meetings", asked Matthew. Kendall responded, "Well, you know Susan was real upset. I could tell she was thinking about the cause…" "Objection! Calls for speculation.", bellowed Attorney Steven O'Connor in his deep voice. "Sustained.", quickly responded Judge Sinclair.

"Let me rephrase the question.", Matthew said as he quickly continued with his examination. "Mr. Kendall could you tell the members of the jury what you observed happening at these so called 'Power Meetings'?" Kendall looked at Matthew, took a sip of water and a deep breath before proceeding. When he started his testimony once again, he continued in his flat tone. "Well, Susan would tell us how important we were to her. She said we were like the school children she used to teach. She told us we needed to help her. She said she had a master plan to save the babies and punish the murderers." Matthew interjected. "Mr. Kendall, could you tell us what that master plan was?" Kendall continued in his non-emotional delivery. "Sure. She told us she wanted to close the abortion clinics by scaring everyone that worked there to death. She figured that if she could scare them good enough then there wouldn't be anybody left to work there. Then there would be no more abortions."

Matthew moved closer to the witness. "Did you agree with the defendant's master plan, Mr. Kendall?", he asked. Kendall replied, "of course I did. I have to…she was my leader. She told us that she spoke to the Lord…and the Lord told her what do do." Matthew leaned on the witness stand. With a raised voice to add a flair of drama, he asked the witness, "Did the Lord tell her to kill Kari McDuffee?"

"Objection!", shouted Attorney O'Connor across the courtroom. "Withdrawn", demurred Matthew. Matthew stepped back from the witness stand. He noted the disapproving stare of Judge Sinclair down from the bench. She obviously was not happy with his last question.

"Now Mr. Kendall, let me turn your attention to January of this year.", continued Matthew. "Were you still a part of the defendant's group, Save the Babies?", he asked. The witness replied, "Yes, I was." Matthew asked, "could you please tell the jury about the last so-called 'Power Meeting' you attended?" "Sure", replied Kendall and he turned to look at the jury as he continued with his testimony. "I remember it was a snowy day. The heat wasn't working too well in the office. Susan was yelling at everyone to hurry up and come in the conference room and meet. I think there were about six of us...let's see, Susan, Tyrone, Ella, Caroline, Wesley and me. I think that's right.", said Kendall as he counted on his fingers those he remembered being in attendance at the meeting. Kendall continued, "Susan...she was so pissed. She said the group 'Our Choice' was getting out of control. She told us we had to teach them a lesson. They had planned a demonstration on Thursday in Newton 'cause they knew we were gonna be there. Susan said she had enough of them and we had to scare them away. She wanted us to get as many people as we could to be there. Then she asked if anyone had a gun. Ella said her father had a 'Dirty Harry' gun."

Matthew interrupted, "could you tell us what happened next?" "Well...", continued Kendall, "...Susan asked her to bring it to the office on Thursday. I remember Caroline was getting real upset. She asked Susan what we needed a gun for. Susan told her to shut up. Susan said we were gonna teach them a lesson." Kendall paused briefly in his testimony. Matthew turned and looked at the jury. The entire jury seemed focused on Carter Kendall and listening to every word he said.

"Please continue, Mr. Kendall", Matthew requested. "Okay", responded Kendall. "Now where was I?...Oh yeah, the gun. I think Caroline left 'cause she was so angry. I'm not sure...but anyways, Susan said to us that she needed somebody to "take care of this". That's her exact words...I remember them. She looked at Wesley. But he shook his head 'no'. Then she looked at me. I looked right back at her. She said, 'I appoint you Carter Kendall. You are my messenger." Those were her exact words too. I smiled at her and said 'I accept'. Nothing else was said and everybody left."

Matthew then inquired of Kendall what happened on the morning of the murder. Kendall testified that he had met the defendant early in the morning at the office. "She handed me the gun and some bullets. Then she kissed me on the forehead. She told me to go Newton and show 'Our Choice' who was the boss." Matthew quickly went over what happened at the protest scene. Even though Kendall remained calm and flat in his testimony, his words were riveting to the jury who paid their entire attention to him. Kendall described how the two groups were shouting back and forth at each other. He described how he pulled the gun out and shot into the crowd. He remembered seeing the young girl fall and then he started to run.

Matthew concluded his direct examination of the witness with a final question. "Is there anything else you would like to tell the jury, Mr. Kendall?" Kendall paused and then said, "...well yeah. I know I shouldn't have shot that girl...but I was listening to Susan. I probably shouldn't have listened to her either. But I did. I'm really sorry and I'm paying the price for my mistake." Matthew looked at the witness, "thank you Mr. Kendall.", he uttered. Then Matthew turned to Attorney O'Connor and said, "your witness."

Attorney Steven O'Connor rose from his chair and strutted around the counsel table toward the witness stand. "Well hello, Mr. Kendall. I'm Steven O'Connor", he began. "Now I know this has been a long day for you Mr. Kendall, coming from prison and all. Do you need a break before we begin?", O'Connor asked. "No...no, I'm fine", replied Carter Kendall. Matthew sat, watched and waited. Just like a pit bull ready to pounce, thought Matthew of his opposition. Attorney O'Connor said, "well if your comfortable. Let's begin. Now a few moments ago you told the esteemed Mr. Schipani that you paid the price for killing Kari McDuffee. Isn't that what you said?" Kendall looking directly at Attorney O'Connor, replied, "yeah…I'm paying the price." Steven O'Connor paused and then asked, "well isn't it true that you got a reduced price? A sale price on prison time?" "Objection!", shouted Matthew. "Overruled", replied Judge Sinclair.

"Well, we're waiting Mr. Kendall. Didn't you get prison time on sale?", asked Steven O'Connor. "I guess", replied an emotionless Kendall. "You guess?", roared back Attorney O'Connor. "You guess Mr. Kendall? You admit you killed a girl and you guess that you got your twenty year sentence on sale?" "Objection!", shouted Matthew as he rose in an attempt to break the momentum that O'Connor was starting to build. "Overruled", quickly ruled Judge Sinclair.

O'Connor continued with this line of questioning. "Now Mr. Kendall, isn't it true that the revered Wallace Cartwright and the district attorney gave you a reduced sentence? Isn't it true that you got a sale price, so to speak, if you would testify against my client?" Kendall looked down into his lap and then said, "Yeah…I told you. I guess so." O'Connor leaned towards Kendall. "Do you think this was a good sale price, Mr. Kendall?", O'Connor quickly retorted back. "Objection!", Matthew loudly announced while slamming his hand down on the counsel table. "Sustained", responded Judge Sinclair.

The cross examination of Carter Kendall continued in this manner for the remainder of the day. O'Connor would ask emotional or sarcastic questions and Matthew would be on his feet objecting. Sometimes the rulings would be in Matthew's favor, sometimes against. Judge Sinclair was fair in her rulings. She ruled as she believed the law was to be applied. When the hour was getting closer to the end of the day Matthew observed Steven O'Connor constantly watching the old school clock on the wall in the courtroom. "What is he up to?", thought Matthew.

There were about five minutes left in the court day. O'Connor continued to hammer away at the witness and clock watch at the same time. His last question to Carter Kendall was, "Sir. Isn't it true that the reason you're here to testify against my client is that you made romantic and sexual advances toward her and she turned you down?" Before a confused looking Kendall could respond, Matthew was on his feet again. It felt like the fortieth time today. "Objection!", he shouted.

Judge Sinclair broke the stride with her inquiry to Matthew. "What is the basis of your objection?", she asked. Matthew replied, "First, your honor, I'm not sure what the relevancy of this is. Secondly, there is no foundation for this question." Judge Sinclair paused briefly. "Attorney O'Connor. The objection is sustained as to foundation.", the judge said. She continued, "Lay a foundation counselor and then I'll determine relevancy."

Steven O'Connor not missing a beat, responded back to the judge, "your honor, before I do that. It will take a little while to lay the foundation and I note that the hour is late. Perhaps this would be an appropriate time to break for the day?", he asked. Judge Sinclair glanced across the courtroom at the clock. "I agree with you. The hour is late. This is a good time to break. Court will be in recess until the morning.", the judge said. She motioned to the court officer who instructed the jury to follow him. "All rise", ordered the other court officer to those remaining. Judge Sinclair exited out the left door as the jury proceeded out the right door of the courtroom.

Matthew stood at the counsel table with Peter Casner. Matthew's face was red in anger. Steven O'Connor had planned it perfectly. The day had ended with a cliff hanger. The jury would have the night to wonder if there was a sexual relationship between the defendant and the witness. Matthew knew that he had been out classed by his former law school peer. All he could say to Peter was "son of a bitch!", as he grabbed his briefcase and swiftly walked out of the courtroom.

Matthew and Peter went for a quick beer and then parted company for the evening. Morning would come real soon and Matthew had a lot of work to do. The cross-examination of Carter Kendall had damaged the government's case significantly, in Matthew's opinion.

Matthew spent the evening in his home library reviewing the transcripts and notes of his interviews with Kendall. There was no mention of any romantic relationship between Kendall and Atchinson. But it also appeared that the question had never been asked. This could totally undermine the case, thought Matthew. It would give Kendall a motive to lie about the murder. He was a spurned lover. He would say anything to get back at Atchinson. Matthew spent the rest of the evening sequestered in his library trying to figure out a way to rehabilitate his star witness.

The call came at seven thirty the next morning. The trial was canceled for the day. Judge Sinclair had gotten ill last evening. Matthew was sure that this was not a blessing in disguise. Yes, it would allow him time to talk to Kendall about this allegation. But it would also give the jury more time to think about the allegation.

Matthew drove to the prison where Kendall was to be held for the next twenty years. They met for about an hour. Kendall insisted that there was no romantic relationship between them. "I don't like skinny old white bitches. I like big healthy girls!", Kendall told Matthew. They reviewed his testimony. Kendall remained consistent with his accounting of the events in January.

Matthew was driving home from the prison when his car phone rang. It was Romello Glassman, the clerk to Judge Sinclair. The judge would be out for the rest of the week. Her appendix had chosen this time to burst. She would be in the hospital for a few days to recover from the emergency appendectomy. "Great", thought Matthew. "More time for the jury to think".

Matthew chose to go to the apartment rather than back to the office. The 'big move' was this weekend. He still had some more things to pack before he and Scott moved to Cambridge. Adam had already moved his stuff over and was in the process of cleaning the new house.

Matthew hated moving. The disorganization drove him crazy. He felt rushed to put everything where it belonged. The highlight of the move over the weekend was when his parents arrived on Sunday with an extra guest. When they entered the kitchen Matthew was in his bedroom. He could hear the pitter patter of little paws on the linoleum kitchen floor. It was Diana. She was finally home! He ran out of the bedroom and to his beloved dog. He hugged her as she licked his face and wildly wagged her tail.

That evening Rosa insisted upon making dinner for everyone. Adam, Scott, Janice and Jose joined Matthew and his parents for dinner. They enjoyed a traditional Italian feast with many bottles of Lambrusco, her favorite wine. "God, I love that woman", thought Matthew, "but to have to endure that wine!"

Monday morning arrived and Judge Sinclair was back on the bench. The remaining cross examination of Carter Kendall lasted only for the morning session. It was just as stinging as last week. Kendall denied that he and the defendant ever had a romantic relationship. But Matthew believed that some members of the jury were questioning the credibility of this witness. Matthew conducted a short redirect examination to clear up a few things that were brought out on cross examination. But he purposefully stayed away from the subject of the supposed romantic relationship.

The government rested their case. The defense in the following week brought forward several character witnesses and members of Save the Babies. These witnesses directly challenged the government witnesses about the level of control Susan Atchinson had over the group. They portrayed Atchinson as an engaging leader, not a controlling one. Matthew guessed it would be a toss up for the jury on who to believe from the group.

The final highlight of the trial was the taking of the witness stand by Susan Atchinson. She had insisted upon it against the advice of her counsel, Kathleen McEwan. But the highlight was not for the government, rather it was for the defense. Atchinson, who was on the stand for two days, dressed in a cardigan sweater with a gold crucifix prouncely hanging outside of her sweater. She presented as a credible, sincere and sober witness. Atchinson testified that she was intimidated by Kendall. She testified his size and strength scared her. She also testified that Kendall made sexual advances to her on many occasions. In a teary voice, Atchinson testified that on one occasion Kendall tried to rape her, but that she was able to stop him. Finally, she testified, "I had to throw him out of the organization. That was way before the unfortunate tragedy in January."

Matthew had to play his cross-examination of Atchinson well. He could not be as accusatory and cut throat as he wanted to be. It was clear that the jury liked this witness. To attack her would backfire in his face. Matthew only conducted a short cross examination. It was not helpful to the government's case. He could not rattle Susan Atchinson as hard as he tried; even though his attempts were gentle. She politely responded to all his questions. Her responses were frequently laced with the phrases, "the Lord", or "Jesus". Atchinson insisted she would never break the law. She testified that she would never condone murder. "I love all life, Mr. Schipani", she told Matthew.

The morning of the closing argument Matthew met with Wallace before going to court. He expected to have his head handed to him. He told Cartwright that he anticipated the jury would acquit. Cartwright was not upset with Matthew. He said, "we deal with what we have. The facts make the case. The facts didn't work here. Lawyers don't win cases, facts do." Matthew was relieved. As he walked into court he thought about what he might have done differently in this case. He could not think of anything. Maybe Wallace was right, thought Matthew. The facts make the case.

Matthew's closing was brief. He highlighted to the jury the evidence that they had heard about the defendant, her control and the mission of her group. He did not address the relationship that was alleged. He tried again to portray Susan Atchinson as a controlling leader who commanded Carter Kendall to kill Kari McDuffee. He spoke about the tragedy of cutting short this young woman's life. When Matthew sat down he realized that much of his closing argument sounded like his opening statement. He wondered if this was a mistake. But he really didn't have much else to work with. Carter Kendall was not the star witness he thought he would be. Steven O'Connor had taken care of that.

Kathleen McEwan's closing was much stronger. She played up the political card in the case. She asserted that this trial was all about re-electing and Attorney General and that the prosecution of the defendant was the "ticket to get the pro-choice vote". Matthew listened closely. He was impressed by Kathleen McEwan. "I wish I was in her shoes", he thought.

Judge Sinclair excused the jury for the afternoon to begin their deliberations. When the jury left Matthew walked over and invited Kathleen McEwan to lunch. They went to the deli around the corner from the courthouse and enjoyed a nice lunch. They discussed the case for awhile, but then changed the subject to Christmas shopping. Matthew enjoyed the fact that he could battle with attorneys inside the courtroom and still be able to enjoy them socially on the outside. They returned to the courtroom only to find out that the jury would not have an answer today.

The call came at eleven o'clock the next morning. The jury had reached a verdict. Matthew knew that this was not a good sign. The jury had not deliberated that long. He left his office and walked across the street to the courthouse. While sitting at the counsel table waiting for the entrance of the jury he turned and looked into the galley of the courtroom. The galley was filled with what appeared to be supporters of the defendant. The judge entered the courtroom followed by the jury.

"Madam foreperson, have you reached a verdict?', inquired Judge Sinclair. "Yes we have.", responded the young blond woman as she stood in the jury box. "Please hand the verdict to the court officer", instructed Judge Sinclair. The officer took the slip to the judge who read it and handed it back. He brought it back to the foreperson. "Will the defendant please rise?", asked Judge Sinclair. Susan Atchinson and her attorney stood at the counsel table. Judge Sinclair then said, "on the sole count of the violation of civil rights, how does the jury find?" The foreperson responded, "not guilty." There was some minor applause in the galley. Judge Sinclair peered over the bench with a disapproving look. The judge continued, "on the sole count of conspiracy to murder, how does the jury find?" The foreperson affirmatively responded, "not guilty".

The courtroom erupted into applause. The judge yelled "order" and the applause abated. Judge Sinclair looked at the jury and said, "ladies and gentlemen of the jury you are hereby discharged with the thanks of the court." She then looked at the defendant and said, "Ms. Atchinson, the jury has reached its verdict. This case is dismissed. You are free to go." The applause began again, but it was brief in duration. The judge and jury exited the courtroom. The trial was over. Matthew and Peter walked over to Kathleen McEwan and shook her hand. The day was done.

Their first Christmas in the new home was a festive occasion. Scott, Adam and Matthew took advantage of the vacant third floor apartment and turned it into a dance hall. They had a large Christmas party with many friends. The music pumped and the alcohol flowed. Adam was trying to matchmake any single man or woman he could at the party. "Nobody should be alone on Christmas", he told Matthew. His efforts were successful for at least two couples.

Matthew spent the traditional Christmas holiday in the Berkshires with his family. There was a new addition at the dinner table. His sister Maria's fiancee, Alfonso was soon to become a part of the family. Matthew highly approved of Alfonso. He was a kind and gregarious man. "Maybe he can bring Maria out of her shell", he told his mother.

The winter passed quickly and Matthew was happy about that. Even though it was a mild winter by New England standards, Matthew still toyed in his mind about moving south. He did this every winter. "It should only snow on Christmas eve", he would tell anyone who would listen. "Then it should all melt away." Matthew hated the cold and the snow. He tried cross country skiing one winter to make it more palatable. It didn't work.

Adam had begun to work at a small law firm in Salem. Matthew wasn't sure if Adam was happy with his new job, but it was helping to pay the bills. Their new house was starting to take shape as the spring approached. They decided to rent the third floor apartment even though the renovations were not to the level that Scott had wanted them to be. The extra income allowed them to make changes in their own apartments sooner than expected.

Work continued to go well for Matthew. Wallace Cartwright kept true to his word. He never criticized Matthew for the Atchinson case. In fact, Wallace put Matthew on another heavy duty case. It was a organized crime case involving racketeering. The case was being tried in Worcester county and each morning as Matthew would drive on the Pike he hoped that he would be successful. Otherwise he was sure that his career as an Assistant Attorney General would be short lived.

CHAPTER 7

FOLLIES WITH PHILLIP

April 1987

It was a bright Spring day and Matthew had resolved that he was going to walk the Common at lunch. His secretary, Amy buzzed the line. "Phillip Styles is on hold", she said. Matthew replied, "I'll take it". "Hi Phillip, how are you?", asked Matthew. "Good…very good", responded Phillip. He continued on, "I have great news for you Matthew. Ruth has been nominated to the superior court by the Governor!" Matthew replied, "that's fantastic! How does it look?"

Phillip happily stated, "it looks real good. She knows two people on the confirmation council and they really like her. She should know by the end of the month." "Fantastic!", Matthew said once again. "Please give her my congratulations." Phillip responded, "I will. But I also called to find out what you and Adam are doing Memorial Day weekend. Do you have any plans?" Matthew thought briefly and then said, "none that I know of. Why what's up?" Phillip then invited Matthew and Adam to Provincetown for the weekend. A friend of Phillip's had a home there and offered it Phillip anytime he wanted to use it. "Let me talk to Adam tonight and I'll let you know tomorrow", Matthew told his friend.

Matthew hung up the phone and reached for his jacket. He was going on his walk. But then Percy Jacobs, another assistant in the office walked into Matthew's office and sat down. "I was just heading out the door. What's up?", said Matthew. Percy said in reply, "the giant is going to be calling you any minute." Matthew looked perplexed. "Why? What did I do now?", he asked Percy. Percy chuckled and said, "oh please. Ever since you won that racketeering case you've become the golden boy in Wally's eyes." Matthew blushed and said, "so go ahead. Why's he calling me?" Percy then explained. "It seems like the gentle giant wants you to head an investigation of your old stomping grounds. DCP supposedly has been taking federal funds allotted to them and mismanaging the funds. The funds mysteriously vanish from the programs they are designed for and wind up in the payroll account. Wallace thinks that there's problems at the top. Commissioner Blodgett is bullshit. She thinks she can handle it herself. She's not happy about us looking over her shoulder and..." Percy was interrupted by telephone. It was Amy. The Attorney General was on hold.

"Hello Wallace. How are you", said Matthew to his boss. Percy began to get up and leave but Matthew motioned him to sit down. The Attorney General told Matthew that there were "problems over at your old place". He told Matthew that he wanted to take control of the situation and issue a press statement. "I want to be the spokesperson here. I think somebody may leak it from the inside. I want to talk to the newshounds first. Then the damage can be controlled.", said Wallace Cartwright. Matthew smiled when Wallace called the press, "newshounds". He hadn't heard that word in years and yet it fit Wallace. "You know the place better than anyone else in the office. So I want you to check it out. I presume you'll accept the assignment.", said the Attorney General to Matthew.

Matthew of course accepted the assignment. How could he turn Wallace Cartwright down. He had become his work surrogate father to Matthew. Before their conversation ended Matthew asked if he could have someone assist him. Wallace told him to "take whatever man power you need". So Matthew told him that he would have Percy Jacobs personally assist him. "That's fine with me", said the Attorney General.

As Matthew suggested Percy to assist him he looked over at Jacobs. He was mouthing the words "fuck you" to Matthew and smiling at the same time. When Matthew completed his conversation he reached over his desk and extended his hand to Percy, saying "welcome aboard partner!" Percy just grimaced.

The investigation of DCP was over almost before it began. Once the Commissioner was aware that the Attorney General's office was ready to fully tear apart the agency, she folded. Commissioner Blodgett cooperated with Matthew and handed over all the information he had requested. Matthew completed his investigation with the recommendation that Wallace charge the Commissioner and the director of operations at DCP. He also recommended that they be fired immediately from their posts. In the art of political compromise, Wallace Cartwright struck a deal where the funds would be restored and the Commissioner and her top managers would resign. No criminal charges would issue. The agreement would be kept somewhat under wraps. The image of the agency would not be forever tarnished in the news.

The week before their trip to Provincetown, Matthew and Adam stood beside a beaming Phillip Styles and Octavia Moon. They were in attendance at the swearing in of Ruth Rogers as a superior court judge for the state of Massachusetts. Matthew was also very proud. Ruth was an honest and good woman. She was nominated to the judgeship on the basis of her skill and knowledge of the law. She had no political connection. She received the job on merit. Ruth's appointment showed that politics did not always make the judge.

The following weekend in Provincetown was fun as usual for Matthew. They spent the day shopping and eating more than they should. The three of them were standing on the outside deck of a gay bar during tea dance when Phillip asked Matthew a very important question. Matthew was looking out on the ocean when Phillip said, "Matthew were down a partner now. Octavia and I have talked about it. We don't want to promote any of the associates. I don't think any of them are ready yet. So honey,…how about leaving the government payroll and coming to work for us and make some real money?" Matthew was taken back by the offer. He hadn't expected it. He was also very flattered. To him, Phillip and Octavia were consummate lawyers. To have them ask him to become a partner in their firm was a high compliment. Matthew told Phillip that he would "seriously give it some thought" and let Phillip know next week.

They changed the tone to a lighter subject. Matthew and Adam were admiring the muscular shirtless men in their shorts walking around the deck of the bar. Phillip said, "oh, to be young again!" They laughed. Phillip then turned to Adam. "I have to tell you this story. I know Matthew's already heard it, but too bad!", an excited Phillip began. "A couple of weeks ago", he continued, "I went shopping for a gift for Ruth. I bought her a judge's robe. It was beautiful. Good material, no cheap stuff. But anyway, so before I wrapped the robe I decided I needed to see how it fit. Now it didn't look as good as my pink taffeta, but I didn't look too bad! So, I'm home in the apartment with Ruth's robe on. I started to prance around in the house. I kept yelling "guilty! guilty! guilty!". Thank God nobody was home!" Adam broke out in laughter. Matthew laughed as well. The story was just as good the second time around. The vision of Phillip running around the house with the robe of justice on was hysterical to Matthew. "He probably had nothing on underneath", thought Adam to himself, as he smiled.

On the ride home to Cambridge at the end of the weekend, Matthew and Adam began discussing Phillip's offer. It certainly was lucrative and Matthew thought it might be time to make a move. He wanted to broaden his legal background. A general practice would help him to do that. But Matthew was also reticent. "I need to talk to

Wallace before I do anything", he told Adam. Adam agreed with Matthew. Wallace Cartwright had been good to Matthew and he should give him the courtesy of letting him know before he made any move.

A few days later Matthew approached Wallace Cartwright about the offer. His conversation with the Attorney General was just as he expected. Wallace was very supportive to him. He said although he didn't want to lose Matthew, "I think you being an assistant AG for the rest of your life would be much below my expectations for you. I think you can achieve much more.", said Wallace. Matthew thanked the Attorney General. Wallace Cartwright responded with a big bear hug of Matthew before he left the office. "Don't worry. You'll be back somehow.", said Wallace as he walked out the door.

Matthew sat down for a moment in his office. He wiped away a small tear in his eyes. Wallace Cartwright was not only a good boss, he was a good friend. Matthew knew that he would miss the day to day contact with him.

Matthew called Phillip to tell him that he accepted the offer. Phillip was elated. But Matthew still had a mixture of emotions in his soul. It would be difficult leaving his job and Wallace Cartwright. But he knew that this was a good opportunity for him. Octavia got on the phone and expressed her joy about Matthew joining the firm. She was able to lighten him up a little and Matthew was also able to joke with Octavia. "Remember. I need two buff male secretaries!", he said to her. She responded, "not until I get them first!" The firm of "Moon, Schipani and Styles" became an entity on the bright, sunny early July day.

September. For some reason this month always provided Matthew with daunting challenges. It was a month he dreaded. It also seemed out of place for him to loath the onset of September. The month began his favorite season of the year. But as September progressed, Matthew waited for the shoe to drop and doom to set in. And the shoe did drop once again this September, as it had done so many times in the past.

His mother Rosa called Matthew one September afternoon. She was calling to deliver the news that her brother and his uncle, Francesco was moving back to Massachusetts from California. He had purchased a home in the bedroom community of Agawam. Rosa was elated. But Matthew was not. Inside his stomach was churning. He gave his mother a non-emotional response to the news. The events of ten years ago seemed like another life; lived by another person. So far behind him and now back again. The old memories were moved to the center stage of his mind again. Matthew told his mother that he decided to come to the Berkshires for the weekend. "We need to talk", he said. She replied, "Okay. I'll see you Saturday. I'll have dinner ready." Matthew hadn't told Adam what happened in California. In fact, he hadn't told anyone, except Scott. That took him a long time to do when he did it. Now he felt as if he needed to expose his 'secret', especially to Adam. The night before he was leaving to go to his parent's home, Matthew was in Scott's apartment reliving his life in California. He was sharing with Scott his new fears, which came from his old fears, about having his uncle living so close. Scott told him that time changed people. Maybe he was overreacting. Scott also didn't understand why Matthew felt the need to tell his mother. "Why do you have to tell her when she really doesn't need to know that crap?", he asked Matthew. Adam walked into the apartment as Scott finished his question. The question went unanswered.

Adam quickly took control of the conversation, taking advantage of the silence as he walked in. He complained about the "horrible week" he was having at work. "I don't know if I'm cut out to be a lawyer", Adam told Matthew and Scott. Then he announced that his best friend, Joseph Stevens was coming to spend the weekend. "We are going out and partying!", Adam exclaimed. Seeing no response from either Matthew or Scott, he asked, "what's the matter? Did I do something wrong?" Matthew paused momentarily and said, "no, honey, you didn't do anything wrong. I'm going to my parents for the weekend. My uncle Francesco is moving back to Massachusetts in a few weeks and I need to clean up some things from the past." Adam looked at Scott and said, "that's the mafia dude, right?" Scott shook his head affirmatively. Adam asked Matthew, "do you want me to cancel with Joseph and come with you?" Matthew replied, "no, I'll be fine. You two enjoy the weekend. You deserve it." Adam again inquired, "are you sure? I can just do it another weekend." Matthew said, "no…it's all right. Just dealing with the past sometimes can be real shitty. Anyway, I'm tired. You two hang out. I'm going upstairs to bed."

Matthew got up from the table. He leaned over and kissed his best friend and his boyfriend good night. He walked up the stairs to his apartment. Matthew wasn't out the door a minute when Adam asked Scott, "what's happening with this uncle Francesco shit?" Scott replied, "it's really not my place to tell you. Talk about it to him when he comes back."

The next day as Matthew got off the Mass Pike at the Lee exit, he thought, "I could do this damn trip in my sleep!" He had been back and forth on the turnpike more times than he could count since he moved east to go to law school. He drive down the narrow street to his parent's home. He looked at the leaves on the trees. They were just starting to turn. Another few weeks and the brilliant fall colors would appear on the trees throughout the Berkshires. It would be peak season for the 'leaf peepers', as the locals called the tourists who came to the Berkshires to appreciate nature's majesty. Some people would come from as far as Florida to see the leaves turn. Matthew loved the fall in New England, especially in the Berkshires. He loved the colors on the trees appearing over time. He recalled the many pictures he had taken of the trees over the years.

As he pulled in the driveway and turned off the car, he sat and gazed out at the trees to the side of his parent's house. They were in different stages of turning color. Matthew's favorite colors were leaves of red and gold. He remembered as a child playing in the woods near his house and hunting for the most brilliant leaves. He remembered his elementary school project where he took some leaves of red and gold and glued them on construction paper. He was so proud of that project. He couldn't have been more than seven years old. He smiled at his remembrance. It was a simpler time; a happy time. He had been blessed with a wonderful childhood. While walking up the driveway Matthew thought that if he asked his mother if she could find that elementary school project, he was sure she could. Rosa never liked to throw things out. Matthew was sure that if they looked hard enough in the attic he would find his project stored among his brother and sister's projects. "Maybe I'll look this weekend", he thought.

The morning came after Matthew spent a restless night in his old bedroom. Matthew and his mother decided to go for a walk through the woods behind the house. Matthew spent many playful hours in these woods as a child, and as an adult he enjoyed walking through them. Matthew and Rosa talked a great deal about many different things. His relationship with Adam, his new job, money, and all the other things that a parent and child share. Matthew and his mother walked slowly through the woods. Matthew picked up various leaves off the ground that had fallen. He was looking for red and gold ones. He found a few which made him happy. But it was too early in the season to find a treasure. The leaves needed a few more weeks. "Mom", Matthew said quietly admist the woods. "I wanted to tell you why I left California so quickly all those years ago." Rosa stopped walking and Matthew stopped with her. Her mother's intuition came into play and she spoke before her son could say another word. "Honey, that happened a long time ago. You don't have to tell me anything if you don't want to.", said Rosa in a concerned tone to her son. Matthew replied, "but I want to." Rosa said, "okay…if you want to." They began to resume their walking.

"You know that after I graduated USC money was really tight.", Matthew said to his mother. She shook her head "yes". He continued, "well, Uncle Francesco helped me out. But the way he helped was wrong. He was involved in smuggling goods over the border to the United States. He asked me to make pick ups and deliveries, so I did. He paid me really good money." Matthew paused and looked at his mother. Matthew did not detect any look of surprise on her face, so he went on. "I did it because I needed the money. I knew then, and I certainly know now, it was wrong. The other thing that Uncle Francesco would do is he would get me guys to have sex with. It was a reward when I did a good job." Matthew was clearly ashamed about his last statements. His voice trailed off as he spoke them. His mother could see the shame in her son's face. Rosa put her hand to her son's cheek and stroked it. "You were young honey. We all do things when we were young that we would never do now.", she told her son. Matthew replied, "I know…but the sad thing is, a part of me was enjoying it…well, at least until that night I called you and asked you to fly me home."

They sat on a log under a big birch tree. Matthew continued on with his story. "That night…the reason I was so upset was that one of Uncle Francesco's friends, Patrick, had given me a job to do and I really screwed it up. Patrick came over to the house. He was ranting and raving about me to Uncle Francesco. I still remember it as clear as if it happened yesterday. He called me a 'goldilock faggot'. Then he came into the den where I was sitting. He grabbed me and threw me against the wall. He just picked me up like a sack of potatoes and tossed me. My whole body slammed against the wall. My head hit it too. I fell to the floor. Patrick kicked me a couple of times. He told me to 'get up cocksucker'. I struggled to my feet. I looked and there was Uncle Francesco standing behind Patrick smiling. I went to ask him for help when Patrick punched me in the mouth. My mouth was bleeding real bad. I tried to fight back…but Patrick was huge…he beat the shit out of me. Uncle Francesco just stood there and let it happen. "Rosa reached over and held her son's hand with a reassuring grip. Matthew stopped talking. He was crying. The pain of ten years ago was as deep now as it had been then. Matthew rolled his head into his mother's should and cried.

After a few moments, Matthew leaned away from his mother. He wiped his tears from his eyes. "I never told anyone else about it until a couple of years ago. I told Scott…but I didn't want anyone else to know." Rosa said, "that's all right honey…it goes no further…it's over…that was the past. You're an adult now, no one can ever hurt you again." She kissed her son and held him once again. "Please don't tell Dad.", Matthew asked his mother. She assured him she wouldn't. They stood silently for a moment and then turned and began to walk back toward the house. The conversation that Matthew had delayed for ten years ended there in the woods. It was never brought up again.

Before leaving Sunday morning to return to Cambridge, Matthew and his parents joined his brother Anthony for breakfast. Anthony had recently won a special election and was a selectman in Stockbridge. He had reservations for the best table at the Running Brook Inn, one of Stockbridge's famous bed and breakfast establishments. They had an enjoyable and hearty breakfast. Matthew kissed them all good-bye and began his ride home on the Mass Pike. The ride he could do in his sleep.

Uncle Francesco never returned to Massachusetts. A few weeks after their discussion in the woods Matthew received a telephone call from his mother. She wanted to relay the information that the house sale in Agawam had "fallen through" and Uncle Francesco decided to stay in California. Matthew didn't inquire any further, but he was sure that his mother was instrumental in her brother's decision not to move back to the east coast.

Just before the Christmas 'recess', as Phillip liked to call it, the firm received a new client. Arthur Martin, a twenty seven year old gay man would become one of the firm's most important clients. Phillip had briefed Octavia and Matthew before Martin arrived for a meeting at the office about the case. He had decided that the case was so important that they all needed to work on it together. Little did Matthew know, this would be the last case he ever worked on with Phillip. Just this past summer Phillip had been diagnosed with HIV. He had told Octavia about it right after finding out. But he decided to keep it from Matthew. He wanted to wait "until the time is right", he told Octavia.

Arthur Martin walked into the conference room of the office. He greeted Phillip who then introduced Octavia and Matthew as his partners. "Kinda cute!", thought Matthew as he shook Arthur Martin's hand. This client and the case that was at their door was about an incident of 'gay bashing'. It was a direct test of the new "Hate Crimes" statute that had only been passed five short months ago in Massachusetts. Arthur Martin wanted to sue the City of Boston and its police department. He wanted to sue for what he saw as their participation in, and indifference to, an event of gay bashing that occurred just last month.

For the benefit of Octavia and Matthew, Martin detailed what happened last month. Martin had left a gay bar called the 'Pink Triangle' at closing hour. He decided to go for a walk in the park that abutted the bar, in the Fenway section of Boston. Martin was clear that the purpose of his walk was to find a man to have sex with. The park was notorious as a gay 'cruising' area. Martin walked through the park and eventually he found not just one man, but two, whom he believed to be friends. While Martin began detailing the events, Matthew was furiously writing notes. Martin went on with his account of that evening. "I was blowing the two of them. They were really into it and all. I was on my knees...I was having a great time! Then smack! I felt this bang to my temple. The tall one...his name is here", said Martin pointing to a document and pushing it to Octavia. "The tall one, ", he continued, "...he took out a gun and hit me in the head with the handle. I fell over. The Puerto Rican one then started to kick me all over...my head, my chest, my legs...His name is George Santiago. Then the tall one started to kick me too. They were calling me names, like 'cocksucker' and 'queer' and you know…The Puerto Rican kicked me the most. I crawled up in a ball and tried to make it stop, but they kept on kicking!"

Matthew put his pen down for a moment. Arthur Martin was becoming emotional. Matthew slid the box of tissue toward Martin. "Thank you", said Martin wiping his eyes and blowing his nose. He then continued on, "So where was I? Oh yeah, they kept on kicking. I think they were getting loud, because I heard a voice yell 'police'. They must have attracted attention. I really didn't see anything. It was dark and I was balled up with my hands around my head. They stopped kicking me for a few seconds. I heard one of them, I think it was the tall one, say 'he offered us money to suck our dicks'. Then I heard the same deep voice that yelled 'police', say "goddamn queers! Why don't they all move to San Francisco!" Martin took a dramatic pause and then continued on. "Then the kicking started again! I couldn't believe it!", said an astonished Martin. "It didn't last very long, but it really hurt. And I swear…I swear on a stack of Bibles, that when I opened my eyes for a second to take a look, one of the guys kicking me was in a uniform! It finally stopped when I heard another voice that I hadn't heard before, say "I think he's had enough". The next thing I remember was being at the police station and asking for some ice and a towel. My lip was all swollen and my mouth was bleeding. My head was killing me. They took their fuckin' time before they got the ice for me. Then I was charged with solicitation." He took a deep breath. Arthur Martin was exhausted from his replay of the events to the attorneys.

Matthew continued to write and Phillip asked Arthur Martin a question. "Do you have the name of the police officers that you dealt with that night?", he inquired. "Oh yes!", proudly responded Arthur Martin, as he grabbed another piece of paper out of the manila folder he had brought with him. "It's right here", he said to Phillip. Phillip took the paper, glanced at it for a minute and then handed it to Octavia. She put on her reading glasses, looked at it briefly and then passed it to Matthew. Phillip continued to ask questions as Matthew looked at the document. "Thank God", he said to himself. The police officers names on the sheet were not names he recognized from his tenure at the Attorney General's office. The paper named Officer Robert O'Leary and Sergeant Thomas Chaffey as the responding officers on the fateful evening.

By the time the two and a half hour interview was over Matthew's hand was ready to fall off from all the writing he had done. Arthur thanked them all profusely for listening to him and for taking the case. Phillip escorted them out of the conference room. He returned shortly thereafter. The three of them sat around the conference table. Octavia was the first to speak. "If all this checks out we have one major lawsuit here!", she said. Phillip agreed, "that's why I want us all to work on it together. I think you Octavia should be the lead counsel in the case. Let's have a woman as the spokesperson on this case rather than another gay man. It will show that women care about gay rights as much as gay people do.", he concluded. Matthew agreed. They decided that they would also have their seasoned paralegal, June, be part of the team.

Phillip looked over at Matthew and said, "see what favors you can call in over at Boston PD. Let's find out about this O'Leary and Chaffey." Matthew shook his head in agreement. "This is going to be an explosive case!", Matthew thought. The meeting ended with the three of them gathering their papers and heading toward their offices to begin their tasks on the Martin case.

The cold winter wind was blowing in Matthew's face a few weeks later as he walked down the slushy sidewalk in front of the Superior Court. He had to meet Phillip and Octavia at nine thirty. They were scheduled to be in Judge Jackson's courtroom for the Martin case. Phillip's 'Christmas present' to the City of Boston was Martin's civil complaint against the city, the mayor, the police department and the two individual police officers in this case. The complaint alleged a violation of the new "Hate Crimes" law. The city responded immediately with a Motion to Dismiss. The city asserted that Martin had filed a complaint which failed to state a claim upon which relief could be granted. It was a standard motion. Octavia was scheduled to argue the opposition to the motion. Matthew and Phillip were to be present in court as part of the team that Phillip had established for the case.

Motion session in Judge Jackson's courtroom historically moved swiftly. The judge believed that either the party bringing the motion had the law on their side or they didn't. There weren't any shades of gray to Judge Jackson. It was cut and dry. No artful argument was necessary. Just state the law and the judge would make his decision. In the Martin case, Judge Jackson told City Solicitor Roberto Lopez that he didn't have the law on his side. The motion was denied. The Martin case would proceed on. The judge ordered discovery to be completed in a timely fashion and scheduled a pre-trial conference in sixty days.

When they returned to the office Phillip was on a roll. "This is a battle!", he announced. Phillip had a specific outline and schedule for the case. He assigned tasks in conformity with that schedule. He announced that the schedule must be adhered to without exception. The Martin case was the predominate case in the firm. Matthew knew that Phillip knew how to prepare a winning case. He believed that with Phillip's leadership the Martin case would be a winner and affirm the new statute.

A month into the case, with the discovery deadline rapidly approaching, Matthew decided that he needed a vacation. He was overwhelmed with the Martin case. It was very complicated and the time involved was immeasurable. He also had other cases that he needed to attend to. It had been quite a while since he had been on vacation. Between work and his normal case of the winter blues, Matthew was becoming very depressed. He called his friend Ted at the travel agency. He and Adam would take a brief trip to Florida. "The sun will do me good", thought Matthew.

As March roared in like a lion, Matthew and Adam flew out of the northeast and headed south. They spent a week going between Fort Lauderdale and Orlando. They did some sightseeing, but primarily spent time relaxing on the beach. Adam talked about looked for teaching jobs at various law schools in the Boston area. The day to day functions of a trial lawyer were not enjoyable to him. Matthew encouraged him in his plans. The warm Florida sun and the Atlantic Ocean was refreshing to both of them. It gave Matthew the much needed stamina required to return to New England for the last few weeks of winter. Although brief in its duration, Matthew and Adam decided that their trip was one of the most relaxing ones they had ever taken.

A week after returning home Matthew woke in the middle of the night to the telephone ringing. Adam was asleep in the bedroom. Matthew had fallen asleep in front of the television, laying on the sofa. He jumped up when he heard the ring. He was half awake and somewhat disoriented. As he struggled to get the phone, he banged his knee into the coffee table. "Jesus Christ!", he exclaimed as he went down on one knee and reached to grab the phone with his left hand.

"Hello", Matthew mumbled into the phone. It was Octavia on the other end. "I'm real sorry to call you at this hour", she said. "It's okay…what's up?", said Matthew. Octavia spoke in a very soft tone. "It's Phillip. He's in the hospital. He's really sick…they brought him in about two hours ago. Darryl called me to let me know. I thought you should know too…" Matthew interrupted, "what's wrong?" Octavia struggled a moment to speak. Then continuing in her soft tone, she said, "I'm not really sure. I think its the flu or pneumonia. He's at County General. I called them…they said we could come at six. I wanted to know if you wanted to go with me". Matthew instantly responded, "of course I want to go. Do you want me to drive?", he asked. Octavia said that she would drive. They arranged to meet outside Matthew's house at five thirty. "I'll stop and get coffee", she said to him and then hung up the phone.

Matthew turned on the light and went over to the sofa. He sat down and looked at the television. An old black and white movie that he was sure he had seen was playing, but he could not recall the title. He lit a cigarette and watched the movie for a few minutes. Finally, he figured out the title of the movie. It was *Witness for the Prosecution*. "Damn lawyer movies!", he said out loud. Suddenly Diana came out of the bedroom and walked across the floor to him. He must have woken her. "Come here baby", he said to his dog. He patted the couch and she jumped up on it. She twirled around on the couch a few times and then laid down with her head on his lap. Matthew sat smoking with one hand and petting his dog with the other. He watched the movie for awhile longer.

Matthew had a feeling that there was something really wrong with Phillip. He didn't know why he felt that way, but he was sure that there was something wrong. He thought for a minute about AIDS, but then he disregarded it. He decided he was becoming AIDS phobic. Everytime he got sick, Matthew was convinced he had AIDS. He didn't, but the fear was always there.

Morning came rapidly and he found himself riding in the car with Octavia, drinking his coffee and not saying much. When they pulled into the parking spot, Matthew unbuckled his seat belt and turned to Octavia who was turning off the ignition. "Before we go in", he said. "I have to ask you this. Does Phillip have AIDS?" Octavia looked out the windshield for a moment without responding. Then she turned to Matthew. "I'm afraid so. He wanted to tell you himself...he wanted to wait for the right time...I'm sorry.", she said. Matthew shook his head and did not say a word. "When we go in there, let him tell you. Don't let him know that I told you...okay?", said Octavia. Matthew sadly responded, "I'll wait for him to tell me".

Octavia went into Phillip's room first. After about ten minutes she came out, grabbed Matthew by his arm and said, "go ahead". Matthew walked into the room. There was Phillip lying on the hospital gurney with its stark white sheets and blankets over him. Phillip was sweating. He had an oxygen mask covering his face. There were a few machines to the side of the gurney. The male attending nurse handed Matthew a green mask for his face. Matthew looked at him quizzically. "Put it on", said the nurse. Matthew held the mask for a moment and then put it on the chair. He refused to wear it. Matthew walked over to the bed and held Phillip's hand. "Hi sweetie", he said in a soft voice to Phillip. Phillip motioned with his other hand to a small table on the opposite side of the gurney. Matthew walked over to it. There was a pen and pad on the table. Matthew grabbed it, saying "do you want this?" Phillip shook his head affirmatively. Matthew handed the pad and pen to Phillip. Phillip began to write slowly on the pad. As he wrote Matthew pulled up a chair next to the gurney. Matthew grabbed Phillip's other hand and held it while Phillip wrote. Phillip put the pen down on the blanket and handed the pad to Matthew. In scrawled writing, Phillip had written, "I can't talk with this damn mask! I'm really tired. They tell me I have pneumocystis." Matthew took the pad and pen and put it on the floor. He looked at Phillip and tried to hold back the tears. He did, but it was difficult. Matthew said, "just relax honey…relax. Get your rest."

Matthew sat with Phillip for about five minutes until the nurse came in and told him he had to leave. Octavia followed behind the nurse. "We should get going", she said. Matthew rubbed Phillip's hand, stood up and said, "We'll be back later. Get some rest…I'll see you in a little bit. I love you…" Matthew turned away from Phillip. Octavia blew a kiss to Phillip. He waved back at her. Matthew and Octavia walked out of the hospital room silently and hand in hand.

The day was not a productive one for either of them at the office. Matthew and Octavia both had their calls held, with the exception of emergencies. The paralegals attended to routine calls. Matthew told June, the senior paralegal that if anyone wanted to talk to Phillip to tell them, "he's out on medical leave. Nothing more!" Matthew and Octavia decided they would deal with any pressing issues on Phillip's cases later.

Matthew called Adam to tell him about Phillip. As he relayed the news, Matthew broke down on the telephone. Adam did the same. "I don't know what to do", Matthew told Adam. Adam said, "you do what you can. That's all Phillip wants. You need to call Scott and Janice. They really should know so they can go see him." Matthew agreed. They decided that they would meet after dinner and go to the hospital together to see Phillip. Matthew then made the calls to Scott and Janice. He cried through both of them. It was difficult news to relay. He could hear his friends hurt in their voices when they heard the news. Matthew hated to be the bearer of such bad news. He had always left that job to his mother. But she couldn't help here. He had to do it himself.

The next month was an emotional rollercoaster for Matthew. He would be happy one moment and lashing out the next. Phillip had made it through the pneumonia, but he was very weak. He had to stay at home and in bed for some time. Matthew spent many evenings at Phillip's house. He would help him to eat, wash up and clean around the house for Phillip. Matthew would also read to Phillip as he was laying in bed. Matthew found the time he spent reading to Phillip to be the most enjoyable. It was as if the only thing that existed at that time was the story he was reading. Everything else, including Phillip's medical condition, was excluded. Only the story counted. Matthew was reading classic books to Phillip that he had only heard about. He wondered if Phillip was enjoying this time as much as he was.

The Martin case was progressing, but now Octavia was at the helm. Rose Barrows, an associate in the firm was now a member of the team. She was a bright, young woman who was filling in for Phillip. She understood that this case had been "Phillip's baby", and she respected that. She showed her respect by her diligence on the case. When the pre-trial conference date came for the Martin case, Matthew decided he would beg off and let Octavia handle it by herself. He needed to attend to some of his other cases that had taken a backseat between the Martin case and Phillip's illness. Matthew was becoming increasingly depressed about Phillip. Adam was supportive to him, but understood that Matthew had to deal with this himself. It was the first time Matthew ever had someone so close become sick with the AIDS virus. It was emotionally and physically draining on him.

The pre-trial conference on Martin went off without a hitch. Octavia handled it with her usual finesse and class. The case would progress to trial. An October trial date was scheduled. Matthew knew that he couldn't beg off at that point. He needed to be an integral part of the trial.

Matthew was also keeping to himself a lot at home since Phillip had gotten ill. He rarely did anything social. He felt guilty about keeping separate from Adam and Scott, but they never complained. They knew he needed his space. Matthew also knew he needed his space to work through this issue. He would seek space by going on walks by himself, or going to the library at Harvard just to be alone. But many times he felt incredibly alone. Alone emotionally, not physically. He needed the physical solitude, but the emotional loneliness was difficult. He knew he had to deal with and accept Phillip's illness. He had to do it alone. He couldn't have someone else carry the burden for him. He had to find the strength on his own to deal with his friend's condition.

In late July, Phillip returned to the office with the purpose of planning for his retirement. He had made the decision that he could not return to work. He was closing down his portion of the business. He decided to take the next few weeks to put things in order. He would come into work for half days and try to accomplish as much as he could. When he didn't meet his goals for that day, Phillip would become very frustrated and angry. Both Octavia and Matthew told Phillip to take his time, he didn't need to rush. Phillip curtly responded, "I don't know how much time I have left. I have to get this done!"

Phillip made the decision to move in October to Florida. He was going to live with his sister Joanna. He believed that the warmer weather would be good for his health. "I won't be able to make it through another New England winter", he told Octavia and Matthew. The thought of Phillip moving away from Massachusetts made Matthew very sad. He felt that the distance would put an end to their relationship. A permanent end. Yet he knew that Phillip was right. The Florida weather would be good for him. "Maybe he'll be able to hang around long enough to beat this thing", Matthew told Adam.

Matthew found himself laden with doubts about whether he wanted to continue with the firm once Phillip retired. He thought it would be too emotionally upsetting for him to work in the office without Phillip there. He shared his feelings with Octavia. She understood. She always understood. Matthew's respect for Octavia had grown so much since they worked together. She was a brilliant lawyer. Matthew admired her skills in protecting and advancing her client's interests. Matthew's respect for her was only enhanced by the way she was dealing with Phillip's illness. He marveled at her eternal optimism. Octavia truly believed that the world was a wonderful place and the most people were good and kind. In the darkest hour, Octavia could find the light. Matthew knew that if he decided to leave the firm he would miss working with her a great deal. But he took solace in the fact that if he made the decision not to work together anymore, he knew he had found a friend for life.

Matthew started to come out of his depression. He was dealing with Phillip's illness. But the dreaded month of September was setting in. "Please let me make it through this month this time", Matthew thought. He did, and without incident. It was a break in the September doom cycle. "Maybe its not cursed after all", Matthew told Scott over a cup of coffee. Scott responded, "it is just an old folklore you have yourself believing in. See the month passed without the sky falling!" Matthew shook his head to agree, but the doubt remained in his mind.

However, there was one minor odd occurrence during the month of September that Matthew quickly remedied. For about a week he and Adam were getting obscene phone calls at home. They did not recognize the voice on the other end of the phone. It was a male, but the voice was obviously disguised. They deal with it by hanging up the phone or taking it off the hook. But the calls escalated to the point of becoming violent. The last call was the one that made Matthew change his phone number. The caller said, "Matthew...I'm looking forward to the day I get you alone, drag your ass down an alley and cut off your cock and shove it down your throat!". After Matthew slammed down the phone he called the police who advised he change his number to an unlisted one. Matthew promptly did so the next day.

The week before Phillip was moving the Martin case was scheduled for trial. The city had requested a continuance. Matthew and Octavia agreed to it. They did not want to have their last few days with Phillip cut short by the trial. The trial was set out for a new date at the beginning of the year.

On Saturday, Matthew, Octavia, Adam, Scott, Janice and a host of Phillip's friends rented a boat for a whale watch out of Gloucester. Phillip loved whale watches. He wanted to go on one more before he moved. It was a rainy, dreary gray fall day, but that did not dampen spirits aboard the tiny whaler. The whaler left the shore and entered the choppy seas off of Gloucester. Their four hour trip was filled with many whale sightings. Matthew marveled at the size of the whales. They were huge. They would come right up to the boat. Matthew was amazed at how trusting the whales were, given man's history of savagery towards them. They were so meek for such large creatures. Phillip was snapping away with his camera. He must have gone through three rolls of film. The day was an exceptional one. Only one person got sick on the boat, but quickly recovered. As the boat bounced back and forth in the rough waters, Matthew looked over at Phillip. "He looks good", thought Matthew. Phillip had regained some of the weight he so quickly and dramatically lost when he first got sick. Phillip's face had regained its color. He had rosy cheeks again.

On this day out in the choppy waters of the Atlantic Ocean watching a marvel of nature, Phillip was smiling and laughing. It had been a long time since Matthew had seen Phillip happy. But today, he was smiling. That bright, white smile. The twinkle had returned to Phillip's eyes. Matthew thought how wonderful it was to see him smile again. When the boat began turning and returning to shore, Matthew stared at his friend's smiling face. "This is how I want to remember you, Phillip", thought Matthew.

CHAPTER 8

GOOD-BYE DEAR FRIEND

April 1989

Matthew stared off into the puffy white clouds and the blue sky ahead. He was pressing the speed limit on the Mass Pike. He had done this trip so many times before, yet today he felt rushed. When he recently became the chief legal counsel for the Division of Child Protection, Matthew promised that he would be visible in the community. Hence, he was driving west to appear at a forum entitled "Reforming the Child Welfare Laws".

The forum was being held in Springfield. Matthew was one of the guest speakers at the forum. The audience he was to address included social workers from DCP and private agencies, as well as local law enforcement personnel. Matthew hoped that some local legislators would also be present to hear his call for stronger child protective laws and stronger punishments for child abusers. Matthew remained cognizant of the fact that he had to tone down some of his true feelings today. He did not want to offend Governor Stuart Alley, who was his ultimate boss. The Governor was sitting on the fence about whether he would give his endorsement to stiffer child welfare laws. Matthew pulled off the exit and through the toll booth. He would be on time. "Thank God!", he thought. Matthew parked his car in downtown Springfield and walked spiritedly to the building where the conference was being held. The city appeared dirty and deserted to him on this bright spring day. He wondered if Springfield had seen its better days. Such potential as a city, bordering the beautiful Conneticut River, thought Matthew. Yet, the "Massachusetts Miracle" seemed to have skipped right by the City of Springfield.

Matthew was met at the reception table by Janice Pierce. "Hi hon!", she said with a big hug and kiss. Janice was coordinating the conference. She grabbed Matthew by the arm and walked him down the hall to the main auditorium. "There's about six hundred people here", she said as they walked. "Wow! A great turnout!", Matthew responded. While they were walking Matthew chuckled inside. Here he was being escorted by his friend with whom he had made a meteoric rise in power and stature in the child welfare community since they first met several years ago. Janice was the director of the DCP office at Cape Cod, having recently transferred there. Matthew was in charge of the legal department for DCP. Here they were, two dear friends who not too long ago, would be spending their weekends alternating between responding to child abuse calls and partying at the local gay bar. Matthew had a big smile on his face as Janice opened the door into the auditorium.

Matthew walked in and the applause started. He looked around and saw many dear friends, old and new, that he had worked with over the years. While walking to the dais he looked over to his right and saw his friends from the Berkshire DCP office. They were on their feet applauding. Matthew had a warm feeling of gratitude inside. Matthew waved at the audience. He was red with embarrassment. He went onto the platform and shook hands with various people, some he knew and some he didn't. He sat next to his friend Frank Livingston.

The conference began with his old boss, who was now his boss again, Kevin Michaels making the opening remarks. Michaels had been appointed Commissioner of DCP by Governor Alley two years ago. He was a strong cheerleader for Matthew when Wallace Cartwright had floated the idea of Matthew returning to DCP as the chief legal counsel. Michaels made brief introductory remarks and then turned the microphone over to the Deputy Commissioner for Western Massachusetts, Frank Livingston.

Matthew was third in line to speak. He enjoyed the speakers that had preceded him. They were inspiring and opinionated on the issue of child welfare. Frank Livingston was the perfect master of ceremonies for the conference. He kept it moving in an orderly fashion. Matthew was half listening when Frank was detailing Matthew's accomplishments as a way of introduction. His mind had drifted to when he first met Frank. Frank was one of Matthew's first supervisors when he was a child protective investigator. Frank was one of the first openly gay men in the agency. He was also one of the most respected men at DCP. He was a true leader. Matthew had always said that Frank knew more about child protection than anyone else in Massachusetts. Kevin Michaels had made a smart choice when he elevated Frank to the Deputy Commissioner position. "And so, may I present to you our very own chief legal counsel, Matthew Schipani!", concluded an excited Frank. Matthew quickly regained his focus, stood up and headed to the podium.

About half way through his speech Janice Pierce slipped a note on the podium in front of Matthew. He looked down at it without missing a beat in his speech. The note said, "Judge Rogers just called. She said it's urgent!". Matthew acknowledged the note with a note to Janice and then continued with his remarks. As the time went on Matthew began to become anxious. He decided to cut trim down his speech. Matthew skipped a few pages in his speech and went into his closing. Matthew ended his impassioned speech with a call to all those in the room. "Let me enlist you in this fight!", he said with an animated and elevated voice. "A fight for justice for children! We need to let those on Beacon Hill hear our voices. The voices of those who care about and protect the children of this Commonwealth. Our voices for justice for abused children! Our voices to shake the legislature which continues to treat child abuse lighter than it treats animal abuse. Let me pose this question to you as a motivator to raise your voices. Why is it in Massachusetts that if you abuse your cocker spaniel, you may serve more time in prison than if you abuse your child? Isn't something wrong here? It just doesn't make sense! So, join us! Enlist now! Raise your voices and shout with your votes! It's time to protect the children of Massachusetts! Thank you very much." With that powerful conclusion, the room erupted into applause. A loud ovation greeted Matthew as he stepped down from the platform and headed toward the exit.

"Judge Rogers' chambers please", Matthew uttered into the phone. "Judge's lobby. Linda Galvin speaking", answered the other end. "Linda, this is Matthew Schipani. Ruth just called me. She said it was urgent", Matthew sternly said. "Yes, Attorney Schipani. Please hold on. She wants me to get her off the bench for your call.", said Linda Galvin.

Matthew held on the phone for just a few moments when he heard what he thought was his friend's voice. "Matthew", said a shallow and low voice. "Ruth, is that you?", asked Matthew. "Yes, it's me…Joanna Styles just called me about an hour ago. Phillip took a real down turn this week. He's lost his sight…he's on oxygen. She doesn't think he'll make it much longer", said Judge Rogers very softly. "Oh, Christ!", was all Matthew could respond. "He wants to see you…", said the judge with her voice trailing off. "I'll call right now. I'll get back to you, okay?", responded Matthew. "Yes please do", sadly replied Judge Rogers through her tears as she hung up the phone.

Matthew reached in the inner pocket of his suit jacket and found his address book. He located Joanna Styles telephone number and quickly dialed the phone. "Phillip had been doing so well…the Florida weather was good for him", thought Matthew. The phone only rang once when Phillip's sister, Joanna picked up the phone. "Joanna. It's Matthew Schipani", he said. "Oh thank goodness Ruth got a hold of you", Joanna Styles replied. She continued, "He's going quickly Matthew…it's not going to be much longer. All he's been talking about is that he needs to see you. He really wants to see you…"

Matthew stood silently with the phone in his hand. He managed to tell Joanna, "I call the airline right now. I'm in Springfield. Bradley Airport is only a half hour away. I'll be there before dinner." Joanna mumbled a quiet "thank you". Matthew hung up the phone and began to dial Ted at the travel agency.

Matthew walked back to the auditorium. He motioned from the back of the room to Janice. He motioned her to come off the podium. She followed him outside to the hallway. Matthew told her about Phillip's condition. Janice began to cry. They sat down on the small bench outside the door for a moment. "I'll make apologies for you…just go", she said to Matthew. He kissed Janice on the cheek and turned to leave. "Please tell him that I love him", Janice shouted to Matthew as he walked away.

The flight to Tampa was quicker than Matthew wanted it to be. Joanna's husband met him at the airport. They drove in silence back to the house. Upon his arrival, Joanna hugged Matthew so hard he thought she was going to squeeze the air out of him. She held onto him for a long time. Phillip was asleep in the other room. Matthew ate dinner and Joanna checked periodically on Phillip. As he was drinking a cup of coffee after dinner, Joanna came out of the room. "He's somewhat awake…I didn't tell him you were coming.", she told Matthew. Matthew got up and began to walk to the bedroom door where Phillip was. Joanna touched him on the shoulder and said to him, "don't be shocked at how he looks. He's not in any pain right now. They have him doped up. Remember he can't see you so you'll have to let him know that your here." Matthew shook his head and opened the door. He walked in quietly shutting the door behind him.

Matthew stood quietly and looked at his friend. It had been six months since he last saw Phillip. The change in his appearance was incredibly dramatic to Matthew. It looked as if his friend had age twenty years in the past six months. His face was gaunt and gray. A tube of oxygen ran under his nose. Almost all of his blond hair was gone. An intravenous tube protruded from Phillip's right arm. Matthew's friend looked like a very old dying man. Tears came silently down Matthew's cheeks. He wiped them away with his hands. "I can't cry...it will upset him", thought Matthew. Then remembering that Phillip could not see him, Matthew allowed the tears to continue to stream. He did not wipe them away.

He walked toward the bed and said softly, "Phillip, it's me Matthew." With that statement Phillip tried to raise his hand. Matthew went over, grabbed his hand and sat on the edge of the bed next to his friend. "I'm here for you honey", Matthew said to Phillip. Phillip attempted to speak, but words could not come out of his mouth. Matthew took his index finger and put it over Phillip's lips gently. "Don't try to talk.", he said. Matthew went on, "I'm here...just relax. You don't need to talk. I know what you're thinking...I'll talk for a bit." Matthew rubbed Phillip's head with the cool washcloth that was on the side of the bed. Phillip was sweating profusely. Matthew continued to repeat softly over and over, "it's okay...I'm here."

Matthew held onto Phillip's hand and sat in silence. He stared at the bedroom wall. He could feel the anger building up inside of him. Since Phillip had become symptomatic with AIDS everytime the subject was brought up, no matter what the setting, Matthew would become furious. He blamed the government, he blamed the religious fanatics, he blamed anyone he could. "Why can't this virus be cured?", Matthew would say. He would go on to rant that the "power structure" in the country was purposefully not trying to find a cure for AIDS. "Who cares about faggots and drug abusers anyway? They're probably thrilled we're all dying!", Matthew would profess.

These were the thoughts that were now in his mind as he sat next to his dying friend.

Matthew continued to rub Phillip's hand. "It's okay honey. We're all here for you", he said to Phillip. Matthew looked at Phillip and saw one tear come from his eye down his cheek. "Don't cry honey", Matthew said as he wiped it away. Phillip opened his mouth. Matthew leaned in over towards Phillip. "I love you", Phillip was able to whisper to Matthew. "I love you too", said Matthew through his tears. Matthew began to become overwhelmed with emotion. He didn't want Phillip to hear the distress in his voice. He decided that Phillip should rest, and he should leave the room so he could regain his composure. "Listen honey, you need to rest. I'm going to sit with Joanna and Bill. I'm not going anywhere. I'm here for you. I'll be back in a little bit, okay", Matthew said. Phillip shook his head "yes". Matthew leaned over and kissed Phillip. He got up and walked slowly out of the room.

Matthew closed the bedroom door behind him and proceeded to the kitchen table where he sat down. He didn't utter a word. Joanna and Bill were silent as well. Matthew looked down at the glass table. He saw his reflection in it. It was the reflection of a sad, scared and hurt man. Joanna got up and walked into the room with Phillip.

About five minutes later Joanna returned to the kitchen. She sat at the table and said in a hearty voice, "that little shit!". Her husband Bill said, "what?". Joanna looked at Matthew and said, "I didn't tell him you were coming. I wanted it to be a surprise. So when I went in there I asked him, 'were you surprised Matthew came?'. You know what that little shit said to me? He said, 'no. I knew he would come' ". Joanna smiled and Matthew smiled back at her. "This is so important to him…and to us.", she told Matthew. "I needed to be here. He was always there for me. I want to be here.", Matthew said with continued sadness in his voice.

Later that evening a hospice nurse came. She told Matthew and the family that Phillip probably would not make it through the next day. She told them that they needed to tell Phillip it was okay to let go. They needed to give him permission to die. That evening, when Matthew went in for the last time before going to bed he tried to tell Phillip it was okay to die. He couldn't. So like the good lawyer and social worker, he chose the middle road. "Phillip, fight if you want to…but if you're too tired, it's okay…you can go. We'll be fine…you've prepared us to handle it." Matthew weepingly told his friend.

That evening as he was tired to get some sleep Matthew realized that he had compromised. He hadn't told Phillip it was okay to die, to let go. He had chosen the easy way out. But he began to question whether he should tell Phillip that it was okay to give up the fight. His catholic teachings came into play. "Didn't God want us to fight to live?", Matthew thought. Then he began to get angry with God. "To hell with God! If he loved us so much he wouldn't let this happen!", thought Matthew. Then he began to get angry with himself for being so angry with God lately. Matthew reached over to turn out the light. He saw the telephone on the table and exclaimed, "Oh shit! I didn't call Adam!"

Matthew reached down in his briefcase and found the number of the hotel that Adam was staying at in Washington, DC. He had been there for a week for a conference on the federal judiciary. Adam joined two other new faculty members at the law school for the trip. He had been really excited about it. Matthew dialed the number quickly. "Room 1532", Matthew said when the hotel picked up. After about six rings Adam picked up the phone and mumbled, "hello?" He had been sleeping. Matthew rattled off quickly to Adam what was going on. Adam asked, "where are you now?" Matthew replied, I'm at Phillip's sister's house." Adam responded, "do you want me to fly down in the morning?" Matthew told him "no" and that he believed his friend would be dead in the morning. "Can you please call Ruth tomorrow and let her know what's happening?", Matthew asked Adam. "Of course I can honey", Adam reassuringly replied.

"What about Octavia and Scott?", Adam inquired in a concerned tone. Matthew replied impatiently, "don't you remember? Scott's still in Germany. I don't know how to get in touch with him. Octavia's at her mother-in-law's in New York City. Ruth was trying to reach her. I don't have the goddamn number!" Adam responded, "okay sweetheart. Just try to calm down. Get some rest. Please call me if anything happens or if you change your mind and want me to come. I love you." Matthew responded, "I love you too, Adam", and he hung up the phone. Matthew turned off the light. He closed his eyes. He knew he needed some sleep. Tomorrow would be a difficult day.

Phillip's labored breathing in the morning was not a good sign. Matthew knew that the end was near. He had to tell his friend it was okay to die. On his second trip into the bedroom that morning, Matthew did just that. He told Phillip it was time to let go. "Time to move on to a better place", he said. This was very difficult for Matthew, but he knew it had to be said. Matthew repeatedly gave permission to Phillip to "let go" on his many subsequent trips into the bedroom that afternoon. The phrase "let go" was easier for Matthew than to say that it was "okay to die". For some reason that phrase didn't sound so morbid to him.

The day was a long and stressful one. It was a death watch. Matthew, Joanna and other relatives alternated back and forth into Phillip's room. Matthew was also on the telephone all day. He spoke with Janice, Adam and Ruth. Octavia still could not be located. Matthew took a few quick solitary breaks during the afternoon. He sat on the chaise lounge in the backyard in the hot Tampa sun, trying to relax. The sun was powerful and draining. Its effects were somewhat calming to Matthew. The heat washed over his body and cleansed him to continue the vigil.

As the sun began to set over Tampa, so did the sun set on Phillip Styles life. Matthew had gone back into the bedroom for what would be his final time. Phillip struggled to removed his law school class ring from his right hand. Matthew helped him take it off. Phillip took the ring, placed it in Matthew's hand and attempted to speak. Matthew looked at Phillip and asked, "do you want me to have this?" Phillip weakly responded, "yes". Matthew placed the ring on his left hand and took his hand grasping Phillip's.

Phillip's breathing was becoming more shallow even with the oxygen. Matthew was becoming anxious. At times he thought that Phillip had died, but only a few moments later there would be another breath. This went on for over an hour. Then, there were no more breaths. Phillip Styles was dead. AIDS had claimed its newest victim. Matthew held onto Phillip's hand and cried. Joanna entered the room. She summonsed the others. Matthew sat silently in the room for about an hour with them. No one spoke. Finally, the hospice nurse came into the bedroom. "I think it's time to go", she politely said. Matthew kissed Phillip's forehead and left the room.

The flight back to Boston was very difficult for Matthew. He felt as if he were in a time warp. Matthew kept looking out the window of the airplane at the puffy clouds passing by. "Was Phillip among those clouds?", he thought. Matthew ordered his third glass of Chablis. He ordered this wine in Phillip's honor. It was his favorite. Matthew toasted the clouds as they passed over the wing of the airplane. He toasted the clouds in memory of his friend.

The memorial service was to be held in Springfield. This was where Phillip had spent the major part of his life. Joanna had asked that Matthew give the eulogy at Phillip's memorial service. Phillip had been cremated and Joanna brought the ashes with her to the service. The day of the memorial service was extremely taxing on Matthew. He knew that he had to maintain his composure during the eulogy. Phillip would have wanted that. Matthew had written up a eulogy that he was intending upon reading. He thought this would be easier. But when he was called on to speak, Matthew disregarded his notes. He spoke from his heart.

Matthew spoke slowly. It was difficult for him to get the words out. Matthew looked around the church as he spoke. He saw many dear friends of Phillip's who were also his friends as well. The sorrow expressed on Octavia's face was overwhelming. They were intently listening to Matthew. Matthew saw Phillip's former law professor in the back of the church. She was openly crying.

Matthew began to close his eulogy. His voice had become stronger as he had been speaking. He closed with, "...Phillip was a community activist both in his role as a social worker in New York and later as an attorney here in Massachusetts. Children were his passion. He was a strong advocate for the social, psychological, and legal needs of the children in this state. Phillip fought many court battles against uncaring parents and an uncaring beauracracy. He did this so that the children he represented could have a better chance at a healthy and happy future. In illness, Phillip remained a role model for this community..." Matthew paused briefly and took a deep gulp.

"Phillip continued his advocacy for the civil rights of persons with AIDS and gay persons in general.", Matthew continued. "He helped to establish the People with AIDS coalition here in Springfield, and when he moved he was a founding member of the coalition in Tampa." Matthew stopped speaking again. He was wondering if he was losing track. He cleared his mind while he gripped the disregarded written eulogy he was holding in his hands. He clenched it for strength and then he began to speak again. "I want to conclude by talking to you about Phillip's death. We can't ignore it. It was a cruel death, a painful death...an unnecessary death. AIDS cut short a brilliant and vivacious life. But Phillip died with dignity. He accepted his illness and put his best face forward. He did not complain. When it was time to die, Phillip moved on to the next stage of existence with grace. And so, we too must move on...We have to let go, but we can never forget Phillip Styles. We can hold on to his memory by adopting his concerns and commitments as our concerns, our commitments, for our time. We need to insure that Phillip's causes, child welfare and AIDS awareness, become our causes too. Together, we can take the power of his memory and use that power to help advance the struggles he so valiantly fought for. This would be the best gift that we could give to the memory of Phillip Styles."

Matthew was beginning to lose his composure. He looked down for a moment, then raised his head and continued to speak. "So, we say good-bye to a dear friend. You are in a better place Phillip. There is no more pain. We will miss you, but we will never allow ourselves to forget you. Thank you for enriching our lives by being a part of our lives." Matthew turned and bowed his head to the minister and left the altar.

Matthew walked back to the church pew and sat down. Adam and Janice on each side of him, gripped his hands. He looked at them both solemnly sitting with tears streaming down their faces. He looked across at the next pew. Scott and Octavia were sitting together. Their tears and sadness were overwhelmingly expressive. Octavia was visibly shaking. Matthew thought, "I hope I never have to go through this again…I hope I never have to see these people in such pain." The ceremony concluded with the song, *And He Shall Raise You Up*. It was a beautiful song filled with hope. Matthew took solace in the hymn.

Matthew took several days off from work following Phillip's service. He had to put things in perspective. He spent a great deal of time alone, thinking about Phillip. He tried to force the horrible memories of those last few days to the back of his mind. He wanted to remember the good times. The times they worked together, the times they thought together about the law, and the times they played together. Those social times, the 'follies with Phillip', as he called it, were the most happy memories that Matthew had. "Maybe that's all I'll remember someday", he thought.

Matthew returned to work. He dove right back in. It would help him to move on. He continued with his legislative agenda for stiffer penalties for abusive parents. Matthew appeared at the State House for hearings on proposed legislation to make child abuse punishment longer and more severe. Matthew was a strong and vocal advocate for this cause. Matthew's legislative ally, Representative Dexter Donnelly, was impressed by Matthew's ability to captivate the audience of usually bored and apathetic legislators. Matthew had the ability to translate facts, figures and statistics into a meaningful, personal and compelling argument for stricter laws.

Adam continued to enjoy his position at the law school. He found teaching much more satisfying than his brief stint at practicing law. He also enjoyed the leisurely schedule of academic life. He had a lot of free time. Scott had completed the remodeling of the third floor of their house. Matthew's aunt, Gloria Tanzinni, was prepared to move in the next month. She had just retired after having been a nurse for over thirty years. She needed to move to a more economical place. Matthew was happy that his 'favorite aunt' would be living in their house. She was engaging and had a wonderful sense of humor. It also meant that with Aunt Gloria living in Cambridge, Matthew's mother would come to visit more often. Matthew was happy about that as well.

Summer was approaching and Matthew was bound and determined that he was going to take some time off this summer. He wanted to work on his tan. "I'm sick of being pasty white", he told Adam. Adam constantly reminded him of skin cancer. "Why do white people always want to be darker? I don't get it", he said to Matthew. During their annual Memorial Day trek to Provincetown, Matthew spent most of the afternoons lying out on the deck of the guest house to achieve his desired tan.

On Memorial Day itself they left Provincetown early. They had planned a surprise party for Janice and Jose. It was their two year anniversary. The party was not only a surprise, but it was a big hit! Adam's friend, Dalton Beauvais, the exclusive clothing designer had given the most desirable gift of the evening. It was matching outfits from his store on Newbury Street. Adam played matchmaker once again that evening. He had invited his best friend, Joseph Stevens to the party. Joseph was trying to break into professional ballet dancing. He had been working at his trade for several years. He was suppose to go for an audition the day after Memorial Day, but Adam had convinced him to come to the party. Adam had decided a few weeks earlier that Joseph and Dalton would make a 'cute couple', which by the end of the evening they did. Adam's matchmaking had worked again!

At one point during the party Janice and Matthew sequestered themselves in the kitchen to talk about the latest crisis at DCP. The newspapers were trouncing on the agency and its Commissioner, Kevin Michaels for a debacle over a decision about a foster child. Matthew had just explained that Commissioner Michaels and he would be making the decision by the end of the week, when Jose walked into the kitchen. "Shop talk?', Jose asked in a disapproving tone. Matthew apologized and Jose replied, "that's okay, but come on…rejoin the party!" Janice looked at her husband and said, "you're right honey". She reached for her wine glass with one hand and grabbed her husband's arm with the other. "Come on sweetheart! You're the hostess with the mostest!", she said laughingly to Matthew. "I'll even get the DJ to play *I'm Coming Out!*, so you can show us that fancy dancing you do!", Janice chortled as she walked out the kitchen door returning to the party crowd. A few moments later Matthew heard Diana Ross proclaiming, *"I'm Coming Out!"* and so Matthew 'came out' of the kitchen lip synching the words to the song. The group danced and laughed.

The month of June was a busy one for Matthew. He had many social plans and his work schedule was increasingly busy. The annual AIDS Walk in Boston was part of his calendar. Matthew walked with the usual crew: Adam, Janice, Scott, Ken and George. The walk was an enjoyable venture for Matthew, even though its purpose was rooted in sadness. Matthew looked around the Boston Common and moved with the walk down Commonwealth Avenue. He was sure that the crowd walking this year was the biggest he had seen. He was not sure if this should be interpreted as a good sign, or a sign that more and more lives were affected by HIV.

The day for the walk was a beautiful hot and sunny June day. Matthew and Scott joked and googled at the beautiful shirtless, muscular young men who were part of the walk. Every time a man would walk by that they liked they would make a joking remark to one of their friends. Scott saw a man in his late twenties during the walk. He looked like Sylvester Stallone with a tan. Scott exclaimed, "delicious!" and they all laughed. Adam called them "old queens!". They were walking along the Charles River with the Esplanade as their final destination. Matthew found a sense of anger was enveloping him. "what's wrong?", asked George, who could tell by just looking at Matthew that the frivolity of an hour ago was gone. Matthew curtly responded, "nothing" as he continued to walk with the crowd. But something was definitely wrong. Matthew was very troubled and very angry. This year the AIDS Walk was personal. He hadn't known anyone who had died from AIDS when he walked in the past. This year he did, and the walk was about Phillip. Matthew was very angry.

By the time they reached the Esplanade, Matthew had excused himself from the group. His anger had reached its peak and he was desperately seeking a place to be alone among this large crowd. Unbeknownst to Matthew, as he searched for his place Adam was following slightly behind. During his search he saw a man who looked eerily like Phillip. He did a double take. Of course, it was not Phillip. But this only made Matthew more upset. While he was looking for his spot Matthew was crying as he searched. He finally found a small area under a tree near the Charles River. He sat on a stone that was placed there. A few moments later Adam advanced and sat down on the stone with Matthew. Without uttering a word, Adam reached and put his arm around his lover. Matthew sobbed and Adam wiped away the tears. They sat together quietly gazing at the river. Adam knew what was going on inside Matthew's head. But he also knew that words were inadequate at this time. Several minutes passed when they heard the band playing in the background on the stage erected at the end of the walk. "Let's go back", Matthew said to Adam. They walked hand in hand back through the crowd and rejoined their friends.

A week later as Scott and Matthew were enjoying coffee and the Sunday papers, Scott told Matthew that he had met a new man. "I hope this is it!", he said to Matthew. The new man was a thirty year old medical student at Tufts University in Boston. His name was Andrew Prosser. He was originally from Chicago. Matthew hadn't met him yet, but he could tell from Scott's conversation about Andrew that Scott was falling in love. As he put down the *Parade* magazine, Matthew said, "why don't you invite him to the dinner party next Saturday?"

Matthew had planned a dinner party to celebrate Ted and Pete's fourteenth anniversary. They were an unusual couple among gay men. They had been together longer than any couple Matthew knew. Their relationship deserved a celebration. Adam, of course would be doing all the preparation. He did it so well and found enjoyment from it. Adam had also invited Joseph and Dalton who were hitting it off tremendously. "You can afford to take one night off from work", Matthew said to Scott. Scott pondered and then said, "I guess I could. It would be fun and you can satisfy your curiosity!" Matthew chuckled, "I can't wait to meet Mr. Wonderful!", he said.

"Matthew you have two calls holding", said his administrative assistant, Tracy Brookstein. How Matthew hated Monday mornings! In fact, he hated the morning in general. He would tell friends not to call him in the morning. "I'm usually not awake until noon", he would say. Matthew barked into the phone, "who is it?". Tracy responded in her normal pleasant tone, "Boston Gazette on line two about McFadden and James Dennis is on line three." Matthew said, "Ask James if I can get back to him later. Give me the Gazette."

Matthew pressed the speaker function on his phone. "This is Matthew Schipani", he said. "Hello", said the voice on the other end.

"This is Alfie Stone from the Boston Gazette." Matthew replied dryly, "yes, how can I help you Mr. Stone?" The reporter said, "I'm calling about the McFadden case. Can you tell me what's going on with the case?", Alfie Stone asked. Matthew replied, "the Commissioner will be holding a press conference tomorrow. You will get the details then." Without giving the reporter a chance to respond, Matthew said, "see you there" and pressed the button on his phone to disconnect the call. Matthew called the Commissioner. "Kevin. We need to meet on McFadden. I've got the damn press calling me!", Matthew said in an animated voice. The Commissioner set a meeting for the afternoon.

The McFadden case had the potential to destroy the image of the agency and in particular, the career of Commissioner Kevin Michaels. DCP had placed two black children that were in the state's custody in a black DCP foster home. When the foster parents decided to move to Florida because of a family crisis, the local DCP office refused to allow them to take the children with them outside of the state. The biological parents of the two children were both incarcerated for felony crimes. Their legal rights to the children had been terminated by the court. The state had permanent custody of the children.

The two children, Rebekah and Roy, had been living with Stanley and Karen McFadden for over four years. They were ages six and seven respectively. They spent most of their young lives in the care of the McFaddens. When an agreement could not be reached between the local DCP office and the McFaddens, the local office removed the children from the foster home even before the McFaddens had left Massachusetts. The children were not placed in another black home, but rather a white DCP foster home, as there were no black homes available.

The McFaddens ultimately canceled their plans to move. They dealt with their family crisis from a distance. They let the DCP office know that they decided to stay in Massachusetts so Rebekah and Roy could be returned to them. But the local office balked at that idea. The McFaddens continued to try to negotiate with the local office but they were not successful. Seven months had passed. The McFaddens attempt at going up the chain of command, calling their representatives and even a letter to the Governor had all fallen on deaf ears. They became increasingly frustrated as time went on. When all had failed, the McFaddens went to the press. For the two weeks the local newspapers and television stations were having a field day with the story.

Matthew's meeting with Commissioner Michaels went very well. He liked the fact that once Kevin was presented with a problem he would make a decision and take ownership for that decision. The Commissioner managed the agency in Harry Truman style. The buck stopped on Kevin Michaels' desk. Matthew and the Commissioner agreed that the local office was clearly wrong in their refusal to allow the children to be returned to the McFaddens. Matthew asserted that the office staff were being punitive and not acting in the best interests of these children. "They're stubborn control freaks. They don't like to be told what to do", Matthew said of the local DCP staff. Kevin Michaels turned to his chief legal counsel and said, "the children will be returned to the McFaddens in the morning. We'll hold a press conference in the afternoon to announce the decision."

When Matthew got up to leave the office, Kevin Michaels said, "I'm letting Steve Hadley go immediately". Hadley was the director of the local DCP office that made the contentious decision. Kevin held his hands up in an open fashion and said, "he had the final call. He could have stopped it before it got out of hand. But he chose to ignore it. I think it was racist and incompetent. I won't have that here." Matthew shook his head in agreement, but added, "I don't know if it was racist, but it was definitely wrong." Matthew walked to the door of the Commissioner's office. Kevin Michaels said, "be at the press conference tomorrow." Matthew shook his head affirmatively.

The press conference the next day went successfully. The newspapers would have to find somebody else to crucify this week. The children were back where they belonged. Matthew returned to his office after the conference and began returning phone calls. He called James Dennis. Dennis was the director of the Webster DCP office. It was one of Matthew's favorite offices. Located in a rural area south of Worcester, Matthew had gone to this office many times since his return to the agency. The office reminded him of his years past in the Berkshire DCP office. The staff in Webster were a dedicated group of professionals who were concerned about the well being and safety of children.

"Hi James. What's happening?", asked Michael. "Same old stuff. Different day.", replied James Dennis. Matthew said, "sorry it took me two days to get back to you. It's been crazy here." James replied, "I know you've been busy. I saw the press conference. I thought it went well. I'm just calling on a minor issue. It's a reference check." Matthew asked, "okay. Who is it?"

James Dennis shuffled his papers so loudly that Matthew was able to hear it over the phone. "Okay. Here it is", said James. He continued, "the guy applied to be a social worker. His name is Craig Talbot. He listed you as a reference." Matthew's eyebrows raised, he gulped and the inflection in his voice was raised as he queried, "Craig Talbot? Is that the name you said?" James Dennis shuffled his papers again. "Yeah, Craig Talbot", he told Matthew. Matthew exclaimed, "you gotta be shitting me!" James paused for a moment and then asked, "why? What's wrong?" Matthew asked if the office had done a computer check and James replied that he believed they had. "Well", said Matthew. "…if it's the same Craig Talbot, and I only know one, he's a fucking psycho! Pardon my language. I took him away from his parents many moons ago when I was a social worker back in the Berkshires."

James interrupted, "he's in his twenties, a white guy. His resume says he graduated from MIT." Matthew shouted, "that's the one!"

James said, "well I guess he's a non-hire. I can't believe that the computer did not pick it up! That's weird though…why would he give you as a reference?" Matthew replied, "shows how fucked up he is!" James Dennis quickly changed the subject. "How's the summer tan coming?", he asked. "I'm as handsome as ever!", replied a chuckling Matthew. The conversation ended with Matthew accepting an invitation to come to the Webster DCP office. "You know how much I like to visit", he told James Dennis, and marked it in his calendar book.

That evening sharing pasta with his Aunt Gloria, his mother and Adam, Matthew made them all stop eating and assemble in front of the television set for the local news. The third story on the newscast was the McFadden case. Standing right next to DCP Commissioner Michaels was Matthew. The television anchors made the agency look heroic in the decision. Matthew thought, "well Kevin's job is safe, for now at least." Matthew grabbed the remote and turned off the TV. They walked back to the dinner table. His mother pinched his cheek and said, "my handsome TV star!". They all laughed and returned to their pasta.

That evening in bed Matthew and Adam were sharing work stories. Matthew interrupted Adam. "Oh! I forgot to tell you!", he said excitedly. Then Matthew discussed the telephone call from James Dennis. "That's fucking bizarre!", said Adam. Matthew rolled over and turned out the light saying, "I know…it's disturbing, isn't it?" He pushed his head into the pillow and fell fast asleep.

The next morning the phone on his desk buzzed. "I've got to turn that ringer down!", Matthew said out loud. He picked it up. "Hi Matthew, it's Dexter Donnelly", said a cheerful Tracy as she put the call through. "Hi Dexter", he said. "Matthew, it's gonna pass the senate!", said an exuberant Donnelly. Matthew stood up from his chair, "that's fantastic!", he cheered into the phone. They were talking about a bill which increased significantly prison terms for abusive parents. "Now if the old bastard will sign it", said Donnelly referring to the Governor. "I think he will", said Matthew. "But I'll give Shannon Watson a call. She's always got the dirt. I'll see what she knows". Donnelly retorted back to Matthew, "haven't you had enough of reporters this week?" Matthew laughed and then said, "I know. But she's one of the ones I can trust...one of a very few." Donnelly said, "well, I have to go. Keep me posted!" With that comment their conversation ended.

Another few days passed and what seemed to be a routine day wouldn't turn out to be so routine at all. The morning started out well, but an event in the afternoon overshadowed the accomplishments of the morning. Matthew arrived late for work and when he walked in Shannon Watson was on hold. He went to his office and picked up the phone.

"Nice fucking hours you keep!", Shannon said in her typical sarcastic tone laced with her New York accent. "Fuck you!", responded a laughing Matthew. Shannon quickly replied, "well honey, as I've told you many times...you name the place and I'll be there with my whip!" They both laughed and Matthew said, "promises, promises!" Then he inquired, "so what's the good word?" Shannon replied, "well, it is a good word. The old fart is going to sign the bill. You've got the law!" Matthew took his fist and punched the air yelling out a loud "yes!"

Shannon continued in her conversation. "The 'gov' is going to hold a press conference next week. I hear you're going to be invited. I'll be there, so after the press conference we can do the 'wild thing' at a sleazy hotel!" Matthew laughed and said, "can I bring a few of my friends?" Shannon replied, "at least ten or twenty, I hope!" Matthew thanked his friend for the information and concluded their conversation with, "lunch is on me".

Matthew looked at his watch. He was late for a meeting on the seventh floor. He grabbed his suit jacket off the coat rack and quickly walked to the elevator. Matthew arrived on the seventh floor and slipped into the room as Frank Livingston was speaking. Livingston stopped and turned to Matthew. "Just to bring you up to date", he said to Matthew, "we've confirmed the date in January." Matthew nodded his head. Livingston was talking about a celebrity fund-raiser that he was in charge of putting together. The fund-raiser was being sponsored by the agency not only to raise funds for DCP, but also to increase awareness about child abuse in Massachusetts. Livingston dead panned, "I'm sorry to tell you Matthew, but Diana Ross sends her regrets!" Everyone in the room began to laugh.

"Seriously though", continued Livingston. "We do have our celebrities. Bailey Adams the comedienne has made a commitment. Steven Fox was already on board as was Suzanne Cardy. And just yesterday, James Davenport, the soap opera star sent word that he would come." "Ooh", exclaimed Sally McNulty, one of the staff members present. "he's so fine!', she exclaimed as she was blushing. Matthew asked, "who is he?" Sally fidgeted and then perked up in her chair. "He used to be a model", she said. "But now he's on Santa Fe Times. It's on channel seven at two o'clock. I tape it so I can watch it on the weekends!", said Sally with glee. Matthew laughed.

Frank continued to explain the details of the fund-raiser for about the next half hour. Matthew was impressed, but he always found Frank impressive in his work. It was a novel idea that Frank had come up with and it could really help the cause of preventing child abuse. "Too bad they didn't invite Diana Ross...she would have come", thought Matthew. He closed his eyes and briefly saw himself in his fantasy meeting his idol and shaking her hand. This would fulfill one of his unachieved life time dreams.

Matthew returned to the office and held a brief meeting with the DCP legal directors from the various offices throughout the state. It was about four o'clock when the meeting broke up. Matthew returned to his private office and looked at the stacks of paperwork mounting on his desk. While flipping through the stacks he called Adam to tell him that he would be working late. He had to get some organization in the mess that sat on the top of his desk. He was reviewing a policy memo when he heard Tracy yell, "you can't go in there!" Matthew got up from his chair only to see the door to his office fly open. Craig Talbot was standing in the entry way of Matthew's office. He had aged somewhat since Matthew had seen him in Harvard Square a few years ago. Craig was clearly agitated as he moved into the office. He was huffing, his fists were clenched and he stared right into Matthew's eyes. "You fucking faggot!", Craig yelled at Matthew. Tracy had followed Craig, and with that comment she turned away to return to her desk to call security.

Craig's face was bright red. He screamed, "you fucked up me getting that job!" He moved closer to Matthew. Matthew looked at him directly. In a calm voice, Matthew said, "Craig. Sit down. Let's talk." Craig responded at the top of his lungs, "Fuck you! Didn't I make it clear long ago that you would pay for what you did to me? You're trying to ruin my life. I can't even get a job because of you, you goddamn queer!" Matthew motioned to the chair. "Craig, please calm down. Sit down. We'll talk." Craig yelled again. "No I won't sit down! You sit down mister hotshot faggot lawyer!"

"Excuse me!", came a stern voice and a tap on Craig Talbot's shoulder from behind. It was Jonas Kilpatrick, one of the staff attorneys in Matthew's office. "You're going to have to leave now", said Kilpatrick firmly. Craig turned and got right in front of the face of Kilpatrick and screamed, "you leave asshole! This is between me and him...I'm not going anywhere!" At that point, two security guards pushed Kilpatrick aside gently and reached for Craig. He reached out to punch one of the security guards. The two then tackled Craig in Matthew's office. Craig went flying over one of the wing chairs seated in front of Matthew's desk. The security guards lifted Craig from the floor. They spun him around on his heels and lifted him off the ground slightly, walking him out of the office. As he was being forcibly ejected from Matthew's office, Craig turned his head and said, "I'll kill you motherfucker...I'll kill you!" Craig continued to scream his threats as he was being walked down the hallway by the security guards.

Tracy ran into his office. She came over and put her arm around a visibly shaken Matthew. "Sit down...I'll get you some water", she told Matthew. She quickly returned with the cup of water and asked, "are you okay?" Matthew took the water and said, "yes. Thank you." Jonas reappeared in the office and told Matthew, "he's left the building". Matthew said, "thank you, Jonas. Thank you for coming to my rescue.", and he reached out to shake Jonas' hand. "Any time" replied Jonas as he left the office.

Tracy sat with him for a few minutes. She too was very upset. She insisted that Matthew go to court tomorrow and getting a restraining order against Craig. Matthew declined. "It won't happen again", he assured Tracy. "Plus, getting a restraining order will only escalate him further." Tracy expressed her disapproval on his decision. She told him to pack his things up. "You've done enough today. I'm walking out with you. You shouldn't leave alone.", she told Matthew. Matthew replied, "I've got a lot of work to do. You go home...get out of here. I'm okay, I'll be fine. See you tomorrow." Tracy stared at Matthew and said "no, I want you to leave, but since you are so stubborn, I am staying too!". And she did.

When Matthew got home that evening Adam was already asleep. Matthew decided not to wake Adam with the news about Craig Talbot. It would only upset him. Matthew did go downstairs and talk to Scott about it. "I think Tracy's right, you should get a restraining order", Scott told Matthew. Matthew once again declined, saying, "he's got problems. I don't want to make it any worse for him."

It was eight o'clock on the Saturday morning following the Governor's news conference when Matthew's phone rang. It was his mother. "Good morning, mister news star", she said to her son. Matthew replied, "what do you mean?" Rosa said, "you didn't get the paper yet? You made page one. There's a picture of the Governor signing that new law you wanted and you are standing over his shoulder watching. In fact, the article credits you for getting the law to pass." Matthew smiled, saying to his mother, "I'll walk down to the store and get it. By the way, Mom. Who wrote the article?" His mother yelled, "Franco! Bring me the paper!" A moment later she said, "some reporter named Shannon Watson." Matthew replied, "mmm" and he smiled broadly.

CHAPTER 9

DISTRACTIONS

July 1990

It had been seven months to the day they had met. Adam was in San Diego. He was attending a two week conference on legal realism in the law school curriculum. Matthew was lying on the bright white sand of a beach in Barbados. James Davenport handed him a rum and punch, saying "here you go sweetie". Matthew replied, "thanks" as he took a sip of the refreshing drink. James asked, "I'm going for a swim. Do you want to join me?" Matthew responded, "I'll be there in a minute". James Davenport walked into the blue green calm waters of the Caribbean as Matthew laid back on the lounger to enjoy the sun.

Matthew and James had met on a cold wintry night in downtown Boston at the DCP fund-raiser that Frank Livingston had organized. Matthew spotted James as soon as he walked into the room to take his seat on the dais. Adam didn't even notice James until later in the evening when he spoke. James Davenport was a 26 year old biracial actor. He had chiseled features and deep blue eyes. Matthew was sure that James would stand out in any crowd. He had that 'star look' about him. He carried himself like a movie star.

At the end of the evening Matthew went up to thank the participants at the fund-raiser. He shook hands and briefly conversed with all the celebrities that came to lend their support. Matthew walked over to the stunning James Davenport to thank him as well. Davenport shook Matthew's hand firmly and beamed a broad, bright smile. They exchanged pleasantries for a few moments. Matthew shook Davenport's hand again to say good-bye. With his other hand Davenport gave Matthew a folded piece of paper. "It's my number", he said to Matthew, then adding "give me a call. I live in New York". Matthew stared into those deep blue eyes and stammered an "okay". As Davenport turned away he said to Matthew, "don't forget to call!" Then he walked away. Matthew stood there in astonishment and thought, "he's so beautiful!" Matthew blushed as he turned and walked back to his table, bumping right into Adam. Adam grabbed his jacket and they left the fund-raiser.

That evening Matthew and Adam were recounting the night and talking about how the fund-raiser went. Matthew asked Adam, "what did you think of that guy James Davenport?" Adam responded, "he's really cute…but he's not that great of a speaker. He needed a TelePrompTer to pull it off. You know what they say…great looks, no brain! Why what did you think of him?" Matthew shrugged his shoulders and answered his lover, "oh…I guess the same."

And now, on a hot July day, unknown to Adam, Matthew was in a foreign country with the person that he confided to Scott had become his 'mistress'. Mr. James Davenport. Matthew sat up and got off the lounger. He walked into the calm Caribbean sea. The water temperature was about eighty. Matthew relished the warm flowing feeling of the water as he descended deeper and deeper into it. He swam out towards James. They met in the water and Matthew leaned into him and kissed him. "Are we still going to Bridgetown tonight?", Matthew asked. James responded affirmatively and turned in the water. "Follow me", he said to Matthew.

They swam out to a raft that was about two hundred yards out into the water, held down by an anchor. They mounted the raft. The hot Caribbean sun quickly dried them both. James said to Matthew, "can you believe we have to leave here tomorrow?" Matthew shook his head and said, "I know…it's gone by so quick. But I've really had a terrific time. Thank you so much." James smiled back at Matthew. They sat on the raft for a few moments quietly enjoying the sun. Matthew jumped back into the sea. James followed. They swam to the shore and at the beach they grabbed their drinks and walked to their room.

"I'm going to shower off", said Matthew to James as he closed the bathroom door behind him. The cool shower water rained down on Matthew. He began to shampoo his hair. His eyes were closed and he was scrubbing his scalp. As he rinsed off, he opened his eyes. There was James in the shower with him. Matthew jumped. "You scared the shit out of me!", he exclaimed to James. James smiled, kissed Matthew and reached for his penis. James began to stroke Matthew's penis. Matthew tilted his head back under the shower spout. Matthew groaned in ecstasy. They both reached their climax in the shower a short time later. They washed each other off and tumbled into bed for an afternoon siesta.

That evening as they drove on the 'wrong side' of the road, as Matthew called it, he constantly noted the poverty on the sides of the road. When they got closer to the capital city of Bridgetown, Matthew turned to James and said, "I can't believe the way these people have to live. Look at those shacks." Matthew pointed to a hill on the side of the road that was dotted with little open air shanties that served as homes. "I guess we don't realize how lucky we really are", opined Matthew to James. They spent the evening enjoying the tourist areas of the capital city, but once again on the ride back to the hotel Matthew began concentrating on the stark contrast between the wealth of the tourist area and the poverty of the rest of the island. It was disturbing to Matthew. He mentioned it again to James, who just shrugged his shoulders and stared out the window as they continued to drive.

Matthew continued his diatribe about the inequities of the living conditions as they were crawling into bed for the evening. He had been going on for about forty five minutes. "...I mean just go down the road a few miles and you've entered the back woods of Appalachia...it's so unequal..." Finally James had enough. "Come on Matthew, stop! You're not going to solve the economic problems of Barbados tonight. Turn off the light. We have to leave in the morning and I need my sleep.", he said to Matthew. Matthew reached over and turned off the light. James was right, he thought. But so was he.

The next day when Matthew boarded the commuter flight from New York back to Boston he blew a kiss good-bye to James. The brief hop back to Massachusetts gave Matthew time to pause and evaluate what he was going to do about his future and this relationship with James Davenport. He was in love, no maybe in lust, with James. But he was also living with and committed to Adam. They had been together a long time, they had history. He loved Adam deeply too. Yet, Matthew could not get over the fact that this quasi-famous man, James Davenport had the 'hots' for him. It inflated his ego. At the same time, Matthew wondered if he was just one of the many ports in a storm for this extremely good looking celebrity. As the small commuter plane touched ground at Logan Airport, Matthew shook his head as if to excise thoughts from his mind. He didn't want to think about his affair with James and the impact it was having on his relationship with Adam. He decided to ignore this conflict, at least for now.

Ken Rivers picked up Matthew at the airport. Matthew had confided in Ken last month about his relationship with James. While they were putting Matthew's luggage into Ken's Saab, he asked Matthew, "so how was it?" Matthew replied that he had a good time on his brief vacation. "Barbados is a beautiful country. The people are lovely. You should try to go there sometime", he said to Ken. Ken looked at Matthew and sarcastically responded, "I don't have a movie star to pay for my trip!". Matthew replied, "fuck you!"

Ken helped Matthew bring the luggage up to the apartment. They sat an had a few drinks together. Matthew explained that he was conflicted about the relationship with Adam and James. "You need to sort it out", Ken told Matthew. He went on, "remember all the times we used to have sex. We had to stop it…it was screwing things up. Things are much better this way, aren't they?", he asked. Matthew replied that they were. While he and Ken had frequently had sex together many years ago, and they both found each other sexually exciting, it was complicating their relationship. They made the mutual decision to stop having sex and just continue to be close friends. Their relationship benefited from that wise decision made a long time ago. Matthew asked Ken, "so how's your love life?" Ken, in his usual catty tone replied, "well, not as good as yours. But, I met this guy last week. His name is Alfie. He's really cute." Matthew poured another drink and said, "Alfie? That's a different name. Where's he from?" Ken replied, "he lives in the south end with his ex-lover. He's thirty two, about six feet tall. He's a reporter for the Gazette. I think he said he's been there about five years." Matthew interrupted, "what's his last name?" Ken responded, "Stone. Why do you know him?" Matthew sat down at the table, handed Ken his drink and said, "I think I may. I might have talked to him about a case or something in the past. The name sounds familiar. It is a distinctive first name."

That evening Matthew and Ken went out to dinner together. While eating dessert Ken told Matthew that he was thinking of returning to school for a masters degree in business. Matthew was supportive, "you can do it. You need to do it. I know you don't want to work at that bank for the rest of your life!" Ken then again brought up the subject of Adam and James. "So when is your wife coming home?", he asked Matthew. "I'm picking him up Monday night.", Matthew replied. Ken looked at Matthew straight in the eyes and said, "when are you going to tell him about mister movie star?" Matthew replied, "I'm not...and he's not a movie star! He's only a soap opera actor." Matthew paid the bill and they called it a night.

Monday morning arrived with its usual speed and surprise. The weekends always seemed so short. The day began with a conference about the latest legal crisis that the Division of Child Protection was embroiled in. The crisis was a case that presented the age old conflict between the power of the state and the belief in religion. The facts of the case were not complicated, only the ramifications were. The facts involved a six year old girl named Megan Sharpe who was suffering from leukemia. He parents belonged to a recognized religious sect in Massachusetts called the "Church of Power and Healing". The church teachings provided that the use of modern medicine and medical treatment was against God's will and strictly forbidden. Viruses, illnesses, and even accidental injuries were to be treated by the 'teachers' of the church, without the benefit of modern medicine. These 'teachers' would pray over the stricken member and implore God to heal them.

Last month, Megan Sharpe failed to attend her specialized school program in Lynn for several days in a row. The teachers became alarmed and called her parents, Anita and Warren Sharpe. Mrs. Sharpe told the teachers that Megan was sick and they were praying for her recovery. One of the teachers called back and begged Mrs. Sharpe to call a medical doctor. Anita Sharpe thanked her so politely for her suggestion, but declined saying it would violate their religious beliefs.

A few more days passed and Megan did not appear. The vice principal of the school called and tried to convince both Anita and Warren Sharpe to seek medical attention. Once again they declined, stating that they would trust God to heal their daughter. The vice principal filed a neglect report with the local DCP office alleging that the parents failure to secure medical treatment for Megan was placing her at risk. The report was investigated. The parents were cooperative with the investigating social workers, but they refused to get any medical treatment for Megan. When pressured by the social workers, Warren Sharpe explained that they had the religious freedom to make this choice. He cited by memory the state's spiritual healing statute as legal authority for refusing medical treatment for their child. The social workers tried but could not change the parent's minds.

The local DCP office made the decision to petition the juvenile court for an emergency order to remove Megan from her parent's custody in order to secure medical treatment. The DCP staff alleged that failure to act would lead to the child's death. The order was given by the court and Megan Sharpe was removed from her parent's custody and brought immediately to North Shore General Hospital. At the hospital, over the protests of the parents and with the consent of the DCP social workers, Megan Sharpe was given medical treatment. A day later her condition had stabilized and it appeared that she was out of medical danger. Anita and Warren Sharpe hired an attorney while Megan was laying in the hospital receiving medical treatment. Their attorney filed an appeal with the state appeals court to overturn the juvenile court order.

The appeals court directed the case to the Supreme Judicial Court of Massachusetts, the state's highest court. In taking this action the appeals court noted for the record that this case, "…presents an issue of extreme public importance which requires a determination by the Commonwealth's supreme court." The Supreme Judicial Court, noting that Megan was still receiving the contested medical treatment, put the case on the 'fast track'. The court ordered that the matter be heard in fifteen days. Matthew had received the notice of hearing in the mail this Monday morning.

Matthew dialed DCP Commissioner Kevin Michaels. "Kevin. I got the notice on Sharpe today. It's a short order. The argument is in two weeks. We need to set up a meeting as soon as possible." The Commissioner agreed and also asked Matthew to contact the attorney general's office for assistance on the case. Matthew had Tracy get in touch with the attorney general's office. A quick connection was made and Matthew found himself on the phone with his old boss, Wallace Cartwright. They exchanged pleasantries and small talk. Matthew then turned the conversation to the Sharpe case. He gave Cartwright a thumb nail sketch of the case and then requested that someone from the attorney general's office be present at their case conference, which was set for tomorrow. He was surprised when the Attorney General said to him, "I'll be there myself. I need to be on top of this. This is a big issue for the future." Matthew thanked the Attorney General and happily concluded, "see you in the morning Wallace!"

He quickly dialed the Commissioner. "The Attorney General himself is coming tomorrow!", Matthew reported to Kevin Michaels. "Oh shit!", responded Michaels. "That doesn't make it sound to good. To have your old boss here makes it look like we're going to lose…but, I guess we might as well know right up front. So, I'll buy the donuts. What are Cartwright's favorite?", Michaels asked Matthew. Matthew chuckled and replied, "why 'Boston Creme', of course!". Kevin laughed and said, "of course! Then 'Boston Creme' it is!"

That evening Matthew and Adam were catching up on the day's events and Adam's seminar in California. Adam looked at Matthew and said, "how come you're so brown? Did you lay out in the sun all the while I was gone?" Matthew looked away for a moment and then replied, "yeah. I wanted to get a good tan. It's summertime you know." Adam responded curtly, "I know it's summer. It's also called skin cancer! I told you to cut that shit out!" Matthew quickly changed the subject to their upcoming 'couples dinner' in two weeks.

Their couples dinners were becoming a new tradition over the past year. But every time they scheduled one the guest list would grow. Janice and Jose were the staple of the group. Scott and now his 'main squeeze', as he called Andrew were regulars. Ted and Pete would try to come into the city for the dinners as well. Matthew always enjoyed their company, and especially liked Ted's famous desserts. Adam wanted to invite Dalton and Joseph this time. Matthew enjoyed their company as well. It was a match that Adam had put together and it was working out well. He took pride in this new relationship. Matthew thought that Joseph was a good friend for Adam. He was always there, in good times and in bad, just like Scott was for him. They would be friends forever, he thought. Matthew then said, "I want to invite Ken. He's got a new boyfriend named Alfie. I think they would have fun."

Adam looked up from the table with a disapproving look. "So when doesn't Ken have a new boyfriend? They never last. Plus, the list is too long. They'll have to come another time." Matthew was getting angry. "He's my friend. I want him here this time, not another time!" Adam shot back, "he's your old fuck buddy. You know he gets on my nerves. He's a bitchy queen! He can come over another time." Matthew raised his voice. His anger was clear. "Look! I said I want him here. No discussion. That's it!" Adam looked at Matthew. He could read his anger, so he acquiesced. "It's not worth fighting about. Just remind him that he has to make something to bring with him", replied Adam in a tone of defeat.

The next morning Matthew and Commissioner Michaels anxiously waited with their staff for the arrival of the legendary Attorney General. Matthew was staring out of the huge window of the Commissioner's office. The view was spectacular. The window captured most of the Boston skyline. Matthew's thoughts were drifted as he stared out the window. He was thinking of James Davenport. "How did I get myself into this? I'm becoming obsessed with him. I tape the goddamn soap opera just so I can watch him. I'm sure Adam thinks that's weird...or something's up...", Matthew mused. His commiserating was interrupted by Doris Albright, the Deputy Commissioner of DCP. "The Attorney General is here", she announced. "Show him in", said a sober Kevin Michaels.

Wallace Cartwright knew how to enter a room. Any room. He was a magnetic presence. As the Attorney General entered the spacious office of Kevin Michaels, he walked directly toward Matthew. He pumped Matthew's hand in his standard jovial greeting. Matthew thanked Wallace for coming to the meeting. "I'm glad to be here!", exclaimed the Attorney General.

Matthew ushered Wallace to the chair at the head of the table. He sat down next to his old boss on the right, while his current boss took the chair at the opposite end of the conference table. Other agency attorneys and senior staff sat on each side of the long cherry conference table. Matthew outlined the facts of the Sharpe case for all assembled. He then provided a brief overview of the legal issues that the case presented. "The appellate issue here is whether the state's intervention power to protect children can override parental choice regarding religious practices. This case squarely pits the public safety power of the government against religion. It is a classic case of separation of church and state.", said Matthew while flipping through the yellow legal pad in front on him.

He continued, "Now the statute, chapter 362, section 41 is not clear on this issue. The statute provides that parents can utilize spiritual healing and treatment for their children. But it is ambiguous. It does not explicitly differentiate between emergency or life threatening cases, versus routine illnesses that children get. However, because the statute specifically excepts out certain routine immunizations, it is a fair reading that the statute is only applicable to routine medical care. That it my interpretation on what the legislature intended in 1948 when the statute was authored. The only amendments came in the sixties, and those amendments were for further routine vaccinations and the like."

Matthew looked over his shoulder at the Attorney General. Wallace Cartwright was intently listening to his former assistant. Matthew went on. "As far as the case law, the only decision is the <u>Fulmante</u> case. It's a 1972 SJC decision, but it's not really on point. The court in that case upheld the exclusion for vaccinations for children for specific non-catagious diseases that were specifically enumerated in the statute. However, we can use this decision as some authority to support our argument. Our argument is that the statute is only applicable in routine, non-life threatening medical conditions. Now that's where were at. This is my analysis…it's not the only analysis. I'd like to hear from you about how we should tackle this case.", Matthew said to those assembled around the table.

The discussion began around the conference table. It was a lively and intelligent one. Kevin Michaels tried to guide the discussion. Michaels kept reiterating that if DCP's authority to intervene was not upheld in cases such as this, children would be put at risk. Cartwright became a passive observer of the discussion. He would occasionally take notes. Matthew watched his former boss during the discussion. Wallace seemed to be immensly enjoying the lively debate. As the conversation began to wind down after about 20 minutes, Matthew summarized. "We agree that DCP's authority to act has to be affirmed", Matthew began. "If it is not, then we are beginning to slide down a slippery slope that will put children at risk. We'll also have parents invoking bizarre religious beliefs as a way to justify child abuse." Matthew turned to the Attorney General and asked, "who do you think should take the lead on this case? Us or your office?"

Wallace Cartwright pushed against the table and slid his chair out. His magnificent presence towered over the room. He looked at Matthew and said, "I think you should take the lead Matthew. You have made a cogent and persuasive argument here today. You and your staff know the dangers better than anyone else if this case fails. I think you personally should make the argument to the seven old men up on the hill." With that, the Attorney General returned to his seat. Matthew blushed slightly and did not speak. Not a moment passed when Kevin Michaels chimed in, "I agree with the Attorney General. Matthew, I think you should argue this case." The meeting ended without much more discussion. Matthew would argue the case at the supreme court. Both the Commissioner and Attorney General offered any support to Matthew that he needed for this case. They were united in agreement that this was a monumental case for future child welfare practice. Matthew fondly said goodbye to Wallace. "How I miss that man!", he thought.

That evening while sitting in his home library, Matthew began to plot the case and the argument out. He called Octavia at home. Matthew told her that he was given the assignment to argue the Sharpe case in front of the state supreme court. He asked Octavia if she had time to offer a helping hand in his preparation. She responded, "of course I do. You know I always have time for you!" Matthew wanted an objective, out of agency opinion about his strategy for the case. He could think of no other lawyer he respected more. They agreed to meet on Thursday. As their conversation was concluding, Octavia added, "…oh, by the way, the Martin case is settling. The city made a decent offer and Arthur is going to take it." Matthew replied, "that's good!" Octavia asked, "do you think Phillip would have thought I sold out?" Matthew assured her that their dear friend would not have thought that by accepting the settlement Octavia had sold out on the issue of gay bashing. "You did what your client wanted. There'll be another case just like it. It's only a matter of time. That statute has no teeth." Their conversation ended with confirmation of their meeting on Thursday.

The dinner party was a success, large group and all. The food and its presentation were wonderful. Ted had made a cake he called "Chocolate Decadence", which Matthew absolutely adored. It was full of fat and calories, but Matthew didn't care. He took a second piece. He would go to the gym an extra day to make up for it. "Rationalization, what a beautiful concept!", Matthew thought to himself.

Despite the success of the evening Matthew was preoccupied during most of it. His mind was alternating back and forth between the Sharpe case and James Davenport. "I've got to figure this out", he kept telling himself. When Matthew did pay attention during the party he noticed that Ken and Adam seemed to be getting along. "That's a relief!", he sighed. Matthew did not like that Adam and one of his closest friends could not get along. However, Matthew wondered if they were being civil to each other because of Ken's date, Alfie Stone. The attractive young reporter was enticing everyone with his stories about the city, crime and politics. He became the focus of the party that night. He was relishing all the attention and was one of the last persons to leave the party.

Two days before the argument was scheduled to be heard at the Supreme Judicial Court, Matthew's evening preparation was interrupted by a phone call. It was James Davenport. He was unexpectantly in Boston for the weekend. After saying "hello", Davenport asked Matthew, "where's your boyfriend?" Matthew replied that Adam was over his friend Joseph's house, and then angrily said, "I told you not to call me at home. It's too risky!" James Davenport replied, "relax for Christsake! He's not home. You should get rid of him anyway. Obviously he's not satisfying you or you wouldn't be so quick to run to me!" Matthew paused momentarily and then replied in a curt tone, "you called me. I didn't call you." Davenport said in return, "that's right I called you. I'm at the Four Seasons, room 1154. Are you coming over or what?" Matthew said, "I don't think so. I've got too much to do. I have to argue a major case in court in two days...plus, I don't know when Adam will be back." James replied, "well I'm here if you change your mind. A little sex might do you good...calm you down!", and then he hung up the phone.

Matthew did change his mind. About forty five minutes later he found himself in the midst of wild sex with James Davenport in the hotel room. The sex was very enjoyable and did provide a much needed stress outlet for Matthew. They didn't talk very long after their encounter. James apologized somewhat for making the comments he did about Adam. Matthew didn't respond to the apology. Matthew rushed back home from the hotel. His "catholic guilt", as he called it set in. The cheating on Adam had to stop. "This is ridiculous", he thought. "I'm just feeding my ego with mister gorgeous. It's just sex…there's no future here. I'm just getting my rocks off with a hot guy…" He sped down Mass. Ave. towards home, all the while beating himself up over the just concluded sexual encounter.

When Matthew got home he could not concentrate so he decided not to return to his work. He went to bed. He wasn't in bed ten minutes when he heard Adam come in the house. A few moments later when Adam crawled into the bed beside him, Matthew pretended to be asleep. Adam reached for Matthew's penis and began to stroke it. Matthew mumbled, "I'm really tired…how about tomorrow", and then rolled away from Adam. Adam decidely turned over with a grunt of disapproval.

"May it please the court", began a well dressed Matthew Alexander Schipani in the traditional greeting offered by lawyer's to the highest court in the jurisdiction. The Sharpe case was beginning. Matthew was standing at the lectern of the Massachusetts Supreme Judicial Court. The seven justices of the court richly robed, were staring down at him. This court was truly supreme. Although newly erected last year, it maintained the majesty of an old courtroom. No veneer furniture here. Rich, deep mahogany tables and a large judge's bench behind which the justices presided in their maroon leather chairs. "This is how the supreme court should look.", thought Matthew.

The time allotted for his argument was only fifteen minutes. He had prepared for almost a month and it all came down to these fifteen minutes ahead of him. But nothing goes as prepared. The first ten minutes of Matthew's time was consumed by questions from the bench. The justices peppered him one after the other with questions. They seemed focused on the state's intrusion upon the freedom of religion. Matthew began to feel a tone of hostility from the bench.

The supreme court was a "hot bench", which meant that they asked a lot of questions. Today it seemed "hotter" than normal.

The light on his lectern flipped on. This meant he only had two minutes left in which to conclude his argument in support of the state's position. Seeing the light, Matthew shifted his argument from the last question by Justice Schwartz. "Your honors. If I may summarize for the court.", he stated. Firmly Matthew went on, "the state Division of Child Protection receives over seventy five thousand calls of suspected child abuse each year. The child protective social workers investigate these calls and they take action to protect the children of the Commonwealth. At times that action must include the removal of children from their parents custody to insure that there will be no more abuse, neglect or even death. These are among the facts of the case presented here today. Megan Sharpe was in severe medical distress when the DCP social workers made their decision. The evidence at the trial court level showed that but for the actions of the social workers, the child would have died. Child protective social workers took protective action. They had no choice. The parents would not allow medical attention. The child needed this attention. The social workers brought the child to receive that life saving medical attention."

Matthew quickly continued on. "The statute at issue strikes the appropriate balance. It recognizes the freedom of religion and religious beliefs in a modern society. However, it also recognizes the wonders of modern medicine. The statute only provides that religious treatment and exemptions may be utilized in routine, non-contagious and non-life threatening situations. It does not authorize a parent to place their religious beliefs on their child to the child's medical detriment. It does not authorize the sacrifice of children in the name of religious freedom. Rather, it chooses the middle road. It respects parental choice, while insuring that children receive required medical treatment. The absence of any exemption for extreme medical conditions or life threatening illnesses, is a clear message from the legislature that those conditions are not within the scope of the statute." He took a breath and continued. "In <u>Prince vs. Massachusetts</u>, the Court held many years ago that parents do not have a right to make martyrs of their children. This was what the parents were attempting to do here with the child. <u>Prince</u> remains controlling law, and the Court should following the reasoning of <u>Prince</u> and hold it controlling in the instant matter."

"In conclusion, the actions of the DCP representatives were well within the scope of the government's parens patriae power to act in the best interests of children when their parents cannot through negligence, inability or refusal to do so. To allow parents to invoke religious beliefs to the detriment of their child's health or survival would be contrary to the strong public policy interests of this Commonwealth in protecting children. We urge that this court affirm the action of the trial court, and by doing so, affirm the Commonwealth's history of protecting children. Thank you your honors." Matthew concluded as the red light on the lectern went on. He had made his argument just within the time frame set by the court.

Three months passed when the call came from chief clerk Marilyn Whately. The Sharpe decision was completed and would be issued at two o'clock. Matthew decided that he himself would go pick up the decision. He didn't want anyone else to see if before he had the chance. The bench had been hostile. The decision could go either way, and Matthew wanted to be prepared before it became public record. As the clerk handed Matthew a certified copy of the decision he thanked her and quickly walked away. He found a secluded corner in the grand hallway of the court building. Matthew opened the manila envelop and pulled out the decision. It was a long decision, about twenty type written pages. Matthew flipped to the back page of the decision. He focused on the last few sentences in the final paragraph. The decision stated, "...for the reasons outlined above, we hold here today that the actions of the Division of Child Protection were within their statutory mandate. These actions, and in particular the removal of the child from her parent's custody and subsequent authorization of medical treatment, did not violate the religious freedoms of the Appellants as guaranteed by the First Amendment and Article I of the Massachusetts constitution. The welfare and protection of the children of this Commonwealth are the paramount considerations of this court. They outweigh any religious choice of a parent, especially when that religious choice causes harm or possible death to a child. Accordingly, the trial court decision is affirmed."

Matthew smiled. He put the decision back into the envelope. He couldn't have said it any better. Justice for children had been served this day in Massachusetts.

CHAPTER 10

TIME TO PUT THINGS IN ORDER

October 1992

It had been a nasty break up, times two. First, Matthew and James Davenport decided that their relationship had to end. The distance and the fact that it was an affair with sex as its focus, just meant it couldn't go on anymore. But even though James agreed that it had to end, he was still angry with Matthew. He called him a "wimp" and told him if he was a "real man" he would "dump" Adam. But Matthew wasn't prepared to do that. He and Adam had too much together. They had been through so much. The good and bad times. They had a history together. Even though Matthew had a sexual relationship with James, when it came to Adam it was more than sex. He truly loved Adam. But he also knew that he had to tell Adam about James. He owed that to Adam and to the relationship.

The evening that Matthew chose to tell Adam about James began routinely as many others did. They completed dinner when Matthew explained they needed to talk. Matthew disclosed his relationship with James Davenport. Adam at first did not seem surprised. But as the conversation went on Adam began to become angrier and angrier. He stormed out of the room and went for a long walk. Matthew waited up for awhile, but eventually went to sleep alone. The next day Adam told Matthew that they needed to talk. He decided that he was moving out. The relationship was over. Matthew was astonished at Adam's quick decision to end the relationship. It was not the response he expected. Yet, Adam would not waiver. He was firm, and he was leaving Matthew.

Adam moved out the following week. As he was bringing his final items to the car he turned to Matthew and slowly said, "I am so disappointed in you. Here you are, a successful lawyer, with lots of friends and a wonderful family. You had everything. We had everything. We had so much together. But you couldn't keep your dick in your pants! You disgust me. I never want to see you or talk to you again!" Then Adam reached up and slapped Matthew across the face and walked out. Matthew stood there dumbfounded.

The slap did not hurt, but the shock of it did. Adam and Matthew had never had any physical confrontation during their entire relationship. The slap was more symbolic than it was anything else. Matthew knew he was wrong. "I deserve to be slapped", he told himself. Matthew spent the rest of the weekend crying and smoking. Scott checked in on him periodically, but Matthew wanted to be alone. He had brought this on himself and he would have to deal with it by himself.

Three weeks later Scott and Matthew went to see Diana Ross in concert. She was performing with the Boston Symphony Orchestra, opening their holiday season concert series. This was Matthew's eleventh Diana Ross concert. He was thrilled as usual. However, when Diana sang *Endless Love*, Matthew broke down like a baby. The powerful song always made him misty eyed, but this time between the performance of the song and the ending of his relationship with Adam, Matthew's emotion could not be controlled. The separation was much more difficult than he ever thought it would be.

Matthew returned to his old pattern of having sex with Ken Rivers. He enjoyed sex with Ken, and although it had been many years since they had been together, Matthew found Ken as sexually exciting as ever. It was awkward at first, as they had moved beyond this part of their relationship. But Matthew's desire for sex was intense, and Ken was a comfortable partner. They were good friends who enjoyed each other's bodies and sex. There was no emotional attachment to the sex. It was fun. Matthew commented to Scott one evening after Ken left, "you know…he's as hot in bed as he was ten years ago." Scott sarcastically responded, "well he gets enough practice! I'm sure he's great!"

Matthew began to contemplate the idea of being single on a long term basis. He could never have another relationship like he did with Adam. He would never love someone so much and so deep. So, maybe being single was the way to survive in the gay world. Just be single, have a few men to safely fulfill your sexual needs and focus on other things in life. Then Matthew thought that this was a sad commentary on gay life. He had a true love at one time. It was possible in the gay world. Maybe it could happen again. Maybe not.

At work Matthew was facing a professional life without Kevin Michaels. The Commissioner was looking for new work. The Governor's race was in a few weeks and Stuart Alley was not running for reelection. Michaels knew that once a new Governor took control he would be out of a job. He was campaigning for Susan McGinty, but she was way down in the polls against Lloyd Dickerson. Michaels made it very clear that he wouldn't even try to keep his job if Dickerson got elected. "He's a goddamn bigot. I won't be associated with someone like that!", Michaels told Matthew and anyone else who would listen.

Lloyd Dickerson subsequently beat Susan McGinty in the election. However, his victory was by a closer margin than expected. The public had given up on the election. Many registered voters had decided to stay home rather than cast their ballots. Matthew's boss,

Kevin Michaels, tendered his resignation as Commissioner of DCP a week after the election.

The holiday season was particularly difficult for Matthew. It was his first Christmas alone in a long time. He didn't even bother to decorate, with the exception of his grandmother's porcelain Christmas tree which he put out on the mantle. It was more in her memory than in the Christmas spirit. Adam had dropped a Christmas gift off at Scott's apartment for Matthew. Matthew was embarrassed by this. Given the way their relationship ended and Adam's comments that he never wanted to see Matthew again, Matthew had not bought a gift for Adam. On Christmas Eve, Matthew tried to keep his mind off Adam. He focused on his sister Maria's new baby boy, Peter. Christmas in the Schipani family was also somber that year due to the absence of his brother Anthony. His brother was a reserve captain in the Air Force. He was not home for the holidays. He had been deployed right after Thanksgiving to the Middle East. He was a part of the crew that was enforcing the no-fly zone established after the Gulf War. The family did not know how long Anthony would remain in that global hot bed.

Matthew went to Dallas, Texas in February to visit an old friend from law school who had relocated there shortly after the bar exam. Matthew spent a great deal of time alone while visiting his friend Cathy Reed. She was an up and coming corporate lawyer in Dallas. She invited him to come visit as soon as she had heard about the breakup with Adam. One bright morning Matthew went out for a jog by himself with his headphones. He was listening to Bette Midler sing *Wind Beneath My Wings*. It reminded him of Phillip. His hero…his friend, his mentor. He smiled as the thought of their many dinners together during law school, their law practice together, and most importantly, the knowledge of life that Phillip shared with him.

Matthew also thought about Phillip's final days. He had done a good job of blocking out those painful memories in his mind during the past few years. But now as he jogged, he purposely chose to remember that time. He was able to put a different perspective on it. It was a good perspective, a healthy one. He thought about what a dear friend Phillip had been to him and how he in turn had been able to return that friendship by being with Phillip when he died. Matthew started to feel as if he was finally coming to terms with Phillip's death. Phillip was gone, but he was not forgotten. His memory would always live.

One night Cathy and Matthew decided to go to the Cedar Springs area to a gay bar. The bar was called *Trash Disco*. It specialized in disco songs from the seventies. Matthew was in heaven while the music played. He met a young man, at least ten years younger than him who tried to pick him up. He was very flattered. They danced a few dances but when the bar was closing Matthew politely turned down his offer to go home with him. Matthew knew that the ghost of Adam was still in his mind. Yes, he was having sex with Ken, but that was safe. This would be risky. He would feel as if he was cheating on Adam, even though they had been broken up for several months by now. As bizarre as this thought sounded, at some level it made sense to Matthew.

Matthew's last day in Dallas was spent at Dealey Plaza, where President Kennedy was assassinated. Matthew's first impression as he walked the grassy knoll was how small the area actually was. Television made things look so much bigger. As he stood in the middle of the street he looked up at the corner of the Texas Bookstore Depository where the gunshots supposedly came from. It just didn't seem right to Matthew. Then he looked over to his left and saw the fence behind the grassy knoll. That made more sense to him.

Matthew took the tour of the Bookstore building. It had been turned into a museum. The elevator went directly to the sixth floor where Lee Harvey Oswald supposedly shot the fatal bullets. Matthew gazed out of the window where the gun was to have been pointed. He had the view of the sniper. It was a bird's eye view of the street below. Matthew began to get an eerie feeling. This was the ground that Oswald walked on before being a part of one of the most disturbing crimes in this century. When Matthew walked out he signed the book that had been placed for visitors. He noticed in a child's handwriting on the page opposite his a message that said it all. "I'm sorry he shot you", wrote the little boy above his signature.

Driving back to Cathy's apartment Matthew was very quiet. He thought about how he had cried while standing in the plaza trying to imagine that horrible day in Dallas almost thirty years ago. He was too young to have known John F. Kennedy personally or to have voted for him. Yet, he knew of the legend. Matthew's mother had worked on President Kennedy's successful campaign. He did remember vaguely his mother crying as he and his father watched the black and white television reports of the assassination. To Matthew, John Kennedy stood for hope and a vision for a better world. Camelot had died that day in Dallas and with it the hope of a young generation.

Upon Matthew's return to work things at DCP seemed to be moving along routinely. The new Commissioner, Nicole Perkins and Matthew were getting along fine. But it certainly was not like when Kevin was at the helm of the agency. Matthew continued to enjoy the people he worked with, and Tracy always provided him with a warm smile that would make his day. Janice was now working in the same office as Matthew. She had been promoted once again. She was now the program director at DCP. Matthew particularly enjoyed the fact that he could see one of his dearest friends not only after hours, but during the work day.

Matthew also was spending more social time with Octavia and her husband Brandon. Matthew found them to be wonderful company. They would spend many an evening over a pot luck dinner and many glasses of wine, solving all the problems of the world. Octavia's practice continued to do well, but she admitted that she was lonely without Phillip and Matthew.

Matthew began dating another man. He was an attorney that Matthew had met at a gay bar association meeting right before he left for his vacation in Texas. Michael Bailey was two years older than Matthew. They had been on several dates, slept together once, but there were no "sparks" for Matthew. His mind and his heart still belonged to Adam. He knew this relationship was going nowhere, but he enjoyed the companionship.

He had only seen Adam once since their breakup and that was just by coincidence. Matthew had just completed an argument in the appeals court and was preparing to leave the clerk's office when Adam walked in. Matthew was taken back by seeing Adam, but politely said "hi", to which Adam replied the same. Matthew asked, "what are you doing here?". Adam responded that he and two other professors at the law school had filed an amicus brief on a case pending before the appeals court. That was the extent of their encounter. Matthew went home that night, visibly shaken and drank himself into a crying sleep.

Matthew also began to receive hang up phone calls at home in the middle of the night. He remembered how a few years back he had received disturbing threats over the telephone. He had changed his phone number then, and he decided to do the same now. At first he thought it might be Adam making the calls given their encounter. Then he realized that Adam would not resort to this. It was unlike him. But the calls were annoying and changing the number did the trick. The calls stopped.

Scott was single again and Matthew and he would joke about growing old and being alone. "We can buy a beach house and sit on a deck in rocking chairs looking out at the ocean", Scott told Matthew. Matthew wondered if this was a premonition of his future. Well, at least he would be with his best friend, he thought. Matthew also took his time alone to catch up on old friendships. He purposefully made a trip to the western part of the state to spend some time with Sharon and Louise. Their friendship had drifted apart over the years and Matthew was not going to let it get any further apart. They had been so good to him in his hour of need when he left Darren all those years ago. Matthew spent three enjoyable days with Sharon and Louise and their two adopted daughters, Nicole and Patricia.

A funeral brought Matthew and Adam together again. In the midst of death, Matthew and Adam's relationship was reborn. It was September, of course. That dreaded month for Matthew. September, the month their mutual friend Dalton Beauvais tragically died. Dalton had been coming out of an office building late at night in downtown Boston, when a drunk driver lost control of his car. The car jumped the sidewalk and hit Dalton. He never regained consciousness. Adam had called Matthew at work to tell him the bad news. They had not talked since their fortuitous meeting at the appeals court that day. Three days later they were at Dalton's funeral in Arlington. Adam sat beside his best friend Joseph in the front row of the church.

While the casket was wheeled out of the church at the end of the ceremony Adam had to hold Joseph up so that he could follow the casket down the aisle. Matthew watched Joseph and his ex-lover follow the casket. He thought about how short life was, and how tragic and testing it could be. He also thought about how much he admired Adam, who was standing right beside his friend in his hour of need. A few days after the funeral Matthew called Adam at the law school. "Do you think it would be possible for us to go out for a cup of coffee?", he asked. Adam accepted without hesitation.

Their coffee break was a sober one. They talked a great deal about Dalton and how Joseph was holding up. Matthew remarked about how short life was and how in the end all that matter was that people loved one another. Adam agreed, saying "sometimes tragedies like this put things in perspective. The little things in life don't matter anymore, including the mistakes you may have made. All that counts is if people are kind and good to one another." Matthew shook his head in agreement. He asked Adam if they could see each other again. They made a date for dinner the following week.

The following week, during their dinner date at Chez Pierre in Harvard Square, they talked about all aspects of their relationship, including the affair with James Davenport. They went for a walk after dinner on the exceptionally warm fall evening. They walked down by the river. The bright fall moon shined above the thin clouds in the sky. As they strolled along the Charles behind Harvard, Matthew stopped Adam and said, "do you think we could try it again?" Adam shrugged his shoulders quietly saying in response, "I don't know. I'm not sure it would be the right thing to do. Then on the other hand maybe we should be together again. There's no doubt how much we care about each other. But, right now Matthew, I'm just not sure. I'm sorry I can't give you an answer". They continued to walk along the side of the river without further conversation.

Just before Thanksgiving Adam called Matthew. "I've thought about what you said a few weeks ago. I'm willing to try again if you are." Matthew beamed on the other end of the phone. "Yes, I am!", he cheerfully replied. Matthew sighed a huge sigh of relief. In a world where few get a second chance, he had just been given one. He was not only extremely happy, he was very thankful.

The next week after another dinner date Adam returned to Matthew's apartment. Diana greeted Adam with a high pitched bark. She had truly missed her friend, and now he was back home. That evening their sex was terrific, but Matthew took more comfort in the ability to fall asleep in the same bed with Adam and holding the man he truly loved as they fell off to sleep.

It had been a year since their separation, but Adam's return to the apartment and Matthew's life was easy. It seemed as if everything returned to normal. Matthew was upbeat again. His friends noticed a positive change. The holiday season this year was one of happiness. His mother and father were overtly expressive in their joy when Adam joined them for Christmas dinner.

The annual New Year's party at Ted and Pete's seemed like old times. It was a new beginning and Matthew was determined that this time he wasn't going to screw it up. The love of his life was back. The loss of Dalton had shown that life was too short to let go of what really mattered. What really mattered to Matthew was Adam. He was given a second chance. He was determined that this time it would work. Life was too short to let this relationship end again. Adam was his soulmate, the love of his life. He was going to do everything in his power to make sure that Adam and Matthew were together forever.

CHAPTER 11

NOMINATION

June 1994

It had been three months to the day since that fateful call in the middle of the night announcing that Wallace Cartwright was dead. Matthew was staring off into space and looking out the window of his office when Tracy announced that the Governor of Massachusetts was on hold for Matthew. "Good afternoon, your excellency", Matthew forced himself to say into the telephone. How he despised this man, and yet he had to be polite. After all, he was the Governor of Massachusetts.

"Matthew", began Governor Lloyd Dickerson, "I'd like to meet with you to discuss your future in state government." Matthew cautiously responded, "is there something wrong?" A lightened voice of the Governor responded, "no, the exact opposite!" Matthew was scheduled to meet with the Governor on Thursday, "2 p.m. sharp", said the Governor. "You know how I can't stand it when people are late. So make sure you're here on time." Matthew dutifully responded, "I will be."

That evening Matthew explained to Adam about his telephone call from the Governor. Adam held onto his theory about the death of Wallace Cartwright. "Remember?", Adam began. "Remember the day he died. Remember how I told you there was some conspiracy behind Cartwright's death. Well maybe fatso has unlocked it and that's what the meeting is all about!", concluded an excited Adam. Matthew looked at Adam with a doubting face. "Oh please…there is no conspiracy", he told Adam. Adam wanted to go on with his conspiracy theory, but the look on Matthew's face indicated he would have none of it.

Matthew had not divulged to anyone, even Adam, the true circumstances of how Attorney General Cartwright had died. Rather, he went along with the public story that Wallace had died from natural causes. He did so not because he liked Lloyd Dickerson, but rather because he revered Wallace Cartwright. Wallace deserved this, thought Matthew. He should remain a hero even after death. Heroes don't overdose on medication. The secret would remain safe. Matthew would not let the true circumstances of Wallace's death, no matter how innocent they were, to come from his lips. It was the one thing he and Lloyd Dickerson agreed upon.

While Matthew was driving into work he remembered he needed to call Ted about his airplane tickets. He had planned to leave Friday morning to for Houston, Texas. He was attending a three day national conference on child abuse. Matthew was among the many speakers at the conference. His panel was to address criminal sentences for children who were the perpetrators of abuse. He was looking forward to the conference. He dialed the phone from his car. The novelty of the car phone had quickly worn off. It was no longer a status symbol. Everyone had a car phone these days. It was almost an essential. Matthew viewed it as another accessory for the "info '90's", as he called the decade. He waited on hold for Ted to pick up. Matthew looked at his beeper sitting on the passenger seat. Another accessory for the decade. Matthew had a theory about everything. He had decided that the 1990's was the information decade, like the '70's was the "we" decade and the '80's was the "me" decade. Information itself had become a commodity. Whoever had the most information on any given subject had the power, and won. Access to that information via computers, car phones, faxes, etc. defined who moved ahead and who fell behind, according to Matthew's theory. He was determined that he would not fall behind so he bought into purchasing all the essential accessories. Ted picked up the phone. "It's all set, Matthew. You leave at 6:30 in the morning. I've booked your seats as well." Matthew thanked his friend and recradled the car phone. Traffic was moving very slowly this morning. A typical Cambridge to Boston commute. Thirty minutes to go just over three miles. Matthew sat at the light and lit a cigarette. He made a deal with himself that he would only smoke three today.

The car phone rang while he waited. Matthew picked it up. It was Shannon Watson, the reporter and his friend. "Where are you going Thursday afternoon?", she asked Matthew. Matthew responded, "is this a friend question or an official question?" Shannon gleefully responded, "both!" Matthew, ever the attorney and bureaucrat, who mastered the art of answering a question with a question, asked, "where did you hear I was going on Thursday?" Shannon knew Matthew was being evasive. Her voice reflected her impatience. "I heard you're meeting with fat boy", said Shannon so irreverently referring to the Governor of Massachusetts. "Oh really?, replied Matthew. "What are we meeting about?", he asked. Shannon responded, "About you becoming the Attorney General!"

Matthew dropped the car phone from his hand. He swerved to avoid hitting a parked car on Memorial Drive. He reached for the dangling phone by its cord and pulled it back up to his ear. "Are you there?", he heard Shannon Watson inquire. "Yeah, yeah, I'm here", replied Matthew. There was a momentary pause and then Matthew asked, "can you meet me for coffee in about fifteen minutes?" Shannon said, "sure. Scott's place?" Matthew responded, "that's fine. See you in fifteen." He called work and said he would be a little late. Tracy's laugh appeared too knowing for comfort.

When he arrived at his best friend's coffee shop Shannon was already seated drinking a cup of coffee and munching on a bagel. She and Scott were in deep conversation as Matthew joined them at the table. "Good Morning", he said to them. Scott motioned over to a waiter. "Get Matthew a cup of mocha java and a blueberry muffin, please.", he said to the waiter, anticipating Matthew's order. Scott said, "do you mind if I sit with you a bit?" Shannon shook her head saying, "I don't mind. It's good for my image. To be seen with two hot men. Of course neither of you could give a shit I spent three hundred bucks on this outfit!". Matthew chuckled and responded, "oh I care honey. The outfit enhances your voluminous breasts!" Scott laughed so hard he began to choke. He reached for Shannon's coffee and took a gulp.

Shannon, the consummate reporter changed the tone of the conversation almost immediately. "So what are you and the gov going to talk about tomorrow?", she asked Matthew. He knew that the cat and mouse game of answering a question with a question would not work in person with Shannon. So he decided to tell her the truth, which was like telling her nothing. "I honestly don't know", stated Matthew. He added, "he told me to be there at two and so I'm going to be there at two on Thursday." Shannon looked at Matthew closely. He knew she was trying to read his face to detect any falsity. She could see none. He really didn't know why he was meeting with the Governor. So Shannon decided to tell him the "scuttlebutt" that she had heard through the grapevine. "My understanding", began Shannon, "is that fat boy has scheduled a press conference for 3 o'clock on Thursday. He's meeting with you and Gerry Kilpatrick before the press conference. Between the two of you, one is going to be nominated by fat boy for Attorney General. Rumor has it that it's you big guy!".

Matthew looked at Scott without saying a word. Scott smiled and raised his eyebrows. Matthew's face had an expression of confusion on it. He looked at Shannon and said, "I don't get it. What benefit would Dickerson get by nominating me?" Shannon replied, "maybe he thinks you're the best one for the job?" Matthew looked at her, smirked and said, "c'mon Shannon. We both know how this Governor operates. There's an agenda here, but I don't know what it is. If all this is true, which I highly doubt anyway...but for the sake of argument, if it's true, what political gain would Dickerson have by nominating me? He's not exactly fond of 'those queer boys', as he called us last year. Remember?" There was a pronounced pause in the conversation. Shannon grabbed a piece of Matthew's half-eaten muffin. She took a sip of her coffee and said, "I think you hit the nail on the head. Fat boy wants the gay vote. This is a way to get it. You are a respected, openly gay attorney. You're active in a lot of community organizations. You've been around for awhile. You even worked for the legend himself!" Matthew interrupted, "no. I don't think..."

Shannon put up her hand and spoke again rapidly. "Let me finish. This is perfect for fatso. You have the name recognition. You have no skeletons in the closet, for lack of a better phrase. He nominates you and come election time when he's pressed about his 'queer boys' remark, he points to you and he's absolved. That's how the fat wonder thinks." Scott interjected, "too neat." Matthew looked at him and said, "I agree. It's too superficial. Too obvious. The public will see through it and you guys in the press will tear him up!" Scott shook his head in agreement with his friend's analysis.

Shannon turned and grabbed her purse off the back of the chair. "Yes, I know its obvious. But fat boy does things like this all the time. Remember the power plant issue in Hampden last month? He's not the brightest bulb, pardoning my play on words. He thinks this will help him. That's why he's doing it." Matthew once again shook his head "no", but Shannon persisted. "Look", she said commandingly, "I know politics." Matthew went to say something but Shannon once again raised her hand. "Let me finish", she said and then went on. "Fat boy knows he's got to get as many votes as possible. He's got to cross every demographic line and pull a few votes from here and there. If he doesn't, he's out, and he doesn't want that. So he gets you to promote him in the gay community. Gay people vote, they're concerned about the future. They'll show up at the polls. If he can get the gay vote it will swing him into victory lane and that's all that fatso cares about."

Matthew looked at her and responded, "well, I still think it's shallow. But if that it what is his motivation, I don't think I'm the one. I'm not going to be a quiet 'queer boy' for anybody, including Lloyd Dickerson." Scott responded, "you go girl!" with a laugh. Matthew and Shannon laughed also. Matthew said, "speaking of going, I've got to get going." Shannon stood and so did Matthew. "I should go too", she said. "Let me walk you out", Matthew replied. Shannon leaned over and hugged Scott, "I'm waiting for that shrimp dinner you promised!", she said. Scott said he would call her. They both waved to Scott and walked together out of the coffee shop.

Shannon was parked next to Matthew in the lot. As he opened his Volvo door, Shannon said, "don't worry. I won't crucify you in the paper if this happens. You know that don't you?" Matthew smiled, "of course I do. You have always been good to me." Shannon replied, "I could be better if you let me!". Matthew laughed loudly said, "you are the horniest woman I have ever met!" They gave each other a hug and Matthew drove away to his office.

Thursday arrived and Matthew found himself sitting in the overstuffed, puffy wing back chair in front of the Governor's desk. Matthew was staring at the portrait of James Michael Curley behind Governor Dickerson's desk. The former mayor of Boston, Governor of Massachusetts and outlaw, watched over the shoulder of the latest occupant of the corner office. Matthew found Curley to be fascinating. As he stared into Curley's eyes, he heard the door open behind him. He stood, turned to greet Governor Lloyd Dickerson who was extending his hand. The handshake seemed weak to Matthew. "Thank you for coming. Please sit.", instructed the Governor. Matthew sat down and watched the Governor strut around the desk to his chair. Matthew focused on the 'beer belly' of Lloyd Dickerson protruding over his belt. "Can't he afford a tailor?", thought Matthew as Dickerson sat down.

"Well, I guess you're wondering why I summonsed you.", said the Governor to Matthew. "Yes, I was curious", responded Matthew. The Governor began, "well, it goes like this. Wallace is dead. You know that. Bradford is over there playing attorney general. I need him here. He needs to help me run the ship. Plus there's an election coming up in a few years. He needs to take care of that too. So anyway, I was thinking. Who would Cartwright want to fill out his term? So I did some research. Well, actually Eunice did it, but anyway…" The buzzer on the Governor's phone rang and interrupted him. He raised a finger, "Excuse me", said Lloyd Dickerson. The Governor picked up the receiver.

Matthew looked behind Dickerson. He was drawn to the portrait eyes of the long deceased Curley. He heard Dickerson mumbling on the phone, but Matthew wasn't paying attention. He kept looking at the portrait. Dickerson' sudden raising of his voice startled Matthew. Dickerson yelled into the phone, "tell the bitch to get it done by Friday or her hot black ass will be on the curb looking for a job." The Governor slammed the phone down. He looked up at Matthew and guffawed saying, "affirmative action…causes more problems than its worth!" The Governor shook his head and leaned back in his tall chair. He leaned with such force that Matthew wondered if the chair would hold his large girth. The momentary thought of the chair collapsing under the Governor made Matthew smile.

"So where was I?", asked the Governor. "Oh yeah", he began. "Wallace…so Wallace is dead. I need an Attorney General. So I had Eunice pull your file. You didn't do that bad when you were over there with Wallace. You lost Atchinson, but anyone would have lost that mess. But you won Scarletti. Now that was pretty good. I'm sure those guys cooling their jets in Walpole aren't very happy with you.

Since you returned to DCP you've been keeping that place out of the papers. Not bad…"

The Governor leaned back in his chair once again. He clasped his hands together with a smile on his face. "So here's the deal", he said to Matthew. "I nominate you for Attorney General. You get the job, you pick whatever agenda you want. I'll make sure you get your budget requests and all that stuff…" Matthew interrupted, "for what in return?", he asked. The Governor paused and then said, "the homosexual vote. I need it to be re-elected. Goddamn liberals. They think I'm too conservative. I really don't mind you people. I just get a little uncomfortable around a lot of homosexuals. But I've always been nice to you Matthew haven't I?" Matthew confusingly looked at the Governor and shrugged his shoulders.

After a few silent moments passed, Matthew asked, "Am I suppose to hide that I'm gay? Because if that's what you want, I can't do it." The Governor boisterously replied, "Oh no…no. I'm not asking for that. I'm just asking for your support in the next election." Matthew sat quietly and looked at the Governor. He was thinking, "is this a sell out or an opportunity?" He wasn't really too sure of his answer, but he decided that the opportunity was there. He should take advantage of the opportunity. If Dickerson became an asshole, he would just resign, thought Matthew.

Matthew waited a few moments to ponder and to let Dickerson realize that he wasn't going to just jump at the job offer. Then Matthew asked, "I'll have firing and hiring authority over the whole office as well?" Dickerson replied, "of course." Matthew asked, "will I have the ability to set out legislative agendas that may run counter to yours?" Dickerson rubbed his chin and then replied, "I don't want to intrude on your ability to set your agenda. I would only ask that you give me the courtesy of letting me know what you will be setting out before you do it." Matthew replied, "does that mean you would have the right to veto it, so to speak?" Dickerson responded, "no, no…I just want to be prepared. I don't want us publicly disagreeing. It wouldn't look good if the man I made attorney general ran diametrically opposed to me on certain issues. I'm just asking for the courtesy call."

Matthew sat quietly again for a minute or two. He sat up in the chair and looked at Dickerson, then looked at Curley, and back at Dickerson. "Okay. I accept your offer.", he told the Governor. "Wonderful! Wonderful!", exclaimed Lloyd Dickerson. They stood up and shook hands. Dickerson then said, "I have an idea…yes! Let me be spontaneous! I'm going to call a news conference in a half hour. Let's announce it today!"

Dickerson motioned Matthew to sit again. "I'll get my press secretary. Let's do it! Is that okay with you?" Matthew responded calmly, "that's fine." Dickerson galloped out of the office to the outer office. Matthew could overhear him commanding his staff about whether the press room was set up and ready. While sitting in the inner office Matthew remembered his conversation a few days ago with Shannon Watson. Dickerson had already scheduled a press conference for 3 o'clock. "Great way to start a working relationship, with a lie", thought Matthew.

Dickerson came back into the office. "It's a go", he told Matthew. "We'll do it in about fifteen minutes. I'll have Jacob bring you down when everyone is ready. I have your bio sheet. Here's a copy. If anything is wrong, correct it and hand it to me before I begin to speak. Any questions?", hurriedly asked the Governor. Matthew asked if he could use a phone. The Governor brought him to a small sitting room off the office. "Don't be long", he warned Matthew as he closed the door to the room.

Matthew called Adam at the law school. His office said he was in class. Matthew said it was an emergency and he needed to be interrupted. Adam came to the phone shortly thereafter. He immediately inquired, "is your father all right?" The memories of Franco's bypass surgery were still fresh, even in Adam's mind. Matthew said, "he's fine. Turn on Cable News at three. You'll want to see it. Please call Scott and Janice and ask them to do the same." Adam replied quizzically, "okay. You want to tell me what's going on?" Matthew said, "no. Watch the news. It'll be fun!" Matthew then dialed his parents in the Berkshires. His brother Anthony picked up the phone. He must be visiting, thought Matthew. "Are Mom and Dad home?", Matthew asked. His brother said they were outside in garden. "Tell them to watch Cable News at three. You watch it too. I think you'll like the news." His brother said, "okay" and Matthew hung up the phone. Matthew got up and walked back into the Governor's office. A man introduced himself as Jacob. "They're ready. Follow me please", he said to Matthew.

Matthew met the Governor in the hall outside the press room. He followed the Governor through the door into the auditorium. Coming in the opposite door he could see Bradford Collins and the Lieutenant Governor. They all ascended the staging behind the podium. Matthew surveyed the crowd of reporters. He saw Shannon Watson in the second row. When their eyes connected she gave him the "thumbs up" sign. Matthew smiled. He also saw Alfie Stone, the reporter who his friend Ken had dated a few times.

The Governor began his remarks, "My dear friends in the media…". "That's an oxymoron", thought Matthew as he turned his head to pay attention to the Governor. Dickerson went on beginning his statement as he did all his press conferences. "I have a brief announcement and there will be no questions to follow. I have the pleasure today to announce to you that I am sending the name of Matthew Alexander Schipani to the senate as my nominee for the next Attorney General of Massachusetts. Many of you know Attorney Schipani, who is standing here to my right. Matthew Schipani served as a deputy under our dear Attorney General Wallace Cartwright. In fact, it was Wallace who first spotted this bright young man and recruited him right out of law school. Attorney Schipani was responsible for single handily bringing down the Scarletti gang in Worcester when he was working for Wallace."

Dickerson continued on, "For the last five years Attorney Schipani has been the chief legal counsel of the Division of Child Protection. He has been a leader among child advocates. In fact, he's on his way to Houston, Texas tomorrow morning to be one of the principle lecturers at a national conference on child abuse. Attorney Schipani is responsible for the passage of the 1989 statute which increased the penalties for perpetrators of child abuse in Massachusetts. I believe that Matthew Alexander Schipani will be a strong and energetic Attorney General. That is why I have selected him. He will keep true to Wallace Cartwright's vision of justice. A vision that I have always shared in. Therefore, I urge the state senate to rapidly confirm this talented man as the next Attorney General of Massachusetts. I now present to you Attorney Matthew Alexander Schipani."

Matthew shook the Governor's hand. He had not prepared any remarks, so he would have to shoot from the hip. The flashbulbs and the camera lights were blinding to him. He began, "I would like to thank his excellency, the Governor for the honor he has bestowed upon me. I accept this nomination with gratitude and humility. To be called to fill in the shoes of our dear friend…my dear friend, Wallace Cartwright, is an immeasurable task. But I promise you and the people of Massachusetts that I will do my best to measure up to the standards and integrity that the late Attorney General established. I will be happy to meet with the press when I return from Texas next week. Today I just want to express my thanks to the Governor and my hope that if confirmed, the people of Massachusetts will find me a faithful and diligent civil servant. Thank you very much."

Matthew stood back from the podium. Bradford Collins came forward and said, "thank you everyone. Good day." Matthew turned and waved as he walked off the staging. He heard what sounded like a familiar voice among those yelling questions say, "don't you think a faggot's a little wimpy compared to Wallace Cartwright?" He turned briefly, but Governor Dickerson grabbed his arm and continued to escort Matthew to the door.

While walking down the hall Matthew in an irritable tone said to the Governor, "did you hear that question? It's started already. I hope you're prepared!" The Governor stopped walking and said, "I'm prepared or I wouldn't have nominated you. I can deal with it. Can you?" Matthew shook his head 'yes'. The Governor then said, "I want you here Tuesday morning when you return from Texas." Matthew replied he would be there, shook the Governor's hand and linked up with Shannon Watson who was coming down the hall. She gave him a big hug and they walked out the State House door together. Matthew asked, "did I do all right? He didn't tell me that I was going to speak!" Shannon replied, "you did fine." Matthew then asked, "who made the faggot remark?" Shannon smirked and said, "Alfie Stone. Ironic isn't it? He's the biggest queen I've ever seen!"

When Matthew returned to his office at DCP he was greeted with a standing ovation by his staff and led by Tracy. She came up to him and gave him a big bear hug. "I'm so happy for you!", Tracy exclaimed. Steven Rusk, a lawyer in the office popped open a bottle of champagne and began pouring. The hastily put together celebration was enjoyable for Matthew.

That evening Matthew, Adam, Janice, Jose and Scott enjoyed dinner at Matthew's favorite Italian restaurant in the North End. La Napoli was an exclusive restaurant that Matthew had discovered shortly after he moved to Boston from the west. Ever since he was a regular patron, Guiseppi, the owner gave Matthew the traditional italian kiss on the cheeks as he welcomed them for dinner. "I saw you on TV today. Such a handsome boy…you do a good job for us, won't you?", asked Guiseppi. Matthew replied that he would try his best. Matthew ordered his regular at La Napoli, mussels over a bed of linguine with red sauce. La Napoli's food was almost as good as his mothers. Almost.

When they returned to the house Matthew's answering machine had twelve calls on them. Adam wrote down the calls, but Matthew decided there was only one more person he wanted to talk to that evening. He called his parents. His father told him how proud he was of him. Rosa, his mother, cried on the phone as she expressed her joy and pride. His sister Maria and her husband were also at his parents. They too joined in congratulating Matthew. Matthew promised to come and visit once he returned from Houston next week.

Matthew took the time in Houston not only to learn more about child abuse, but also to reflect on the major change in his life and the awesome responsibilities that he would be assuming if his nomination was approved. Apparently his colleagues at the conference believed he would be confirmed. His placard on the dais entitled him as the "Attorney General Designee" of Massachusetts. On the second day of the conference Matthew took advantage of the early recess to get some exercise. He decided to go running in Memorial Park. This popular park, set in Houston's downtown area was famous for its beauty and the fact that former President Bush was a frequent jogger there. Matthew's jog was invigorating for him. It gave him time to think about the road ahead. He would be trading his privacy for a very public life. The whole issue of his sexuality would become public knowledge throughout Massachusetts. He was sure that the local tabloids would have a field day with his sexual orientation. But Matthew decided the loss of privacy was worth it. If this happened he would have the opportunity to make many changes. "The opportunity to do good.", as Phillip used to tell him during their conversations about what the real role of a lawyer in society was. The opportunity was too big not to have seized it. The loss of privacy was clearly outweighed by the possibility of becoming a successful gay leader. This was a role that Matthew always aspired to, and now it was at his front door.

That evening Matthew took a raincheck on the dinner dance party so that he could spend more time alone. He walked around the Market Square area of downtown Houston. He was struck by how clean the downtown area was in comparison to downtown Boston. But, downtown Houston was a daytime downtown. By night, most of the streets were vacant. This evening he only saw a few people out walking. Matthew walked into a small narrow bar in the Market Square area. He later learned that it was the oldest bar in Houston, having been built in the 1800's.

Matthew sat alone at the bar and ordered his second draft beer. In the background the song, *Someone To Watch Over Me*, was playing on the jukebox. It set the tone for this comfortable, intimate setting. The orange chandelier lamps provided dim lighting which accented the relaxed atmosphere. Matthew was very calm, enjoying his solitude. He focused on the large portrait of a grand southern belle that adorned the bar wall. The worn portrait illustrated a woman of splendor, from another place and time. The memory of this evening would become his most enjoyable one for the conference in Houston. Much more than the substance of the conference, Matthew would recall the solitude of the weekend as the most enriching for him. It gave him time to strategize for the chaotic future that certainly was waiting for him at home. It also gave him time to be thankful for the chance he was given.

As Matthew got off the plane at Logan Airport in Boston he was greeted by a group of reporters. "No", he didn't have any comment. "Obviously, I haven't read the articles. I have been in Texas for four days.", he told the reporters. "Yes. I would be happy to meet with you tomorrow to discuss it.", said Matthew as he waited for the luggage to come off the plane. Adam met him outside in the parking lot. Matthew was surprised when Adam offered to drive, he knew how much he hated the city traffic.

Matthew was greeted at home by a barking Diana. He hugged and kissed his now graying dog. "Want a soda or something?", asked Adam. "Yes, please.", replied Matthew. Adam handed him a soda and a glass. "Thanks", replied Matthew. They sat in the office library of the house as Matthew went through the mail that came over the past few days. Adam said to him, "I cut out all the articles about you and saved them. They are on the credenza.", said Adam pointing. Matthew turned around and retrieved the articles. There were nine of them. Adam said, "the one about your mother is the best!" Matthew looked perplexed and said, "my mother?" Adam replied, "yeah, they tracked her down outside the Red Lion Inn and cornered her for an interview. It's on the bottom. She was great…read it."

Matthew flipped to the bottom of the pile. He pulled out the article. The headline read, "Attorney General Designee's Mother Says Sexual Preference Doesn't Matter". Matthew began to read the article. Only two paragraphs into it he began to smile. His mother Rosa was no wallflower. She told the press that they were "ridiculous" bringing up the issue of Matthew's sexual preference. Rosa went on to say what Matthew did "in his home has nothing to do with his ability to be a great Attorney General. He will be a great one, too.", she concluded. Rosa accused the press of being "absurd" and going to any lengths for copy, including, "driving all the way out here to the Berkshires to bother an old woman."

Matthew read the rest of the articles as well. They were a mixture of praise and criticism. The Boston Chronicle did not even raise the issue of sexual preference. That paper, which was usually the standard by which all others were gauged, gave a fair accounting. The paper indicated that Matthew was a skilled attorney, with wide experience in government service. The paper did however, express a concern that his young age may be a factor against him. But the paper encouraged the senate to approve his nomination.

The Boston Gazette's two articles focused completely on the issue of homosexuality and how it affected Matthew's ability to be an effective attorney general. What angered Matthew the most about these articles is that their criticism and assertion that his sexual preference disqualified him as Attorney General, were penned by Alfie Stone. Stone, a gay man who had dated Matthew's friend, Ken Rivers. Stone, a gay man who had been a dinner guest in Matthew's home. Now, Alfie Stone was one of Matthew's leading critics. "It's great to have fighting from inside your group.", said Matthew to Adam.

Finally, Shannon Watson's articles were as she promised. Writing for the Boston Ledger, the conservative paper in the Boston area, Watson and the editor of the paper declared that "the sexual preference of Matthew Schipani is irrelevant to this ability to be Attorney General of this Commonwealth." In fact, the article referred to Rosa Schipani's interview and agreed that the press was being "absurd" in raising this issue. The paper strongly supported Matthew's nomination, "on the merits of his performance as a respected attorney in this state."

Shannon's articles were probably the most important, thought Matthew. Her paper had a large and broad readership, despite its conservative leanings. Overall, thought Matthew, the press was good. But he found himself focused again on Alfie Stone's articles. He could not get beyond his anger about them. "Talk about selling out", Matthew said to Adam. "That's a true sell out. Abandon your brothers and sisters and join the bandwagon that discriminates against your kind. That's really sad!"

Matthew met with Governor Dickerson the following morning. The meeting with the Governor went better than he expected. He was concerned about the press, but Dickerson was not. In fact, Matthew noted that the Governor was in a better mood than he had ever seen him. He wasn't his cross, mean-spirited self. Matthew wondered what that meant. Governor Dickerson said to Matthew, "Senator Lee Danders will be your only problem at the confirmation hearing. So try to smooth him over before the hearing", advised the Governor. Matthew asked, "when do you think the hearings will be?" The Governor responded that he believed the hearings would be next week and may only take a day or two. "I think most people have their minds already made up. There is no need to worry about it. I wouldn't have nominated you if I didn't think you could be confirmed", Governor Dickerson told Matthew.

That evening Matthew and Adam were joined for dinner by a now single Scott and Adam's best friend, Joseph. Joseph was doing much better since losing Dalton in the accident. He even joked about dating again. Scott, on the other hand was not doing well about being single. He and his latest love had recently broke up. They realized that no matter how much they cared about each other, they had outgrown each other very quickly. They decided there was no future for them. So they ended it before it got any harder. But it was still difficult. The normally jovial and engaging Scott was quiet and reserved this evening.

Adam expressed that he and Joseph wanted to throw a dinner party this weekend to celebrate Matthew's new job. Matthew cautioned against it, saying it was premature. Adam continued to push the idea. "Just a small party…about ten of us and your family", he told Matthew. Scott agreed with Adam and was all for the party. Finally, Matthew relented and agreed to the party.

The dinner party that weekend was another success. Matthew joked with Adam that he should forget the law and open a business throwing dinner parties. Adam, certainly had the flair for throwing a wonderful party. Matthew noticed that Adam always seemed the happiest when he was entertaining guests. "Maybe he should forget this law school professor stuff and go to culinary school", thought Matthew. The highlight of the evening was Janice's announcement that she was pregnant. Everyone broke into spontaneous applause and hugs around the dinner table. "A wonderful new life for two wonderful people", thought Matthew. When Adam was serving dessert, Scott called Matthew to the phone. He had answered it as he was the closest.

Matthew grabbed the receiver and spoke into the mouthpiece. "Hello", he said. On the other end he heard a voice say, "nigger cock sucker! You think you're going to be the top cop? I'll show you nigger lover. I'll get you, you little faggot…" Matthew hung up the phone. It was clear to Scott that whomever was on the other end had upset

Matthew. His face had turned sheer white. Scott said, "who was that?" Matthew tried to compose himself and look as normal as possible. "Just a pain in the ass reporter", he lied.

While Adam was serving coffee after dessert, Matthew asked Octavia if she could join him for a moment in the library. He motioned to her husband to come as well. Matthew really enjoyed Octavia's husband, Brandon. He was vice president of a small insurance company in Marblehead. Brandon was a skilled negotiator and people person. He knew how to read people and assess them quickly.

While they were in the library Matthew explained to them about the phone call he had just received. Brandon said, "I thought you were unlisted?" Matthew replied that he was and he couldn't understand how someone could get the phone number. Octavia said, "well if it happens again I would let the police know." Brandon asked, "did you recognize the voice?" Matthew said that he didn't. Octavia added, "I think you may get more of this until your off the front page of the papers." Brandon shook his head in agreement, "It's probably nothing, the timing just makes it seem worse", he said to Matthew. Matthew changed the subject. "Before you leave to go finish your coffee, I wanted to ask you something.", he said to Octavia. "Shoot.", she replied. "Well, if all this goes through and works out…", Matthew said, "I wanted you to consider coming to the Attorney General's office. Your the best lawyer I've ever known and I need someone I can trust and rely on." Octavia was clearly surprised by the offer. She paused for a moment and then told Matthew that she would definently think about it. "This is role reversal in a way", said Matthew referring to when he went to work with Octavia. Now he was the one extending the invitation.

The hall where Matthew's perfunctory confirmation hearings were happening was without the benefit of air conditioning. So on this hazy, hot and humid July day, the ten senators on the committee hurriedly questioned Matthew. They wanted to return to their air conditioned offices as soon as possible. However, Senator Lee Danders did not let the heat affect the length and number of his questions. After asking a series of questions regarding the law and Matthew's agenda if he were to become the Attorney General, Danders began to probe the personal side of Matthew's life.

Matthew believed that these questions were irrelevant, but he followed the Governor's advice and remained as polite and responsive as he could. The final back and forth between Matthew and the senator was even conducted with grace. Senator Danders asked, "now you testified a few minutes ago that you are a catholic, isn't that right?" Matthew responded, "yes, that's correct." "Well then,", continued the senator, "how do you reconcile your homosexual lifestyle with the teachings of The Bible?" The senator's diction was marked by his intonation and pronunciation of every syllable of "homosexuality", when he asked this question. Matthew paused a moment and then with a smile said, "I don't try to reconcile them." The senator looked back at him and bellowed, "that's because you can't!" Matthew gleefully responded, "Senator. My God accepts everyone that loves Him and loves his fellow human being. I don't want to bore you with a theology lesson because I don't think it is relevant. The role of religion and politics was dealt with by a great man from Massachusetts, John F. Kennedy. I think he defined the separation appropriately. I promise to keep my religion out of my public duties. Do you promise the same, senator?" The panel of senators, with the exception of Lee Danders, broke into laughter. Senator Danders was clearly annoyed, and responded, "no more questions."

The inquisition was over. Matthew took a deep breath. He did not find the hearing to be intellectually challenging. But, confirmation hearings are not about intelligence. They are about politics. They give the politicians an opportunity to present their views on various issues in the context of a hearing. It was just an exercise in politics disguised as a selection process for executive and judicial appointments. Matthew never heard so many ten minute questions in his life! But most of the questions were pretty benign. No new ground was broken and no revelations were made in this small, hot chamber of the Massachusetts State House.

As Matthew left the State House walking toward Beacon Street with Adam he began to chuckle. He shared with Adam his dream from last night that he had about the confirmation hearings. In his dream he was a black Matthew Schipani with Anita Hill hair. A bespectacled senator bearing a strong resemblance to Justice Thomas questioned Matthew from a bright red and white striped bench. In his dream the senator barked at him, "isn't it true that you used your position to promote gay black men into positions of power?" Matthew responded in his dream, "no! no! Its all lies!" To which the senator responded, "bring on the boys!" Then a chorus line of shirtless, muscular black men danced across the red and white bench to the sound of "I Love The Nightlife". Then Matthew woke up.

Adam could not contain himself. "You are such a mess!", he said to Matthew as he laughed while walking. "It sounds more like one of your fantasies than a dream!", said a giggling Adam. Matthew was laughing right along. Then they clasped their hands together and walked past the brownstones on Beacon Street. "Let's get a drink. I think you deserve one.", said Adam. They went to a small, quiet corner bar and sat at a candle lit table. While they were drinking Adam exclaimed, "I got it! I figured out the dream!" Matthew laughed and said, "I don't know if I want to hear it!" Adam pulled his chair close to Matthew's and said, "come on. I have a theory. It's you as Diana Ross. The dancers are all your fantasy men…" Matthew interjected, "please stop! No more of your theories! Plus I would make a very ugly Diana Ross!" They both laughed and finished their drinks.

Three days had passed. The vote was in. Tracy told Matthew that Governor Dickerson was on the line. Matthew picked up the phone and sternly said, "yes, Governor." Dickerson began to speak in a somber tone. "It was a close vote. Closer than I thought it would be. That damn Danders raised a lot of trouble…" The Governor paused and then with a lighter tone said, "Twenty Five to Thirteen. Congratulations, Mr. Attorney General!"

Matthew let out a large sigh and smiled a beaming smile. "Thank you, sir. Thank you very much!", he said to the Governor. The Governor responded, "your welcome. I'll schedule the swearing in for a week from today. Do you want it anywhere special?" Matthew thought for a moment and then said, "is it possible to have it in the Berkshires? My parents are out there and they are getting older. I don't want to have them travel into the city if it can be avoided. Plus, that's where I grew up." The Governor replied, "of course we can do it there. How about at the university?" Matthew replied, "that would be wonderful!" Dickerson burped, "excuse me" he said, and finally, he started speaking again. "Now I know your friendly with Ruth Rogers. Do you want her to do the swearing in?" Matthew replied, "if that's possible it would be great!" Dickerson said, "anything is possible. This is your day. I'll have my girl Friday call the Appeals Court and invite Justice Rogers. I'll call you back tomorrow with all the definite plans. My office will handle the publicity about the swearing in and all that other stuff, so don't worry about it." Matthew thanked the Governor once again and the conversation was ended.

He called Tracy into his office. She jumped up in the air when Matthew told her and ran into his arms to embrace him. He asked her to call the Commissioner and explain that he would be resigning in a week. Matthew did not feel the same sense of loyalty to this DCP Commissioner as he had to Kevin Michaels. He didn't feel obliged to give this Commissioner a personal call. He would submit his written resignation before day's end.

Matthew called Adam, his parents and Scott in that order to share the good news with them. Everyone was elated and proud. Adam saw it as another opportunity for a party. Scott talked about being "best friends with the powerful". Matthew's parents were particularly pleased that the ceremony would be held in the Berkshires. Matthew then called Janice. When she picked up the phone and said "hello",

Matthew said, "Ms. Pierce. This is Attorney General Schipani." Janice let out a scream of joy. She was overwhelmed with excitement. They spent the next thirty minutes on the phone reminiscing about the "old days" and how much their lives had changed.

While Matthew continued to call his friends and professional acquaintances to tell them his good news, people began gathering in the outer office. During his phone call with Octavia he reminded her of his offer the other evening. "I'll need all the help I can get!", he told her. He asked her to think strongly about coming to work with him. She promised that she would and said that she and Brandon looked forward to the swearing in ceremony.

Matthew decided he had called just about everyone he needed to. He had been on the phone for almost two hours. The rest would have to find out through the press. Matthew opened his office door and walked out into the outer office. Another impromptu party had begun in his honor. Once again it was quickly coordinated by Tracy. Matthew graciously accepted the praise and good wishes from his colleagues. It was a wonderful day for him.

The day of the swearing in ceremony was an unusually mild August day in the Berkshires. When Matthew walked into the university auditorium with the Governor to his left and his parents and Adam to his right, the audience rose to its feet in loud applause. They were greeted on the stage by the president of the university. When the applauding stopped, he asked everyone to remain standing. Off to the side of the stage was a single grand piano, the piano player and his friend Janice Pierce with a microphone. Janice sang the national anthem with a strong and soaring vocal range. While she was singing Matthew thought if Janice had ever pursued a professional singing career, she would have been a chart buster. Her performance earned her a standing ovation from the audience.

The university president introduced Governor Dickerson. Polite applause greeted the introduction. Lloyd Dickerson stood at the podium and began to address the crowd. "Thank you President

Downey. My fellow citizens I have the high honor of presiding over the swearing in of Matthew Alexander Schipani as the Attorney General of Massachusetts. It is only fitting that we are assembled here in the foothills of the Berkshires. For this is where our new Attorney General grew up and learned those so important values that parents and the community teach children. Now please indulge me for a minute as I give you some background on Matthew Schipani. It will illustrate to you and to our citizens why I believe that Matthew Schipani will serve this Commonwealth with dignity and honor."

The Governor then began detailing Matthew's educational and experiential background. He followed this with a brief soliloquy about how he believed that Matthew would protect the rights of all of the citizens of Massachusetts, including those who were suffering from discrimination. The Governor touted Matthew as a strong advocate against crime and cited his work to provide harsher sentences for those convicted of child abuse. The Governor concluded his remarks with, "…so ladies and gentlemen, I have told you why I have chosen this talented young man. I think you agree with me that he will be a leader in every sense of the word. Therefore, I now have the honor to present to you the next Attorney General of the Commonwealth of Massachusetts, Matthew Alexander Schipani!" The audience rose to its feet. Matthew shook the Governor's hand and waved to the audience. There was a long, sustained standing ovation.

Appeals Court Justice Ruth Rogers walked over to the podium toward Matthew. Her long flowing black robe followed behind her. The audience sat down. Justice Rogers handed Matthew his bible. It was the bible his grandparents had given him on his eleventh birthday. Rosa had made sure that Justice Rogers had it for the ceremony. They moved to the side of the podium and stood at the end of the stage. The room was completely quiet. "Please place your left hand on the bible and raise your right hand.", began Justice Rogers. "Repeat after me.", she instructed. Matthew repeated the oath. "I, Matthew Alexander Schipani do solemnly swear that I will uphold the Constitution of the United States and the Constitution of the Commonwealth. I solemnly swear that I will uphold the laws of the United States and this Commonwealth. I solemnly swear that I will faithfully exercise and fulfill the duties of the office of Attorney General. I take this position voluntarily and willingly. I will to the best of my ability preserve and pursue justice for the citizens of this Commonwealth. So help me, God."

With the completion of the oath, Justice Rogers said, "Congratulations, Mr. Attorney General", and embraced Matthew. The audience rose to its feet in applause. Matthew looked out at the audience loaded with dear friends, families and neighbors. It was a wonderful sight! Matthew stood drinking in the thunderous applause. He looked around the room and saw so many good friends and important people in his life. He thought this was a tribute to them as much as it was to him. It was because of these people here today that Matthew Alexander Schipani was who he was. He motioned them to be seated and after a few more moments of applause the crowd took their seats.

Matthew began his acceptance speech. "I would like to thank his excellency, the Governor, the President of the University, Senator Callahan, Senator Keezell, Justice Rogers and most especially my family and you my friends, for this honor that has been bestowed upon me today. I wish to thank the people of this glorious Commonwealth for this honor as well and make my pledge to them to be an effective and strong Attorney General." Matthew looked out at the sea of faces and media cameras awaiting his remarks. He continued, "I would like to speak to you today about four different issues. I promise that I will make it brief and won't pontificate too much!" This comment was greeted with laughter and applause.

"First, as your Attorney General I have the duty to the citizens of this state to ensure that Massachusetts is a safe place for them to live and work in. Crime prevention and punishment for criminals will be the top priority of this administration." Matthew was interrupted by applause. He allowed the applause to continued for a short time and then he continued on. "In order to be an effective law enforcement official I only need to look to the model and leadership of my predecessor on this issue. Attorney General Wallace Cartwright was a gentle and quiet man who carried a large stick. Wallace Cartwright fought against crime during his many years of service to this state. I intend to follow his leadership on this issue. Many of you know that Wallace was not only my boss at one time, but he was also my friend. Many of you here today still feel the loss of his passing. I know Wallace is watching us now, and I know that the best tribute to his memory I could provide would be to continue his legacy of tough law enforcement. I intend to do just that!" The room erupted into applause.

"Secondly, the problem of child abuse in Massachusetts has grown to epidemic proportions. When I first began working in child welfare as a caseworker many years ago, the caseloads were high, the problems were complex and the job was tiring. As chief legal counsel for DCP, I saw an agency bursting at the seams with impossible caseloads, extremely complex and violent situations. An agency that was dealing with the most difficult societal problem to face us: child abuse. Child abuse in my mind is the number one societal problem in this state. It is time that we as leaders of this state address this problem with more than lip service."

The applause started again. It was slow and then began to quicken and rise in tone. Matthew continued, "I make another pledge today. That is to the children of this state. No longer will you be silent voices and silent victims. This administration is going to work to reform the child welfare system in Massachusetts, from bottom up. Reforming will begin at DCP and continue through the court system and the legislature. We must help the courts to move these cases with a sense of purpose and compassion. We cannot allow abused children to remain at home, and those children removed from their parents to languish in foster care. We must push the legislature to continue to enact stricter laws in the area of child abuse. We began that effort in 1989 and five years have passed without the legislature taking a lead on this issue. Five years is too long! The problem has gotten worse. We must act together as a society to wipe this scourge from Massachusetts. I promise to be a catalyst for action in this area!" Again there was loud applause which forced Matthew to stop for a moment. "Thank you", he quietly said and then proceeded on.

"Third. I want to thank all of you across this state who understand that homosexuals are not by their definition of being homosexual any lesser citizens than non-homosexuals. I also want to thank you for disregarding the old stereotypes and myths about homosexuality. You did so by approving my nomination. My appointment as your Attorney General reaffirms my belief that old, worn out and untrue stereotypes and myths about gay persons are dying in Massachusetts." Once again there was applause. Matthew interrupted to continue. "This appointment shows that a gay person can and will function in a position of authority. It affirms my belief that Massachusetts is willing to accept all persons no matter what their race, color, creed or sexual preference may be. This appointment should send the message to the legislature that the time for a gay civil rights law is now. We have waited too long!" The audience began a loud and sustained applause. Half of the audience was on its feet. Matthew looked over at Governor Dickerson. He remained in his seat as Justice Ruth Rogers stood next to him applauding.

"In conclusion, my fourth and final point. I would not be here if it were not for a great many people in my life. It would be remiss of me not to share this moment with them and to acknowledge their contributions to the quality of my life. First, I want to thank my family, Anthony, Maria and my parents Rosa and Franco. They taught me the true inner values and beliefs that I have and bring with me to this job. I want to thank my dear man, Adam who has stood by me through all the good and bad times. I want to thank my best friend Scott who loves me unconditionally. I also want to thank dear friends Janice, Octavia, Kevin Michaels and the late Phillip Styles. They have all made me who I am today." There was applause again. Matthew appreciated the applause for his family and friends. He concluded his remarks, "Finally, I want to thank all my personal and professional friends who have given so much to me. With all of your support and the support of the Governor and the people of Massachusetts, I hope to bring honor to this position. I thank you all for being a part of my special day. God bless you!"

Matthew moved away from the podium and forward to the end of the stage. The audience was on their feet applauding. He looked down at his mother and father who were wildly applauding and crying at the same time. Matthew gave a wave, turned and followed the Governor and Justice Rogers off the stage. As he walked out he reached and shook many extended hands. The ceremony was completed. Matthew Alexander Schipani was the Attorney General of Massachusetts.

After a small and intimate dinner at his parents home, Matthew, Scott and Adam drove back to Cambridge. It was a wonderful day but it had been exhausting. Matthew went right to bed. His new career was starting in the morning and he needed his rest.

The alarm clock seemed much louder than normal as Matthew pushed the button to turn it off. He walked into the kitchen, turned on the coffee machine and proceeded to the living room. The *Today* show was on. Bryant and Katie were reviewing the day's events. Diana came over to him wagging her tail. He pet his dog and watched the morning show. A moment later Adam was coming out of the bedroom. "Good Morning!", said a chipper Adam. This was highly unusual for Adam in the morning. He was usually such a grump. Adam brought Matthew's coffee to him. "I've picked out your suit and tie for you. I want you to look spectacular for your first day. I'll even drive you to your new office!", said Adam.

Matthew showered quickly and dressed. Adam was ready and they left for the morning commute. Adam drove through Beacon Hill to the front of the Attorney General's office. Matthew reached in the back seat for his briefcase. He leaned over to Adam who had double-parked so Matthew could get out. "I love you", he said to Adam. Adam replied, "I love you too. I have never been so proud of you as I am today. Now go knock 'em dead!". Matthew and Adam kissed and Matthew got out of the car.

Matthew walked up the marble stairs to the front door of the building. He opened the large door and saw the metal detector and police officer at the entrance. "Good Morning, Mr. Attorney General", said the police officer. Matthew smiled. "Good morning", he said in return. Matthew walked through the detector even though the police officer had motioned him around it. He walked down the hall toward his new office. He chuckled inside as he recalled the greeting he had just received. "Mr. Attorney General", he said to himself. "I like it!", he cheerfully thought.

CHAPTER 12

SETTLING IN

September 1994

Matthew was musing as he stared out of his floor to ceiling office window at the townhouses on Beacon Hill. "Would the boom fall this September once again?", he thought. Then Matthew smiled. "How could it? He was on top of the world!", he thought. Matthew was settling in as the state's first openly gay Attorney General. Governor Dickerson had been true to his word. Matthew had been given carte blanche on staffing his office and requests for funds to support his efforts. It was a good beginning. But there was so much work to do!

The phone buzzed. It was Tracy on the other end. Matthew made sure that he did not leave Tracy behind at DCP. She was a valuable asset, total professional and good friend. He knew that if he wanted his inner office to run, Tracy had to head the administration of the day to day activities. So she came with him. "Octavia's on the line", said Tracy to Matthew. He clicked over to the next line, "yes, dear", he said to Octavia Moon, Deputy Attorney General of Massachusetts. His first legal appointment was his most important. The woman he considered to have the brightest legal mind accentuated by deep compassion, became his first assistant.

"Honey, I just talked to Janice. There's a case about to explode over there and she wanted to know if we could meet next week on it", said Octavia. Matthew flipped through his appointment book. "How about next Wednesday? I'm pretty lean that day." He could hear Octavia flipping through her book on the other end, "it's okay with me. You want me to call her?", she asked. "No, I'll do it. I haven't talked to her in about a week. I need to touch base", Matthew replied. "Thanks", said Octavia as she hung up the phone. Matthew placed a call to his old work place, DCP. "Commissioner Pierce's office, please", he said into the phone. Janice Pierce had been appointed by the Governor as the new commissioner of DCP. Matthew had made the recommendation to Governor Dickerson. Dickerson happily accepted the recommendation by Matthew. He whole heartedly supported Janice's appointment. Now one month into her new job, Janice Pierce was facing a challenge. "Commissioner Pierce's office. Ada Backenhouse speaking" Matthew spoke, "good afternoon Ms. Backenhouse. This is Attorney General Schipani. Is Janice available?" The secretary's voice made a noticeable change to a more attentive tone. "She's in a meeting. But I'm sure I can interrupt." Matthew replied, "would you mind if its not too much of a problem?" Ada Backenhouse replied, "certainly! It's no problem."

A moment passed and Matthew's friend and songstress was on the phone. "Mr. Attorney General", Janice stated. "Oh, please! Stop the formality crap!", Matthew replied. Janice laughed. Matthew then asked, "so you've been there not even a month and I have to bail you out!" Janice chuckled and said, "you know I can't stay away from you too long!" Matthew replied, "look, I know you're in the middle of something. I talked to Octavia. Can you come over here next Wednesday, around two?" Janice quickly replied, "I'll be there! Thank you." Matthew said, "no problem. See you on Wednesday, and don't forget about Saturday afternoon!" "I didn't!", replied Janice. Matthew was referring to their conference in Hyannis on Saturday. Janice and Matthew were speakers at a state-wide conference on child abuse. Matthew loved attending these conferences. He found the speakers to be fascinating. He also thought they were a good method to help professionalize the discipline of child welfare. They had planned to ride together on Saturday. Matthew told Janice that now that she was DCP Commissioner she needed to get rid of her "crackerbox of a car". Janice was shopping for a new car, but hadn't settled on one yet. Matthew would be the pilot of the "yuppie mobile", as he called his Volvo for their trip on Saturday.

The phone buzzed again. "I just wanted to let you know that you're three o'clock is here early", said Tracy. Matthew thanked her and then reached under the pile of papers to a folder marked "Finalists". Matthew was interviewing for his third in line at the Attorney General's office. He made no bones about appointing his dear friend and former partner Octavia as his first assistant. But he wanted to have his third in charge to be a person he did not have a previous relationship with. He thought the objectivity would be helpful and that it would also not give the impression that Matthew was going to only hire his friends.

He pulled the resume of Elizabeth Ann Kragen out of the folder. Her resume was impressive. Attorney Kragen was a graduate of Yale Law School, fourth in her class. She had worked as an assistant United States Attorney in Boston for seven years. She then was a legislative assistant to United States Representative Susan Gaudet. She worked the halls of Congress for six years. She returned to Boston five years ago to join the prestigious law firm of Brathwaite, Johnston and Rome. Now Attorney Kragen wanted to come work at the Attorney General's office. Her cover letter indicated that she had a "strong desire to return to the public sector…working to make the government more efficient and effective to its constituents." Matthew looked at Octavia's notes from the first interview. Octavia had made many positive comments, including "if you feel comfortable with her, hire her! I think we could work together well." Matthew thought, "if Octavia likes her then she's gotta be the one."

Matthew reviewed her references. Representative Gaudet could not say enough about her. Senior Partner, Roy Brathwaite expressed that he would "hate to lose her…but she has a keen legal mind in the area of government service that could be of great benefit to your office." Matthew made a quick call to Adam and then buzzed Tracy. "Could you send in Attorney Kragen please?", he requested.

Elizabeth Kragen strolled gingerly into Matthew's office. He extended his hand to her and then motioned her to sit down. Matthew was in awe over the beauty of this woman who sat before him looking for a job. She reminded him of movie star Meg Ryan. She had exceptional good looks accented by an air of dignity. They talked briefly about general matters and Attorney Kragen's background. Then Matthew focused the interview toward his agenda as Attorney General. "I have a strong commitment to two major issues while I occupy this seat.", he began. "First, I want to advance the issue of child protection. I would like to get your feelings on that issue."

Attorney Kragen paused briefly and then with determination said to Matthew, "I think the way society treats its children is a reflection of the disintegration of society itself. We view children as chattel. We feel that we can control them, beat them and disrespect them. All the while we forget that by doing so we are teaching our children how to act as adults. We are creating a generation that will not have intrinsic moral values. As a society and more particularly as the government, I believe that we need to work towards the elimination of these scars on our children. We have to combat child abuse and at the same time we have to teach the parents how to be effective role models and teachers. When the parents are beyond teaching and their crimes are so unspeakable, then the government must remove those parents from the child's life. I strongly support your efforts in this area and would be vigilant advocate in this area."

This response brought a broad smile to Matthew's face. He wanted a team of child advocates on his staff. "Thank you. I find your view to be enlightened. I think it fits in with my view of this important issue", Matthew said in response. "The other issue", he continued, "is the issue of gay civil rights. I am intending upon asking the legislature to adopt a statute that would prohibit discrimination against homosexuals in housing, employment, medical benefits and public accommodations. I'm sure you are aware of my openness regarding my sexual preference. This office has an open and non-discriminatory policy towards all that work here. I intend to expand that view to the society in general. Do you have any thoughts on this issue and where you would fit in regarding it?", asked Matthew.

Elizabeth Kragen smiled at Matthew and then began. "I don't believe that sexual preference has any place in any type of decision making or eligibility for services, both public and private. I feel that my sexual preference of heterosexual is just as irrelevant to these issues as your sexual preference. I see this struggle as mirroring the civil rights struggles of blacks in the sixties. I would support your efforts in this area." Matthew nodded his head in agreement.

"Finally", he said, "there is one other issue that I would want your assistance on if you were to come to work here. As you know, Governor Dickerson is sending a bill to reinstate the death penalty to the legislature. This office is in the process of obtaining documentation and research on this issue not only here in Massachusetts but across the nation. I have not made a decision about the position of this office or my position on the bill. I have only made it known to the Governor that I would only support a narrowly tailored statute with built in appellate review. But I haven't seen his bill yet. Octavia Moon is coordinating our efforts on this issue. It's an arduous project that has to be completed in a short time. Is this something that you would find to be of interest?"

Elizabeth Kragen quickly responded. "When I worked with Representative Gaudet in Congress, she had me do a great deal of research on various issues. I have always found research to be fascinating. In fact, I believe I am a better in office attorney than a litigator. I like setting policy, doing research and implementing systems. I don't have a personal opinion on the death penalty. I have the same concerns and reservations that most of us do. But I also know that society wants stern punishments to end the overwhelming crime wave. I think it would be a wonderful issue to research, chart out and formulate a position on."

Matthew leaned back in his chair with his hands folded to his lips. He paused for a few moments and looked at Attorney Kragen. She was not only beautiful, but she was also intelligent and articulate. He recalled that Octavia was impressed with her. Matthew leaned forward, rested his hands on his desk and said, "Deputy Attorney General Moon was most impressed with you. If you came here to work, she would be your supervisor. Do you have any impressions from your interview about working with her?"

Attorney Kragen smiled as she responded, "I thought she was delightful. She put me at ease and made me feel as if I had known her for years. I was much more calm with her than I am sitting here with you.", she concluded with her face blushing. Matthew chuckled, stood up and said, "I am pleased to make you a job offer. I'd like to have you here as part of the team. Are you willing to accept?" Attorney Kragen stood up, extended her right hand toward Matthew and said, "I accept", and shook his hand. Matthew proceeded around his desk and walked over to her side to escort her from his office. He motioned to the door. "Talk to Roy Brathwaite. See when it is convenient for him to have you finish up over there. Once you have a date, give Tracy a call and we'll have you on board. The sooner, the better.", concluded Matthew. He opened the door and ushered her out. They shook hands again. Matthew looked over to Tracy and standing next to her desk was Shannon Watson. He smiled, motioned her into his office and followed closing the door behind him.

"Who's the babe?", asked Shannon as Matthew sat down behind his desk. "My new hire, Elizabeth Kragen. She'll work under Octavia.", responded Matthew. "Well…I guess you have to be gay or beautiful to get a job in this place! The office is filled with studs!", said a laughing Shannon Watson. Matthew laughed and replied, "so what brings you here beside my stunning good looks?" Shannon smiled. "I came because I want to do a tag along with you. I want to write an in-depth profile for our Sunday magazine. My editor wants it done for right after Thanksgiving. I know all the sordid details of what goes on at your home, but I want to know all about the 'Attorney General Matthew' for my story. So, will you let me in?" Matthew smiled and said, "how could I say no? Of course I'll let you tag along. You might find it boring though…but you're more than welcome. When do you want to start this exercise?" Shannon replied, "in about two weeks. I'm finishing up an investigative piece and then I'll be free to start." Matthew said, "that's fine…just let me know when." Their conversation was interrupted by the buzz on the phone. "It's Dexter Donnelly", said Tracy. Matthew looked at Shannon. "Go ahead, take it…I'll be by in a few weeks", she said as she blew him a kiss and walked out of his office.

Matthew pushed the blinking button on the phone. "Hi Dexter! What's up?", he asked Representative Donnelly. Donnelly replied, "I was hoping that we could get together next week sometime to begin to go over the draft anti-discrimination statute. I've decided to sponsor it along with Senator Pena once its completed." Matthew responded, "I have to meet with DCP next Wednesday in the afternoon. How about around 4:30 I hook up with you and we can go get a bite to eat and review it over dinner and drinks?" Donnelly replied, "that would be great. I'll meet you at your office and we'll go from there." "Sounds good", responded Matthew. Dexter said his goodbye and Matthew hung up the phone.

The weekend conference in Hyannis was as wonderful as Matthew expected it would be. He found the debate about child welfare to be exhilarating. He never grew tired of this important issue. It was at the core of his being. He was determined to have a positive impact in this area. Before Janice and Matthew returned to Boston they drove further out on the Cape to Provincetown to go to dinner at one of their favorite restaurants. While they were sitting in the Lobster Pot restaurant gazing out at the ocean, Matthew realized how much more he enjoyed Cape Cod in the fall than in the tourist season of summer. It was much more peaceful and relaxing. How he wished they could stay for a few days. But he had dinner plans for Sunday and he knew they had to be on their way back to Boston.

Sunday night dinner by Adam. It was perfect as usual. The food, the presentation, the setting all provided an intimate and comfortable evening for Adam and Matthew to meet Scott's newest love, Dion Renzi. Both Matthew and Adam giggled in the kitchen alone while Scott and Dion sat in the dining room. Dion Renzi was a thirty one year old, tan, gorgeous Italian man. Matthew admired the chest and bulging biceps on this man. Adam thought he looked like he walked out of a magazine. Dion Renzi was noticeably nervous during the beginning of the evening. He was a new lawyer in private practice who was coming to dinner at the home of the Attorney General of Massachusetts. But by the end of the dinner hour, Dion had relaxed and was quite engaging. Matthew hoped that this relationship would work out for his best friend. "It's time for him to settle down and fall in love", Matthew told Adam.

The rest of the evening the four of them spoke about their careers, their goals and where to vacation for the winter. Matthew of course began with his denunciation of the forthcoming winter season. "I want to go somewhere in February. By then I'll have had enough of the snow and cold. I will be ready for a beach", said Matthew in an agitated tone. Scott suggested a return to Hawaii which Adam readily agreed with. But Matthew said, "I want to try somewhere new. What about Mexico?" For the next hour or so they began to discuss various warm vacation spots for a trip that was still five months away. The evening ended with Matthew extending an invitation to Dion to stop by the office for lunch someday to discuss his legal career.

That evening while in bed Adam said to Matthew, "don't you think that was a little out of place for you to ask Dion to come to your office?" Matthew looked quizzically at Adam and said, "why?...are you jealous or something?" Adam sternly replied back, "well I certainly would have reason to be given what's happen before. But that's not it. It just seemed like a come on...I don't think Scott appreciated it." Matthew sat up in bed and looked at Adam, saying, "well I guess I was just trying to be friendly. I know it's tough being a new lawyer out there. You should know that! I thought I would talk to him about openings in my office if he was interested. I don't really think Scott thought my invitation was unusual. I'll talk to him tomorrow about it..." Adam replied, "if he wasn't so gorgeous and didn't have such a great body would you have given the same invitation?" Matthew was becoming angry. "It has nothing to do with him being hot. I was trying to be nice. I'd like to see him and Scott become serious. I already told you that. Don't turn around everything I do just because you're jealous!". Adam looked at Matthew and said, "fine...okay. Just turn the light off." Matthew did as he was asked. Adam rolled over on his side away from Matthew. A moment later Diana jumped up on the bed and snuggled between them. Matthew laid awake staring at the dark ceiling. "I was just trying to be helpful", he thought.

About an hour later Matthew had fallen off to sleep but was awaken by a muzzled bark from Diana. He sat up. Adam remained sleeping. "What's wrong?", he asked Diana. Then he too heard a noise outside. Diana barked a little louder. Matthew got out of the bed and went to the window. He looked down and saw a figure dressed in dark clothing with a small flashlight in his hand. He stepped back from the window. "Shh", he said to Diana. Matthew walked over to the bed and shook Adam. Adam slowly opened his eyes. "There's somebody walking around the backyard", he said to Adam. Adam sat up. Matthew reached in the drawer of the nightstand. He grabbed the Smith and Wesson snub nosed revolver. "I'm going downstairs and check it out...call the police", Matthew said to Adam. Adam got out of the bed and in a strong whisper said, "don't go outside! Just wait until the cops come." Matthew shook his head "no". They both walked over to the window and peeked out. The figure was still in the yard and appeared to be trying to open the cellar window. "I'm going!", announced Matthew as he sprinted out of the bedroom. Adam quickly dialed 911.

Matthew quietly closed the door behind him and walked down the stairs to the front lawn. He slithered along the side of the house in the shadows toward the backyard. As he came around the corner he saw the figure with a flashlight in one hand and what appeared to be a crowbar in the other. Matthew heard a distant siren. "Freeze!", he yelled with the revolver pointed out at the figure. The figure rose and held the crowbar up as his weapon. It was a man, but Matthew could not see his face. He had a ski mask on. The figure began walking toward Matthew. The siren was getting closer. "Don't move or I'll shoot!", commanded Matthew. Matthew stood his ground. The figure approached. Matthew's mind was racing about how close he would let this man get to him before he pulled the trigger.

Suddenly the figure threw the small flashlight at Matthew's head. The light distracted him. Matthew pulled the trigger. The gun went off. The lights in his aunt's apartment and Scott's apartment turned on instantly. Adam came running up behind with Diana to one side and a flashlight in his hand. Diana rushed to the back of the yard barking loudly. Adam shined the flashlight and they watched the figure jump the back fence and run. Scott came running out with Dion in tow. A screech of tire wheels and bright blue lights announced the arrival of the police. "Don't move!", yelled a voice. Matthew raised his hands in the air with the pistol still in his grip. Three or four bright flashlights shined on the group.

"Mr. Attorney General!", exclaimed one of the officers, recognizing Matthew. "He jumped the fence and ran that way!", pointed Adam to the back of the yard. Two police officers ran back to their cruisers and screeched out of the driveway. By this time Aunt Gloria had made her way to the backyard. Matthew motioned them all to the front of the house. A detective car arrived with its flashing blue roof light as they were walking in the door of Scott's apartment.

Once inside they all sat down at the kitchen table. Matthew explained to the police about hearing the noise and his encounter with the masked figure. "You really shouldn't go out there alone", warned one of the officers. Matthew replied, "I know…I just thought I could catch him." A few moments later a state police officer knocked on the door. The Cambridge officer let him in. "Mr. Attorney General, we heard the call and came to assist.", said the state trooper. Matthew told him to sit down. He proceeded to tell the story again. The trooper responded, "we'll have a car posted here tonight if we don't get the guy."

Scott had made a pot of coffee and began to serve everyone. About forty minutes later the officers that had gone in pursuit of the trespasser returned. "No luck", said the young officer to the detective. The state trooper said, "I'll get a car here tonight in case he returns. If it's all right with you I'll send somebody by your office tomorrow so we can review the report and get some more info." Matthew shook his head affirmatively. The police officers rose to leave. Matthew and the others thanked them.

Adam returned to bed but Matthew and Scott joined by Dion and Aunt Gloria, had another cup of coffee. Matthew lit his third cigarette. He was surprised that Scott didn't yell at him. He really didn't like smoking in his apartment. Diana laid underneath the table sleeping. "I think we should get an alarm for the house and the yard", said Scott to Matthew. Matthew shook his head saying, "I don't know. It's a lot of money. Do you think it's really necessary?" Aunt Gloria chimed in, "yes, I do. You know you are the Attorney General. Who knows what nuts are out there? I can help out with paying for it…it would make me feel better too." Matthew looked at her and said, "you don't need to pay for it…that's not fair. I've got the money…if you guys think that's what we should do, I'll talk to the state cop tomorrow about it when he comes by." Scott and Aunt Gloria shook their heads affirmatively.

Matthew butted out his cigarette. "Come on auntie...let me walk you upstairs. Let's leave the love birds alone!" Aunt Gloria got up and kissed Scott. Matthew waved good night to Scott and Dion. He walked his aunt to her apartment and then returned to his. Diana beat him to the bed and snuggled next to a sleeping Adam. Matthew crawled in under the sheets and shortly fell back to sleep.

Monday morning arrived without incident. Matthew was sitting at his desk when the phone buzzed indicating that the state police officer was present to discuss what happened last night. Matthew had Tracy bring the officer in. They discussed briefly the events of the evening and the trooper asked Matthew if there was any one in particular that he knew had a vendetta against him. Matthew thought for a moment or two. The only one he could think of was Craig Talbot, but that was a few years in the past. For all he knew, Craig had moved on. Matthew did not want to implicate him for no reason. So Matthew indicated to the trooper that there was no one in particular that was "out to get me".

Later that day Attorney Roy Brathwaite called Matthew to congratulate him on his choice of Elizabeth Kragen. "I will really miss her. She's quite a talent.", said Roy Brathwaite to Matthew. Matthew replied that he was looking forward to having her "be on the team. I guess since I stole one of your stars I definitely owe you lunch!". Roy Brathwaite chuckled and then said, "I'll take lunch with the Attorney General any day!" They agreed to set up a time in the next month to meet and have a leisurely lunch. Elizabeth Kragen would be joining the Attorney General's office in three weeks.

Matthew was excited and relieved. He now had his senior management staff in place. There were only a few staff attorney positions left to fill. Maybe Dion Renzi would be interested. Matthew insisted to himself that he wasn't considering him because Dion was so good looking. Rather, he was offering a young, gay attorney an opportunity to establish himself. Just like Wallace Cartwright gave Matthew an opportunity many years ago. Adam's jealously was unfounded as far as Matthew was concerned.

However, a call just before the end of the work day would have properly made Adam jealous. Tracy indicated that James Davenport was on hold to speak with Matthew. They had not spoken for a long time since their affair went sour and Matthew lost Adam over the whole thing. Matthew was reticent to take the call, but eventually decided to do so. It was only a telephone call. "Hello", he said into the phone. Davenport on the other end responded, "well hello Mister Attorney General! I'm calling because I'm in town, I pick up the Ledger and on page four there's an article about how the Attorney General of Massachusetts is cracking down on gang warfare. I look to the side of the article and there is your picture! I just wanted to congratulate you!" Matthew smiled, "thank you James. That's very nice of you to call. How is everything going?"

They talked for about ten minutes. James indicated that once his character was killed off on the soap opera, work was getting scarce. However, he returned to his true love, Broadway. He had been in several plays and now was in a touring company of 'Wentworth Palace', a gay farce set in the early twenties. As their conversation was winding down, James indicated he would be in Boston for a month and asked if they could go to dinner. Matthew hesitated and then said, "I think the best way for me to handle this is to ask Adam. It would be really nice to see you again, but I can't jeopardize my relationship over this. How about you call me next week and we'll go from there?" James quietly responded, "that's fine. I don't want to cause any problems. I'm glad for you that you two are back together. But I'll be honest…the thought of getting it on with you would be great. But I know we shouldn't do that…so let's at least try to be friends." Matthew agreed and said, "I'll talk to you next week" and hung up the phone.

That evening Matthew and Scott spoke about purchasing an alarm for the home. They decided it was a good investment and that their safety was paramount. Matthew would call the alarm specialist that the state police officer recommended. Aunt Gloria expressed her approval and relief at the decision to install the alarm.

Wednesday arrived and Matthew was anxiously awaiting the appearance of Janice Pierce. It would be their first "official meeting". Two dear friends meeting in the roles of Attorney General and DCP Commissioner. Tracy signaled that Janice was on her way. Matthew called down to Octavia's office. "Can we meet in the large conference room?", he asked. Octavia said, "we can meet anywhere you want. Did you forget your the boss?" Matthew laughed. He asked Octavia to bring in two assistants of her choice. He was sure that if Janice wanted the Attorney General's office to be involved in a DCP case it was a murky situation that would need a lot of assistance.

Matthew greeted Janice prior to the meeting in his private office. They hugged and kissed as if they hadn't seen each other for years. In actuality it had only been a couple of days. Two dear friends of many years in major roles in state government were about to sit down and attempt to address what would become a major test for both of them. Matthew ushered Janice down the hall to the conference room where they would begin to unravel the crisis.

Matthew and Janice walked into the room and sat next to each other at the conference table. Octavia was seated to Janice's right. "Thank you all for coming today. I'd like to have everyone introduce themselves as there are a couple of faces here I don't know as well.", said Matthew. They went around the table starting with Janice. Octavia Moon was to her right, followed by Jennifer Alexander, Matthew's successor as the DCP chief legal counsel, Doris Keeton, assistant Attorney General, Eric Pimental, assistant Attorney General, Tracy, Matthew's administrative assistant, Jane Walters, director of the Greenfield DCP office and Matthew's old friend, Frank Livingston, DCP deputy Commissioner. Janice asked Matthew if Frank could outline the case for everyone. Matthew smiled, "absolutely!", he said. Frank Livingston began to give the case history on the current crisis at DCP. In 1990, DCP removed two twins named Colin and David from their parents, Candice and Kenneth Baker. The children were three months old at the time of their removal. They had been born cocaine addicted. The parents had a long history of cocaine and substance abuse. DCP social workers tried to work with the family to prevent the removal of the children, but were unsuccessful.

The children were placed in the home of Luis Ruiz and Brian McDermott, two openly gay professional men who were approved by DCP as foster parents. The children remained in this home since their removal from the parents. About six months ago the parental rights of Candice and Kenneth Baker were terminated by the court. They had not successfully freed themselves from their drug abuse and were unable to care for the twins. DCP filed a petition in the probate court on behalf of Luis Ruiz and Brian McDermott to adopt the twins. The matter was heard in the Franklin county probate court. Judge William O'Toole was the presiding justice. Somehow the parents found out about the pending petition. Frank Livingston indicated to the group assembled that he suspected that a social worker in the Greenfield DCP office who was "homophobic" had leaked the information. The parents filed objections to the petition of Luis and Brian to adopt the children. The judge only heard argument from counsel. He did not take any evidence. At the end of the argument, Judge O'Toole ruled from the bench that the two prospective adoptive parents sponsored by DCP were not fit to adopt the twins due to the "abnormal and abhorrent lifestyle." The petition was denied. Luis Ruiz and Brian McDermott were not only devastated but they were also very angry. The judge ordered DCP to place the children in another foster home. DCP refused and the judge indicated that if the children were not removed he may find the agency in contempt. DCP wanted to appeal Judge O'Toole's ruling.

Matthew interjected in Frank's dissertation about the case. "I'm not sure why you feel the need for this office to become involved here. Jennifer and her staff certainly can file the appeal..." Janice turned to Matthew and replied, "I'm concerned that if we don't have your office involved not only will we have a screwed up case, but we may also have a complaint against the agency for violation of civil rights. Luis and Brian are bullshit! They're getting mixed messages from us. The local staff is washing their hands of it and I have indicated that we support them. However, I'm not too sure if they believe us." Janice stopped speaking. Matthew paused for a moment and then looked at Octavia, "any thoughts?", he asked. Octavia replied, "well...first of all, as to the legal issue of violation of civil rights, they have no standing. There is no protection for these two men. There is no protected right to be an adoptive parent. So while I may disagree with the state of the law as it is right now...there is no violation of civil rights." Matthew nodded his head in agreement.

Janice Pierce asked, "may I interject a little more?" Matthew replied, "please...go right ahead." Janice leaned back in her chair and began. "I guess the reason I wanted to bring this matter here is two-fold. First, I believe as an agency our first interest has to be what is in the best interest of a child. If we as an agency can find adults who are willing to care and protect children I don't care what their nationality, creed, orientation or handicap is. I just want dedicated and caring individuals for our children. I know Matthew that this is a position that you always stood for and want to advance." Janice continued, "secondly, I think this case has major ramifications for children throughout the state who are awaiting adoption. I know I'm not a lawyer, but if this ruling becomes the standard I think we effectively close the door on many prospective adoptive resources for our children. I see this issue as a major policy and resource issue for DCP for its future. Bearing this in mind, it is my belief that if your office takes the lead in appealing this and takes the position I think that your office would, I think it sends a clear message to the judiciary that DCP and the state's top law enforcers are only concerned about what is best for a child. That's why I want your help…its beyond the whole civil rights issue. I don't see this case as the rights of the two adoptive parents to be gay parents. I see the case as the rights of Colin and David to have caring parents whose sexual orientation is immaterial."

Matthew pushed his chair back and stood up, just like Wallace Cartwright did a few years ago. He hoped that someday he would have the same presence that Wallace did. He was smiling as he responded. Janice Pierce, the consummate professional whose major concern has always been the welfare of needy children, thought Matthew. Matthew spoke with a deep voice as he began, "many years ago when I met this fine woman", he said putting his hand on Janice's shoulder, "I knew then that she was truly dedicated to the needs of children. I think what you have just said Janice once again reinforces your dedication. When I became Attorney General only a short time ago I made the promise that I would use this office to advance the rights of children and to remove from society the scourge of child abuse. This office will be happy to work with you and your staff on the appeal of this matter. It is the right thing to do. These little boys need parents…that is their primary need. We will do whatever we can to assist you in achieving that goal." Matthew sat back down next to his friend. She was smiling ear to ear.

Octavia then said, "permit me to deal with the nuts and bolts of this case." The discussion began around the table about the procedures necessary to perfect the appeal. Octavia took control of the discussion. Matthew happily allowed her to do so. He knew that if anyone could prepare a case for success on appeal it was Octavia. She assigned the task of the contempt issue to DCP chief legal counsel Jennifer Alexander. Octavia and two assistants from the Attorney General's office would work cooperatively with Jennifer and her staff on the appeal of the dispositional order.

Matthew interjected, "I'm going to have to excuse myself in a minute from this discussion. I'm sorry, but I have another obligation. But I want to make it clear that DCP has the support of this office. Octavia, I am going to ask that when you get a date for appeal that you argue the case to the appeals court. Hopefully they will make the right decision and we won't have to take it to the seven old men on the hill. But if we do, we will…so, with that please allow me to excuse myself. Janice, I'll check in with you at the end of the week." Matthew stood up and gave a casual wave good-bye to the group assembled and then walked out the door back to his office.

Tracy came into the office a few moments later with a pile of papers. "These are for your review when you get a chance", she said to him. Matthew took the papers and motioned Tracy to sit down. He then asked her, "why is it that child welfare issues follow me wherever I go?" She looked at him, grinned and said, "because it's your calling in life. This is what you were truly put here to do. Think about it…you started as a social worker protecting kids. Then you headed DCP's legal division and made major impact in the area of child protection. Now you're here and about to do more. I mean, if it wasn't so important to you why would you have devoted time to it when you gave your acceptance speech?"

Matthew stretched in his chair and said, "I guess you're right…I just hope that what I've done has been helpful. Sometimes I feel like I'm swimming against the tide on this issue. That case we discussed is not that difficult…the judge was way off base. I hope that someday no one will give a shit about the sexual orientation of parents. Who cares? All I care about is whether they can love a child…" Tracy smiled and said, "see…that's what I mean. You're heart is in it. You can make the difference…that's what this is all about." Matthew said, "thank you…I hope so." Tracy stood up and said, "I know so." and then walked out of the office.

About twenty minutes later Representative Dexter Donnelly was at Matthew's door. "Good afternoon sir…are you ready?" said Donnelly. Matthew looked up and exclaimed, "Dexter! Come in please…I didn't realize you were waiting." Donnelly sat down and Matthew said, "just let me call my mother and I'll be all set. I haven't talked to her since the incident over the weekend…I know she's probably crazy worrying." Matthew picked up the phone and began to dial. Donnelly looked at Matthew and said in a confused tone, "what incident over the weekend?" Matthew put up his finger indicating one minute and said, "I'll tell you at dinner."

Matthew then connected with his mother on the phone. She indicated that she and his father would be coming down for the weekend and staying with Aunt Gloria. She then expressed her concern about the incident over the weekend. "It's all right…we're getting an alarm", said Matthew in attempt to calm his mother's nerves. It seemed to do the trick. He ended the conversation with his mother saying, "I'll tell Adam that you two can have a cooking competition!" His mother laughed and said, "see you soon". Matthew put down the phone and said to Dexter Donnelly, "ready?" They both got up and left the office for the restaurant.

Matthew was enjoying his dinner with Dexter Donnelly. Matthew had always found Dexter to be quite engaging. Dexter was now approaching forty five, with graying temples and movie star looks. Matthew noticed a few women in the restaurant doing a double take when they walked by their table. He was sure that these women were noticing the distinguished looking gentleman he was sitting with. They talked about the incident at Matthew's home over the weekend. Dexter expressed his concern and said he was glad that Matthew was installing an alarm. "Maybe you should keep that gun on you all the time as well", commented Dexter. Matthew shrugged his shoulders, "I'm not sure with my performance over the weekend if I should be carrying a gun around. I don't really know if I have the heart to actually shoot somebody."

They then began to talk about the draft statute that Matthew wanted Dexter to sponsor. The proposal would specifically enter the language "sexual orientation" into the already existing state anti-discrimination law. Matthew had a copy of the existing statute. He handed it to Dexter with the arrow he inserted to include the phrase "sexual orientation". The existing statute prohibited discrimination on the basis of sex, race, national origin and religion in the areas of housing, employment, public accommodations and medical care. "I think that this addition would be easier than rewriting the entire statute and trying to get the legislature to approve a brand new statute. It also has the ultimate effect that I think we want by just adding this category of protected class to the existing statute.", said Matthew to Dexter.

Donnelly shook his head in agreement. "I think this would be more palatable to my colleagues. But I also think it will still be a battle.", said Donnelly. Matthew paused, "I know it will. But I think it's necessary that we raise the issue and give it a try." Dexter Donnelly replied, "I couldn't agree more."

They ordered dessert and coffee. Dexter then said to Matthew, "I wanted to change the subject a bit if you don't mind." Matthew replied, "that's fine...what's on your mind?" Dexter said, "it's my son, Peter. He's nineteen, a freshman at Northeastern. He still lives at home. The other day he told my wife that he thought he was gay. She came to me horrified. I told her to calm down and she told me to deal with it." Matthew leaned forward across the table toward Donnelly with an attentive stare. Donnelly continued in a somber tone, "I'm not really sure how to deal with it. Obviously, I don't care if he's gay...but my wife, well she's another story. But that's not really the issue...I can deal with her. I guess I'm just upset that Peter didn't feel he could talk to me about it..."

Matthew interrupted, "I'm not sure if that's true Dexter. You might be reading too much into the fact that he told Karen first." Donnelly responded, "you may be right. But I guess I'm bringing this up because I know it can be difficult for kids to come out and I want to make this as painless as possible for Peter." The waitress arrived with their dessert. Matthew took a sip of the steaming coffee and then said, "Unfortunately I don't think you can totally prevent the pain that Peter will have to go through. The major part of the pain can be removed by your acceptance. But then he's going to have to deal with your wife. If you can get Karen to accept it and be able to deal with it, then that will remove a major obstacle too. But then there's society's response…" Dexter replied, "I guess that's what I'm afraid of. I think I can deal with Karen…I mean, she's going to have to deal with it. I won't tolerate her acting out against him because of this and I think she knows that. She does love her son…" Matthew interjected, "I have no doubt that Karen loves your son, but I know it can be difficult." Dexter shook his head in agreement. "But the society issue…how do I help to prepare him?"

Matthew paused momentarily and then said, "I guess that's the million dollar question. I don't really know if I have the answer. It's going to be tough. I think if he knows that he is always safe at home that will give him the strength to confront society's negative reaction to him. One thing though, don't let him come out in the gay bars. If I were you I would try to channel him to more appropriate and supportive areas. There are a great deal of young gay support groups. If you want I can get you the information." Dexter said, "yes, please…I think that would be helpful." They concluded their dessert with further discussion about Dexter's son. It was a good discussion and Matthew was happy to be of whatever help he could. They parted for the evening with Matthew's promise to call Dexter with the information about the support groups.

While walking home Matthew was thinking about how much he admired Dexter not only as an effective legislator but also as a parent. Dexter was truly concerned for his child's well being. The fact that his son was gay did not affect the way Dexter felt about his son. Matthew thought how Dexter reminded him of his own father. Franco accepted Matthew's homosexuality as one facet of his son's being. To Franco, Matthew wasn't just a homosexual, he was a great many other things. He was a lawyer, a caring individual, an athlete, a bright man, and his son. Matthew was glad to see another father feel the same way about his son as Matthew's father did.

A week passed when Octavia met with Matthew about the DCP case. The order of contempt had been set aside pending resolution of the appeal. Jennifer Alexander had skillfully advocated to Judge O'Toole that the threat of contempt in the face of appeal was not good jurisprudence. Through her advocacy or his fear of reversal on appeal, O'Toole removed the contempt order. The children would remain with Luis Ruiz and Brian McDermott. The appeals court had set the matter for hearing in three weeks. "I really think you're the one who can convince the justices that this case is about the children's rights and not about sexual preference", said Matthew to Octavia. She looked at him and said, "I hope I am. I think that's what the case is all about…but you never know what the court may think. I think it's real risky. They could uphold the trial court and that could send the message that we're all afraid of." Matthew replied, "I guess…but in my heart I don't think they will take the bait. I think that the court will weed through the red herrings and look at the needs of the twins." Octavia smiled, "that's what I intend to try to convince them to do." "You will!", exclaimed Matthew.

The phone rang interrupting their discussion. "It's James Davenport on the phone. I didn't know if I should interrupt…it sounded personal", said Tracy. "That's okay", said Matthew. "I'll come back", said Octavia to Matthew. He shook his head affirmatively. "Hello, James", said Matthew. "Hi…I'm sorry. I know I must have interrupted something. I have to remind myself that you're a big shot now! I can't just call you at the drop of the hat…" Matthew replied, "that's okay…what's up?"

James said, "well I called to see if you talked to Adam yet. I really wanted to go out for dinner sometime this week if that's okay…" Matthew indicated that he hadn't talked to Adam yet. "I've had a hell of a couple weeks…I promise I'll talk to him about it tonight", he said. James replied, "maybe you should invite him along to dinner. It might remove some of the mystery to the whole thing…" Matthew said, "well I don't know about that. But let me think about it. I'll call you tomorrow…I promise". James replied, "okay" and hung up the phone.

That evening after they were done with dinner Matthew decided to bring up the issue of James Davenport to Adam. He told him about the two phone calls he had received. Adam did not look pleased. "I knew he was in town. I saw the ad in the Sunday Ledger for the play. I figured he'd call you." Matthew explained that he would like to see James and go out to dinner, but would only do so if Adam approved. He also explained James offer for Adam to join them for dinner. "Well isn't that so big of him!", replied an angry Adam. Matthew replied, "well I guess by your response that the answer is 'no'." Adam replied, "do whatever you want. I guess I don't really understand why you two need to see each other. It was an affair…it's been over for awhile, or so I thought!"

Matthew reassured Adam that there was no affair going on between James and he. But he wondered if this fell on deaf ears. "Maybe I should have told James 'no' right away and then never told Adam", thought Matthew. But the cat was out of the bag. He had to deal with it. "I would really like to have your approval", said Matthew to Adam. Adam looked at him in anger and said, "I think you do whatever you think you should do. You're not going to get my approval or disapproval. Do what you're going to do and then deal with the consequences." Matthew replied, "well what I'm going to do right now is forget about the whole thing." Adam said, "that's the easy way out…just don't deal with it."

Matthew sat on the sofa in the living room and flipped the channels. "*Jeopardy!* is on. Are you going to play?", he asked Adam. Adam came in and sat next to him. They began to play the game. At the commercial break Adam asked Matthew, "so what about your other trick?" Matthew looked quizzically at him. "What are you talking about?" Adam replied, "Dion. Are you going to give him a job?" Matthew sighed. "I told you last week he has an interview with Elizabeth Kragen a couple days after she starts. It will be up to her. Can't I do anything right?" Adam smirked and said, "Scott better keep an eye out for you…you might steal his boyfriend from him!" Matthew flipped the television off. He stood up over Adam and yelled, "that's not fair! I told you I was trying to help him out! Can't you just believe me? Why would I ever do something like that to Scott? That's just not fair!" Before Adam had a chance to respond, Matthew walked out of the living room and went into the kitchen. He grabbed his jacket and stormed out of the house. He got into his car and went for a drive.

Matthew drove north on the expressway. He put one of his saddest Patti LaBelle tapes on his stereo. He was upset. He truly loved Adam and yet everything he seemed to be doing recently was being second guessed by Adam. He had no sexual desires for Dion. Yes, it was true that Dion was a beautiful and sexy young man. But he was Scott's boyfriend. Matthew was happy about that. He would never do anything to interfere with that. Scott meant too much to him. Damn it, Adam meant too much to him!, thought Matthew.

He got off the highway and reentered going south back towards home. He thought about James Davenport. He decided it would be wonderful to see him again. But it wasn't worth the risk of losing Adam. He would have to call James and tell him that he was sorry, but they couldn't get together. The thought of being without Adam again was too much for him to handle. Matthew wasn't paying attention as he was driving. A heavy rain began to fall on the highway. He kept on thinking about his personal life. Suddenly, he thought he saw something in the road. He went to slam on his brakes. They weren't responding. The car was hydroplaning. He kept pushing on the pedal with all his force. He was swerving. The car was not responding! Suddenly, he felt the impact of his front end hitting against the jersey barrier. Then he felt the air bag pop into his face and smother him.

The next thing Matthew remembered was lying in the ambulance on the way to the hospital. The attendant asked him how he felt. "I'm okay…is anybody hurt?", he asked. The attendant replied, "nobody's hurt except your car…what happened?" Matthew explained how he thought he saw something in the road and that his brakes didn't respond because of the wet road. The attendant shook his head.

About three hours later Matthew was checking out of the hospital with Adam at his side. He had not been hurt, just some bruised ribs, but his car was a mess. The police had it towed to the local state police barracks. They would reconstruct the accident scene. During the ride home Adam was apologetic. "If we hadn't fought you wouldn't have gotten into that accident.", said a contrite Adam. Matthew responded that the accident wasn't Adam's fault. He just wasn't paying attention while he was driving and he probably was going to fast. He was sure that he had seen something though. It looked like a dog or something. Matthew also told Adam that he decided on his drive that he was not going to see James Davenport. "You mean too much to me to let this screw things up again", he told Adam. "Thank you", replied Adam.

The state police investigation of the accident was completed quickly. A week later Matthew received a call from the Captain at the barracks where his car remained. "Well, Mr. Attorney General, I'm not going to give you a ticket for speeding. You probably were only going about five miles over the speed limit. But your car should have stopped…the surface wasn't that wet." Matthew sighed and replied, "any idea what happened then? I've never had a problem with the car before." The Captain replied, "I think somebody may have tampered with the brake lines. Where do you park your car?" Matthew became anxious. He nervously replied, "I…I park the car in my driveway. I don't have a garage. Somebody may have tampered with the brake lines…what do you mean?" The Captain said, "our investigator thinks they were cut so that they would eventually break. Any idea who would do this?"

Matthew was now very concerned. Add this to what happened a few weeks ago with the trespasser at his house and it appeared to Matthew that somebody was trying to hurt him. He told the Captain he had no idea who would cut his brake lines. He also told the Captain about the incident at his house a few weeks ago. The police officer responded, "I think I'm going to give the Commandant a call. I think somebody may have some ill will towards you. You may need to think about protection." Matthew said, "I have an alarm on my house…there's a uniformed officer at my office…what else do I need?" The Captain replied, "maybe a bodyguard." Matthew chuckled, "don't you think that's a little reactionary?" The Captain concluded, "no, not really. I'll talk to the Commandant. He'll get back to you."

A month passed and the decision on what was called *In re Male Twins*, the DCP case with the pseudoymn to protect the identity of the children was issued. Octavia picked up the copy from the court. The appeals court had directed that the matter be remanded back to the trial court. The appeals court found that the probate court judge had made a "dispositional order without the benefit of hearing evidence on the best interests of the children at issue". The issue of whether Colin and David should remain with their gay foster parents would have to be tried at the trial court level. The appeals court was clear that the standard to be applied was the best interests of the children standard.

Octavia and Matthew had to decide what to do now that the case was thrown back in their laps. "Let's give it a couple of days and see whether we want to try it or whether we'll send it back to DCP. I'm seeing Janice this weekend. I'll discuss it with her.", Matthew told Octavia. He rose out of his chair and grabbed his long winter jacket. The weather had taken a major shift toward winter cold. "Come on Daniel. I'm ready to go home.", said Matthew to the undercover state police officer who was assigned to be his bodyguard. He leaned into Octavia and whispered in her ear, "you know they give me this body-guard and I can't even get a cute one at that!" She chuckled and walked away. Matthew waved bye to Tracy as he and the police officer walked toward the door of the building to go home.

The holiday season provided Matthew with a legislative loss. The house had defeated Dexter Donnelly's proposed amendment to the state's anti-discrimination law. "I'm sorry", said Donnelly to Matthew. Matthew replied, "don't be sorry. It's not your fault. We'll try it again…I'm not willing to let go." Later that day Matthew's office issued a press statement expressing the disappointment of the Attorney General over the defeat of the proposed amendment.

The press release concluded, "in this time of good will towards all, I invite the members of the legislature to reevaluate their votes on this important issue. Good will provides that we treat all as equals, no matter what their differences might be. The legislature has by their votes reneged on that good will towards all. I invite the legislature to start the new year in the spirit of good will and to offer up the amendment again for consideration." The release was signed, Matthew Schipani, Attorney General.

He thought maybe it was a hollow message falling on deaf ears. But maybe it would get through to a few. It needed to be said. Matthew was determined that if the legislature would not act, he would have the bill reintroduced at every opportunity he could. "It's about equality and fairness", he would tell his friends.

CHANGES

March 1995

Matthew was a bundle of nerves sitting on the couch petting Diana. He was waiting for Adam to return from the job interview in San Diego. They hadn't spoke since the interview and Matthew knew that he would be ready to attack Adam for information the minute he walked in the door from the airport.

Matthew was uncertain about how he felt regarding Adam getting this job. Sure, it was an interim position, only through the spring 1997, but that was two whole years. Matthew wasn't sure if their relationship could handle the separation. An east coast—west coast relationship would be difficult. Their time together would be minimal. But Matthew did not let his own personal concerns interfere with Adam's professional desires. He supported Adam when they had discussed the position. He encouraged Adam to apply and when Adam received an interview Matthew was his strongest cheerleader. But inside he felt much different. He felt empty. He recalled the days of their separation a few years ago. He wasn't sure he could endure that loneliness again.

Diana jumped off the couch and headed toward the kitchen door. A few moments later Matthew heard Adam pull into the driveway in their new Volvo. The door slammed, the trunk opened and momentarily thereafter Adam was greeting a barking Diana. Matthew walked out into the kitchen and hugged Adam. He took his suitcase from him and dragged it into the bedroom. Then he came back out into the kitchen. "Do you want a drink?", asked Matthew. "I'd love one!", replied Adam. Matthew began preparing Adam a scotch and soda. Adam quietly said, "well, the job's mine if I want it…" Matthew turned, drink in hand and gave it to Adam. He sat down at the kitchen table with him. Matthew feigned joy and said, "that's wonderful…what are you going to do?" Adam paused briefly and then said, "I told them I'd need a week to think about it. It's a great opportunity…to be a Dean of an up and coming law school. Even if it is only for a few years. Then I could come back and get a better position here."

Matthew went to the refrigerator. He grabbed a soda and sat back down at the table. "It sounds like you've already made up your mind", he said in a somber tone. Adam replied, "no, not really. I think we need to talk about how this will impact us. You were pretty good at avoiding that subject before I left. I think we need to figure it out before I make a final decision." Matthew looked at Adam and said, "this is your decision, not mine. I think you have to do what is right for you." Adam angrily responded, "it's our decision…that's the problem. You don't want to deal with it! We need to discuss it and figure out if it's really worth it." Matthew took a sip of the soda and stood up saying, "it's late…let's talk about it tomorrow when we get home from work." Adam shook his head and replied, "fine…avoid it for another day. We'll talk about it tomorrow."

That evening in the middle of the night Matthew woke up. He rolled into Adam and put his arm around his sleeping lover. He squeezed Adam's torso and held him tight. Adam remained sleeping. Matthew stared at the back of his lover's head and held on. He knew in his heart that Adam really wanted this job. Standing in his way would be selfish. But he didn't want to let go…yet he knew he had to.

Matthew closed his eyes and tried to fall asleep. He had an empty feeling in his stomach and in his soul. This was the beginning of the end.

The next day brought Matthew a series of mini-crisis's that needed immediate attention. He felt as if he didn't have the energy to make these decisions but he knew they were his to make. His mind was preoccupied, but he had to put his personal issues aside so he could deal with the pressing legal issues. The first issue was where Matthew would give his address on gay civil rights. He had been approached by his alma mater, Harvard Law School, to be their keynote speaker. He had also been approached by two state colleges and the University of Hartford in Connecticut. Matthew decided that he wanted to return to the Berkshires to make the address, so he told Tracy to call the president of Westfield State and confirm his acceptance.

The next issue was the Baker case. There had been a pre-trial conference yesterday regarding the upcoming trial concerning the twins. Octavia appeared in Matthew's office to give him an update. "I made the argument to Judge O'Toole that he should recuse himself from the proceedings given the appellate involvement. He finally agreed after he berated me about my questioning his judicial integrity. I should find out today who it is assigned to", Octavia told Matthew. "I can't believe the old fart would question you after the ruling he made!", forcefully responded Matthew. Octavia smiled and said, "you know judges…some of them when they put on that robe, they think they're God." Matthew smiled and shook his head in agreement.

Octavia then continued, "I think it will be June before we get a trial date. Thank God the kids didn't have to move! I've been thinking, though…I really think that you should do the trial." Matthew's eyebrows raised. He leaned back in his chair and said, "don't you think that I would be seen as a little too personally involved in this case?" Octavia replied, "no I don't. I think it fits in with where you envision yourself as Attorney General. I also think if you avoid any gay litigation you are caving into the establishment. Take that logic and extend it. If you do then I can't argue any cases involving women's rights. I don't think that's what you really believe in".

Matthew folded his hands on his desk and leaned forward. "It has been quite awhile since I have done a trial, but I guess as always, you're right", he said. Then he continued, "okay...let's do it this way. We'll do the trial together...we'll prepare the case together, appear in court together and do all the publicity together. That will send a better message than me doing it alone." Octavia readily agreed. She stood up and as she was leaving said, "I'll get the entire case file copied for you so you can review it." Matthew replied, "thank you."

"Scott's on hold", Tracy said as Matthew picked up the phone. He clicked over to the next line. "Yes dear", he said to his friend. "I was wondering if you had time for lunch today", asked Scott. Matthew looked at his appointment calendar and his watch. "I can do a brief lunch, but it would have to be around here", he said. Scott replied, "okay...how about 12:30?" Matthew said, "I'll meet you at Mario's, 12:30." and then he hung up the phone.

The third issue that Matthew had to deal with presented itself as he was getting ready to walk out the door to lunch. "Grumpy's on the phone", said Tracy referring to the holding Governor Lloyd Dickerson. Matthew punched the line on his telephone. "Good afternoon Governor. How can I help you?", he said in a cherry tone. A bellowing Lloyd Dickerson responded, "for Christsakes Matthew! Where the fuck is the paper on the death penalty? You promised it to me last week! I have to introduce this bill soon. I can't sit around and wait!"

Matthew quickly responded to the fuming Governor. "I'm sorry. I thought Elizabeth Kragen brought it over to you last week. I reviewed it with her in the beginning of the week. She assured me that she would personally deliver it." The Governor was not calmed by Matthew's response. "Well, tell the bitch to get it over here today!", ordered Governor Dickerson. Matthew replied, "she's on vacation until next week. She's in Hawaii...I'll have my administrative assistant try to find it and get it right over to you." The Governor screamed, "today! Not tomorrow!", and slammed down the phone in Matthew's ear.

Matthew got up from his desk and opened the door. "Tracy...can you come in here for a minute?", he said to his administrative assistant. Tracy immediately came into Matthew's office and shut the door behind her. "The Governor didn't get the position paper on the death penalty that Elizabeth had done. Do you have any idea what happened?" Tracy had a confused look and then said, "she told me last Friday that she was hand delivering it. She left in the afternoon for the State House. I thought she delivered it." Matthew said, "I'm going to lunch with Scott. Please go down to her office, have her secretary get into the computer and see if it's there. If not, unlock the office and go through her files. I need it by the time I get back!" Tracy stood up and shook her head affirmatively. Before he knew it, she was out the door and down the hall toward Elizabeth Kragen's office.

Matthew and Scott had a light lunch. Scott asked how Dion was doing in his job at Matthew's office. Matthew replied that he heard positive reviews regarding Dion. Then Scott asked, "so what's happening with Adam? Is he taking the job?" Matthew put his head down briefly and then said, "I think he really wants to. But he says he wants me to be part of the decision. You know that I don't want him to go, but I can't let him know that. It wouldn't be fair to him." Matthew continued, "he was always so supportive to me in my goals." Scott interrupted, "I think you may have to let him go. If you don't he's going to resent you for it. Then your relationship will suffer more than if he went." Matthew shook his head in agreement. "I know...but it's really hard. I've been avoiding it, but we're suppose to talk about it tonight. I'm going to have to give him my blessing or he won't take the job. I guess I never thought it would end again...certainly not this way", said Matthew as his eyes began to water. Scott extended his hand across the table and put it on Matthew's. "This doesn't mean the relationship is over. It's only a temporary job. You two can fly back and forth to see each other…" Matthew looked at Scott and said, "no…it's over. I mean, we'll try to do that in the beginning. But then the distance will get in the way. The contact will lessen and be more sporadic. The relationship is going to fade away." Scott replied, "no, you're wrong. It doesn't have to be that way. You can make it work…you just have to try."

They ended their lunch shortly thereafter and Scott walked with Matthew to the door of his office. They hugged and Matthew said, "see you tonight", as he turned and went back into the building. Scott waved to his friend. Matthew quickly proceeded to the elevator and then to his office.

Tracy followed Matthew into his office. "We can't find it!", she said in an excited tone. Matthew took his overcoat off and hung it on the coat tree. He went behind his desk and sat down. "No where?", he asked. "No where", she replied. "I don't get it", said a perplexed Matthew. "She knew how important this was…that it had to be done before she went on vacation. I don't understand why it's not on the computer or there's no copies any where." Tracy replied, "I don't either. This doesn't give me a good feeling about her."

Matthew looked at Tracy and asked, "what do you mean?" Tracy got up from the chair, went over and shut the office door and then sat back down. "Well, I wasn't going to tell you this because I thought I may have heard it out of context. But now with this going on, I really wonder." Matthew interrupted, "please, tell me what's on your mind." Tracy began in a concerned tone, "I guess I don't really trust her. About two weeks ago I was going into the copy room on the fifth floor when I heard her and Anita Gunther talking. I stood outside for a minute because what I thought I heard bothered me. Elizabeth was saying that she didn't like a "faggot" being her boss. Anita was quiet and Elizabeth went on to say that she thought that when "he loses the election next year" that she would run for Attorney General. I then ruffled the papers in my hand so they could hear me coming. I walked into the copy room. She greeted me with her pearly white smile and then went on her way."

Matthew put his hand up to Tracy to indicate "stop". He then said to her, "so what do you think it all means?" Tracy replied, "I think she's a snake…she's going to try to set you up somehow. Maybe she just did. She knew how important that paper on the death penalty was and that Dickerson was waiting for it. She knew that he'd be bullshit at you if it wasn't done on time. I don't think she ever delivered it." Matthew said, "don't you think it's possible that it may have gotten lost at the Governor's office?" Tracy in a raised voice exclaimed, "Matthew, don't be so naive! Just watch your back…I don't trust her!" Matthew indicated to Tracy that he would talk to Octavia about this and asked her not to discuss it with anyone else. Tracy readily agreed.

Matthew sat back in his chair for a moment thinking about Elizabeth Kragen. Did she have an agenda to see him fail?, he wondered. He also thought about Tracy's assessment of Kragen. Matthew had known Tracy for many years. She had a keen ability on evaluating people. Most of the time she was accurate. He picked up the phone and asked Tracy to have Octavia come to his office before she left for the day. "Will do", replied Tracy.

Matthew dialed the Governor's office. He apologized profusely to Lloyd Dickerson. The Governor was not pleased. But he indicated that he would wait until Kragen returned from her vacation before filing the bill. "I really need that paper about the constitutional issues before I put myself out on a limb on this issue", the Governor told Matthew. Matthew assured Governor Dickerson that he would deliver the analysis paper to him personally on the day his assistant returned.

That evening Matthew and Adam did not have their discussion about Adam's future career options. Matthew came home to find Adam sound asleep on the sofa. He had left a note for Matthew. "I think I may have the flu…I came home early from work." Matthew walked over to the sofa and pulled the comforter up to Adam's shoulders. He felt his forehead. Adam had a fever. That night Matthew spent nursing his lover with aspirin and fluids. They would not have the discussion this evening.

After a few days Adam recovered from the flu. It was time to discuss his future plans. He had to let the law school in San Diego know his decision in two days. Their discussion was very superficial. Matthew would not engage in discussing how this decision would impact their relationship. "I think you should take the job. It's what you want and I want it for you", Matthew repeatedly said to Adam. Whenever Adam would try to approach the issue of how geography would affect their relationship, Matthew replied, "we'll deal with it." The next day Adam called the law school and accepted the post. He would begin on May fifteenth.

Elizabeth Kragen sat in her office the morning of her return from vacation with a pensive Anita Gunther. "Can you believe that asshole called me at home last night and told me to be in his office at ten thirty?", complained an irritated Kragen. Anita Gunther shook her head saying nothing. "To think he can command me around! I think the power has gone to his head!", said Elizabeth Kragen as her face was becoming red with anger.

Gunther interjected, "what's so important that he wants to meet with you?", she asked. "It's that god damn death penalty analysis for the Governor. I forgot to drop it off at the State House before I left. I guess Dickerson was pissed. But I'm not letting 'queer boy' know that I forgot...I'll blame someone else...", said Kragen. "Just don't blame me!", exclaimed Gunther. Elizabeth Kragen rocked back in her chair and smirked, "how could I blame you? I need you...remember, I plan to run this office soon...I intend to have you with me.", she said. Anita Gunther replied, "this is too big for me...just keep me out of it, all right?". Smarmily, Kragen said "Don't worry honey, I will...now let me go see the boss and try to calm him down.", as she stood up from her desk and walked to the office door.

Matthew was deep in a pile of paperwork when Elizabeth Kragen knocked lightly on the door. "Come in", he firmly told her. Kragen sat down. Matthew began immediately. "Elizabeth, the reason I called you at home last night was I wanted to give you some lead time for today. While you were away the Governor called me and he was infuriated. He never received your analysis of the death penalty. I promised he would have it by the end of today. Do you know where it is?", asked Matthew. Kragen politely responded, "Matthew...I dropped it off at his office the day I left for vacation. Someone over there must have lost it. I also think I gave Tracy a copy of it before I left so you would have your own copy. I have the original on my computer at home...I'll go home now, print it out and personally deliver it again. I'm really sorry if this caused any inconvenience."

Matthew looked squarely at Elizabeth Kragen. He had prided himself on his ability to read people's faces. Yet, it appeared that her face did not show any sign of deception or deceit. Maybe she was telling the truth, he thought. He responded, "thank you. Would you please go take care of that now for me?" Kragen smiled and said, "of course" and then immediately rose from her chair and turned and left his office. She shut the door behind her. Matthew buzzed Tracy at her desk. "Could you come in for a second?", he asked.

Tracy walked into Matthew's office immediately thereafter. She shut the door behind her and sat down. "Did Elizabeth give you a copy of the document before she went on vacation?", Matthew asked Tracy. "No, she did not", emphatically stated Tracy. Matthew mused and said, "well she claims she did. Now if I had to bet money on who to believe, of course I would bet on you. So that raises the next question. Why did she lie about it?" Tracy instantly responded, "I told you a few weeks ago...I don't trust her. She's up to something...watch out for her." Matthew shook his head in agreement. "I don't like this feeling I'm getting about her. You, me and Octavia have to keep an eye on her...I'm starting to feel like Caesar!" Tracy agreed, "I think she's plotting something...I also don't trust that

Gunther woman either. I'm going to talk to Carol…she's down that end of the building. I can trust her." Matthew smiled, "Tracy, thank you…how could I ever survive in this job if you weren't here?" Tracy leaned across the desk and grabbed Matthew's hand and rubbed it with hers. "Don't worry honey…if she wants to start something she's going to have to get past me first!" Matthew smiled and Tracy smiled back as she left the office. "I wouldn't want to be on Tracy's bad list!", thought Matthew smiling.

The coming Saturday evening was a fairy tale come true for Matthew. Several months ago he had been invited to attend an AIDS benefit concert being held on Boston Harbor. The headliner for the concert was Diana Ross. Without hesitation Matthew accepted. He would have front row seats at the concert.

Matthew walked up to the bar with Adam and Dexter Donnelly and ordered a drink. The state police officer assigned to protect him stood off to the right. Dexter's son Peter stood with the officer and Scott and Dion. Matthew got his drink and walked back toward the group. "I think this is my fourteenth concert!", he proudly announced. Scott laughed and said, "I think we should give you a wig and a gown and let you do it…you probably know the show by heart!" The group laughed. They proceeded to their seats. Dexter and Matthew strolled behind. Dexter's son Peter and Adam were deep in conversation. "How's he doing?", inquired Matthew about Dexter's gay son. Dexter replied, "I think he's doing well. He had a couple of dates…my wife didn't freak out. I think events like this are important. He gets to see gay people come together for an important cause." Matthew replied, "I agree. I think this is a healthy way to come out." They walked together to their seats.

About five minutes before the show began Matthew sat frozen in fear next to Adam. Across the aisle he saw James Davenport sitting for the concert. Matthew had turned away quickly, but Davenport had noticed him. Now he was walking over toward Matthew and his group. As he got into the aisle squeezing by people to get to Matthew,

Trooper Frank Hamilton stood up. "Can I help you?", he inquired as he blocked Davenport's access to Matthew. Davenport sarcastically replied, "yeah, you can help me by getting the fuck out of my way!" With that, Trooper Hamilton flashed his badge in Davenport's face. Matthew stood up behind the police officer and said, "it's okay Frank…he's all right." The trooper said, "fine" and sat back down. Matthew extended his hand to Davenport saying, "Hi James…what brings you to Boston?" Davenport replied, "I'm dating one of the dancers in the group performing with Miss Ross." Matthew replied, "that's good…", and then said, "sorry about the distraction…there's some people who really don't like me, so I have to have some protection around." James replied, "no problem" and then looked at Adam and the others sitting next to him. "Aren't you going to introduce me?", he asked Matthew. "Sorry", replied Matthew as he made the awkward introduction of James Davenport to everyone. After a few moments of brief conversation Davenport shook Matthew's hand good bye and returned to his seat.

While the band was walking out Adam commented about Davenport to Matthew. "He's aged…he's not as cute as he used to be." Matthew smiled and then said, "I'm sorry…I didn't know he would be here." Adam replied in a light tone, "you have nothing to be sorry about…now just shut up and enjoy the show!" And enjoy the show Matthew did. All thoughts of Adam leaving next month were suspended as Matthew sat back and enjoyed his idol. While Diana was singing *Endless Love*, Matthew reached over and squeezed Adam's knee. Adam put his hand on top of Matthew's and they smiled at each other. But that was not the highlight for Matthew that evening.

Davenport arranged for back stage passes for Matthew and his friends. At the end of the show Matthew followed James backstage. There was a cocktail party to benefit AIDS. Matthew was introduced to Diana Ross by Davenport's boyfriend. Matthew shook her hand but was so starstruck that he was unable to say anything. All he did was smile. Diana Ross smiled back at him.

For the remainder of the weekend Matthew would not stop talking about how he had met Diana Ross. Scott and Adam joked with him about how starstruck he was. But for Matthew that didn't matter. He had actually shook hands with his idol. That memory would be with him forever.

April 19th. Another routine day was about to begin for Matthew. On the ride into work he and Adam talked about the small dinner party that Matthew had arranged at Scott's restaurant for Adam's going away. "I don't want any surprises!", commanded Adam. Matthew replied, "I promise there isn't. It's a quiet and intimate dinner like you asked." Adam pulled the Volvo up to the curb in front of Matthew's office. Matthew began to open the door and Adam grabbed his left arm, "are you sure you're okay about this?", he asked. Matthew replied, "about what?" Adam said, "you know what…I'm leaving in a few weeks. Are you sure you can deal with this?" Matthew looked at him and said, "yes I'm sure. I've been dealing with it. I've accepted it. I told you I think it's good for your career. What else do you want me to say?" Adam looked down at the seat briefly and then said, "nothing…I just want you to know that this has nothing to do with you. I'm doing this for me." Matthew took Adam's hand from his arm and held it. "I know…it's going to be okay. I love you…we'll work it out." He then leaned over to Adam and gave him a kiss. Matthew exited the car and Adam drove away.

The phone buzzed loudly. Matthew picked it up. "Come down to the conference room quick!", yelled Tracy. Matthew got up from his chair and briskly walked down the hall to the conference room. The large television in the corner was on. About five people had gathered in the room and their eyes were fixated on the television screen. The announcer from CNN was talking over a live picture of a burning building. "…once again, for those of you who are just joining us. A bomb apparently has exploded here at the federal building in Oklahoma City. Emergency crews are on the scene…the building houses many federal offices including the DEA and ATF. There is also a day care on the first floor of the building…" The announcer kept speaking but Matthew was tuning him out. He was completely engulfed by the horror on the screen. Visions of firefighters holding bleeding children in their arms and running from the crumbling building filled the television screen. Adults scurrying around the scene of destruction. Parents yelling for their children.

Matthew stood and watched the screen for about five minutes. Then he couldn't take it anymore. He leaned over to Tracy and whispered, "I'm going back to my office. You stay here…let me know what's happening." She nodded her head 'yes'. Matthew walked slowly back to his office. He closed the door behind him. He dialed Adam at the law school. "Did you see what happened?", he asked Adam as he picked up the phone. Adam replied, "I'm watching CNN right now." Matthew said, "fucked up world isn't it?" Adam responded, "it sure is."

Tracy kept Matthew up to date during the morning about the details of the Oklahoma City bombing. But in the afternoon, the bombing across the country took on a local flavor as the federal building in Boston had received a bomb threat. The Governor closed down the State House just in case. Matthew told Tracy to tell Octavia and Elizabeth to send their staff home. The office would close. He wasn't going to take a risk with anybody's lives.

That weekend Matthew, Adam and Aunt Gloria sat glued to the television as President Clinton led a nation in mourning over the Oklahoma bombing. The deaths of the children haunted Matthew. Once again children were innocent victims at the hands of an adult. Matthew sat on the sofa with tears coming down his face as the President delivered his impassioned speech. Senseless violence in a society that's going mad, thought Matthew.

"Well, Judge Martin has been assigned the case", said Octavia to a half awake Matthew on a dreary Monday morning. Matthew looked up from his desk and motioned Octavia into his office. "Is that good or bad?", he asked her. "I think it's okay. I talked to a friend of mine who practices there. Judge Martin has a fair reputation. She used to be a DA...been on the bench for about five years. I think we'll be okay.", said Octavia. Matthew replied, "good...good. So when's the date?" Octavia looked down at her notes, "June twelfth for pretrial and July eighth for trial. Do you think we can pull it together by then?", she asked. "I think so", responded Matthew.

So the Baker case would begin. Matthew and Octavia would have the opportunity to practice together. Matthew was looking forward to it. It would be fun to be back in the courtroom again. Plus, the case stood for something he really believed it. The twins deserved loving parents. The sexual orientation of those parents didn't matter. Hopefully this judge would agree and Colin and David Baker could get on with their lives in a loving home.

Two days before Adam's party Matthew was walking from his office to Scott's restaurant alone. He had given his protector the afternoon off. He had decided that the around the clock guard was not necessary. There had been no further incidents since the car accident and Matthew was now of the belief that having a state police officer assigned to him was a waste of the tax payers money. "I have to call the Commissioner of Safety", he thought. He didn't need a bodyguard anymore. Matthew arrived at Scott's restaurant without incident. He sat in his regular booth and ordered his normal cup of mocha java. A few moments later Scott joined him. "Everything is all set for the party", Scott told Matthew. "Good...I really want it to be nice", said Matthew. "It will be", responded Scott.

The dinner party was bittersweet for Matthew. He knew he had to put on a happy face for Adam. He wanted Adam to have fond memories of his send off. So Matthew smiled and talked about how proud he was of Adam. He loudly proclaimed that their relationship would weather this disruption. But in his heart he knew that this would not be true.

Their farewell at Logan Airport was difficult for Matthew. Inside he felt completely in turmoil. Yet, once again he put on his happy face. Adam promised to call when he landed in California. They kissed each other good bye and Adam walked into the gate down the ramp to the airplane. Matthew leaned against the wall and put his head down. He was silently crying. On the drive back to Cambridge, Matthew drove in his car in silence. He turned the radio off; he didn't want any cheery music or broken hearted lullabies now. He walked into the house and hugged Diana. He kissed his dog and said, "looks like it's you and me alone again baby", he said to her.

Matthew walked into the living room. He found a card on the coffee table. He opened it up. It was from Adam. It was a beautiful card with the inscription, "To the Man I Love." Matthew read the brief note Adam had written inside. "I know this is difficult for you...but I appreciate how you have supported me in this choice. Please know that I have never loved anyone as much as I have loved you and your family. Please continue to support me in my time of searching and growing. This is not good-bye, it's so long for now. Love always, Adam." Matthew put the card down and cried immensely. Diana laid her head on his lap and stared at her owner.

Commencement Day at Westfield State College and Matthew was the keynote speaker. He got out of his car and walked past a group of about fifteen protesters holding signs. Tracy walked with him. He looked at the signs. They did not have pleasant messages on them. "AIDS is God's Revenge", "Silly Faggots! Dicks are for Chicks!", "Repent for your Sins!". Matthew looked at Tracy as he continued to walk. "Well isn't this a pleasant welcome", he whispered to her. "Assholes!", she responded. The group began to chant, "Queer! Queer! Queer!". Matthew continued to walk. The local police officers came closer to him and escorted him by the group. Tracy stopped and flipped her middle finger at the group. Matthew laughed and tugged at Tracy with his right hand to continue to walk with him. As he turned he saw a familiar face in the back of the group. He was sure it was Craig Talbot. He stared at him briefly. Their eyes met for a moment, and then Matthew continued to walk.

His address was well received by the students. The protesters were kept outside. Matthew spoke of equality for all no matter their race, sex or sexual orientation. He spoke about how he would continue to fight for a statute to prohibit discrimination against gay persons. But Matthew was most proud of his comments regarding community service. Matthew told the graduates, "you now enter the work force and the professional community of this state. I wish you every professional and economic success. You deserve it after your long hours of study and training. But I implore you not to forget those who are less fortunate than you. Take some time from your professional lives to give back to your community. Become involved in your local church, local civil organization, primary school sports, youth groups or other agencies that help the less fortunate. Take time to give back to the community where you live and work. When we all take time to do this we enrich our community and ourselves. We enrich and ennoble ourselves and others. Be an active part of your community."

His comments were greeted with loud applause. Matthew hoped that the applause was an indicator that his message was heard and that a few of the graduates would heed his call.

He left the campus without incident. The protesters had left. Matthew and Tracy drove together to the Berkshires for dinner with his family. On the ride back to Boston Matthew told Tracy that he believed that he spotted Craig Talbot among the group of protesters. "That's that nut case that showed up years ago at DCP, isn't it?", asked a concerned Tracy. "Yes, it is", replied Matthew. Tracy shook her head. "I told you that you shouldn't have gotten rid of the state cop. What if he's the one behind the car accident?" Matthew looked at her as he prepared to take the exit off the turnpike. "But what if he wasn't? I don't want to blame him for something I can't prove." Tracy responded, "just call the state police and have them assign someone to you again please." Matthew replied, "I'll think about it. It was kind of eerie seeing him there."

That evening Adam called. He had been calling every day as promised since he moved. Matthew talked about the college address. He left out any mention of Craig Talbot. Adam seemed to be adjusting well to California. Matthew could tell from the excitement in his voice that Adam was feeling challenged with his new job. It was a good career move for him. Adam asked when Matthew was going to fly out to the west coast. "Let me finish up the Baker case and maybe I can get out there in August or September", Matthew said. Adam replied, "as soon as you can. I miss you a lot." Matthew said, "I miss you too."

A few days later, Matthew and Octavia were sitting discussing the "Elizabeth Kragen Issue", as Matthew had now called it. Over the past several weeks Kragen had been noticeably cold and distant to Matthew. He wondered what she was up to. "How about we have her go out to Philipston to deal with the environmental mess out there?", asked Octavia. Matthew smiled and held up one finger. "That's a great idea! She'd have to be out there for at least three months between investigation and the grand jury. It'll get her out of my hair and away from whatever camp of supporters she has set up here.", he said to Octavia. "I also don't think we want her around her when the trial begins in a couple of weeks.", Octavia stated. Matthew agreed. "I'll call the DA today and let her know in the morning that she should pack her bags and head west!", Matthew said laughingly.

The next morning Matthew met with Elizabeth Kragen in his office. He attempted to portray her assignment as one of great importance. But Matthew could tell from her facial expressions that Elizabeth Kragen knew exactly what was going on. She was being banished from the castle so the king could hold onto his throne. "He's won this one", thought Kragen, "but it's only the battle, not the war." Kragen smiled and shook Matthew's hand as she thanked him for the assignment. Matthew sat in his chair as the door to his office slammed behind a leaving Elizabeth Kragen.

Tracy came into the office a moment later. "Is the bitch gone?", she asked. Matthew smiled, "for a little bit at least. Hopefully she gets the message that she's playing with the wrong person.", he said. "I wouldn't bet on it", said Tracy as she handed Matthew the morning mail and left the office.

Matthew began to sort his mail. One letter appeared odd to him. He grabbed the letter opener and tore the envelope. He pulled out the papers inside. He opened the papers to see his face imposed on the naked body of a man having anal sex with another man. He flipped through the papers. They were all explicit photographs of men engaged in sexual activities. Matthew's face had been copied from newspaper photos and placed over the person in the photo. There was also a brief note in the envelope. It was obviously typed on an old typewriter. The type was worn and uneven.

The note read, "wouldn't the press like to see the attorney general doing what he really likes to do? Sucking cock and fucking butts! You goddamn faggot! I'm watching for you…you're on your way to hell and I have the ticket in my hand!" Matthew put down the papers. He looked at his hands. They were shaking. He picked up the envelope. There was no return address. The postmark was Boston. Matthew picked up the phone and buzzed Tracy, "can you come back in here please?", he asked. When she returned he handed her the papers and the envelopes. She looked at them and read the note. "Can I call the state police please?", she tenderly asked. Matthew shook his head "yes".

He was meeting with Octavia about the letter when Tracy knocked to announce the arrival of Lieutenant Mark Cunningham of the state police. "Show him in please", said Matthew. He stood up, introduced himself and Octavia. Lieutenant Cunningham introduced Trooper Debra Kiley who was with him. Matthew handed the Lieutenant the papers and the envelope he had received. Lieutenant Cunningham reviewed them and then handed them to Trooper Kiley.

"Do you have any idea who is behind this?", asked Lieutenant Cunningham. Matthew said, "I think I may have figured it out". Matthew then explained to Lieutenant Cunningham about the incident at his house with the trespasser and the car accident. "I already know about those matters. I pulled your file", the state police officer told Matthew. "Great! I have a file with the state cops.", thought Matthew. "You said you thought you may know who is behind this. Why don't you tell me about that?", asked Lieutenant Cunningham.

Matthew then explained about Craig Talbot. He went over everything he could remember about Craig. He started with how he had taken him away from his parents when he was a teenager because of abuse. Then he told the state police about the incident at Harvard Square many years ago, as well as the incident when he was chief legal counsel of DCP. Matthew concluded with that he believed he saw Craig present at Westfield State College among protesters when Matthew gave his address at the graduation.

"Well, I think we may have a stalker here", said Lieutenant Cunningham. He continued, "We'll do everything we can to locate and tail this guy. Meanwhile, I think your one on one protection should begin again. I hope you don't have any objections." Matthew looked at Tracy. She gave him a stern look. If he turned down the bodyguard he knew there would be hell to pay with her. "No, I don't have any objections. That's fine", he told the Lieutenant.

Lieutenant Cunningham and Trooper Kiley rose from their chairs. "Don't worry Mr. Attorney General. We'll find him and monitor his every move.", said the police officer. "Thank you", said Matthew as he walked them out of his office. Trooper Kiley said, "we'll be sending over a trooper this afternoon. Kevin Miller will be assigned to you." "Thank you", replied Matthew again.

A few hours later his bodyguard arrived. "A muscular latino man and I get to take him home with me!", said Matthew to Octavia trying to make light of the situation as they stood admiring the handsome state police officer assigned to protect Matthew. They both laughed.

That evening Matthew cleaned up the extra bedroom in the house for Trooper Kevin Miller. Scott came upstairs to see Matthew and when he saw a handsome latin man walk into the kitchen he smirked at Matthew. Matthew laughed inside, he knew what Scott was thinking. Matthew introduced Trooper Miller to Scott. They shook hands and Trooper Miller went back into the living room to watch television. Diana followed him. She was enjoying the company.

"Did you get to hand pick the cop to watch over you?", asked Scott in a lilting tone. "No...but boy did I luck out, huh?", replied Matthew. "Yes you did. He's a stud if I've ever seen one!", said Scott. Matthew responded, "yes he is. A straight stud with a wife and two kids at home." Scott laughed and said, "well, that's his loss." They laughed together. A moment later Dion appeared at the door. He came in and sat down. Once again Trooper Miller came out into the kitchen. Matthew provided the introductions. He also had to repeat his discussion about the handsome state police officer in the other room.

They sat around for about an hour gossiping. Ken Rivers was planning to spend the weekend with Matthew. They were going to go on the AIDS walk together. "This will be my last free weekend. The trial starts next week", Matthew told Scott and Dion. Scott said, "well enjoy it...but don't fuck Ken again, okay?" Matthew laughed, "I can't promise anything!", he said.

That evening as he and Diana laid in bed, with Trooper Miller in the other room Matthew stared at the ceiling. Adam hadn't called in two days. Maybe he was busy...or maybe the drift was starting to set in. Matthew began to feel incredibly alone and empty. Adam was gone and Matthew was sure that he would never be back. He was also sure there would never be another Adam in his life. He had found his true love and now he lost him. It was difficult for him to fall asleep that evening.

The custody trial was here. Matthew and Octavia walked into the courtroom of Judge Antoinette Martin. It was a new courtroom. One Matthew did not like. The veneer and cheap furniture filled the tiny room. But the furnishings of the room was not what mattered here. The only thing that mattered was that Matthew and Octavia were successful in their pursuit of parents for Colin and David Baker. Judge Martin took the bench. "Are the parties ready to proceed?", she inquired. Matthew stood up and stated, "Attorney General Matthew Schipani on behalf of the petitioner, Division of Child Protection. Also present in the courtroom is Deputy Attorney General Octavia Moon." The judge replied, "thank you Mr. Attorney General", and she turned to opposing counsel. "Attorney Mary Ward-McGinley for the parents. Ready to proceed your honor", said Matthew's opposition. The judge then stated, "the Commonwealth may call its first witness." Matthew stood once again and said, "the Commonwealth calls DCP Commissioner Janice Pierce."

Janice Pierce stood from the galley and strolled to the witness stand. She was an incredibly commanding presence. Her walk to the stand alone was elegantly impressive. Judge Martin visibly took note of the stature of the DCP commissioner as she sat down in the witness chair. Matthew began the examination of Janice. It was odd to him to have one of his dearest friends on the witness stand with him asking pointed questions of her. But Matthew was a professional and he played the role. He was the lawyer and she was the state's witness.

"Now Commissioner Pierce, could you summarize from your prior testimony the reasoning that the Division approved and supported the placement of the children in the foster home of Luis Ruiz and Brian McDermott?", probed Matthew with his final question of the witness. Janice pointedly paused for a moment and then stated, "As I indicated when I began my testimony a while ago, the issue for me as Commissioner is that children who are in the state's custody are placed in loving and permanent homes. In this case the biological parents were no longer an option. The court had found them unfit and unavailable to care for the twins. The children were only three months old when they were removed from the parents. They were still suffering from cocaine withdrawal. Mr. Ruiz and Mr. McDermott took the children in and attended not only to their daily needs, but also to their special needs as a result of being born drug addicted. The children remained in that home. They received daily loving care and protection. When the decision was made by the court that the children were permanently removed from their parents, a long term plan had to be developed for Colin and David. Mr. Ruiz and Mr. McDermott were the logical long term plan. They had provided excellent care to the children. The local office staff approved them as adoptive resources. I concur with that decision."

Matthew then asked, "just one final question Commissioner before I let you go. Are you as Commissioner of the state's child protective agency telling this court that the sexual orientation of the parents is not relevant?" Janice smiled and replied, "yes I am. I, as Commissioner, do not care what the race, sex or orientation of prospective foster or adoptive parents happens to be. All I care about is that we have adults who are willing to make a long term loving commitment to children in our care. This case is not about sexual orientation. This case is about Colin and David Baker deserving to have two loving parents who have cared for them since they were three months old."

Matthew turned to Judge Martin and said, "No further questions, your honor" and then sat down at the counsel table. Attorney Mary Ward-McGinley rose from her seat. "I only have a few questions for you Commissioner", she said. Attorney McGinley moved closer to Janice who sat straight up in the witness chair.

"My first question to you is how did you become the Commissioner of the Division of Child Protection?", said Attorney McGinley. Octavia rose from her chair. "Objection! Irrelevant.", she proclaimed. Attorney McGinley turned to Judge Martin and stated, "if I may be heard before the court rules?" The judge responded, "go ahead counselor". Attorney McGinley stepped back and in front of the judge's bench. She addressed the court, "your honor. It is my client's position that this decision is a sham for political gain. I would proffer to this court that the witness became the DCP commissioner because of the political ties she has with the Attorney General…" Judge Martin interrupted, "I'm not sure what the relevance of that is counselor." Attorney McGinley replied, "your honor, I believe it is relevant to show that this decision was not made with the children's best interest at heart, but rather with the goal of promoting the platform of the Attorney General on behalf of homosexuals. This is a political decision to meet the Attorney General's political goals. That is why he is here to argue this case."

Matthew rose from his chair and bellowed, "your honor, I must object! Attorney McGinley cannot state what my reasoning behind trying this case is. If the court desires to know that and believes it is relevant, I would respectfully ask that I be given the opportunity to address that issue." Judge Martin turned to Attorney McGinley and stated, "he's right. The testimony given here by the Commissioner was that this decision was made at the local level and that she approved it. If you want to cross examine here about why she approved it, you may. But the issue of the Attorney General trying this case is irrelevant. Now please proceed on with your next question counselor."

Attorney McGinley then began her brief cross-examination of Janice Pierce. She went over in detail Janice's involvement with the case. Janice was consistent with her direct examination and that her role in this case was limited to the approval of the prospective foster parents and the decision to appeal the trial court's denial of their petition to adopt. "My last question Madam Commissioner", said Attorney McGinley as she began to close her examination, "isn't it true that you and the Attorney General have been friends for almost twenty years?" Octavia and Matthew simultaneously rose from their chair and in unison stated, "objection!". Judge Martin sternly replied, "sustained. Counselor I told you that this subject was irrelevant to these proceedings!" Attorney McGinley looked at the judge and said, "then I have nothing further your honor. Thank you Ms. Pierce."

Judge Martin turned to Janice Pierce and said, "thank you Commissioner. You may step down." Janice Pierce stepped down from the witness stand and walked by the counsel table. She returned to her seat in the small galley of the courtroom. Judge Martin indicated that this would conclude today's testimony in the case. "We'll pick it up on Monday. Does the Commonwealth believe it can finish their case by Tuesday?", she asked. Matthew replied, "yes, your honor. We have four other witnesses, including the prospective adoptive parents. Our case in chief should be done by Tuesday morning." Judge Martin responded, "thank you. Then court is adjourned for today."

After court Matthew, Octavia and Janice went to a nearby deli for dinner. Matthew and Octavia were staying in the Berkshires with Matthew's parents through the conclusion of the trial. It was easier than commuting back and forth to Boston. Janice would leave tonight to return to her husband Jose and her two children, Dennis and Daniel. "Why was she so insistent upon bringing up our relationship?", Janice asked Matthew as they awaited their meal. "I think it was because this is all she has.", he responded. Matthew continued as he sipped his drink. "The evidence is clear here. The placement is in the best interests of the twins. We'll get all that evidence in through the social workers and Luis and Brian. All she can do is try to rebut it by saying that this placement decision was based upon some political agenda. This judge isn't going to let her get away with that. I like the judge…she knows the law and I'll say this with my fingers crossed, I think she will decide that the placement is in the kids best interest because they've been there so long and Luis and Brian love them. Let's hope…", concluded Matthew. Octavia shook her head in agreement.

They concluded their meal quietly but not without conversation about Adam. "Have you talked to him lately?", asked Janice. Matthew replied, "not in a few days. I'll call him when I get back to my mother's". Janice said, "please send him my best. Are you doing okay with it?", she inquired. Matthew responded, "it's getting easier every day...plus I've got James Davenport chasing after me again!"

Octavia laughed and drank her coffee. Janice would not let this comment go by without probing further. "I thought he was following the Diana Ross tour?", she asked. Matthew said, "well he was. But then his Romeo and him parted ways. He's now out looking for another job. I think he wants to return to Broadway, but he has to wait until the end of August before auditions begin. So, he wants to come stay with me for a little bit. I haven't decided what I'm going to do. It would be like cheating on Adam all over again." Janice replied, "well, think it over first. Don't jump with your dick!". Matthew laughed and said, "I know...I'm thinking it through. But he's so cute!" Octavia said, "cute doesn't mean everything." Matthew sighed, "I know."

Matthew did not have the luxury of staying in the Berkshires for the weekend. Saturday evening almost into Sunday morning his Aunt Gloria called Matthew at his mother's house. There had been an intruder who had broken through the alarm system. Matthew's apartment had been broken into. Scott was away for the weekend and Gloria was sleeping. "Are you okay?", asked a very concerned Matthew. "I'm fine. The police are going to stay here tonight.", replied Aunt Gloria. Matthew said, "I'm on my way. I should be there in a couple of hours." Aunt Gloria disagreed, "Matthew wait until morning. Everything is fine here. I'm okay." But Matthew would not hear of it. "I'm leaving now. I'll see you in a bit."

Matthew woke Octavia to tell her what happened. She immediately called her husband Brandon. "I'm heading over there! I'll call Gloria and tell her I'm on my way. See you when you get here.", said an excited and wide awake Brandon. Octavia told Matthew that her husband was on his way over to Matthew's house. "So I'm joining you for the ride", she stated. Suddenly a voice from the parlor behind her said, "not without me you aren't!". It was Matthew's mother. "I'm coming too. I'll stay with Gloria.", said Rosa. Matthew said, "Mom, you don't need to come. It's just a burglary. I don't know why everyone is overreacting about this."

Rosa walked over to right in front of her son. Her posture portrayed her anger. "Don't you tell me that we are overreacting! I know that there is some nut out there who wants to hurt you. How do you know that this nut wasn't the one who broke in?", stated Rosa in a loud and firm tone. Matthew replied, "I don't know. It could have been him." Rosa said, "well, that's exactly my point. And furthermore, how come the state cop that's assigned to protect you didn't come with you for this trial. Do you think the nut won't leave Boston proper in order to hurt you?" Matthew diminutively shook his head 'no', and said, "I just thought it was a waste of money for him to come out here for a week or two. All the incidents have been in the Boston area." Rosa shot back, "that's not true! You told me you thought you saw him last month in Westfield. That's not Boston is it?".

Matthew looked at Octavia. She stood and said nothing. It was clear to Matthew that this person who appeared to want to hurt him had really gotten to his mother. Rosa was adamant. She grabbed her purse and was ready to go. Matthew knew that he couldn't talk her out of it. "Are you going to bring some clothes with you?", he asked. Rosa shook her head 'yes' and went in the other room, saying "it will only take me a minute" as she left.

Matthew sat with Octavia. "I shouldn't have told her about this", he said to his friend. Octavia replied, "no you were right in telling her. She needed to know. Who knows, if this thing gets any crazier you may have to ask that someone be assigned out here to watch your parents. When does your father get back from his fishing trip?" Matthew said, "he'll be back on Wednesday." Octavia replied, "I think you need to fill him in on it too. You know your mother shields him from things ever since the heart attack." Matthew said, "you're right. I'll tell him when I get back."

Their trip back to Cambridge was made smoother and faster by the lack of significant traffic on the turnpike and Matthew's blue police light on the dashboard of his car flashing away in the middle of the night. They pulled up to the house. A state police car remained in the driveway. Aunt Gloria came out to greet them.

Matthew walked into his apartment. There didn't appear to be any major damage, but the drawers of his dresser had been gone through and clothes were all over the bedroom floor. His office down the hall from the bedroom had also been rifled. The desk drawers were on the floor with papers strewn everywhere. The police officer said to Matthew, "we dusted for prints. We picked up a lot of them. We'll sort them out…hopefully we'll find something."

Brandon helped Matthew to put things back together. Octavia went into the kitchen to make coffee. The morning sun was beginning to rise on this warm summer day. Brandon whispered to Matthew, "look…you know how much you mean to Octavia and me. I'm really concerned about your safety. Please don't go anywhere without the cops. Somebody really wants to get to you…" Matthew put his hand on Brandon's shoulder and said, "I know…it just really sucks having to have someone watch your every move and be with you all the time. The only time I can get any privacy is when I take a shit!" Brandon replied, "it's not worth the risk. They'll find this guy and then things can return to normal."

Monday morning arrived at the courthouse without Matthew. The state police had recommended he not make the trip. Octavia filed a motion to continue the case for two weeks. She cited the break in at Matthew's house and asserted to the court that there was a real concern about the safety of the Attorney General. Attorney McGinley begrudgingly assented to the motion. Unfortunately for Colin and David their fate would have to wait a few more weeks.

Matthew only spoke to Adam once during the week. He did not disclose to Adam that there had been a break in. "No need to make him worry about it. He's three thousand miles away", Matthew told Scott. Scott and Dion made Matthew promise that he wouldn't go anywhere at night without the state trooper and one of them with him. "Great, now I have to have an entourage everywhere I go!', Matthew said. Scott trying to make light of it responded, "you always wanted to be a diva anyway...now you have your entourage to follow!". Matthew did not find humor in Scott's attempt, but did acquiesce to his request.

That weekend James Davenport arrived at Matthew's house for dinner. Matthew had made his best attempt to prepare an authentic Italian meal. James was politely appreciative. That night as they laid in bed engaging in sex James said to Matthew, "this is really kinky. Here we are doing it and there's a state cop in the next room waiting to pounce. What if I started to spank you or something...would he come in and blast me away?" Matthew laughed and said, "just be quiet! I think you're turned on that mister muscle is next door to us!" James chuckled and replied, "you want me to ask him to join us?" They both laughed together.

The next morning the telephone rang. It was Adam. Matthew felt a wave of guilt rush over his body as he laid in bed talking to the man he truly loved as the man he had just had passionate sex with lay sleeping beside him. Matthew and Adam talked briefly about when Matthew would be coming out to California. "I think I'm going to have to take a raincheck on next month. This case is much more complicated than I thought. I don't think I'll be done in time.", Matthew told Adam. Once again he declined to tell him about the escalating violence around him.

Matthew could hear the disappointment in Adam's voice. "Well, I'm definitely coming home for Christmas", said Adam. He continued, "school breaks on December tenth. I'll be home a few days after." Matthew replied, "good...good. December can't come soon enough." They concluded their conversation. Matthew hung up the phone and laid back down in the bed. He rolled into James Davenport and held onto him. Davenport continued to sleep. Matthew thought deeply. He began to feel like he was losing control of the romantic part of his life.

"Finally, your honor", stated Octavia Moon as she was winding up her closing argument in the Baker case before Judge Martin on a bright, sunny Tuesday morning. "Finally, the real issue in this case is what is in the best interest of Colin and David Baker. Not what is in the best interest of their biological parents. That issue was decided a long time ago. Mr. and Mrs. Baker are no longer in the eyes of the law, the parents of Colin and David. They have no right to challenge the future that these children deserve. Colin and David Baker's parents are Luis Ruiz and Brian McDermott. The testimony that you heard before you supports that conclusion. Mr. Ruiz and Mr. McDermott have provided for these children since their early age. They have provided them a home with love and protection. The children only know Mr. Ruiz and Mr. McDermott as their parents. They are clearly bonded to these two fine gentlemen. Therefore, we ask this court to approve the petition of Mr. Ruiz and Mr. McDermott to adopt Colin and David Baker. The state's child protection agency sponsored this petition and as the experts in child welfare have asserted that this is in the children's best interest. The evidence adduced at trial supports that position. Your honor, please act in these children's best interest. Give them a home where they can remain for the rest of their childhood. A home with parents that love them. Thank you very much."

Matthew patted Octavia's knee as she sat down next to him. "That was wonderful", he whispered in her ear. Judge Martin began speaking. "I have heard the evidence before me as well as the arguments of counsel. I believe that since this matter has been before the appellate court, that I owe this case and especially these children a full review of all the evidence. Accordingly, I am taking the matter under advisement. I will issue my decision within sixty days. Thank you all very much." Judge Martin rose from her chair and with that so did those assembled in the courtroom. This phase of the Baker case was over. Now the wait for the decision. Matthew hoped that it would be the one they pursued.

Friday was finally here. It was the end of a long week and Matthew was packing up his files. James Davenport sat in Matthew's office waiting for him to conclude the day. He and Matthew were joining Scott and Dion for dinner in the North End. The phone buzzed. "Matthew, you have the bitch on line one and Dexter Donnelly on two", said Tracy. Matthew replied, "have Dexter hold. I'll take Elizabeth first." Matthew clicked over to the line and said, "hello Elizabeth. How is everything going?" Elizabeth Kragen politely responded, "I should be done here by next week. Things moved pretty fast. The district attorney is going to indict the company president next Tuesday." Matthew replied, "wonderful…wonderful. Well once you're done head back here. I have plenty to keep you busy." Kragen responded, "good. I'm looking forward to being back in Boston." Matthew politely said "good-bye" and then clicked over to the next line on his phone. He spoke briefly with Dexter Donnelly about reintroducing the amendment to the state's anti-discrimination law. The same amendment that failed last year. Then he extended an invitation to Dexter to join them for dinner. Dexter accepted. "Bring Peter along if you like", said Matthew. Dexter replied, "I will".

That evening they enjoyed dinner at one of Matthew's favorite Italian restaurants in Boston. He noticed that Peter Donnelly was constantly staring at James. Matthew whispered in James ear, "I think somebody is infatuated with you!". James smiled. Dinner ended and Matthew and his group parted from Dexter and his son. "I'll call you next week about the amendment", promised Dexter as they walked away. "Thank you", yelled Matthew as he waved. Matthew turned to Scott and said, "can we just walk around for a bit before we go home?" Scott replied, "sure. I don't mind." Matthew turned to the undercover police officer saying, "is that all right with you?" The officer replied, "that's fine. Just stick together okay?" Matthew smiled.

Matthew, James, Scott and Dion walked through the North End of Boston with their state police officer escort in tow. They looked inside the shops and restaurants as they walked. Matthew particularly enjoyed this part of Boston. He felt the streets had as much ambiance as the establishments that lined them. They concluded their walk by returning to the parking lot to retrieve their cars to go home. Another state police officer had been assigned as a look out to watch over the cars while Matthew and his friends enjoyed the evening. "I feel like I'm the President or something", he said to James as they followed the state police car out of the parking lot.

A call in the middle of the night brought mixed emotions to Matthew. It was Adam. He was calling to announce that he would be home for the weekend at the end of the September. "I can't stand being apart from you until Christmas.", he told Matthew. Matthew's voice visibly rose in happiness on the phone. When the conversation concluded Matthew pulled the sheets back up. He looked over at James. "Well, he'll be heading to New York in two weeks anyway", Matthew thought. He decided that evening that not only would he downplay the issue of someone threatening him, he would definitely leave out his one month dalliance with James. "I can't let him know about this. He would think it was going on all the while.", thought Matthew.

CHAPTER 14

MOVING FORWARD

January 1996

Matthew was gazing out his office window at the cold dark day below when the phone buzzed on his desk. As he walked toward the desk he thought how depressing winter in New England was to him. "We live in the dark for three months of the year", he thought. Matthew picked up the phone. Tracy announced that Shannon Watson, his reporter friend was on the line. "Put her through", he said. "Hi Matthew", said Shannon Watson. "Hi there! How are you?", he asked. Matthew sat down in his chair. He knew that conversations with Shannon were not short.

"I'm fine", she began. "I was calling to tell you that Alfie Stone from the Gazette is going to be issuing an exclusive next weekend with your deputy, Elizabeth Kragen and I don't think its going to make you happy." Matthew replied, "tell me what you know." Watson continued, "Well it seems that Ms. Kragen doesn't approve of your win last month on behalf of the twins and their gay adoptive parents. According to Stone, she blasts you and claims that you put your political agenda ahead of these children's needs..." Matthew interrupted with a loud, "what!" Shannon interjected, "let me finish. She says that you have an agenda to license gay people to become foster parents so that you can reduce the number of dependent children on the state's rolls..." Matthew once again interrupted, "that's a crock of shit and you know it!" Shannon replied, "I know. But I thought you would like to have some lead time. Her timing is so suspect. Your announcement and everything next month...what's the scoop with her?" Matthew replied, "I think she's a back stabber. She's pulled a couple of things here and made some comments. But I never thought she'd go public." Shannon asked, "so what are you going to do about her?" Matthew responded, "that's the million dollar question, isn't it?"

There were a few moments of silence and then Shannon said, "well, how about this for an idea. I know it's kinda selfish, but how about you give me another exclusive. I'll feature your response to her article. My readership is certainly more important and influential than that rag!" Matthew replied, "mmm...I like it. Okay, you have the exclusive. Let's do it! I'll transfer you back out to Tracy and she can schedule some time for us, okay?" Shannon replied, "okay" and Matthew pressed the transfer button on his phone. He then dialed Octavia's office. "Gotta a few minutes for me?", he asked. "Sure...I'll be there in about fifteen minutes, okay?", responded Octavia. "Okay", replied Matthew.

Octavia's mouth hung open as Matthew explained his telephone call from Shannon Watson. She was completely stunned. "I'll fire the bitch today!", proclaimed Octavia. Matthew raised his hand in a cautionary fashion, "no...no, we can't do that. It will play right into her. We have to think of something else." Octavia said, "you're right. She'll claim you tried to stop her from exercising her right to free speech...oh, what a bitch!" Matthew smirked and said to Octavia, "you and I have dealt with worse..." She replied, "yes, we certainly have." Matthew paused momentarily and then said, "Let's mull it over for a few days. Wait to see what the article says, and after the article is out we'll figure out how to pounce on her." Octavia responded, "yeah, I need a few days because all I can think about

right now is doing nasty things to her! And you know that's not me!"
Matthew replied, "no, it certainly isn't".

That evening Matthew sat with Dion, Scott and Dexter Donnelly
over a pot of coffee and stale cake. They were the campaign committee to elect Matthew this fall for a full term in his own right as Attorney General of Massachusetts. Matthew of course had delegated the
financial operations of the campaign to Scott. If anyone knew how to
spend money and make it work, it was Scott. Dexter was responsible
for the political endorsements from the hill. Dion took on the role of
gopher. He was a hard worker on Matthew's behalf.

The announcement was planned for mid-February at the university in the Berkshires where Matthew had been sworn in as Attorney
General. It was his stomping grounds and he always tried to return
there as much as possible. Matthew was well aware of how people in
western Massachusetts believed the politicians in Boston didn't care
if they existed. Matthew had tried over his short tenure as the Attorney General to go to western Massachusetts as often as possible. He
didn't want the legacy of abandonment attached to him as a politician.

The phone rang and Scott got up to get it. "Is the nigger cocksucker home?", asked a deep voice on the other end. Scott slammed
the phone down. "What's the matter?", asked Dexter. Scott replied,
"it was one of those obscene phone calls again. I thought you were
changing the number, Matthew!" Matthew replied, "it doesn't matter if I change the number. Whoever it is finds my new number and
calls. They must know somebody at the telephone company. I've gotten used to it. The calls don't freak me out as much as before. At least
we haven't had any incidents since last month."

Dexter grabbed a piece of cake and said, "what incident last
month? You didn't tell me about anything." Matthew replied, "oh, it
was no big deal. I was out shopping at Downtown Crossing. I
thought somebody was following me. There was and my protector
arrested him. Nobody got hurt...the case will probably be dis-

missed." Dexter inquired, "was it the elusive Craig?" Matthew said, "no, unfortunately not. I think he's long gone. They never could find him, but I'm sure he was the one who sent the letters. He's probably had enough fun with me and now he's moved onto greener pastures to harass somebody else." Dexter looked at Matthew and firmly stated, "well, I don't know. I still don't like it. But at least you're not pulling the macho bullshit and trying to get rid of your bodyguard." Matthew responded, "well, it's the only way I can get a man to sleep at my house!" The four of them broke out laughing.

The phone ringing interrupted their laughter. Matthew looked at Scott and said, "I'll get it. I don't want you to freak out again!" He picked up the phone. It was Adam. They talked briefly about what was happening in their respective lives. They hadn't talked since Adam returned to California after being at home for Christmas. But their conversation this evening was brief. Matthew was finding that they had less and less to talk about. Their worlds were totally divergent. The commonality was gone. The subjects to talk about were the same: the weather, the job, the family, etc., etc. Matthew ended his brief conversation with Adam and returned to the group. "Adam says 'hi' to everyone", Matthew said. They smiled.

The following Saturday, Matthew found himself at home alone, with no one to call. Scott and Dion had gone skiing for the weekend. Aunt Gloria was back in the Berkshires at Matthew's mother's house. Janice and Jose were on vacation in the Caribbean. She was trying to get pregnant again, she had told Matthew. "I always wanted to have three children. Maybe my vacation will give me my wish!" Matthew hoped that Janice's wish would come true. She was a wonderful mother and Jose was an involved and caring father.

Matthew sat in his apartment with the state trooper watching television thinking about Janice on that Caribbean island. Here he was stuck in cold and dreary New England. He was getting cabin fever and was completely bored.

Matthew decided that he wanted to go out to a gay bar. He hadn't been to a gay bar since he became Attorney General. It was not for fear of being seen in the bar; everyone in the state knew he was gay. He just didn't think that this was the best atmosphere. But tonight, he felt the need to be around gay men and loud music. "I'm going to the Village, Brent", he said to state trooper Brent O'Sullivan. The officer raised his eyebrows. Matthew continued, "I don't expect you to go into a gay bar with me. I can handle myself for a few hours. If it makes you happy, you can drive me and sit in the car." The officer responded, "that would be fine with me, sir." Matthew replied, "I told you to stop calling me sir! For God's sake, you're sleeping in my house. My name is Matthew!" The officer said, "okay, Matthew."

Matthew walked into the bar and went to order a drink. The bar scene hadn't changed in his absence. The same people that were sitting at the same stools at the bar for years were still there. Matthew sipped his beer and leaned against the bar, gazing out at the dance floor. The music pumped while the laser beams and lights surrounded the room. He looked at the crowd. He decided the average age of the men dancing and sweating on the dance floor had to be twenty two. "I'm getting too old for this!", chuckled Matthew to himself. He was rapidly approaching his forty second birthday. "Christ, I could be some of these guys fathers", he thought.

He turned to order his second beer when a man came up behind him and patted him on the shoulder. It was Attorney Martin Santiago, an old friend from law school. "My goodness Matthew! I never thought I'd see you here", said Attorney Santiago as he and Matthew hugged. "How's Adam?", asked Attorney Santiago. Matthew explained the situation with Adam and that he was living in California. "I feel like such an ass!", said Attorney Santiago. Matthew shook his head, "don't worry about it. I'm fine." Santiago then said, "Matthew, this isn't suck up. I need to say this to you. You make me so proud to be an openly gay attorney. You really have made it much easier for all of us. Thank you for being willing to put yourself out there." Matthew blushed slightly and replied, "your welcome...I hope that's one of the things I can accomplish in this job." Santiago replied, "you have. I hope you stay in the job for a long time." The two of them stood at the bar and continued with their discussion. About twenty minutes later and on his third beer Matthew decided he was ready to go home. He was just about to excuse himself from Martin Santiago when a young man, who looked like he was in his late twenties or early thirties came up to Matthew. He was a tall, olive skinned dark haired man. "Would you like to dance?", asked this stranger. Matthew looked at the young man and then pointed his finger into his own chest, asking "me?" The man replied, "yes, you. Would you like to dance?" Matthew replied, "sure" and followed the man out to the dance floor.

While they were dancing to an old disco song redone for the nineties, the young man introduced himself as Salvatore DiMarco. Matthew introduced himself and then motioned to Salvatore to get off the dance floor. They walked back to the bar. Matthew ordered another beer. "Can I get you something?", he asked his new friend. "A beer is fine", said Salvatore. Martin Santiago walked over and interrupted to say good night to Matthew. Matthew invited him to call for lunch and Martin promised that he would.

"So where are you from?", asked Matthew of Salvatore. He replied, "I just moved here a few weeks ago. I'm originally from Palm Beach. I'm starting my masters at Boston College." Matthew smiled, "what program are you in?" Salvatore replied, "accounting...so what do you do Matthew?", he asked. Matthew said, "I'm a lawyer." Salvatore said, "oh, a lawyer! Well I hope you're not one of those that has those annoying ads on TV!" Matthew laughed and said, "no, I'm just a poor government lawyer." Salvatore smiled. Matthew liked his smile. He had perfect bright teeth. It was a wonderful smile. They stood silently for a few minutes and then Matthew leaned into Salvatore and kissed him. Salvatore responded with a strong kiss back.

Matthew and Salvatore returned to the dance floor. Before they knew it the "last call" announcement was being made. They returned to the bar. Salvatore had another beer but Matthew passed. They stood at the bar and Matthew asked, "so where are you going after here?" Salvatore smiled with his perfect smile and said, "I was hoping to your house". Matthew smiled back, "sounds good to me!" Salvatore quickly drank his beer down and they walked to the coat room to retrieve their jackets. "My car is over here. Did you drive or take the 'T'?", asked Matthew. Salvatore replied, "I took the 'T'". Matthew motioned him to the parking lot. They walked towards Matthew's car and Brent O'Sullivan came out of the driver's side of the car. Matthew turned to Salvatore and said, "this is Brent. He's a state cop. I've been getting a few threats lately, so he watches over me. I hope that's okay." Salvatore had a puzzled look on his face and then shrugged his shoulders and said, "sure...no problem."

The next morning Matthew woke before Salvatore. He sat up in the bed and looked at his sleeping friend. He was a very attractive man. Matthew slid out of the bed and went to the kitchen. He turned on the coffee pot. About five minutes later Brent O'Sullivan joined Matthew in the kitchen. Matthew handed him the Gazette. The long awaited interview with Elizabeth Kragen was featured on the front page. "Did you read this?", Trooper O'Sullivan asked Matthew. Matthew replied, "yeah. I looked at it. I knew it was coming."

There was a soft knock at the door. It was Scott. Matthew invited him in. "No work this morning?", he asked his best friend. Scott replied, "no I took the whole weekend off. We wanted to stay today but the room was booked. We got home about three thirty this morning." Matthew handed Scott a cup of coffee. In the distance the toilet flushed. Scott looked at Matthew and smirked, "an overnight guest?" Matthew replied, "shh! Yes, an overnight guest. His name is Salvatore...he's really nice." Scott laughed softly and said, "so you're going to start chasing Italians now? No more black men?" Matthew put his finger to his mouth and said, "shh" once again as he laughed.

"Hi", said Salvatore DiMarco as he entered the kitchen. Matthew introduced Scott to Salvatore. They shook hands. Matthew poured a coffee for Salvatore and invited him to sit at the kitchen table which he did. Salvatore began flipping through the newspapers as Scott and Matthew were talking about Scott's skiing trip. A few minutes later Salvatore confusingly said, "excuse me…but you're the attorney general?" Matthew looked at him and said, "that's me". Salvatore replied, "well, now I'm really impressed! But I think this lady that works for you doesn't like you" as he pointed to the article about Elizabeth Kragen. "I know", said Matthew.

Salvatore and Matthew went out to lunch later in the day in downtown Boston. They parted after lunch and after setting a dinner date for Thursday. Matthew waved good-bye as Salvatore walked into the 'T' station.

Monday morning presented itself not only with a snowstorm but also the storm over the Elizabeth Kragen article in the Gazette. Tracy indicated to Matthew as he walked in that at least ten reporters had called the office for his reaction. Matthew said, "call back Shannon Watson. I want to meet with her sometime tomorrow. And please have Octavia come to my office as soon as possible."

Matthew, Octavia and Tracy sat behind the closed door of Matthew's office and began to strategize about how they would address the "Elizabeth Kragen Issue". Kragen had called in sick to work today so at least they didn't have to worry about her snooping around to see what was going on. The conversation was becoming intense as they mulled over various options to deal effectively with Kragen and the fall out from the article.

The phone rang in Matthew's office. Governor Dickerson was on hold. Matthew picked up the line, "good day Governor", he said. Dickerson bellowed, "Matthew! What the hell you going to do about that bitch? I read the article yesterday." Matthew replied, "we're discussing it now. I want to handle it as gently as possible." Dickerson responded in his gruff tone, "I'd send the bitch packing! Ungrateful slut! How dare she do this to you in full view. Did you have any idea that this was coming?" Matthew replied, "well, I've been watching her lately. I didn't really think I could trust her. But as to the comments she made in the article, I never thought it would be that bad." Dickerson sarcastically said, "well you let me know if I can do anything to help you. Maybe she has a few skeletons in the closet that we can expose. I don't appreciate her embarrassing you. When your embarrassed, I'm embarrassed too. And we both have elections coming up. We don't need this crap now!" Matthew paused before responding to the Governor. It was nice to have his support about this issue, but Matthew knew that Lloyd Dickerson was also concerned about himself. It was he who appointed the first openly gay state attorney general. Dickerson did not want the appointment to fly back in his face at election time. He had an interest as well in making the criticism of Matthew by Kragen turn into old news fast. "I'll let you know what we decide", said Matthew.

The Governor responded, "good. Now there's another reason I called you too. I wanted you to send somebody out to Springfield to work with DA Gray on an investigation." Matthew interjected, "what's going on?" The Governor continued, "well it seems that there's some organized crime group out there that is getting its hands into the lottery. The DA is overwhelmed with the investigation and any manpower we can expend would help. Plus, I think this would be good publicity for both of us if any indictments come out of it." Lloyd Dickerson, always thinking about how it will play in the press, thought Matthew. He responded to the Governor's request. "I'd be happy to send someone out. Can you ask the Commissioner of Safety to give me two state investigators to assist my staff?", he inquired. "Absolutely", responded Dickerson. Matthew said in turn, "I'll call Susan Gray in the morning and tell her that my office will assist. Do you want me to coordinate it directly with her and then report back to you?", he asked. "That would be good", replied the Governor. Matthew responded, "I'll call you next week." Governor

Dickerson said, "good…and let me know if I can do anything to help on the Kragen bitch!" Matthew said, "I will", and hung up the phone.

Matthew filled in Octavia and Tracy about his conversation with the Governor. They were sidelined for a moment about the investigation in Springfield. "Why don't you send Dion and Brenda McManus?", asked Octavia. Matthew thought for a moment and then said, "Brenda would be fine, but don't you think Dion is a little too new?" Octavia responded, "not really. I think he's a workhorse. Plus, didn't Wallace Cartwright many years ago send a new assistant into the middle of a high profile case?" Matthew knew that Octavia was talking about him. "Yes, yes he did.", said a smiling Matthew. "Well, that settles it then doesn't it?", asked Octavia. "I guess it does!", said a chuckling Matthew.

The three of them continued their strategy session about Elizabeth Kragen. After going over a series of options, Matthew decided that he would have Tracy call Kragen at home and tell her to report to his office first thing tomorrow morning. He would confront Kragen directly. Octavia would be present just to have an observer. Matthew decided that he would give Kragen the option to resign gracefully. If she didn't take this option he would farm her out to some investigation away from Boston. Then he would terminate her down the road after he insured that she failed during the investigation. Matthew didn't like this second option. He knew it was setting her up. But Octavia said, "one set up deserves another." Matthew knew she was right. He had to preserve his own job. He was doing too much and getting too far to allow this woman to end it.

The next morning came too rapidly for Matthew. He would have to confront Elizabeth today about her controversial article. Matthew poked in the shower and during his morning routine. He seemed to want to avoid going into work and the inevitable confrontation. He was sure it would be heated and difficult. "Come on Brent, I'm ready to go", Matthew said to his bodyguard. They walked out of the house and headed to the car to begin the morning commute. Even the commute was too fast for Matthew. He was at his office and in his chair much too soon.

Octavia came into his office shortly thereafter. He buzzed Elizabeth Kragen's secretary. "Athena, this is Matthew. Could you have Elizabeth come to my office?", he said into the telephone. "Please hold", said Kragen's secretary. A moment later she came back on the line and said, "Ms. Kragen asked me to tell you that she is too busy to meet with you and to arrange another time." Matthew was furious. His face began to turn red. His voice became stern and he said into the phone, "you tell Ms. Kragen that I am ordering her to be in my office in five minutes! There is no other time…she is to get down here now!", bellowed Matthew. "I'll tell her", said Kragen's secretary in a demur tone. "Can you believe that bitch is playing these games already? She says she's too busy to meet with me. Did she forget who is in charge here?", yelled Matthew as he hung up the phone. Octavia replied, "this isn't going to be pretty. I think she's got a master plan. You're going to have to fire her…she's going to make it difficult." Matthew replied, "I know…but I need to get it over with today. I'm not going to sit and stew about it anymore."

Twenty minutes passed and Tracy knocked on the door. "Attorney Kragen is here for your meeting", she said to Matthew as she rolled her eyes. "Send here in", replied Matthew. Elizabeth Kragen walked in accompanied by assistant attorney general Anita Gunther. "Good morning Elizabeth", said Matthew and Octavia. "Good morning", she replied to both of them. "Anita, I'm not sure why you're here. This is a private meeting", said Matthew. Kragen sarcastically responded, "I know what this meeting is about and I want Anita here as a witness." Matthew sat down in his chair and said, "well, I'm sorry but Anita you will have to leave." Kragen responded, "I told you I want her to stay!" Matthew in the sternest voice he could muster, replied, "I don't care what you want. I'm the boss and I say that she has to leave. Now Anita please excuse us." Gunther looked over at

Kragen and then away. She walked behind Kragen and out the door of Matthew's office.

As the door closed Matthew motioned to the chair and commanded Kragen, "now that the charade is over, please sit down." Kragen sat in the chair in front of Matthew's desk. Octavia sat to Matthew's side and took out her pad of paper. Matthew began, "Now Elizabeth, I'm going to try to say this as calmly and succinctly as possible. The article over the weekend where you gave an interview to the Gazette was a total embarrassment to this office and to me personally. When I hired you I clearly indicated to you that this office had a policy of promoting the civil rights of gay persons. That we would use that policy to enact statutes that give gays the same protections as other citizens. You did not object to that policy, in fact if I remember correctly, you compared it to the civil rights struggles of black in the sixties." Elizabeth Kragen went to interrupt Matthew, "I think..." Matthew put his hand up in a stopping fashion. "I didn't ask for you to comment yet. Just sit there and listen.", he commanded.

Matthew continued as Octavia took notes. "Now, as I was saying. I told you that this was a gay friendly office. That old and tired prejudices would not be tolerated here. Yet in your interview you fell right into the hands of the reporter and emphasized for the press the old and tired prejudices. And you did it with the impritur of this office. That clearly is wrong!" Matthew paused briefly. He could feel the anger building inside of himself. He took a couple of deep breaths and then started again. "The most disturbing part of your interview however for me, was not the disparaging remarks you made about gay people, but rather the way you attacked an issue that has been at the core of my being since I became a professional. You know, very clearly that the Baker case was not about the rights of gay people to adopt!" said an angry Matthew. Matthew's voice once again was becoming elevated. He went on in a now bellowing tone that most likely could be heard through the office walls. "You know that this case was about these two little boys who had loving parents waiting for them but for the bigotry of an old tired judge out in western Massachusetts! You also know that my only desire for the state's abused and neglected children are that they have safe homes where they are loved. I don't promote child abuse, I eliminate it and I have done so for almost twenty years!"

Elizabeth Kragen began to applaud with her hands softly. Matthew stared at her. Octavia's eyes were glued on the smirking face of Attorney Kragen. "Nice speech!", she said sarcastically. Matthew stood up from his chair and screamed at her, "don't you dare sit there and mock me madam!" Octavia reached for his arm and tugged it. Matthew sat down. The room was silent.

About two minutes of awkward silence passed when Octavia began to speak. She was much more calm and business-like than Matthew. She laid it on the line for Attorney Kragen. "The options open to you are two", began Octavia. "The first option is that you submit your resignation effective the end of this week. This office will indicate publicly that there was a parting of the ways, but that we wish you the best. We will publicly state that you were a talented member of this office. The second option is not as palatable. If you do not offer your resignation by five o'clock today, Matthew will go public in his interview with Shannon Watson of the Ledger and discredit you. We will publicly state how you attempted to sabotage this office over the death penalty issue. We will also indicate publicly that you harbored a desire to see the attorney general fail so that you could run your own campaign. You will be fired immediately."

Kragen looked back and forth between Octavia and Matthew. She once again started to speak. Octavia interrupted her. "I didn't ask you to speak. I don't want to hear anything from you! You may now leave this office. If I do not have your resignation by five o'clock, the interview will go forward for publication tomorrow and you can read about your termination in the morning edition! Now, get up and leave!", ordered a furious Octavia. Kragen slowly stood up. She remained staring at them. She walked towards the door, turned the handle and turned her head back. "Fuck the both of you!", she said as she walked out the door.

Shannon Watson was seated outside Matthew's office waiting for her interview. Kragen spotted her and looked down her nose at her. Shannon, never a wallflower, looked straight up at her and said, "what's your problem bitch?" Kragen stopped in her tracks. "Well I guess the wagons have circled haven't they?", she said as she walked away.

Meanwhile, Matthew sat in his office with Octavia. "Thank you for taking over. I was ready to slap her right in the mouth! Wouldn't that have been a great headline!", he said to Octavia. Octavia smiled back, "you were ready to slap her, I was ready to wipe that smug look off her face with my foot!" The phone buzzed. Tracy indicated that Shannon was waiting outside. "Send her in", said Matthew.

Matthew filled Shannon in "off the record" about what had just transpired. Octavia filled in the details also. Shannon remained a good friend of Matthew's. He knew he could trust her. She agreed that if Kragen didn't resign today that she would print her exclusive interview tomorrow. If she did resign, the interview would print next week. They sat for the next hour going over Matthew's position on the issue of gay civil rights in light of the new statute, the current crisis in child welfare and the favorable report about reduction in violent crime in Massachusetts.

The interview received page one attention in the following week's Sunday Ledger. Matthew addressed briefly the resignation of Elizabeth Kragen. "She didn't fit in with the vision and mission of this office that all people are to be protected from discrimination and harm. That not only includes gay people, but it also includes the children of this state.", was the extent of Matthew's criticism of his former deputy. The article also went into great detail about the significant reduction in violent crime in Massachusetts in the last year. Matthew attributed it to the stiffer penalties being enacted by the legislature, many of which he had help to promote and to the "dedication and diligence of our public safety officials. The police and the prosecutors across this state are challenging the thugs and the gangs on a daily basis. The message is clear from this office right on down. If you commit a violent crime against one of our citizens or our children, this state will punish you to the fullest extent of the law. That message is out there and the criminals hear it.", Matthew described by the reporter, "gleefully stated".

It was a cold mid-February day but Matthew's heart was warm inside. He was on hand to witness Governor Lloyd Dickerson sign into law the amendment to the state's anti-discrimination statute. Matthew stood to the right of the seated Governor as he signed the amendment into law, prohibiting discrimination in housing, employment, contracting and medical benefits on the basis of sexual orientation. The cameras flashed and Matthew beamed with joy. Now Massachusetts would join those progressive states across the nation in protecting all the people, thought Matthew.

Lloyd Dickerson reached up from the table and handed the pen that he used to sign the law to Matthew. The Governor loudly stated in front of the reporters as he handed Matthew the pen, "you deserve this more than I do. It was because of your push and tenacity that this law came into being. I congratulate you!". Matthew smiled broadly. "Thank you, Governor", he said as the flashes from the cameras hit his eyes.

That evening Matthew decided he needed to go for a walk. It had been an exciting day and he wanted to stretch out before he went to bed. He began to bundle himself up to face the winter cold. "Where are you going?", asked Trooper O'Sullivan. "I'm just going for a short walk down Mass Ave. You don't need to come. I'll be back in a half hour or so. Stay here and keep Diana company.", said Matthew. "I don't know if that's a smart idea", said Trooper O'Sullivan. Matthew pulled his gloves onto his hands. "Look, I'm so bundled up that nobody will recognize me. I need a few minutes alone. Nobody is going to bother me. Just stay here.", he said to the state police officer. "Are you sure?", asked Trooper O'Sullivan. "I'm sure", responded Matthew.

He walked into the wind on Massachusetts Avenue admiring the many storefronts lining the road. Matthew loved the neighborhood he lived in. There were a variety of different shops and restaurants all within walking distance. No matter what the hour of night, or how cold, there was also life on the street. People walking, shopping and dining together.

The next morning Matthew sat enjoying coffee with Octavia's husband Brandon. He was attending a morning meeting about a mile down the street from Matthew's home and they had arranged to have morning coffee together. Matthew truly enjoyed being with Brandon. He was a worldly man, knowledgeable in many subjects, who had incredible life experience. "I would love to spend all morning here with you Brandon", Matthew said. "But I guess I need to be responsible and get off to work", he concluded with a little sigh. They shook hands as they parted ways.

Sitting in his chair about an hour after he arrived at the office, Matthew had a few minutes of quiet time to ponder his existance. What a blessing he had – he was the first openly gay Attorney General in the state's history. He felt good about the upcoming campaign. He was surrounded at work by talented people that he cared about. Now only if Adam would return home. "All would be right with the world", he sadly thought.

CHAPTER 15

SUMMER PASSAGES

June 1996

Craig Talbot sat in his dingy studio apartment in South Boston and looked out the grimy window at the railroad tracks below. It was a hot and muggy day and the old metal fan was broken. "I don't know how much more of this I can take", said Craig to the teenage boy laying next to him on the bed. The teenager replied, "I know the heat's really bothering me too." Craig looked at him and said, "that's not what I mean. I don't know how much more of this fucking world I can take!" The teenager sat up and said, "calm down man…here take a hit", as he lit the marijuana joint and handed it to Craig. Craig took a deep puff and inhaled deeply. He took another and then handed it back to the teenager. "Ahh…that's better!", he exclaimed.

Craig reached over and grabbed the teenager by the back of his long black hair. He pulled his head toward his chest. "So how about you suck my cock again, faggot? By the way, what's your name again?", Craig said. The teenager looked at him and replied, "my name is Christian, stupid! Sure, I'll suck it, but it'll cost you another fifty." Craig pulled on the teenager's hair forcefully. "Shit! That hurts!", exclaimed the teenager. Craig pushed the teenager's head down into his stained underwear. "You'll suck this cock and you'll do it for free or I'll fuck you up, faggot!" The teenager quickly realized that Craig physically overpowered him. He answered, "okay…okay, man. I'll do it!" Craig cynically replied, "and you'll like it too!"

A world away Adam Lesley sat in the office of the president of the law school. He was there to meet with the president to discuss his application for an associate dean position at Harvard. Adam believed that he stood a good shot at getting the job. He had many contacts still left at Harvard and he felt good about the application process. But Adam had loyalty to this law school. If he got the job at Harvard he would have to leave a semester before the end of his commitment. Adam felt he needed to tell the college president before this happened, just in case it did. But Adam didn't feel the need to tell Matthew. He was afraid that he would raise his hopes. Plus, Adam wasn't sure where their relationship stood. The geography had definitely been a barrier. Matthew hadn't even made a trip out to the west coast. But he also knew that Matthew was very busy. "Dean Lesley, the president will see you now", said the secretary to Adam.

Matthew lay day dreaming on the sandy beach behind the guesthouse in Provincetown with Scott sleeping to his side and the ever vigilant state trooper, Brent O'Sullivan on the towel to the other side. Matthew was taking a week of rest and relaxation from his job. He felt he needed a break. He also had a strong desire to spend some time alone with Scott. Well, as alone as he could be with his bodyguard sleeping in the same room. But, at least he and Scott could be together and enjoy the sights and fun in Provincetown. Matthew was day dreaming of the night before when he and Scott walked into the most popular gay bar in town and saw Jeffrey Caine working there as one of the shirtless waiters. He could not believe his eyes! His old boyfriend from law school days was now working at a gay nightclub for a living. He spoke briefly with Jeffrey, but it was apparent to Matthew that alcohol had taken a toll on Jeffrey's life. While he may have been pumping iron in the gym to keep up his physique, Jeffrey's face looked tired and drawn. "Too much living in the fast lane", thought

Matthew. He had expressed to Scott his disappointment in Jeffrey when they got home the night before. "Such a waste of education and brain power", he had told Scott.

"Ahh, that was great!", said Craig to Christian as he laid back on the worn mattress on the floor. "You sure give good head", he told the teenager. Christian got up off the mattress and went to the sink to get a drink of water. "So how about you let me take care of you instead of that asshole that runs you around?", Craig asked. Christian turned and looked at him saying, "what can you do for me that Malcolm can't?" Craig replied, "well, you won't have to trick as much if you work for me...and you get to suck my big cock anytime you want to!" Christian smirked at Craig and replied, "I'll think about it...you're an asshole, but for an old man you do have a hot body and a great dick! Just don't get your hopes too high, Malcolm might not be too happy about me leaving."

Craig stood up from the mattress and walked over to Christian. "Don't worry about that nigger. I can take of him...you stay here with me and we'll fuck and get high and have a great time." Craig then grabbed Christian by the hips and pulled him into his naked body. Christian tried to move away. "Where you going faggot?", said Craig. "I wanna sit down for a minute...I'm tired", replied Christian. Craig let go of Christian who began to walk back toward the mattress. Craig grabbed his own penis in his hand and walked behind Christian. "How about you sit down on this?", said Craig referring to his penis. Christian responded, "I'm not in the mood...Christ, I just sucked you off! What are you a nympho or something?" Craig stood still. He raised his arm and slapped Christian forcefully across the mouth. "You're the fuckin' faggot boy! Don't you ever call me a nympho again!" Christian held his hand against his mouth. There was blood coming from his mouth. He sat on the mattress and looked at Craig standing over him with an erection. "Now roll over so I can show you what a real man can do!", commanded Craig. Christian cowardly replied, "...no...just leave me alone". Craig pushed Christian down on the mattress and rolled him over. A moment later Craig was pumping his penis into Christian's buttocks. Christian lay his head in silence against the dirty mattress and bit it.

The beeper going off brought Matthew out of his day dream on the beach. It also woke up Scott. Matthew picked up the beeper and looked down at the number. It was Octavia calling. "Can I use your phone Brent?", asked Matthew of his bodyguard. The state trooper handed Matthew the cellular phone. Matthew dialed Octavia. He spoke briefly with her and concluded with, "I'll be there Friday morning." Matthew shut the phone off. "What's up?", asked Scott. Matthew lay back against the towel on the beach. He turned to his protector and said, "Do you know Trooper Brenda Connors?". Brent O'Sullivan pondered a moment and said, "I don't think so...why?" Matthew replied, "well, she was stationed in Brockton. Last night she pulled over a carload of teenagers who were drunk. One of them had a gun. He shot and killed her." O'Sullivan put his head down then looked up and stared out at the ocean briefly. Matthew and Scott were silent.

A moment or two later Scott said, "it's a sick world out there. Do they know who did it?" Matthew replied, "yeah. The caught the killer this morning. He's seventeen years old. Anyway, the funeral is on Friday and Octavia called me to see if I wanted to go. I'm going...I should be there not only for her family but also to send a message." Trooper O'Sullivan agreed saying, "I think you should go too". Matthew responded, "I know. I know you didn't know her, but I guess I want to say I'm sorry to you. It could have been someone you know...shit, it could have been you. I don't know how you do it. I would have never wanted your job." Matthew stopped talking. A minute or so passed and Matthew said to Scott and O'Sullivan, "well, let's get up and change so we can go out to eat. I think I'd better leave tomorrow so I can get back, settle in and then go to the funeral." The three of them stood simultaneously and began to pack up their beach accessories to return to their room.

The funeral was an emotional event for Matthew. He did not personally know Trooper Connors and yet he grieved for her. She had left behind two small daughters who would have to go through life without their mother. Her husband, Mark could barely walk down the aisle in the church. Matthew spoke briefly from the pulpit about the dangers in society and the dangers that police confront on a daily basis. He extended the gratitude and sympathy of the people of Massachusetts to the family of Trooper Connors. He ended his brief remarks with a prayer and then returned to his seat. "I hate this shit", he mumbled to Octavia as he sat down.

Matthew returned to the office after the funeral. He was depressed over the events of the morning. Salvatore had called to confirm their Saturday dinner. He thought briefly about his now regular dating partner. Matthew enjoyed being with Salvatore and yet there was a sense of sadness everytime he was with him. It was as if Salvatore was starting to become a replacement for Adam and Matthew did not want that. But Adam was gone…it had been over a year. He had to move on. But sadly, Matthew realized that things would never be as they once were.

Tracy walked in and handed Matthew a document. "What's this?", he asked. She replied, "it's the speech you asked me to type up for next Sunday." Matthew looked down at the papers and then up at her. "Oh, thanks", he said. Tracy turned and walked out of his office. Matthew began to read the typed version of his speech slated for the annual AIDS walk in Boston next Saturday. The coordinators of the walk had asked Matthew a few months ago to give a speech on the Common before the walk began. Matthew had accepted their invitation. As he read through his speech he began to become angry. He took the papers and through them across his desk.

Matthew leaned back in his chair and closed his eyes. He began to think about how much he hated the issue of AIDS. It had taken from him many dear friends. He had attended many 'AIDS funerals' as he called them over the past several years. He also thought of that day when Phillip had died. He hadn't thought about Phillip in quite sometime. The whole incident had gained some perspective as the years passed by. But today it was very painful for Matthew to think about Phillip. Matthew thought how proud Phillip would be if he were still alive and could see him now.

Matthew returned home that evening exhausted. The funeral had taken its toll on him. Brent took Diana for a walk so Matthew could lay on the couch. He checked his answering machine. There were two calls. Adam and his mother. Adam could wait, thought Matthew. They hadn't talked in awhile. But Matthew would never make his mother wait. Matthew grabbed the phone and dialed his mother's house. After exchanging pleasantries, Rosa said to her son, "have you seen Gloria today?" Matthew replied, "I didn't even go upstairs to say 'hi'. It's been a shitty day. I just came home and collapsed. Brent's out walking Diana for me, I'm so tired." His mother continued on with the conversation. "Well, I called her earlier. I wanted to tell you that your uncle, Francesco died this morning. He had a heart attack last night."

Matthew sat up on the sofa. He did not know what to say. He wondered whether he should feel sad, but he did not. "Are you going to the funeral?", he asked his mother. Rosa without hesitation replied, "no…and neither is Gloria." Matthew asked, "do you think that's right?" Rosa responded, "I disowned him as my brother a long time ago. Gloria feels the same way. It would be hippocritical of me to go to the funeral." Matthew said, "I guess" and then changed the subject. Rosa indicated that she still planned to come out to Cambridge next week to join Matthew and his friends on the AIDS walk in Boston. They concluded their conversation as Brent returned with a now exhausted Diana from her walk.

Matthew called Diana into the living room and said to her, "you ready to go to bed?" Diana wagged her tail. Matthew stood up from the sofa. "I'm not going to eat…get yourself whatever you want. I really need to go to bed", Matthew told the state police officer. "Good night", responded Brent O'Sullivan. Matthew went to his bedroom followed by his faithful dog.

The day of the annual AIDS walk was a picture perfect spring day in Boston. The sky was blue and sunny. The temperature was comfortably warm. The usual group of friends and family joined Matthew for the walk again this year. Matthew was delighted that Sharon and Louise also came out from the Berkshires to be part of the walk. Given his busy schedule and the distance between their respective homes, Matthew had not spent as much time with Sharon and Louise over the past few years as he desired. But this weekend they would be part of the walk and spend the remainder of the weekend at his house. They had plenty of catching up to do!

Matthew was now almost at the conclusion of his prepared speech. The crowd was attentive and appreciative, but they were ready to begin the walk. Matthew pushed aside the typed pages from the podium below him and paused as he looked out at the crowd on Boston Common. "I want to wrap this up with a personal message to you and with your encouragement to help all of us walk and move forward today. HIV has become the leading cause of death for people in Massachusetts between the ages of twenty five and forty five. It is robbing a generation from us. A generation of skilled, bright, talented and loving individuals. HIV continues to cross all socio-economic lines in this state and in the nation. And yet, it is still thought of as the 'dirty disease'; one that we blame the victim for acquiring. We need to use our energy today to move beyond that. When someone gets cancer no one sits around and contemplates how they got it. No one sits around and tries to put blame on the victim. When someone has heart disease, no one blames them for it. But going into the second decade of this pandemic, people are still casting blame and bigotry when it comes to AIDS. I ask you today to use the symbol of this walk to stamp out the blame throwing and labeling." The audience applauded and Matthew took a sip of water from the glass sitting on the table to the side of the podium.

He continued, "This walk is truly about education. Let us together educate those around us, not only today as we walk through the streets of Boston, but everyday. Let us educate our colleagues, our school mates, our neighbors, our families. Let us educate others that this virus is not one of blame but rather one of sadness for it robs from us our friends, lovers and neighbors. Who really cares how someone got the HIV virus? I certainly don't! Does the knowledge of the source of the infection vitiate the fact that the person still has HIV? No, it does not! Do we establish classes of people with HIV? Absolutely not! Should we only be compassionate towards those who received the virus through medical procedures and less compassionate to homosexuals and drug users? I say not!" Applause interrupted Matthew's speech.

Matthew strongly continued on, "when we fall into the trap of blaming and classification that mainstream society would try to ensnare us into, we do a disservice to all our brothers and sisters with HIV. Let it be said once again here and now, AIDS is a human issue! It is a virus that wreaks havoc on the human body, no matter what your race, sex or orientation is. AIDS is not discriminatory. It toils on the body of all its victims with the same intensity no matter how that victim acquired it." He raised his voice and intoned, "so let me finish by saying use today to put an end to the blame game. Use today to start to educate and teach compassion. This would be the best end product of our walk today. I know you join me in looking forward to that magical month of June when we no longer have to walk this walk because a cure has been found. Let us take that magical hope and use it constructively to educate our community about caring and compassion. And let us take that hope for a cure into our hearts and minds and if we really believe…really believe, then that magical month of June when there is no longer an AIDS walk will come. It will come! Thank you all very much. God bless you and keep on walking!"

The audience gave Matthew a loud and sustained round of applause. He smiled as he waved to the audience. Matthew shook hands with the Governor and other dignitaries assembled and then jumped down from the staging into the audience. Matthew walked towards his group of friends to join them in beginning the walk. As he did, many people came up to him, hands extended or arms extended to hug him. Matthew thanked them all and smiled brightly as he made his way back to his friends. Trooper O'Sullivan diligently walked behind Matthew through the crowd, but did not interfere with the positive human contact Matthew was receiving. "He deserves this", thought the trooper.

Across town in his dingy apartment Craig Talbot stood leaning against the counter cutting an apple with his dirty steak knife. "So how much did you make last night?", he asked a half awake Christian. "About three hundred", groggily responded Christian. "Three hundred...Jesus. That's jack shit! How much does that nigger take from you each night?", yelled Craig as he moved over toward Christian. Christian sat up on the mattress, pushed his hair back out of his face and mumbled, "he took a hundred last night...why?" Craig sat down next to Christian. "I think you should give the jungle bunny a boot! Tell him you're working for me now..." Christian softly told Craig, "I'm not really sure if that's a smart move. I don't think you're gonna be able to protect me the way Malcolm does..." Craig yelled, "fuck you! That's bullshit! You're done working for Malcolm today. I own you now and if that nigger doesn't like it he can come see me! It'll be his last trip to this side of town."

Christian did not respond to Craig. He sat and wondered how he could get out of this mess. Craig had given him a place to crash and sometimes the sex was great, but Christian thought "this guy's fuckin' crazy!" He resolved to take a few days to plan how to get away from Craig. "I gotta get away from this crazy bastard!", thought the young teenager as he took another hit from the marijuana joint.

Several days had passed since the successful annual AIDS walk in Boston. Once again this year millions of dollars had been raised to treat and care for those with the virus. Matthew was reading the article on the distribution of the funds in the Ledger when Tracy buzzed to let Matthew know that Dexter Donnelly was here for their luncheon date. Matthew got up and walked out of his office to a waiting Donnelly. He patted him on the back and they went to leave the office for lunch. "I made a reservation at Scott's if that's all right?", Matthew asked Dexter. "That's fine", replied Donnelly. "Do you want to walk or ride?", Matthew asked. "It's nice out. I'd rather walk if that's not a problem with Brent", answered Donnelly. "No problem", replied the state police officer.

Matthew and Dexter sat enjoying their steamers and crab salad in the rear booth of Scott's very successful restaurant. Brent O'Sullivan picked at a Caesar salad. Scott came over to the booth and sat down with them. "Did you ever call Adam back last week?", Scott asked Matthew. "No, in fact I didn't. I've been so busy that I forgot. Why?", asked Matthew. Scott said, "I think you should call him. He told me he has some news for you." Matthew questioned, "is something wrong?" Scott responded, "nothing is wrong. I think you'll be happy with his news." Matthew's interest had been peaked. He would call Adam tonight when he got home from work.

That evening Matthew anxiously dialed Adam in California. His call was answered by Adam's machine. Matthew left a message for Adam to call. But Adam did not call that evening and Matthew rolled around in the bed wondering what Adam's news was. "Maybe I can get Scott to tell me tomorrow", he thought.

Matthew was deep in the midst of reviewing Dion's case summary regarding the lottery scam in Springfield when Tracy called into the office to indicate the Adam was on hold for Matthew. "Well hello, stranger", Matthew cheerily said to Adam. "Hello, honey. How are you?", asked Adam. Matthew replied, "busy as shit, but otherwise everything is going good. What about you?" Adam responded, "I'm doing well. I have some exciting news that I wanted to tell you. Is now a good time or should we talk tonight?", he asked. Matthew said, "please…now! I tossed and turned last night wondering what you were calling about. Please tell me you won the lottery and your taking me away from all this!" he said laughing. Adam paused momentarily and then said, "well, unfortunately not. But I think you'll be happy to hear this anyway." "Okay", said Matthew. Adam began, "I was calling to let you know that I interviewed for an associate dean position at Harvard. I didn't let you know when I was there for the interview because I didn't want to get your hopes up. Anyway, the interview went really well. I got a call last week from the Dean and he has offered me the job. I'm really excited about it and…" Matthew interrupted Adam. "Really excited? You should be damn proud of yourself! That's terrific! Absolutely wonderful! Will it start next fall?, he excitedly asked Adam.

Adam began again. "Well, that's the other half of the news. I spoke to the president of the law school here and told him I got the job. He was very happy for me. The job at Harvard starts in January. They're going to let me out of my contract a semester early here. They had no problem with me leaving, in fact the president of the school was very supportive. So, another reason I was calling to see if I could get room and board from you."

There was silence on the phone. Matthew paused as he listened to the words bounce around in his head. Words he had always hoped he would hear. Matthew said through a teary voice, "room and board? This is your home. It's still your house. Of course you can come back!" Adam sighed a sign of relief and said, "I hoped you would say that. I wasn't sure if somebody had replaced me." Matthew quickly responded, "honey, I haven't had time for anyone and furthermore no one could replace you!" Adam laughed. "I'm not sure if we can pick right up where we left off, but you know we are getting to be two old queens and I think the only ones left for us is each other", he said in a light voice to Matthew. Matthew replied, "We were always for each other. This is fantastic news! Do you think you'll be home for Christmas?", he asked. Adam replied, "I'll be done here December fifteenth. It'll take me a few days to pack and then I'd like to come back." Matthew said, "just let me know when to pick you up at the airport." They continued their conversation briefly and Adam ended with, "I've never stopped loving you." Matthew gleefully said, "I love you too. This is going to be wonderful! Call me in a couple of days so we can talk again."

Matthew spent the remainder of the day calling his friends and family to announce that Adam would be returning to Massachusetts for good in December. His mother noted the lightness in his voice. She remarked that he hadn't seemed this happy in quite sometime. Matthew readily agreed. His conversation with Janice was marked by her whooping yell of excitement when Matthew shared the news. Matthew laughed and changed the subject. He asked her, "so when are you going to tell me? Is it a boy or a girl?" Janice replied, "Jose and I decided not to know until the baby is born. But I hope its another boy. I've always wanted to have three sons." Matthew asked, "when is your due date again?" Janice replied, "late September." He responded, "well at least there'll be something nice to celebrate in that dreaded month." Janice chuckled.

Summer was passing quickly. It was already August. Matthew spent the weekend in the Berkshires with his family. His mother was having her traditional August cookout and family reunion. Matthew enjoyed his time away from the city. He spent time playing with his sister Maria's children and philosophizing with his brother Anthony. Matthew had spent his first night in the Berkshires visiting with Ted and Pete. They reminisced about the 'old times'. They were thrilled to hear about Adam's return for the holidays. "You'll have to come to New Year's this year!", said Ted to Matthew. Matthew woke late in the morning to enjoy the rest of this lazy hot Sunday with his family. The guests were arriving for the cookout. Meanwhile, across the state Craig Talbot was spending a very different August weekend.

"I think you need to learn a lesson!", exclaimed Craig in a loud voice at Christian. The young teenager cowered in the corner of the small room. He had been bruised severely by Craig after their altercation about Christian's refusal to completely part ways with his pimp Malcolm. "You know what I think would be good for you faggot boy?", said a very angry Craig. "I think my fist up your ass would show you who was in charge!", Craig yelled. "Please...please, stop!", cried a terrified Christian. "Stop it...please!", Christian cried again. Craig came over and sat down next to Christian in the corner of the room. "How about you suck my dick to calm me down?", he said as he unbuttoned his jeans and pulled down his pants. Christian reached over and began to stroke Craig's half erect penis. He then placed it in his mouth. Not two minutes later Craig was ejaculating into Christian's mouth. "Now, that's better...I'm gonna save the fist for later.", said Craig sarcastically as he pulled his jeans up from his ankles.

Craig went over to the counter and picked up a half rotten apple. He grabbed the steak knife and began cutting it. Christian laid back against the wall on the mattress and closed his eyes. He was exhausted. Craig slowly ate the apple and stared at the naked teenage boy propped against the wall. Craig thought how Christian reminded him of himself when he was young. "But I wasn't a fuckin' faggot like this one and that Schipani asshole!", thought Craig as he continued to eat his apple. Christian began to snore. The sex and booze from yesterday and today was taking its toll. He was able to fall asleep while half sitting up. Craig was intently staring at the teenage boy. He ate his last piece of apple and threw the core into the dirty sink water burgeoning with dishes and garbage. Craig held the dirty steak knife in his hand. He rubbed the knife back and forth between his palm. He stared at the steak knife and stared at Christian. Back and forth: the knife and the teenager.

Craig quietly went down on all fours. He took the steak knife and put it in his mouth, clenching it with his teeth. He began to slither across the small room in a stalking fashion. He slid onto the mattress on the floor. Christian remained snoring against the wall. Craig pulled the knife out of his mouth. He held the handle in his hands. He reached back as a baseball pitcher would and then plunged the knife directly into the throat of Christian. Christian's eyes popped wide open. Craig pulled the knife out of Christian's throat. Blood was spurting everywhere, including all over Craig.

Craig took the knife and wildly began thrusting it into Christian's body. The teenager was unable to move or resist. He lay slumped against the wall. Craig continued to stab into the teenager's body. He stabbed his chest, his face, his stomach and his arms. He stabbed in a fast and repeated motion. He continued for about two minutes. Craig's teenage prostitute laid dead in a pool of blood on a now blood soaked mattress. Craig stopped stabbing. He held the bloody steak knife in the air and laughed a heinous laugh. "This is so fuckin' easy!", he exclaimed out loud.

Craig stood up from the mattress. He threw the knife down on Christian's body. Craig took off his jeans and threw them over Christian's face. He leaned down and grabbed Christian's penis. Craig took the limp and now dead penis and put it in his mouth and sucked on it for a few seconds. "Now that's a killer blow job!", he laughingly said. Craig then moved out of the small room and into the bathroom. He took a shower to wash off the blood. He watched with delight as the blood streamed down the drain of the tub. "That's what you got waiting for you Schipani!", yelled Craig as he punched the tiled wall in the shower. "That's what you got coming!", he said over and over.

Ninety miles away Matthew felt the tug at his shirt which made the hammock he was lying in begin to swing. It was his three year old niece tugging at her uncle. "Uncle Matt can we go swing?", she asked him. Matthew sat up in the hammock and put his feet on the ground. "Come on honey, let's go", he said to his niece as they ran across the yard to the swing set.

Craig Talbot took the lifeless body of the teenage boy and wrapped it up in the torn, frayed and filthy imitation oriental rug lying on the floor. He was sweating profusely as he wrapped the rug around the body. It was literally dead weight. He left the body wrapped in the middle of the room and went outside the apartment and down the hall to the pay telephone. "Hey, Kenny…can you come over here real quick?", Craig asked his friend on the phone. "Sure…give me about an hour." Craig hung up the phone and walked back to the apartment.

It was two hours later when his friend showed up at the apartment. A stench had begun to fill the apartment from the dead body. Craig showed him the body of Christian wrapped in the rug. "Holy shit! What the fuck happened?", shouted the shock friend of Craig Talbot. Craig put his finger to his mouth saying, "shut the fuck up will ya! Look, this little faggot tried to come on to me. He got me drunk…I passed out and woke up and he was suckin' my dick! I pushed the little shit off of me and he started coming at me. I grabbed the knife…anyway, who gives a fuck! One less faggot around here!" Kenny sat down on the rickety chair in the corner. He put his hand to his forehead. Craig said to his friend, "I need you to help me get rid of him. Can we use your brother's truck?"

Kenny reached for the roach in the ash tray on the table. He lit it and took a couple of puffs. "Well, Craigy my boy…I'll help ya, but it's gonna cost", said Kenny. Craig sat down in the other chair, grabbed the joint and said, "how much?" Kenny replied, "five hundred". Craig looked him squarely in the eye and said, "I only got three…that'll have to do. How about it?" Kenny replied, "fine…three now and three later. A little bit of interest for my efforts. I'll give you a couple of weeks." Craig responded, "okay. But I want the faggot outta here tonight!" Kenny looked at Craig and said, "you got a phone?" Craig answered, "down the hall there's a pay one." Kenny stood up, walked toward the door and said, "I'll be back in a few" and walked out the door of Craig's apartment.

Evening came. Matthew threw the coins into the toll basket as he took the exit to head home. It had been a long weekend, full of activity but he had enjoyed it. If traffic was light on Mass. Ave. he would be in bed before one. Across town Craig Talbot and his friend pulled the dead body of the young teenager out of the back of the rusted Ford pickup. They dragged it through the mostly abandoned park. The park had seen better days. But those days were long ago. Now the grass was overgrown, hypodermic needles were everywhere and the smell of urine, vomit and other unidentifiable odors filled the hot steamy air.

They dragged Christian's body into the beginning of the small wooded area abutting the rear of the park. Craig broke a couple of tree limbs off the trees above. He threw them haphazardly over the body in a crude attempt to camouflage it. Kenny stood by and smoked a cigarette. When he was done Craig said, "rest in peace homo boy". He turned to Kenny and said, "let's get out of here before the niggers see us", he said. Kenny laughed. "I'm packin'. We see any niggers and it's huntin' season!" They walked back through the overgrown grass. They saw a group of about five men huddled under the broken down pavilion smoking crack. Craig said, "one of the niggers will take the blame for this. This was ingenious Kenny…dump the queer in niggerland!" Kenny laughed as he opened the door to the truck. A moment later Kenny and Craig pulled out of the park and headed toward the highway. The skyline of Boston was lit up amist the haze in the distance.

Finally, the heat wave broke during the middle of the week. Matthew had convened a dinner party at his house to plan the upcoming election campaign. With Adam on the west coast, his mother Rosa became the hostess of the party. The dinner of course was an Italian meal. The food as always was wonderful. Matthew sat on the floor in the living room surrounded by twelve of his dearest friends as they planned the election strategy. Scott went over the state of finances for the campaign. To Matthew's delight there was sufficient money to make it through the election. He knew that if he trusted Scott with the task of raising funds it would be done with ease and effectively. Dion had mapped out the schedule for September and October for Matthew's various campaign speeches and appearances. Matthew had made it clear that he wanted to travel all over the state. That was why last winter he had chosen his home town in western Massachusetts to make the first, formal announcement. He didn't want the voters to think he was another Bostonian politician who forgot that the border of Massachusetts extended to New York and not to Worcester. The endorsements were lining up thanks to Dexter Donnelly. In fact, Matthew noted on this evening that Dexter was in better spirits than he had been in a long time. His son Peter had also joined them that evening.

The next morning was marked by an incident that angered rather than scared Matthew. Brent O'Sullivan was driving Matthew to work in his Volvo through Harvard Square as he had done so many times in the past. As they turned behind the square and onto Mt. Auburn street Matthew noticed the sunglassed, helmeted biker speeding up next to their car. He remarked to Brent, "you know we should bike into work. They get there as quick as we do with this damn traffic." Brent chuckled and kept his eyes focused on the car in front of him and the rear view mirror up to his right. As they slowly proceeded through the traffic lights, Trooper O'Sullivan noticed that the sunglassed bicyclist was keeping pace with them and following directly behind.

The Trooper followed the cars proceeding slowly in front of him through the intersection under construction. The bicyclist kept pace and then accelerated to the driver's side of Matthew's Volvo. Trooper O'Sullivan looked out his driver's window and saw the bicyclist looking at him. The man on the bicycle had a big, broad smile. The Trooper looked ahead as the traffic continued at a snail's pace. The man on the bicycle reached into his back pack and pulled out a brick.

Suddenly the brick came smashing through the windshield of Matthew's car. It landed on the right leg of Brent O'Sullivan.

O'Sullivan veered the car to the right. He couldn't see 'where he was going but the car came to a quick stop when it hit the curb. Before Matthew knew it, Brent O'Sullivan was out of the car with his gun waving in the air. Matthew got out of the rear door of his Volvo. He began to run after Brent O'Sullivan. The bicyclist was peddling fast and furious. O'Sullivan pointed his gun at the bicyclist but then lifted it into the air. There were too many people walking through the streets for him to shoot the gun. An inaccurate shot could mean tragedy for an innocent pedestrian on his or her way to work. Brent O'Sullivan stopped running and stood in the middle of the road. Matthew caught up to him shortly thereafter.

"Fuck!", yelled Brent O'Sullivan as he turned to walk back to the car. Matthew said nothing. As they got closer to the car a police cruiser was already there diverting the traffic. Brent O'Sullivan identified himself. Matthew walked around the car. There was minor damage to it. He leaned against the hood waiting for the tow truck as Trooper O'Sullivan and the now present four police officers stood talking. "Mister Attorney General, why don't I take you into work?", said one of the police officers to Matthew. "Thank you", said Matthew as he and Brent O'Sullivan got into the back seat of the police car. While riding to the office Matthew was peppering Brent with questions about whether he was all right. Brent was starting to become annoyed with him. "I told you, I'm fine! I just can't believe I lost the bastard!" he yelled. Matthew decided he had questioned enough. They rode in silence the rest of the way to the office.

The morning incident set Tracy right off. "It's getting worse! I can't believe that they can't find the person that is doing this! I'm sure its that Craig weirdo…" Matthew attempted to calm Tracy down, but she would hear none of it. "You need more than one police officer guarding you", she stated. Matthew replied, "please! I refuse to live my life like this. Next thing you'll say is that I need a bulletproof limo to come to work!" Tracy turned on her heels and replied, "not a bad idea!" Matthew shook his head as Tracy closed the door behind her.

That evening Matthew and Adam had a delightful conversation. Matthew was beginning to look forward to Adam returning even though it was still four months away. They talked about the election campaign, Scott's romance and Adam's new job. What Matthew did not talk about was the event of the morning and the other incidents of violence that had happened since Adam had moved. He purposefully left that out.

"They'll catch whoever it is before he gets back", Matthew told Scott that evening. Scott shook his head in disagreement. "I don't know about that. I think if this gets any worse you should let Adam in on it." Matthew did not agree. "He's three thousand miles away. There's nothing he can do about it. I would appreciate it if you didn't say a word to him about this." Scott replied, "I won't. You know that you can trust me. But I'm more nervous now then I've ever been, even more so then when that guy tried to break in." Matthew shrugged his shoulders.

Dion piped in, "I'm concerned too. I've scheduled you to be all over the place in the next few months. You better talk to Brent about getting some more protection when you're on your road trips." Matthew replied, "I'm sure my guardian angel has already taken care of that. Brent is so protective it's ridiculous. He's been beating himself up all day because that guy got away from him. I'll tell ya, if he wasn't straight I could fall in love with that man! I always feel safe when I'm with him." Scott responded, "I hope so. I'm just waiting for something really bad to happen." Matthew responded, "nothing bad is going to happen. Everything is going great. The election looks good, my staff is great and Adam will be back home where he belongs before we know it! Let's stop brooding and be happy!"

Dion grabbed a bottle of wine out of the refrigerator. He poured three glasses and handed Scott and Matthew theirs. Dion raised his glass and said, "let's toast to being happy and to victory in November!" Scott and Matthew clicked their glasses with Dion and drank their wine. "Good year!", exclaimed Matthew as he took another sip of wine.

It was eight o'clock in the morning and Matthew was sitting in the conference room of Governor Dickerson's office surrounded by Bradford Collins to his left and three others to his right that he really didn't know. "Well, should I sign it now or wait until after the election?", the Governor asked Matthew. Governor Dickerson was referring to a bill that Matthew had championed in the spring which had recently passed the house and senate. The bill provided for stronger penalties for those who would discriminate against persons with HIV or AIDS in the areas of employment, housing and medical care.

Matthew drank from his second cup of coffee this morning. He looked at the bill typed out on the paper in front of him. He and Octavia had reviewed the proposed statute in detail prior to offering it through Candice Miller, the state senator from Cambridge. The proposed statute was constitutional and could withstand any challenge. It was one of the many initiatives that Matthew had identified as important during his term as attorney general. He wanted Dickerson to sign the bill into law.

Matthew put down the paper and looked across the table at Lloyd Dickerson. "I think you're asking me for a political opinion rather than a legal one", he said. Dickerson wiped off the crumbs from his fourth donut with a linen napkin. "No, Matthew I'm asking you for your opinion as the attorney general of this state", responded Dickerson firmly. Matthew looked at him saying, "well if you remember Governor, I was the one who pushed for the bill to be introduced. So of course I think you should sign it. I think timing is very important on this. If you don't sign it now it dies as a matter of procedure. Then it will have to be reintroduced next session. That will delay it and who knows with how the election turns out whether it will stand a chance of even being reintroduced."

Dickerson sipped from his mug and replied, "so I guess I should sign it now then, right?" Matthew said in return, "yes, you should sign it now. It is the right thing to do. It sends the right message. It's constitutional…it won't be overturned. So as the attorney general I am telling you that the bill is legally correct and as the state's top law enforcer I am telling you that it is good public policy that this state should enforce." Dickerson stood up from his chair and announced, "then I'll sign it. We'll do it tomorrow. Bradford you coordinate the vermin from the press to come in during the afternoon. Make sure you get Candy Miller here too. She should get some of the credit, and I need her district to win reelection!", he bellowed.

Collins closed the cover of his folder in front of him on the table and stood up. The others stood as well, so Matthew joined them. They began to walk out of the conference room. Dickerson walked the other way toward his inner office. "He didn't even ask me to join him at the ceremony", thought Matthew. "What a jerk!", he said under his breath. As Matthew and Brent O'Sullivan walked down the marble halls of the State House he heard Bradford Collins running and yelling behind him. "Matthew! Matthew…wait!" They stopped walking and turned. Collins came up to them. "I forgot to invite you tomorrow. Can you be here?", asked Collins. Matthew smiled and said, "yes. Of course I can be here." Collins replied, "good. I'll call you in the morning and let you know what time." Matthew thanked Collins. He turned to walk towards the exit. "Such a dweeb!", he mumbled to Trooper O'Sullivan who laughed in return.

Matthew woke up Sunday morning to find Diana cuddled right next to him. He looked at the clock. It was only seven thirty. "Damn!", he said as he admonished himself for waking up so early. He wanted to sleep late this Sunday morning. He went over and shut the window in the bedroom. It had gotten very cool during the evening. Matthew returned to the bed. Diana moaned as he tried to slip under the comforter next to her. He put his head back down on the pillow. Ten minutes later his phone was ringing. He reached over

Diana and grabbed the phone. "Hello?", he said. The voice on the other end began singing. "I love you...I love you...yes I do! I love you!" It was an intoxicated Adam. Matthew responded, "what are you doing? It's five in the morning out there!" Adam sang, "I just called to say I love you! I just called to say how much I care, I do! That's a Stevie Wonder song you know! You want me to keep singing it?" Matthew was laughing. "No...you can sing to me another time. Go to bed! I'll call you later."

Matthew hung up the phone and sat up in the bed. "Come on Di Di! Let's get up. There's no sleep today for the weary", he said to his dog. Diana jumped down off the bed. Matthew walked out of the bedroom and into the kitchen. "Good morning", he said to Brent O'Sullivan who was sitting at the table with his glass of milk and the Sunday paper. "I'll make a pot of coffee", O'Sullivan said to Matthew. "Thanks. I'm taking Diana out back", he replied as he opened the door to go down the stairs to the back yard. He looked behind him and saw Brent O'Sullivan following. "Brent! I'm just going to be out in the back yard! It's no big deal. Just go back and read your paper." O'Sullivan gave him a scowl as he turned on the stairs and went back into the apartment.

Later that morning Scott and Matthew were sharing the paper over coffee and donuts. Matthew glanced at an article about a teenage boy found dead in Shady Knoll park. He had been stabbed forty seven times. The police spokesperson indicated that they believed it was drug related. Matthew frowned, "God damn druggies", he said out loud as he turned the page to the next story.

Matthew sat on the back porch that evening with Scott and his aunt Gloria drinking coffee and talking about how quickly the summer had passed. It wasn't even Labor Day yet and the heat of summer had given up its grasp in favor of cool fall winds. "Crazy New England weather", Scott said. They sat and talked about the campaign. The next ten weeks Matthew would have to set his sights and energies full steam ahead on the campaign season. It would begin on

Labor Day weekend. Matthew felt good about the coming race. On this cool August evening he truly believed that he would be elected attorney general in his own right come November. The march to election day was on!

CHAPTER 16

THE LEAVES FALL

September 1996

Craig Talbot sat down on his new mattress stolen from the bedding shop down the street and gulped down his fourth beer. "Hey Kenny! We gonna take the road trip or what?", he yelled at his friend who was in the bathroom of the apartment. "Yeah…yeah, yeah. Just hold onto your hat! I'll be there in a minute", responded Kenny. Craig drank the remainder of his beer and waited for his friend to join him. Kenny came out of the bathroom, fastening the belt on his jeans. "How about we get some honeys before we go?", asked Kenny. Craig yelled, "I don't feel like fuckin' no bitch right now! I've got business to take care of." Kenny said, "fine…okay. What's the hurry anyway?" Craig responded, "I gotta take care of this before the end of the month." Kenny reached down with his hand to Craig and pulled him up from the floor. "Well, let's head north then!"

Matthew looked at Tracy sitting in the back of the police cruiser and began to laugh. "I've never made it down Route Six this fast!", he said as the siren of the state police car cleared the traffic ahead of them. "Well, you're an important guy, you know!", she said with a chuckle. Matthew leaned forward in the seat to Trooper Brent O'Sullivan who was riding shot gun. "Do you think they know that I'm just in a rush to get to the gay bar?", he said with a laugh. Brent O'Sullivan laughed and said, "I won't tell anybody if you won't!"

It was Labor Day weekend in Massachusetts. The last weekend of summer and a heavy traffic weekend on Cape Cod. Matthew was on his way to deliver a campaign speech in friendly Provincetown. Not only did he want to make sure that he didn't abandon his roots in western Massachusetts, he also wanted to insure that he kept his contact with the gay community. He had become a leader over the past few years, a role that he had always desired in the gay community. He certainly could not abandon his constituency at election time. But this was more than just about votes. It was about listening to his gay brothers and sisters and hearing their voices and their concerns. Matthew believed that this would be one of his favorite campaign swings.

He had arranged to stay overnight in Provincetown at the small guest house that Ken Rivers had purchased during the summer. Ken had put all of his savings into this business venture. Matthew had wished him the best. He had hoped that some publicity would assist Ken as well. He promised Ken to ask his friends in the press to write where he stayed in Provincetown. Any form of publicity would help his friend in this very competitive tourist market.

The driver turned off the lights and siren as the police car turned onto Commercial Street in Provincetown. "Is it okay if we go with the flow of traffic?", he asked Matthew. Matthew said, "yes, let's look at all the beautiful people!" To try to speed down Commercial Street would be a big mistake. The street was lined with pedestrians and bicycles traveling about. Matthew preferred safety over speed as they got into town. He also enjoyed people watching on this bright, but cool day. He laughed at the men who insisted that summer was still here and walked down commercial street in shorts with their shirts off. "They must be freezing!", exclaimed Matthew as he pointed to two muscular men holding hands walking down the street. Tracy responded, "I'm sure they are. I brought some sweaters. Look at that tree…it's beginning to turn." Matthew followed Tracy's pointed finger to the oak tree behind the jewelry shop. Yes indeed, the leaves on the tree were losing their summer green and turning fall colors. Fall was coming early to Massachusetts this year.

They pulled into the driveway of the guest house. Ken came out the side door to greet them. He hugged Matthew firmly and kissed Tracy. Ken showed them to their rooms for the weekend. Brent O'Sullivan and Trooper Dennis Lee would share the room across from Matthew in the guest house. Matthew threw his suitcase on the bed and went down the stairs to the kitchen of the guest house. "I'm ready to walk!", he announced. Ken replied, "I've got some time. Can I join you?" Matthew shook his head 'yes'. He grabbed his light jacket and Tracy's arm and followed Ken out the side door. They weren't halfway down the driveway when he heard Brent O'Sullivan yell, "where do you think you are going?" Matthew stopped in his tracks and turned. "We're walking down Commercial Street. I'll be fine. I've got Tracy to protect me!", he said to the state trooper. Brent walked up to them. "You're not going any where without me. Matthew shrugged his shoulders and said, "okay. Then come join us. I'm in a shopping mood!"

Matthew, Tracy and Ken along with their escort spent the next few hours going in and out of the many shops lining Provincetown. Matthew bought a few things for his nieces and an outfit for Janice's soon to be born baby. He bought a blue one. He too believed that Janice was going to have another son. He also purchased some miniature hanging wooden fish for Adam. He was going to mail them to him in California. Adam had begun a collection many years ago. Everytime Matthew and Adam would come to Provincetown he would buy another fish to add to his collection. Matthew had the store keeper wrap them carefully and box them to be sent in the morning mail following the holiday. He wrote a brief note that he put in the box. "These fish are swimming to find their way home…Soon they'll be returning to their home on the Atlantic." He showed Tracy the note and said, "corny, isn't it?" She laughed and replied, "put it in the box. He already knows you're sappy anyway!"

Craig Talbot and his friend drove through the backwoods of New Hampshire trying to locate Gus' Gun Shop. The old Ford pickup bounced along the rock and sand road. They finally found the shop set back from the road under three towering maple trees. They got out of the car and walked into the gun shop. "Hi there fellas!", yelled the gray bearded man behind the counter to Craig and Kenny. "Whatcha lookin' fer?", he asked. Craig walked over to the glass encased counter and leaned on it. "I'm looking for a rifle…not too sure what kind I need.", he told the old man behind the counter. "Well whatcha wanna do with it?", asked the old man. Craig responded, "I want to hunt from a distance." The old man moved toward the left and Craig followed. The old man asked, "whatcha hunting?" Craig replied, "fast game". The old man inquired, "how much ya wanna spend?" Craig said, "Not too much. But I gotta make sure it's good. I need something good."

The old man came around the glass case and stood in front of Craig and Kenny. "Howja find out about my place here?", he asked Craig. Craig smirked and said, "an old army buddy told me about it. He told me I could get a good deal and nobody would know I had been here. Is that what you can do for me old man?" The old man said, "you ain't no feds are ya?" Craig and Kenny laughed in unison. "Do we look like feds?", asked Kenny. The old man replied, "nope, you sure don't!" He motioned Craig and Kenny to follow him through a door. They walked behind the old man into a small dark room in the back of the store. The old man unlocked the combination lock on the closet door and opened it. He bent over and pulled out a wide wooden chest with a lock on the handle. He reached into his pocket, pulled out his keys and unlocked the lock. Craig and Kenny stood behind the old man. They were peering over his shoulder as he fumbled through the box.

The old man pulled out a black rifle and handed it to Craig. It looked almost new. "What's this?", asked Craig. The old man proudly replied, "that's an AR 15 semiautomatic. Can't get it anymore since Clinton got his way. That'll probably do ya good!" Craig looked at the dull black finish of the rifle. He held it against his shoulder and peered through the scope attached to the top of the gun. He pressed his finger against the trigger. "Feels good", he said as he took the gun and threw it to Kenny. Kenny caught the rifle and inspected it as well. "So how good is it with a fast target?", asked Craig. The old man replied, "depends on how good a shot ya are." Craig boasted, "I'm real good. Military trained." Kenny looked at Craig with a puzzled face. Craig had never told him that he had been in the service. The old man said, "it's a beauty. Give ya a good deal on it".

Kenny handed the rifle back to Craig, who looked through the sight on it again. Craig asked, "how good is it from a distance?" The old man replied, "it's accurate at two hundred yards…even if you're not that good of a shot. It'll blow a hole the size of my hand!" Craig smiled and looked at Kenny. He rolled his eyes at Craig. "So you got the ammo for this too?", Craig asked. The old man responded, "sure do. Got plenty up front." Craig said, "well let's go up front then" and motioned toward the door with the barrel of the rifle. The old man locked the trunk and pushed it with his foot back into the closet. He locked the door and then motioned Craig and Kenny toward the door out of the room.

They returned to the front of the store. The old man handed Craig three boxes of fifty .223 caliber bullets. "These'll blow ya a good hole!", he said to Craig. Craig asked, "so how much for everything?" The old man rubbed his balding head and tugged at his gray beard. "It's a beauty ya know…real special piece…" Craig interrupted, "yeah, yeah…How much?" The old man said, "eight hundred and an extra 'C' note for me to forget I ever saw you."

Craig looked at Kenny who raised his hands in an "I don't know" fashion. He then reached into the pocket of his dirty jeans. He pulled out a wad of fifties and twenties. He counted them off on the glass case separating him and the old man. When he reached nine hundred he put the rest of his money in his pocket, reached for the boxes of bullets, tossed them to Kenny and then picked up the rifle. He looked at the old man and said, "glad I never saw ya!" and walked out of the store.

Morning had come to Provincetown. Matthew was reading the Sunday paper out on the deck of Ken's guest house. Dion Renzi had arrived about an hour earlier to join Matthew in the campaign activities in the afternoon. Matthew wished all his campaign appearances could be like this. He didn't have to give a prepared speech, rather he would go to the theater club and mingle with people in return for donations towards his campaign. There would even be a drag show as part of the agenda. Matthew really enjoyed drag shows. He loved watching men impersonate some of his favorite singers. If they did it with style Matthew would actually feel as if he were actually present with Barbra, Bette, Liza and of course, Diana. He was hoping that the show today would be a professional one.

Dion looked up from the section of the paper he was reading and said to Matthew, "so when are you going to push for gay marriages?" Matthew put down his paper on the table. "Dion, please let me get through this election first!", he said. Dion smiled but continued to press the issue. "No, I'm serious. I think that it is something that you should push for." Matthew responded, "I agree. But as with all things, we have to wait until the timing is right. Who knows what is going to happen in this election. Even if I get elected, I'm not too sure about Lloyd Dickerson. He's pissed off enough people over the years that the anti-Dickerson vote may just push him out of office. Then we'll have to wait and see what the new Governor would do with these type of issues."

Dion would not let go of the topic. Matthew hadn't answered his question satisfactorily. Dion continued, "I think Dickerson will win. His opponent has no money for the campaign. And remember,

Dickerson has a lot of favors to call in. So let's presume he wins. How long are you going to wait before you raise the issue?" A frustrated Matthew responded, "let's just hope I win first. Take it one step at a time. I promise you if I win you and I will sit down and try to figure out how to tackle this issue. Okay?" Dion smiled and said, "okay".

The campaign meeting was a success. The meeting raised over five thousand dollars for Matthew's campaign. He enjoyed sitting and talking with people about their issues and what they expected from him as the openly gay attorney general should he get elected. He found that his gay constituents were not only concerned about gay issues, but were also concerned about those issues that all other citizens worried about. They were concerned about violence in the streets, the rise in youth violence, domestic violence and child abuse, as well as discrimination issues. Dion quietly took notes as he sat to Matthew's right while Matthew spoke with many lesbians and gay men.

The drag show was all that Matthew hoped it would be. He thought the performers were wonderful. He also appreciated the time, effort and artistry of their work. It wasn't just men putting on a wig and a dress and getting on stage to perform a song or imitate a star. It was about hard work and illusion so that people would really believe they were watching the star being portrayed. Matthew found the performance of Shirley Bassey's *This Is My Life* to be most compelling. The drag queen began the song in full drag. By the time the song reached its peak and to the completion, the drag queen had become the man he truly was under the makeup and the clothes. The message of the song and the interpretation brought Matthew and the others to their feet in applause.

The work week had been going well until Matthew picked up the Wednesday morning edition of the Gazette. The headline featured an article by the closeted reporter, Alfie Stone. The article detailed how former Deputy Attorney General Elizabeth Kragen was throwing her hat into the race as an independent candidate for attorney general. Matthew was halfway through the article when Octavia came rushing into his office. "The gall of that bitch!", exclaimed Octavia as Matthew motioned her to sit down. "Did you read what she said?", Octavia asked in a heightened voice. Matthew put down the paper and folded his hands. "Octavia…come on, didn't you expect this? She'll get no where with it. She just wants her claim to fame for a few shining moments." Octavia hastily responded, "I wish I could be as calm about this as you are. I think she may cut into your votes and you could lose the race!" Matthew replied, "I disagree. I think she will attract those voters who wouldn't have voted for me anyway. I think my opponent should be more worried than I am."

Matthew's gut instinct was confirmed the next morning when Shannon Watson called him. "The paper took a poll yesterday. Kragen doesn't even dent your lead. We still have you ahead two to one.", she told Matthew. Matthew sighed a sigh of relief. "Well, that is good news. So how about lunch on me for delivering that wonderful news?", he asked. "I'll be there…tell me when", she happily replied.

Matthew and Shannon Watson dined outside at a streetside cafe on Newbury Street in the Back Bay. Matthew had just filled her in on how excited Adam was to receive the fish he had mailed from Provincetown. "This is going to be a hell of a Christmas party this year!", she exclaimed. "Am I invited?", Shannon asked. Matthew smiled saying, "aren't you always?" Shannon shook her head and said, "Yes I am and I'll be there again this year with bells on!" Matthew laughed at his friend.

Across town Craig laid back with his hands folded behind his head on the pillow as the thin young black boy was sucking his penis. "Watch the teeth!", he yelled at the boy. The young boy stopped briefly and then returned to his duty. A few minutes later Craig was moaning, "here it comes!". The young boy took Craig's penis out of his mouth. "No! No!…swallow it!", commanded Craig. A moment later Craig sat up and pushed the young boy away from his crotch. The boy sat on the edge of the mattress sweating from the intensity of the sexual activity. "You can jerk off if you wanna. I'll watch ya.", Craig said. The young boy replied, "nah…I'm okay. How about that joint you promised me?" Craig stood up and went over to the table. A moment later he returned to the mattress, lit the marijuana cigarette saying, "here take a hit" as he handed it to the boy. "So what's your name?", Craig asked his sex partner. "It's Marvin", he replied.

Craig took another puff of the cigarette and handed it back to Marvin. "So you got a place to stay?", he asked. Marvin shook his head, "no, I've only been here a couple of days. I've been looking for a place to crash. I don't live around here. I'm from the Bronx." Craig asked, "how old are you?" Marvin replied, "seventeen". Craig smiled, took another hit and then said, "you can stay here if you want. You just gotta give me lots of head and when I want it, okay?" Marvin replied, "sounds okay to me! You've got an awesome body!." Craig replied, "I know!"

Craig went into the bathroom and jumped in the shower. He was talking in the shower as he lathered himself. "Schipani's a nigger lover! Schipani's a nigger lover! He's a fuckin' dead nigger lover!" Marvin came to the door, opened it and asked, "were you talking to me?" Craig yelled, "no! Shut the fuckin' door. I'll be out in a minute." About five minutes passed when Craig walked out of the bathroom with the towel wrapped loosely around his waist. "Here, I wanna show you something I'm real proud of", Craig said to Marvin. He went into the closet and reached under the bundle of dirty clothes. He pulled out the AR 15 rifle and showed it to Marvin. "Don't worry…it's not loaded", he said.

Craig handed the rifle to Marvin. He took it and said, "cool…what's it for?" Craig replied, "hunting. I'm going at the end of the month. You wanna go with me?" Marvin said, "sure…why not". Craig said, "you know what my gun's name is?" Marvin laughed and asked, "you have a name for it?" Craig replied, "yeah. You wanna know what it is?" Marvin disinterestedly said, "I guess." Craig responded, "Matthew". Marvin looked at him and said, "how come you named it that?" Craig said, "it's my old boyfriend's name". Marvin doubtfully said, "oh, okay" and then asked if he could shower. Craig said, "sure...maybe if you're lucky I'll come in with you." Marvin turned and walked toward the shower. Craig stared at Marvin's naked buttocks and mumbled, "gonna fuck that tight nigger ass tonight, oh yeah!"

Matthew decided to take advantage of the coming weekend to refine his speech that he intended to give not once, but three times in the coming week. "There's only a few ways you can say the same thing", Matthew told Dion as they reviewed the speech. Dion responded, "hell, even president's give the same speech over and over during the campaign." Matthew smiled. It would be a light weekend in comparison to the ones to follow. He only had one campaign appearance and that was early Saturday evening in Marblehead. Then the multitude of outdoor appearances would begin.

Matthew had wanted to have his political rallies outside in public areas and colleges. He believed that he would attract a wider audience. Dion had taken care of Matthew's request. He had twenty four outdoor appearances scheduled between now and two days before the election in November.

"Are you going to stay up here all night and bother me or are you going downstairs to your boyfriend?", asked a chuckling Matthew of Dion. His campaign assistant responded, "you are getting to be an old queen! It's only eight thirty and you're ready for bed!" Matthew looked at Dion and said, "I need my beauty sleep you know!" Dion laughed. His laughter was interrupted by the telephone. It was Adam. Matthew signaled Dion to leave. Dion smiled and waved as he walked out the door to return to the apartment below.

Matthew and Adam were on the phone for over an hour. Now that Adam was returning home in a few months, Matthew found that they once again had a lot to talk about. They talked about their relationship in great detail. Both of them had decided that they could pick up where they left off. They viewed the past year and a half as just an interruption in the cycle of their relationship. The conversation ended with an exchange of "I love you" between the two of them.

"Brent do you mind taking Diana for a walk? I really want to go to bed", Matthew asked his bodyguard. Brent stood up from the sofa where he was watching *Larry King Live* on CNN and said, "no problem. Come on Diana, let's go for a walk!" Diana jumped up from the floor and with tail wagging followed the police officer to the kitchen door. Matthew heard the door slam behind him as he went into the bathroom.

He just put his head down on the pillow when the phone rang again. "Matthew", asked an unfamiliar voice. "Yes", he replied. "Are you home alone?", asked the voice. Matthew turned on the light and said, "who is this?" The voice responded, "it's your old buddy Craig Talbot, Matthew. I'm calling to say 'hi'" Matthew's mouth dropped from the receiver. He held the phone against his cheek. Then he pointed it back towards his chin and said, "what do you want Craig?" Talbot responded, "I want you…I've wanted you for a long time." Matthew put his feet on the floor. He sat up and took the cordless phone with him as he went out into the living room. Brent O'Sullivan was still outside with Diana. He would have to try to string Craig along until he got back.

Matthew said, "well Craig, that was a long time ago. So why are you calling me?" Craig responded, "I just wanna tell you that I think about you a lot. In fact right now I playing with my rock hard cock while I'm on the phone with you!" Matthew rolled his eyes as he walked toward the kitchen. He didn't say anything. He pulled out the kitchen chair and sat down in it. "Craig, why did you call?", Matthew asked. Craig responded, "I've been trying to get a hold of you for a long time now. I even came to your house one night but you had the cops chase me away." Matthew sat in silence for a moment. So that was Craig that evening, as he had suspected it was. "Well, what do you want to talk to me about?", asked Matthew.

There was a few minutes of silence and then Craig said, "are you hard right now?" Matthew answered, "no". Craig said, "why don't you take it out and beat off with me? I'm sure you've got a great cock!" Matthew replied, "Craig just tell me why you were calling. I really have to get to bed." Craig's voice turned deep and angry. "You don't wanna jerk off with me?", he asked. Matthew replied, "no…just tell me what you want from me".

Craig's voice raised and became angrier. He said, "I get it. I'm not a nigger and you love niggers. I know all about that nigger cock you suck. I've been watching niggers go in and out of your home for a long time. Well guess what? I got me a coon boy of my own. You'd like him…a pretty little boy with a big thick dick!" Matthew interrupted. He didn't want to hear anymore. "Craig I gotta go. Please don't call here anymore, okay?" Craig yelled into the phone, "I call you anytime I want you fuckin' faggot! You know you want me! I can't wait for the day I see you alone. I'm gonna tear up your tight white ass with my huge cock and shoot my load up you!" Matthew pulled the phone away from his face and pushed the power button to 'off'. He placed the phone down on the kitchen table. He looked at his hands. They were shaking.

Matthew got up from the chair and went to the refrigerator. He grabbed a beer and twisted the cap open. A moment later Brent O'Sullivan walked in with Diana. He unleashed her and placed the leash on the table. Matthew went to the cupboard and gave her a dog biscuit. O'Sullivan was hanging his jacket on the coat tree when Matthew said, "Brent could you sit down for a minute?" O'Sullivan replied, "sure" and looked at Matthew. He could tell from Matthew's face that something was wrong. "What's the matter?", asked Brent as he sat down in the chair. Matthew proceeded to tell O'Sullivan about the conversation that just took place as Brent was walking the dog. O'Sullivan reached in his jacket and pulled out a pad and pen. "Go over it again in detail for me. I need to take notes.", he told Matthew. Matthew tried to remember exactly what Craig had said. He was sure that he wasn't as accurate as he should be. "It was all sexual", Matthew concluded.

O'Sullivan got up from the table and went to the phone. He called the barracks. Matthew heard him talking in the background as he reached for another beer. O'Sullivan hung up the phone. He told Matthew, "there'll be a crew here in the morning to set up a tap. Don't answer the phone tonight…in fact, take it off the hook." Matthew did as he was told. He went into the library and took the phone off the hook and left the receiver on the desk. A few moments later he heard the annoying buzzing come from the phone. It stopped after a couple of minutes.

That evening Matthew laid in bed debating who he was going to tell about the phone call. He knew that he would have to tell Gloria and Scott. They lived in the same house as Matthew. He had to be concerned about their safety. But he decided against telling Adam. He didn't want to upset him. Things were going to return to normal at some point and he didn't want Adam rushing home in an effort to comfort him. "Just let everything play itself out", Matthew told himself.

The next morning Matthew rose to the noise of a hammer in the kitchen. He got up, put on his shorts and walked out into the kitchen. There were three police officers with a lot of equipment on the kitchen floor experimenting with his phone. He said "good morning" them, to which they politely responded "good morning" back.

The weekend passed and Matthew had not received another phone call. He tried to put the disturbing call out of his mind as he reviewed his speech set for the afternoon on Boston Common. This was an important speech. There would be lots of press coverage. He dubbed today "Boston Common Day". Thankfully the weather had cooperated. It was cold outside but the sun was shining. He looked out his office window and noticed that some of the trees had begun to turn gold. "Sweater weather is definitely here", he said out loud.

"Talking to yourself again?", said Tracy as she came into his office. Matthew smiled. "What's up?", he asked. "Nothing. I just wanted to know if I could come with you this afternoon", she asked. "Of course you can", he replied cheerfully.

It was an old-time political rally with bunting, flags and signs. There was even a band. Matthew was filled with joy as he ascended the stairs to the stage set up on Boston Common. His voice was clear and loud as he proclaimed that he was a candidate for election as the state's attorney general. "I am proud of the accomplishments that we have made over our short time in this office. But our job is not done yet. We need your help and your votes", he implored the audience.

Matthew reviewed his accomplishments in legislation and social policy during his tenure as attorney general. "But I have a vision that builds upon these accomplishments. A vision that needs more time to put together the blocks to reach the top, to reach our goals. We need to come together to build our community. We need to build a stronger, safer and more compassionate Massachusetts. We do that when we as a community set our priorities, set our sights and move forward with deliberate pace on our mission towards a better Massachusetts." Matthew's speech was once again interrupted by applause. It had been the ninth time during this long speech that his remarks had been interrupted. "And so I say to you in closing, together we can work to make Massachusetts a safer place. A state where children play in the streets without fear of danger or harm. A state where adults can raise families in prosperity and with the assurance that their jobs will be safe from discrimination or illegal activities. A state where our elderly will be protected, revered and honored for their life time of achievement and wisdom. Together we will join in passing laws that protect all our citizens no matter what their race, age, sex or orientation may be! Together we will join in re-establishing that sense of community, where one neighbor looks out for the other; helps the neighbor in need. Together we will move into the next century with a sense of purpose, fairness and justice for all! Thank you very much and God bless you!"

Matthew concluded his speech with a double-handed wave to the applauding audience. He noticed the placards bearing his name being raised in the air. The band struck up a patriotic theme as Matthew walked off the stage to his right and to the rear. Matthew walked in between the four state police officers assigned to him, with Tracy scrunched onto his arm. Matthew waved as he walked to the awaiting limousine. He turned for a final wave and noticed the protesters off to the right waving their placards in the air. The one bearing the message, "It's Adam and Eve, Not Adam and Steve!", made Matthew laughed. But his laughter quickly faded when he noticed who was caring the placard. It was Craig Talbot.

"Brent! Brent!", exclaimed Matthew as he stopped in his tracks. Trooper O'Sullivan came to his side. Matthew pointed in the direction of Craig Talbot. "There's Craig Talbot!", he exclaimed. O'Sullivan blurted, "mother fucker!" and grabbed the state trooper standing next to him. "C'mon!", he said as he pushed briskly through the crowd. Talbot saw the uniformed officer and the man in the suit approaching from the distance. He dropped his sign and turned around. As he ran from the Common he knocked down anyone in his way. Meanwhile, Matthew was being pushed into the limousine, which began to drive away quickly in the opposite direction. O'Sullivan continued his pursuit. Talbot continued his running. Talbot was in lead and winning.

That evening Matthew and Brent O'Sullivan had their first fight. Matthew had arranged to spend sometime with Dexter Donnelly's son Peter. He had decided he wanted to walk with Peter down by the Charles River and to be alone with his friend's son. Matthew told O'Sullivan that he could not come with him. O'Sullivan still fresh from his unsuccessful pursuit of Craig Talbot attempted to order Matthew not to go walking without him. Matthew reminded him that he was the Attorney General and technically, he "outranked"

O'Sullivan. This made Brent furious. "I don't give a shit what you say, I'm going with you!", yelled Brent O'Sullivan at Matthew. Matthew replied, "I'll say it again for the fifth time. You're staying here! I'm not going to talk to Peter about intimate things with you breathing down my shoulders! Now get over it!"

Matthew grabbed his jacket and went and stood out on the porch waiting for Peter Donnelly to show up. Inside Brent O'Sullivan dialed Scott's phone on the floor below. He told Scott how Matthew had refused to allow him to go on the walk. Scott said, "stubborn little bitch!" and O'Sullivan agreed. Scott suggested that they follow Matthew. They would walk together behind Matthew and try to be as covert as possible. "Let him try to pull that I'm in charge shit with me!", said Scott to Brent O'Sullivan.

About an hour later Matthew and Peter quietly strolled along the Charles River. It was a cool fall night. The full moon reflected off the river. The ducks quietly waded at the shore. Peter smiled as they walked toward a bench placed on the riverside. "Can we sit?', he asked Matthew. They sat down and looked out at the river and the brownstones across the water in Boston. They sat silently. Matthew looked at the brownstones on Beacon Street and recalled his first apartment with Scott many years ago. He smiled as he gazed at the buildings. His thoughts were interrupted by Peter. "One thing I really want to do was to be an actor. I always wanted to be in a play or on Broadway." Matthew turned to Peter and said, "then go for it! New York isn't that far away. Make some calls, get an agent and go for it!" Peter responded, "I'm not sure if I'm good enough." Matthew replied, "you'll never know unless you give it a try! I'll call a friend of mine who used to be on TV and was on Broadway for awhile." Peter smiled broadly and said, "you would do that for me?" Matthew put his arm around him and said, "yes I would do that for you!" Peter replied, "thank you". Matthew smiled at him. Matthew was happy he could do something, even if it a was a little thing like this, for his dear friend Dexter.

The next morning Matthew asked Tracy to try to track down his old boyfriend, James Davenport. Tracy didn't take too long to complete her search. Davenport was on the phone for Matthew. Matthew explained to him about Peter Donnelly. Davenport said he would "love to meet him. I'll be in New York next weekend. Here's the number." Matthew wrote down the number and thanked James. "Any chance at you joining him?", Davenport asked Matthew. Matthew replied that he couldn't. "I have a heavy campaign schedule ahead of me", he said. The truth be known, Matthew could have made a trek to New York. But he decided in his mind that if he did this he would jinx his returning relationship with Adam by running off to New York to be with Davenport. "That's all I need to do is to start this up again!", thought Matthew. They exchanged pleasantries and the conversation was ended. Peter Donnelly was elated when Matthew called. Moments later Dexter Donnelly was on the phone thanking Matthew for his efforts on behalf of his son. "This means a lot to him, and a lot to me", Donnelly told Matthew. Matthew replied, "you're a good friend, Dexter. Anything I can do to help you or Peter is minimal to all you have done for me."

Matthew spent the afternoon in central Massachusetts on campaign swings. He repeated his "Boston Common" speech at a small park in Webster for a group of about three hundred. He noticed his old friend from DCP days, James Dennis in the crowd. At the conclusion of the speech Matthew purposefully walked into the crowd and towards Dennis. They embraced as they greeted each other. Dennis told Matthew that he was "rooting" for him and that he was sure Matthew would get elected. Matthew thanked his friend from the past for his support. While driving back home Matthew sat silently in the back seat and thinking about his friend James Dennis and his time at DCP. They were happy memories for Matthew.

Matthew was deep in conversation with Adam when his mother walked through the door. He waved at her and motioned her to the left over dinner on the stove he had prepared. Rosa declined Matthew's cooking. "Yes, Ted said it's all confirmed. Don't worry about it!", Matthew said to Adam. He was talking about his trip to California two days after the election. Matthew had decided that he needed a vacation after the election and now that Adam was returning at Christmas he did not fear seeing him in California. It would be a nice vacation and time together before their lives started up again. "Do you want to talk to my mother?", he asked Adam. "Yes", replied Adam. Matthew handed the phone to Rosa. She smiled as she took the receiver from her son.

Scott, Dion, Kevin Michaels, Janice and Matthew reviewed the campaign financial statements over coffee that evening. The campaign was going well and their television advertisement costs would be covered. "I want to blitz the air waves the week before", Matthew said to Scott. Scott replied, "don't worry. We've got enough to cover it. The studio will have the commercials done by next week. Everything is going as planned." Matthew replied, "That's good because I really think that TV advertising is the way that campaigns are won or lost and I…" He was interrupted by the telephone. "Excuse me", he said as he picked up the phone.

"Hello", Matthew said into the receiver. "Well, hello nigger lovin' faggot!", screamed the voice on the other end. It was Craig Talbot. Matthew motioned with his finger rapidly pointing to the mouthpiece of the phone. Brent O'Sullivan put on his earphones and pressed the tape recorder. Trooper Maxine Brennan began dialing on the other line. Matthew began to speak. "Who is this?", he asked knowing full well it was Craig. "You know who it is faggot!", responded Craig. Matthew maintained a calm voice and asked, "well, what do you want?"

There was a pause in the conversation. Matthew could hear Trooper Brennan in the background speaking on the phone. Brent O'Sullivan was illustrating with his hands for Matthew to stretch out the conversation. The police were trying to pinpoint the location of the call. Talbot starting speaking again, "I saw your ass the other day on the Common. I blew you a kiss. Did you see me?" Matthew replied, "I did...but you took off". Talbot said, "that's because you sent your goons after me!" Matthew looked around his living room. His mother and the others were silently listening to his every word.

Craig Talbot continued, "do you think those goons can protect you?" Matthew asked, "do I need to be protected from you Craig?" Talbot replied, "not if you let me suck your cock you don't! Then I'll be where I belong...between your legs and in your bed, fucking the attorney general up the ass!" Matthew responded, "I don't think that's going to happen Craig." Talbot replied, "that's cause you love niggers! You love that big black cock don't you?"

Matthew remained calm. He tried to change the subject. "Craig", he began, "it's obvious that you want to talk to me about something. Maybe we should meet and talk. What do you think about that?", Matthew asked. Talbot yelled in response, "We'll meet, you can count on it mother fucker! But it's gonna be on my terms...not with your goons around." Matthew said, "that's fine. Just tell me when." Craig responded, "no...that's my little secret. I'm gonna surprise you! And the first thing we're gonna do when we get together is fuck! I'm gonna pump your tight lilly white ass! I'm gonna show you who the real man is Schipani, and it ain't you!" Matthew anxiously said, "Craig, let's get this over with. Tell me where we can meet". Talbot replied, "So you're ready to let me fuck ya, is that the deal? Hey, queer! You got a watch on Schipani?" Matthew confusingly responded, "yes. Why?" Talbot said, "well, I figure your goons have traced where I am by now. I've been turning you on long enough in this conversation. So I gotta hang up before the boys in blue get here. But don't forget, my big cock will be up your ass before you know it!" The phone line went dead. Matthew stood with the receiver held to his side. Then he placed it back in the cradle.

About five minutes later Trooper Brennan came into the living room. "The call was made from a pay phone on State Street near Quincy Market. By the time the unit got there he was gone. I'm sorry." Matthew replied, "that's okay. They tried. I'm sure there will be a next time." Matthew looked at his mother and his friends. Everyone had been quiet. Janice broke the ice. "Come on! We have work to do!", she said as she grabbed the papers off the table and they began to return to the campaign work.

"Do you mind if I come with you next weekend to the Berkshires?", Tracy asked Matthew as he sipped his morning coffee and went through the pile of papers on his desk. Matthew looked up and said, "getting to be quite the political animal aren't you?" Tracy sat down in the chair in front of his desk and replied, "I'm really enjoying the campaigning. I didn't think I would but it's been pretty exciting." Matthew smiled and said, "I'm glad. I thought you would feel left out. Of course you can come with us next weekend. We're staying at my parent's house. They have plenty of room in that old rambling house." Tracy asked, "who is coming, because I don't want to be in the way." Matthew replied, "Don't worry about it. It'll be you, Scott, Octavia, Dion and me. And of course, Brent!"

Tracy asked, "what about Janice? Is she coming too?" Matthew replied, "she's too close to delivery. The doctor doesn't want her traveling that much. This has been a difficult pregnancy for her. So she'll be at home." Tracy responded, "well, if it's no trouble, I'd really enjoy being there." Matthew replied, "no trouble at all. We'll have fun!"

Across town the morning sunshine fell on the face of Craig Talbot's sexual partner, Marvin. "Now you sure you're not gonna say a word? Cause if you do, I'll kill your ass. I'll cut your big cock off and shove it down your throat, just like the Colombians!", Craig yelled into Marvin's face as he sat on the young boy's chest. Marvin replied, "I told you…I promise, I won't say anything!" Craig responded, "prove it to me!" Marvin said, "how? What do you want now?" Craig replied, "you know what I want!" Marvin responded, "c'mon Craig…we just did it last night!" Craig said, "too bad! Now roll over and prove it to me! Show me I can trust ya or I'll beat your black ass to a pulp!" Marvin did as he was commanded. He rolled over onto his stomach. Not even a minute later Craig Talbot was inside of him. Marvin laid face first into the pillow. Marvin was crying, but he did not want Craig to see it. He was terrified. "I gotta get the hell out of here!", Marvin anxiously thought.

The following week went whipping by for Matthew. It was now Friday afternoon and he was getting ready to leave for the Berkshires. He would be spending three days there, culminating in an outdoor speech on Monday at the University. Dion had also planned a host of other minor events throughout the hill towns. Matthew quickly packed up his briefcase and slammed the middle drawer of his desk shut. He grabbed his jacket and walked out of the office. "Ready?", he said to Tracy who grabbed her jacket from her chair. "Ready!", she replied. They walked down the corridor to the exit of the building. Brent O'Sullivan followed. He would be their driver to the Berkshires. Scott and Octavia would ride out together on Saturday morning. Gloria was already at his parent's house helping his mother prepare for Sunday's dinner. Rosa had invited many of Matthew's friends from western Massachusetts to dinner. Matthew was excited about seeing his old friends, many of whom he had to his regret lost touch with over the past couple of years. The busy nature of their schedules had prevented them from spending time together.

It was two thirty in the morning when Brent O'Sullivan went into Matthew's old bedroom at his parent's home and shook Matthew to wake him. Matthew opened his eyes and looked at Brent. "I'm sorry, but I need to talk to you", he said to Matthew. Matthew turned on the light. Diana raised her head from the pillow and sat up. Matthew reached over and pet her. "Can't it wait?", he asked. Brent replied, "I'm sorry. I don't think it can." Matthew said, "let me get dressed. I'll meet you in the kitchen in a minute." Brent O'Sullivan walked out of the room.

Matthew put his feet on the floor and looked around the bedroom. His mother hadn't changed it since he lived there so many years ago. The furniture remained in the same places they had been when he lived in this room many years ago. Even his poster of *The Wiz* remained on the wall. He pulled his shorts on and walked out of the bedroom door. Diana jumped down off the bed and followed him.

Matthew walked into the kitchen and sat down at the table with Brent O'Sullivan. "So what's up?", he asked his bodyguard. O'Sullivan began the conversation. "I'm leaving in about an hour to drive back to Boston. I got a phone call from my Captain. A young black teenager appeared at Boston PD tonight telling a story that made them nervous. It was about you." Matthew raised his eyebrows and said, "continue". O'Sullivan went on. "It seems this young teenager had been living with Craig Talbot for a few weeks. Well Talbot told him something that really scared the shit out of the kid. The kid took off tonight and headed to the nearest precinct. He told his story. They have him in custody and I'm on my way to talk to him." Matthew asked, "well, what is his story?" O'Sullivan spoke slowly and deliberately. "It seems that Craig told the young kid that he had a beef with a famous guy in the state. He never really named you as the person. But Talbot said the guy was gay and he was responsible for Talbot being gay. He told this kid who's name is Marvin, that he was going to 'pay back the guy for making him gay'." Matthew stood up and went to the refrigerator. He grabbed a soda out from the shelf. "You want one?", he asked Brent O'Sullivan. "Please", responded O'Sullivan. Matthew grabbed another soda and handed it to the police officer. "Go ahead", he said to Brent.

"So the kid asked him what he was going to do and Talbot said he was going to kill the guy. That's when the kid got really nervous so he slipped out of the apartment while Talbot was sleeping. The kid's from the Bronx...we're in the process of having him checked out to make sure he's not a wacko. And he told us that Talbot had a rifle. We ran a computer check on guns purchased in the metro area. If he's got a gun, he didn't buy it there or he bought it illegally." Matthew interrupted, "how could he get a gun without a permit?" Brent

O'Sullivan scoffed, "come on Matthew! You should know better than anyone else how easy it is to get a gun." Matthew shook his head in agreement. O'Sullivan took another sip from the plastic bottle. "Anyway, the Captain thinks the kid is legit. He described the gun and everything. So they send a unit over to where the kid says Talbot is staying. He's not there and it looks like he left in a hurry. There's only remnants of useless stuff left behind, but we're checking the place out. Of course, there's no gun there. So I decided I wanted to check this kid out personally. That's why I woke you." Matthew lit a cigarette and said, "you honestly think Craig Talbot would want to shoot me?" O'Sullivan stoically replied, "I honestly don't want to take the risk. Think about it…he's got the balls to call you at home and say all that sexual shit. Plus, we reviewed the transcripts of the last phone call. He talks about you becoming his boyfriend and everything. I think he's obsessed with you for whatever delusional reason he has in his sick mind."

Matthew inhaled deeply on the cigarette. "So how long are you going to be gone?", he asked. O'Sullivan replied, "Just today. I'll be back tonight. I'm not going to miss the picnic, that's for sure!", he said with a smile. Matthew asked, "you don't want me to cancel the outings today do you?" Brent O'Sullivan replied, "no you don't have to, but I'm having the local guys assist our men with security. But if we can't locate Talbot I want you to really think about the university speech on Monday. You have it scheduled outside and it's going to be a lot more difficult securing the area than if it was in the auditorium or somewhere else." Matthew paused a moment and then said, "well, I'll think about it, but you know I've prided myself on these outdoor rallies. It allows more people to be there and I can get my message across easier." O'Sullivan said, "just promise me you'll think about it, okay?" Matthew responded, "I will".

There was a knock on the door. Brent O'Sullivan answered. It was a uniformed state police officer, a person Matthew did not recognize. He was here to take O'Sullivan to Boston. Brent said his good-bye to

Matthew and handed his car keys to a now awaken Trooper Maxine Brennan. He followed the other state police officer out the door to the driveway for his early morning ride. "Do you want me to sit up with you?", asked Maxine Brennan. Matthew smiled and lit another cigarette. "No, that's okay...please go back to bed", he said. Trooper Brennan responded, "okay. Good night", and she walked out of the kitchen down the hall toward the den where she had been sleeping on the pull out couch. Matthew remained sitting at the kitchen table.

He sat up for about an hour before he returned to his old bedroom and his old bed. "God damn September!", he said as he turned out the light and rolled over grasping onto Diana who had her head across his chest. Matthew lay with his eyes closed thinking about how he loathed this month and how many Septembers had presented crisises for him. But he also remembered how he had gotten through them all one by one. He assured himself that he would get through this one as well. With that comforting thought in his mind Matthew drifted off to sleep.

He spent Saturday touring around the hill towns of western Massachusetts with Dion and Tracy. Matthew noticed as they drove that the leaves had turned quite early this year. The rapid change in temperature in August had brought fall to the Berkshires about three weeks earlier than normal. But Matthew also reveled in the colors of the trees. He loved the shades of red, gold and orange that dotted the hillsides.

That evening Matthew returned just before dinner. Scott and Octavia had arrived. Rosa had sent out for pizza. Matthew and Dion went over the events during the day. It had been a positive campaign day. As Matthew was drinking his second beer with pizza the phone rang. It was Adam. He took the call in the other room. "I can't wait to see you!", exclaimed Adam. Matthew replied, "I'm looking forward to it too. It'll be here before we know it." Adam noticed the flatness of Matthew's voice. Something was wrong. So Adam asked, "what's the matter?" Matthew replied that he had a busy day campaigning and that he was tired. He continued in his determination that he would not tell Adam about Craig Talbot. Adam persisted. He knew something was going on. He could tell it in Matthew's voice. Adam said to Matthew, "you know what month it is. I know that for some reason September brings a challenge every year to you. Do you mind telling me what it is?" Matthew responded, "it's nothing. There's no challenge this year. I think that's an old myth that I established for myself. You remember some Septembers when everything was fine." Adam replied, "I also remember some fucked up Septembers too!". Matthew continued in his denial that there was any problem present.

Matthew changed the subject of the conversation to what events Adam had planned for him when he came to California. They talked for about another twenty minutes reviewing a tentative itinerary. They ended their conversation with their exchange of "I love you". Matthew gingerly hung up the telephone.

Matthew rejoined the group in the kitchen. Rosa had put coffee on and Matthew asked for a cup. The knock on the kitchen door was followed by it opening and Brent O'Sullivan appearing. "I saved you a piece of pizza", said Rosa as he walked in the door. "Thank you", said Brent as he grabbed the vacant chair at the kitchen table. Rosa brought the pizza over on a plate and handed it to Brent. "Do we need to talk?", Matthew asked. "It can wait for a bit", responded Brent. Scott and Octavia looked at each other with puzzled looks.

Matthew sat in the library of his parent's home with Brent O'Sullivan. As Brent spoke Matthew stared around at the library. He loved this room. That was why he had tried to replicate it in his own home. The paneled walls were lined with floor to ceiling bookcases on two walls. But the cases did not contain law books, rather they contained his father's collection of antique and classic books. The third wall was adorned with certificates that both his father and mother had received from various civic groups for their many years of community work. This was where Matthew got his calling for community service, from his parents. The final wall was decorated with mounted fish that his father had caught over the years as a amateur fisherman. That was the only wall Matthew had not replicated at home. He thought fishing was a boring sport.

"Have you been listening to me?", asked O'Sullivan in an irritable voice. Matthew turned his head back to his bodyguard. "Yeah, I've been listening. You have no idea where Talbot is. He probably has a gun and wants to kill me, and you want me to cancel my speech on Monday." O'Sullivan interjected, "well that's about it". Matthew said, "I'm not canceling the speech on Monday and I'm not moving it indoors. I can't live my life being afraid of this guy. I've become a goddamn prisoner! I won't live like this!"

Trooper Brent O'Sullivan waited a moment before responding to Matthew's ranting. Then he said to Matthew, "I know that this isn't the easiest thing, but I think you need to think about your safety first. We can't guarantee that if your outdoors on the lawn of the university." Matthew sternly replied, "I'm sorry Brent. I know you've done everything possible. But how much of my life do I have to give up because of some psycho? I just can't do it anymore. I'm going ahead with the speech. This is my home town. These are my people. I want them to hear me."

O'Sullivan shook his head and then put it down into his hands. He rubbed his eyes and then looked up. "Will you at least think about it tomorrow?" Matthew responded, "I've thought about it. I'm not changing my mind." O'Sullivan replied, "well how about a bullet proof vest? Will you at least do that for me?" Matthew sighed and paused, saying, "Okay, I'll do that, but that's it. This speech is important to me. The setting is important. I'm not going to alter it." O'Sullivan then said, "we have to tell people here. Your parents are coming to the speech…Tracy, Scott, Octavia, Dion…they need to know." Matthew shook his head and looked to the ceiling. "I know you're right, but I just don't like it. My parents will be a fucking nervous wreck! We'll tell them tomorrow…let's not spoil the rest of the evening. Come on, let's get back out there before they drive themselves crazy wondering what's going on." Matthew stood up and motioned to the door. O'Sullivan got up and Matthew followed as they went to the living room.

The Sunday picnic was a smashing success. The cookout was marked by its Italian accent on food. Not only were there the traditional hamburgs and hot dogs, but there was also lots of pasta, sausage, Italian chicken and antipasto. Matthew's mother and his aunt had spent a great deal of time and effort in the preparation. Matthew's friends appreciated the effort and complimented his mother and aunt repeatedly. Matthew enjoyed seeing the many friends that he hadn't seen as often as he wanted to in the recent past. He spent time talking with Ted about his upcoming vacation to California and what tourist traps he had to see while he was there. He played with Sharon and Louise's children. Kevin Michaels and Matthew's father, Franco spent the afternoon under the willow tree debating the upcoming presidential election. Diana ran around chasing his brother's new puppy and his sister Maria ran around chasing her children.

At one point Matthew and Scott went for a walk in the woods behind the house. Matthew halted Brent O'Sullivan from coming with them. Brent did not put up a fight. While walking through the woods Matthew told Scott of the threat from Craig Talbot. Scott became very upset and started to cry. Matthew put his arm around him as they walked. "Don't be sad…everything will be fine", he told his best friend. Scott put his arm around Matthew exclaiming, "I don't know how you're dealing with this shit! I can't stand it anymore!" Matthew firmly replied, "That's why I refuse to give in. If I run and hide I'll be giving the sicko exactly what he wants. I can't do that. That's not me. I'm a fighter and no crazy fucker is going to run my life!"

Scott motioned Matthew to a log under the tree. They sat down on the log and looked out through the forest. Matthew reached down to his feet and picked up some leaves. He found fallen leaves of red and gold. He held them in his hands and then gave them to Scott. "You know these are my favorite colors don't you?" Scott smiled, "yes, I know. Red and gold...I remember the story from when you were little." Matthew smiled. Scott leaned over and kissed Matthew on the cheek. Matthew grabbed Scott by the head and held him to his shoulder. Scott wrapped his arms around him and they sat holding onto each other without saying a word.

Scott leaned back and said to Matthew, "I need to tell you how important you've been to me". Matthew put up a finger to his mouth and said, "shh". Scott continued, "no, I need to say it." Matthew replied, "Scott, you're acting as if this psycho is going to get his way. Don't worry about it. Everything will be fine." Scott said, "It's not just that. I think sometimes we forget to say things to each other and time just flies by." Matthew responded, "I know how you feel about me. You know how much I love you. We don't need to say it. It's in our hearts. We will always love each other, no matter what". Scott began to cry again. Matthew tried to make light of the situation. "Stop it you big queen! How would it look for our friends to see this tall, lanky hunky man crying!" Scott wiped the tears from his face and smiled. "We better head back", he said to Matthew.

That evening after everyone had left the home except for the core group that was remaining for the speech tomorrow, Brent O'Sullivan assembled people in the living room. He explained the latest news on Craig Talbot. Matthew's mother stood up as O'Sullivan was finishing and said in her strongest and firmest voice, "Matthew, you cannot give that speech tomorrow!" His father Franco expressed his agreement. Matthew turned to his sister and brother and said, "I suppose you agree too?" They both shook their heads in agreement. Matthew stood up and addressed his family and friends. "I know you all may think this is crazy, Brent certainly does. But, I've decided that I cannot and will not live my life running in fear about this crazy guy. I can't give into him. I'll have the police with me tomorrow...in fact,

I've even agreed to wear a bulletproof vest. But I can't compromise anymore. Christ, I'm the attorney general! I shouldn't be afraid of some psycho. What kind of message does that send?" Octavia interrupted. "I think you need to be concerned about your own personal safety above everything else Matthew". He looked at her and firmly replied, "I can't let that get in the way. Am I suppose to curtail the rest of this campaign because of this nut case? I won't do it! I'm going to continue with the outdoor rallies. They've become a staple of the campaign. Just like Clinton did with his bus trips. If I stop now, Talbot wins. I'm not going to allow that."

It was clear to the rest of them that Matthew had his mind made up. "Plus, why is everyone so worried about tomorrow? The nut case is out in the eastern part of the state. Christ, he knows we're onto him! He's probably hit the road fast and is headed south.", Matthew concluded, exhausted from the defense of his decision. The tension was thick and hung in the air. No one uttered a word for a couple of minutes. Finally, Matthew's sister Maria said, "well, let's do something. We can't sit around here all night and brood." Matthew responded, "I agree! Let's do something fun!"

Three miles down the road a rusted out Ford pickup stopped at the intersection near the entrance to the University. "Thanks Kenny", said Craig Talbot as he climbed out of the truck with his duffel bag over his shoulder. His friend turned the truck around and drove off quickly down the road toward the highway. Talbot began walking toward the woods that abutted the university's south lawn. He noticed the worker's packing up their tools. The staging for tomorrow's event had been built. Talbot slipped by them without notice. He walked about five hundred feet into the woods and found a small clearing.

Talbot laid down his duffel bag, open it and pulled out a blanket. Talbot laid down using the bag as a pillow and threw the blanket over himself. He lit the marijuana cigarette and gazed up through the now thinning fall trees at the many stars in the bright crescent moon sky. "Tomorrow is gonna be a great day!", he spoke to himself.

A bright, warm Monday morning arrived in the Berkshires. Matthew was hurrying everyone around the house to get ready so they could leave on time to go to the university for his speech. Three miles down the road Craig Talbot was counting out the .223 caliber bullets as he loaded them into the rifle. Once he fully loaded it he began his ascent up a tall oak tree. Craig climbed to about thirty feet up where he found a strong and sturdy limb to sit on. His brown camouflage outfit blended in with the tree trunk and the fall leaves.

Talbot put the rifle to his shoulder and peered through the scope of the AR 15 down at the podium on the stage about one hundred yards below him to the right. The barrel of the rifle protruded slightly through the leaves on the limb. It was hardly noticeable. Craig continued to look through the sight. He could clearly see the microphone sticking up from the podium. "A sitting duck!", he whispered out loud laughing.

Matthew gave his Aunt Gloria a kiss good-bye. She decided to stay at the house rather than go to the university. She really couldn't tolerate crowds. He tried to put his suitjacket over his sweater, but found it difficult with the bullet proof vest on underneath. "God damn it!", he said as he struggled with the jacket. Rosa came up from behind Matthew and helped him put the jacket on. He shook it into place. "Let's go!", he commanded everyone. As Matthew walked to the door Diana began circling around his legs. "She's been a pest all morning!", Matthew said to Tracy. "She loves her Daddy!", Tracy replied laughing. "I know, but ever since I've been up this morning she hasn't left me alone! She seems to be upset about something", he concluded. Matthew crouched down and gave Diana a kiss on the snout and hugged her. He then ushered the group out the door to the awaiting cars.

Franco went to shut the door behind his wife. The telephone rang. Franco turned and went to the wall to grab it. "Hello", he said. It was

Adam. "He's just gone out to the car to leave for his speech. Do you want me to get him?", Franco asked. Adam responded, "no that's okay. I'll talk to him when he gets back. Tell him good luck for me." Franco responded, "I will" and hung up the phone. He then walked out the door to join the group waiting to leave for the university.

The short ride to the university with the state police escort was quiet. Franco told his son that Adam had called and wished him good luck. Matthew smiled, but he seemed to be focused elsewhere. He knew that this was an important speech. It was to his home town. His people, his neighbors, his peers. Matthew wanted to be totally on cue. He had to show his community that he could do it not only for himself but for them as well.

They pulled up behind the library that was adjacent to the field where Matthew would deliver his speech. He walked with his police escort toward the stage. There was a small band playing off to the left of the stage as they walked through the crowd toward the stairs. The audience was applauding as Matthew led the contingency with Scott, Octavia, Dion and Tracy right behind his parents and his brother and sister. His entourage with the exception of Octavia took their seats in the front row. Octavia followed Matthew and the state police, led by Brent O'Sullivan up onto the stage. The band stopped playing and Matthew waved to the enthusiastic applause that greeted his arrival on stage. He walked behind the podium, shook hands with the mayor and the university president and took his seat.

Craig Talbot sat perched in the tree watching the events below through the scope of his rifle. He followed the bulls-eye in the center of the scope around the stage. He focused in on Matthew who was seated to the right of the podium. "If only you knew you sorry bastard!", Craig said to himself as he laughed. "The faggot's fur is gonna fly any minute now!", he said chuckling in a sinister tone.

The university president had just concluded his remarks and turned the microphone over to the mayor who was in charge of the introduction of Matthew. Matthew looked at Octavia sitting next to him. He grabbed her by the knee with his hand and smiled at her. Octavia grabbed his hand, held onto it and smiled back at Matthew. He turned to Brent O'Sullivan and noticed that he and Maxine Brennan were actively scanning the crowd. Matthew looked out at the crowd. He saw many familiar faces. He also saw a contingency of police posted at each entrance and in the back of the audience. "And so, ladies and gentlemen and children, I proudly present to you our hometown son, Attorney General Matthew Schipani!", bellowed the mayor in a cheerful tone.

Matthew rose and the band began to play. The audience applauded and the placards bearing Matthew's name were being pumped up and down in the air. Matthew shook the hand of the mayor and the university president and walked to the podium. He stood behind the podium. Matthew continued to wave and appreciate the applause. "Thank you…thank you very much!", he said as he motioned with his hands for the audience to sit down. A few minutes of applause lingered on and then the audience sat to be addressed by their favorite son.

Craig sat like a bird on the limb and continued to watch through the scope of the rifle. Matthew had begun his speech. Craig could hear the speech through the speaker system set up on each side of the stage. "The faggot's really into it now!", Craig said as he held his finger against the trigger. Below Matthew was speaking about one of his favorite subjects, the protection of children. "And so, over my many years I have worked to insure that the children of this state can live in a home where they are free from fear of abuse or danger. A home where they have parents who love them dearly and strive every day to make sure that their children's future is bright and healthy." The applause once again interrupted Matthew's speech.

Talbot heard this part of the speech crystal clear. "Yeah, sure you bastard, you protected children! You didn't protect me faggot! You turned me into a queer!", he yelled. Craig Talbot put the rifle to his shoulder and looked through the scope. He found the face of Matthew in his scope. He moved the rifle so that Matthew's face was square in the bulls-eye. Talbot squeezed the trigger of the rifle. The thunderous explosion rocked in Talbot's ear and its impact pounded against his shoulder. He squeezed the trigger again, two more times. Two explosions accompanied the projectiles as they searched for their target.

Matthew was mid sentence when the first bullet struck him in the right temple. His head exploded from the impact and blood spurted everywhere. Matthew fell down immediately on to his side on the floor of the stage. The other two bullets flew over Matthew's head and hit the back of the stage leaving flying wood splinters and two holes in their path. Pandemonium ensued. Matthew's blood gushed all over the stage and on Octavia. Brent O'Sullivan jumped over Octavia and covered Matthew. Maxine Brennan pulled Octavia down from her chair and onto the floor of the stage and laid over her.

The crowd was screaming and pushing as people began to run from the field. Matthew's mother and father stood up and stared ahead. They could not move. Scott leaped from his seat and vaulted onto the stage. He ran over to Matthew and laid down beside him. He grabbed Matthew's bleeding head from the floor of the stage and held it in his hands. He turned Matthew's head and looked at his face. Matthew's eyes were rolled back in their sockets. Scott reached down and pushed the bloody hair from Matthew's forehead. He leaned into Matthew's chest. He could not hear a beat. Scott turned to look over his shoulder. Rosa and Franco were standing to his side frozen in place with their mouths covered. Scott could not respond. The sound of screams and yelling were muffled by many sirens in the distance. Scott cradled Matthew's head in his hands as tears flowed down his face and Matthew's blood stained his lap.

Four days passed since the horror on the stage at the university. Scott followed behind Rosa, Franco, Anthony and Maria as they walked down the aisle of Saint John's Roman Catholic Church. He held tightly onto the arm of Adam as they walked. Octavia held the now overdue Janice as they proceeded behind Scott and Adam. Following them was the flag draped casket containing the body of Matthew Alexander Schipani. They filed into their seats in the pews at the front of the church. The priest began the ceremony.

At the time for the homily the priest deferred his remarks to Governor Lloyd Dickerson and to Scott. Dickerson spoke first. He spoke briefly and poignantly. It was one of the only times that the public had actually seen their Governor truly moved by emotion rather than by politics. When he finished he bowed to the priest and returned to his seat.

Scott grabbed Adam's hand tightly and squeezed. It was his turn. He got up out of his seat and proceeded to the lectern. Janice slid over to Adam and held his arm. The heavily medicated Adam sat dazed with tears running down his face. Janice wiped the tears from his face with her hand.

Scott began to speak. He would make Matthew proud. He spoke slowly and was able to keep his emotion in check so that he could complete his remarks. He knew that Matthew would not want him to be crying in front of the church. Scott spoke for about five minutes and then paused for a moment. He needed a break before continuing. Scott drank a sip of water from the glass on the table to the side of the lecture. Scott continued on with his remarks. "Matthew Schipani was not only a wonderful and thoughtful person, but he was my best friend. The type of friend that many of us will never have…and I know I will never have again. He was a person who loved unconditionally. We shared wonderful, splendid times and dark and hard times. We also shared many deep and intimate times and events together. We loved each other profoundly through all of those times. We never stopped loving each other." Scott paused for a moment and wiped his eyes.

"Matthew loved everyone. He cared about everyone. He was always trying to make things better, not only for his family and his friends but for all the people in this state. He fought for children. He fought against discrimination, against crime and he fought for what he believed in. Matthew fought for justice. He never gave up and never stopped fighting. Only the bullet of that troubled and sick man stopped Matthew. And now he is gone...taken from this earthly plane and home to God. Heaven is now a better and a brighter place now that Matthew has joined his God."

Scott looked out at the parish. Those assembled were paying full attention to his every word. The silence in the church was deafening. He took another sip of water, looked down briefly to regain his composure. Scott continued with his remarks. "You must never forget that Matthew loved all of you. He loved you deeply and intensely. He loved his family with all his heart. He always talked about how much they had given to him not only as a child, but also as an adult. He loved Adam more than he ever loved any other. And though they were separated, Matthew never stopped loving Adam. He looked forward with happiness for their reunion. A reunion that now will not happen. And Matthew loved us...each and everyone of us here today, in his own special way. That is what we must remember about Matthew."

Scott's voice was beginning to crack and warble. He took a deep breath and continued on to conclude his remarks. "Matthew took the power of his love and tried to change things to make the world a better place. I think he did that, and I know you do too. I believe we can all say that children are safer today in this state because of Matthew Schipani. That was his mission in life. To protect the children. And he did it with power, grace and compassion."

"So, I want to say to Matthew today as he is watching us from heaven: Matthew we thank you. Thank you for all you did to make this world a better place in your brief time with us. Thank you on behalf of all those you touched and saved. Thank you for the love and for the deep and lasting impact you had on our lives. We are better people, kinder people and wiser people for having known you. We love you and we will always keep you in our hearts."

Scott stepped away from the lectern and walked slowly back to his seat. He sat down and put his head in his hands and began to sob. He could no longer maintain his composure. He looked up through his tears and turned to Adam. Scott put his arm around an intensely crying Adam and held him to his chest.

Matthew's dear friend Janice also would have made Matthew proud at the funeral ceremony. Janice Pierce joined a solo pianist and sang the communion song at the mass. She performed without flaw, in a soft and soothing voice the hymn *Amazing Grace*. Rosa sat and listened to the lyrics. They comforted her during this most horrible hour in her life. Janice sang, "Amazing Grace, how sweet the sound, that saved a wretch like me. I once was lost, but now I'm found, was blind, but now I see…T'was grace that taught my heart to fear, and grace my fears relieved. How precious did that grace appear, the hour I first believed…Through many, many dangers, toils and snares, I have already gone. T'was grace that brought me here thus far and grace will lead me home!"

Matthew was buried at the family plot in the hills of the Berkshires on this cold fall day. The ground surrounding his casket was covered with fallen leaves of red and gold. As those assembled sang the *Battle Hymn of The Republic*, Governor Lloyd Dickerson handed the folded flag of Massachusetts that draped Matthew's casket to Rosa and Franco Schipani. The song was ending, "…in the beauty of the lillies Christ was born across the sea. With a glory in his bosom that transfigures you and me. As he died to make men holy, let us die to make men free. While God is marching on!" As the mourners concluded with the refrain, Franco took the folded flag and handed it to Adam. Adam held it tightly to his bosom and closed his eyes as the song ended.

A quiet and somber week had passed since Matthew's funeral. Janice was lying in bed in the maternity ward with her newborn son in her arms. Her loving husband Jose sat on the bed to her side and gazed down at the face of his new baby. He looked at his wife, smiled and kissed her gently on the forehead.

Janice looked down at the angelic face of her third son staring up at her. Matthew Alexander Pierce Gonzalez lay in the safety of his mother's arms. Comfortable and without a worry, surrounded by his loving parents. A new Matthew Alexander had entered the world, ready to take his journey and make his impression on the world. The torch had been passed.

0-595-24131-X

Printed in the United States
6385